DUDLEY PUBLIC LIBRARIES

The loan of this book may be renewed if not required by other readers, by contacting the library from which it was borrowed.

GL

The Bosses

COLLECTION

August 2019
Forbidden Nights with the Boss

September 2019
Becoming the Boss

October 2019
Seduced by the Boss

November 2019
Flirting with the Boss

January 2020
Desired by the Boss

February 2020
Claimed by the Boss

March 2020
Taming the Boss

April 2020
Ruled by the Boss

Desired by the Boss

LEAH ASHTON

JENNIFER LEWIS

CATHERINE MANN

MILLS & BOON

First Published in Great Britain 2020
By Mills & Boon, an imprint of HarperCollins*Publishers*
1 London Bridge Street, London, SE1 9GF

DESIRED BY THE BOSS © 2020 Harlequin Books S.A.

Behind the Billionaire's Guarded Heart © 2017 Leah Ashton
Behind Boardroom Doors © 2012 Harlequin Books S.A.
His Secretary's Little Secret © 2016 Catherine Mann

Special thanks and acknowledgement to Jennifer Lewis for her contribution to the *Dynasties: The Kincaids* series.

ISBN: 978-0-263-28073-9

0120

BEHIND THE BILLIONAIRE'S GUARDED HEART

LEAH ASHTON

For Jen – who writes beautiful messages in cards, talks with her hands, and giggles at all my jokes.

Thank you for all your help with this book, and for your belief in my writing.

You're fabulous, Jen. I miss you.

PROLOGUE

THE SUNSET WAS PERFECT—all orange and purple on a backdrop of darkening blue. Just the right number of clouds stretched their tendrils artistically along the horizon.

The beach, however, was not so perfect.

It had been a warm Perth day, so April Molyneux hadn't been alone in her plans for a beachside picnic dinner. Around her, people congregated about mounds of battered fish and chips on beds of butcher's paper. Others had picnic baskets, or brown paper takeaway bags, or melting ice cream cones from the pink and white van parked above the sand dunes.

There were beach towels everywhere, body boards bouncing in the waves, children building sandcastles, women power walking along the beach in yoga pants, gossiping at a mile a minute. Then a football team jogged by, shirtless and in matching deep purple shorts.

April wanted to scream. This was *not* what she'd planned.

This was *not* a private, romantic, beachside *tête-à-tête*.

Evan lay sprawled on their picnic blanket, his back turned away from April as he scrolled through his phone.

Today was their wedding anniversary. Three years.

#anniversary #threeyears #love #romance

Right now April felt like dumping the contents of the gourmet picnic box she'd ordered all over his head—sourdough baguettes, cultured butter, artisan cheeses, muscatels and all.

'Do we *have* to do this?' Evan asked, not even looking at her.

'You mean spend time with your wife on your anniversary?' Her words were sharp, but April's throat felt tight.

The sea-breeze whipped her long blonde hair across her eyes, and she tucked it back behind her ears angrily. She sat with her legs curled beneath her, a long pale pink maxi-dress covering her platinum bikini. She stared daggers at Evan's back. His attention was still concentrated on the screen of his phone.

'You know that isn't what I meant.'

She did. But she'd spent weeks leading up to today, posting photos of their wedding to her one point two million followers.

#anniversary #threeyears #love #romance

She'd organised for the Molyneux family jet to take them up north, up past Broome. She'd found the perfect—*perfect*—private beach. She'd had the stupid picnic box couriered up from Margaret River, and she'd had her assistant organise a gorgeous rainbow mohair picnic blanket, complete with a generous donation to the Molyneux Foundation.

And then Evan had called from work as she'd been packing her overnight bag. He'd asked if they could cancel their trip. He didn't really feel like going, and could they stay home instead?

Coming to this beach had been the compromise.

It wasn't even about the beach, really. Just the photo.

All he needed to do was smile for the camera and then they could go home and eat their fancy picnic in front of the TV. Or order pizza. Whatever. It didn't matter. And Evan could eat silently, then retreat to his study and barely talk to her for the rest of the evening.

Just as he did most nights.

Again, April's throat felt tight.

Finally Evan moved. He shifted, sitting up so he could face her. He took off his sunglasses, and for some reason April did too.

For the first time in what suddenly felt like ages he looked directly at her. Really intensely, his hazel eyes steady against her own silvery blue.

'I don't think we can do this any more,' he said. Firmly, and in a way that probably should have surprised her.

April pretended to misunderstand. 'Come on—it's just a stupid photo. We need to do this. I have contractual obligations.'

For product placement: The mohair blanket. The picnic box. Her sunglasses. Her bikini.

Donations to the Molyneux Foundation were contingent on this photograph.

Evan shook his head. 'You know what I'm talking about.'

They'd started marriage counselling only a year after their wedding. They'd stopped trying for a baby shortly afterwards, both agreeing that it was best to wait until they'd sorted things out.

But they hadn't sorted things out.

They'd both obediently attended counselling, made concerted efforts to listen to each other...but nothing had really changed.

They still loved each other, though. They'd both been clear on that.

April *knew* she still loved Evan. She'd loved him since he'd asked her to his Year Twelve ball.

To her, that had been all that mattered. Eventually it would go back to how it had used to be between them. Surely?

'I'll always love you, April,' Evan said, in a terribly careful tone that she knew he must have practised. 'But I don't love you the way I know I should. The way I should love the woman I'm married too. You deserve better, April.'

Oh, God.

The words were all mashed together, tangled up in the salty breeze. All April could hear, repeated against her skull, was: *I don't love you...*

His lips quirked upwards. 'I guess I deserve better, too. We both deserve that love you see in the movies, or in those books you read. Don't you think? And it's never been like that for us.'

He paused, as if waiting for her to say something, but she had nothing. Absolutely nothing.

'Look, I would never cheat on you, April, but a while ago I met someone who made me think that maybe there was a bigger love out there for me, you know?' This bit definitely wasn't practised—his words were all rushed and messy. 'I respected you too much to pursue her. I cut her out of my life and I haven't been in contact with her. At all. I promise. But I can't stop thinking about her, and I...'

His gaze had long ago stopped meeting hers, but now it swung back.

He swallowed. 'I want a divorce, April,' he said with finality. 'I'm sorry.'

She could only nod. Nod and nod, over and over.

'April?'

Her throat felt as if it had completely closed over. She fumbled for her sunglasses, desperate to cover the wetness in her eyes.

'Let's just take this stupid picture,' she said, her words strangled.

His eyes widened, but he nodded.

Awkwardly, they posed—only their shoulders touching. April took the photo quickly, without any thought at all... but amazingly the beach in the photo's background was perfectly empty just for that millisecond as she pressed the button on her phone.

To her followers it would seem perfect.

A private beach, a handsome, loving husband, a glorious sunset...

Silently she cropped the image, then added her caption and hashtags.

Three amazing years with this guy! #anniversary #threeyears #love #romance

But she deleted the last hashtag before she posted it:

#over

Hugh Bennell's gaze was drawn to the black door at the top of the grey stone stairs. The paintwork and brass door hardware all looked a bit dull—and not just because the sun was only just now rising on this rather dreary London morning. A handful of leaves had gathered where a doormat should be, and a single hopeful weed reached out from beneath the doorstep.

He'd have to sort that out.

But for now he simply wheeled his bike—lights still flashing from his pre-dawn ride—straight past the steps that led to the three-storey chocolate and cream Victorian end-of-terrace, and instead negotiated a matching set of steps that led downwards to his basement flat.

Inside, the cleats on the base of his cycling shoes clicked on the parquet flooring, and his road bike's wheels squeaked noisily. He hung the bike on its wall hanger, immediately across from the basement front door. Above it hung his mountain bike, and to the right of that was the door to one of his spare bedrooms.

That door was painted white, and the paintwork still gleamed as fresh as the day he'd had the apartment painted. He noted that the brass knob still shone—in fact his whole house shone with meticulous cleanliness, just as he liked it.

Hugh settled in at his desk after a shower, his dark hair still damp. The desk was right at the front of his apartment, pushed up against the window. Above him foot traffic was increasing as London got ready for the workday. From his viewpoint all he could see were ankles and feet—in heels and boots and lace-up shoes. The angle was too acute for anyone passing to see him—he'd checked, of course—so he could leave his blinds open, allowing natural light to filter across his workspace.

He placed his mug of tea on the coaster immediately to the right of his open laptop. Beneath that lay the day's to-do list, carefully formulated and handwritten the previous evening.

He'd always loved lists, even as a young kid. He remembered his mum's bemusement when he'd stuck a list above his bedside table to remind himself what to pack for school each day of the week. He'd found it calming to have it all written out—a much better alternative, he'd thought, to his mother's panicked realisations at the school gate and her frantic delivery of forgotten sports shoes at morning break.

'A neat freak with lists!' His mum had laughed. *'How could you possibly be mine?'*

To the bottom of his list for today he added *Paint front door and polish brass.*

He was certain the team at Precise thought his penchant for paper lists eccentric for a man who owned and ran a multi-million-dollar mobile app empire—but then, the team thought him eccentric for many more reasons than that.

A reminder popped up on his screen for a nine a.m. appointment, and he clicked through to sign in for the online meeting. Already four of the five other attendees were logged in, their faces visible via their webcams in a grid to the right of screen.

But in Hugh's box there was only the generic grey silhouette—he never chose the video option, and he kept the camera at the top of his laptop taped over just in case.

Because, for Hugh Bennell, maintaining his privacy was non-negotiable.

He was in control of exactly what he revealed to the world.

His laptop dinged as the final attendee arrived.

'Looks like everyone's here,' Hugh said. 'Let's get started.'

CHAPTER ONE

Six weeks later—London

APRIL FELT GOOD.

She was thirty-two, and her first ever job interview was today.

Sure, she'd been interviewed for the couple of internships she'd had back at uni, but they didn't count. Today was her first real-life *I actually really, really want this job* interview.

That was significant.

She smiled.

Around her, the Tube train was packed. Everyone looked completely absorbed in their own world—reading a book, swiping through a phone, gazing out of the window into the blackness of the tunnel.

Nobody noticed her. Nobody realised how momentous this day actually was.

Since her disastrous wedding anniversary there'd been weeks of numbness for April. There'd been shock, then anger, then the awfulness of telling her mum and her sisters, Ivy and Mila. There'd been weeks of meetings with lawyers and endless discussions about property settlement. There'd been tears and wine and long conversations.

Time had seemed to go on and on. Especially at night, when she'd been alone in her ridiculously too big concrete-and-angles home. Mila had stayed a few nights to keep her company—but she had her own life and a partner to worry about. Her mum had stayed every night for a fortnight, determinedly focusing on the practicalities of lawyers and legal details. Ivy had brought her son, Nate, to visit regularly—although she had been mortified when the toddler had accidentally pushed a salad bowl off the table, shattering it into millions of pieces.

'Don't worry about it,' April had reassured her. 'It's one less thing we need to decide who gets to keep.'

At first, sorting out the things that she and Evan had bought together had seemed vitally important. Maybe it was the focus it had given her—or maybe there was more of her ruthless businesswoman mother in her than she'd thought.

But as the weeks had worn on, and she'd spent more time staring at her ceiling, not sleeping, all their *stuff* had begun to feel meaningless.

As it probably should for a woman with a billion-dollar family trust that she held with her sisters.

So Evan could have everything. Of course he could have everything.

I don't love you…

April didn't sugar-coat what Evan had said. He'd wrapped it up in superfluous words to blunt the blow, but that didn't hide the reality: Evan didn't love her. He'd never loved her—at least not the way April had loved him.

In those endless nights she'd analysed that relentlessly.

How could she not have known?

I don't love you.

You.

Who was she, if not married to Evan?

The feminist within her was horrified that she could even ask herself this question. But she did. Again and again:

Who was she?

This woman Evan hadn't loved enough. This woman who had been oblivious to the end of her marriage.

Who was she?

She was thirty-two, single and had never worked a day in her life.

Her home had been a wedding gift from her mother.

Everything she'd ever bought had been with a credit card linked to the Molyneux Trust. She had been indulged by a family who probably didn't think her capable of being anything but a frivolous socialite. Why would they? She'd applied herself to nothing else. Her days had been filled with shopping and expensive charity luncheons. Her evenings with art gallery openings and luxurious fundraising auctions. She'd spent her spare time taking photos of herself and posting them online, so millions of people could click '*like*' and comment on her fabulous perfect life.

What a sham. What a joke.

She hadn't earned a cent of the fortune she'd flouted to the world.

And her husband hadn't loved her.

She was a fraud.

But no more.

April smoothed the charcoal fabric of her pencil skirt over her thighs. It wasn't designer. In fact it had probably cost about five per cent of the cost of her favourite leather tote bag—which she'd left back home in Perth.

She'd left everything behind.

She'd booked a one-way ticket to London and opened up a new credit card account at her bank—politely declining the option to have the balance cleared monthly by the Molyneux Trust. From now on she was definitely paying her own way.

She'd also located her British passport—a document she had thanks to her mother's dual citizenship of both Australia and the UK.

Only then had she told her family what she was doing.

And then she'd ignored every single one of their concerns and hopped onto her flight the next day.

Now here she was. Three days in London.

She'd found a flat. She'd bought reasonably priced clothes for the first time in her life. She'd researched the heck out of the environmental sustainability consulting firm where she was about to have an interview.

Oh—as she noted her long ponytail cascading over the shoulder of her hound's-tooth coat—she'd also dyed her hair brown.

She felt like a different person. Like a *new* person.

She even had a new name, of sorts.

The name that was on her birth certificate and her passport: April Spencer.

Like her sisters, she'd made the choice to use her mother's surname within a few years of her father leaving them. But she'd never bothered having it formally changed.

Turned out that had now come in handy.

Today she didn't feel like April Molyneux, the billionaire mining heiress whose life had collapsed around her.

Today she was April Spencer, and today she had a job interview.

And for the first time in six weeks she felt good.

As Hugh probably should've expected, it had rained through the remainder of September and then most of October. So it was a cool but clear November morning when he retrieved the tin of black paint from beneath his stairs and headed out from his basement to the front door of the main house.

It was just before sunrise, and even on a workday Islington street was almost deserted. A couple walking a Labrador passed by as he laid out his drop cloth, and as he painted the occasional jogger, walker or cyclist zipped past—along with the gradually thickening traffic.

It didn't take long to paint the door: just a quick sand-down, a few minor imperfections in the woodwork to repair, then a fresh coat of paint.

Now it just needed to dry.

The door had to stay propped open for a few hours before he could safely close it again. He'd known this, so he'd planned ahead and dumped his backpack—which contained his laptop—in the hallway before he'd started work. Now he stepped inside, his work boots loud on the blue, cream and grey geometric tessellated tile entryway.

He yanked off his boots, grabbed his laptop out of his bag and then on thick socks padded over to the grand staircase ahead of him. To his left was the first of two reception rooms on the ground floor—but he wasn't going to work in there.

Instead he settled on a stair third from the bottom, rested his laptop on his jeans and got to work.

Or at least that was the plan.

Instead his emails remained unread, and the soft beep of instant message notifications persisted but were ignored.

Who was he kidding? He was never going to get any work done in here.

It was impossible when his attention remained on insignificant details: the way the weak morning sunlight sauntered through the wedged-open door to mingle with the dust he'd disturbed. The scent of the house: cardboard packing boxes, musty air and windows closed for far too long. The light—or lack of it. With every door but the front door sealed shut, an entryway he remembered as bright with light seemed instead gloomy and...*abandoned*.

Which, of course, it was.

He hadn't stepped foot in here since the day he'd moved into the basement.

Back then—three years ago—it had been too hard. He hadn't been ready to deal with this house.

Hugh stood up, suddenly needing to move. But not out through the front door.

Instead he went to the internal door only a few steps away and with a firm grip twisted the brass knob and yanked the door open.

He hadn't realised he'd been holding his breath—but he let it out now in a defeated sigh. As if he'd expected to see something different.

But he'd known what was in here.

Once, this room had been where his mother and her second husband had hosted their guests with cups of tea and fancy biscuits.

That would be impossible now. If any antique furniture remained, it was hidden. Completely. By boxes. Boxes that filled the room in every direction—stacked neatly like bricks as tall as he was—six foot and higher.

Boxes, boxes, boxes—so many he couldn't even begin to count.

Hugh reached out to touch the nearest box. It sat on a stack four high, its plain cardboard surface slightly misshapen by whatever was crammed within it.

Some of the many boxes that surrounded it—beneath, beside and beyond—were occasionally labelled unhelpfully: *purple treasures…sparkly things.*

Others—the work of the woman Hugh had employed to help his mother—had detailed labels and colour-coded stickers: a relic of Hugh's attempts to organise his mother's hoard into some sort of system.

But his mother had resisted—joyfully creating ridiculous categories and covertly shuffling items between boxes—and in the end her frustrated assistant had correctly informed Hugh that it was an utter waste of time.

Which he'd already known—but then, what option had he had?

Doctors, specialists, consultants…all had achieved nothing.

How could they? When his mother knew exactly what she was doing?

She'd been here before, after all. Before Len. When it had been just Hugh and his mum and her hoard. And her endless quest for love.

With Len she'd finally had the love she'd searched for for so long. A love that had been powerful enough to allow her to let go of all the things she'd collected in the years since Hugh's father had left them. Things she'd surrounded herself with and held on to so tightly when she'd been unable to possess the one thing she'd so badly wanted: love.

Without Len his mother had believed that her hoard was all she'd had left. And, despite still having Hugh, despite his desperate efforts, it hadn't been enough.

He'd been helpless to prevent the hoard that had overshadowed his childhood from returning.

Hugh closed his eyes.

There was so much *stuff* in this room that if he walked another step he would walk into a wall of boxes.

It was exactly the same in almost every room in the house—

every living space, every bedroom. Except the kitchen, halls and bathrooms—and that was only because of the staff Hugh had employed and his mother's reluctant agreement to allow them into the house each day.

So that was all he'd managed: to pay people to keep the few bits of empty floor space in his mother's house clean. And to clear a safe path from her bedroom to the front and back doors in case of a fire.

Really, it was not all that different from how it had been when he'd been ten. Except this time he'd had loads of money to outsource what he'd only barely managed as a kid.

And this place was a hell of a lot bigger than the tiny council flat he'd grown up in.

He opened his eyes, but just couldn't stare at those awful uniform boxes any more.

Back in the entry hall, Hugh grabbed his laptop and backpack, ready to leave…but then he stilled.

The new paint on the door was still wet. He wasn't going anywhere.

But he also wasn't going to be able to work—it would seem that three years had done nothing to ease the tension, the frustration and the hopelessness that those damn boxes elicited within him.

Even waiting another three years—or ten—to deal with them wasn't going to make any difference.

They'd still represent a lot more than they should.

They needed to go. *All* of them.

This house needed to be bright and light once again. It needed to breathe.

So he sat back down on the bottom step of the grand old staircase, knowing exactly what he was going to do.

It was time.

It had started with confusion at the supermarket checkout.

'Do you have another card?' the checkout operator had asked.

'Pardon me?' April had said—because, well, it had never happened to her before.

It had, it seemed, happened several times to the not particularly patient operator—Bridget, according to her name tag. She'd studied April, her gaze flat, as April had tried what she knew to be her correct PIN twice more.

And then, as April had searched hopelessly for an alternative card—she'd cut up every single card linked to the Molyneux Trust back in Perth—Bridget had asked her to move aside so she could serve the next in a long line of customers.

April had dithered momentarily: was she supposed to return the Thai green curry ready-meal, the bunch of bananas and bottle of eye make-up remover to the shelves before she left?

But then the weight of pitying stares—possibly only imagined—had kicked in, and April had exited the shop as fast as she'd been able, her sneakers suddenly unbelievably squeaky on the supermarket's vinyl flooring.

Now she was at home, still in her gym gear, on her butter-soft grey leather couch, her laptop before her.

For only the second time in the four weeks since she'd been in London she logged in to her internet banking—the other time being when she'd set up her account at the bank. Her fully furnished flat didn't come with a printer, so she'd have to scroll through her credit card statement onscreen.

But it was still easy to see the reason for her mortification at the checkout—she'd maxed out her credit card.

How was that even *possible*?

She'd been so careful with her spending—more so as each still jobless week had passed.

She hadn't bought any new clothes for *weeks*. She'd stopped eating at cafés and restaurants, and had instead become quite enamoured with what she considered a very English thing: convenience stores with huge walls of pre-made sandwiches in triangular plastic packaging. And microwaveable ready-meals for dinner.

They must only be costing a few pounds a meal, surely?

She *had* joined the gym, but that had seemed very cheap. And fortunately the flat came with Wi-Fi, so she hadn't had to pay for that.

So where had all her money gone?

Five minutes later she knew.

With pen and paper, she'd documented exactly where her money had been spent.

Her rent—and four weeks' deposit—was the biggest culprit. Only now did it dawn on her that even if she *did* get one of the many, many jobs she'd been applying for, her starting salary would barely cover her rent. With absolutely nothing left over for sandwiches in plastic triangles.

She flopped back onto her couch and looked around her flat.

It was small, but—if she was objective—not *that* small. And it was beautifully furnished. *Expensively* furnished. Her kitchen appliances were the same insanely priced brand she'd had back in Perth. Her small bathroom was tiled in floor-to-ceiling marble.

She even had a balcony.

But she couldn't afford a balcony. She couldn't afford any of this.

Because she didn't have any money. *At all.*

Not for the first time in four weeks, she wondered if she'd made a terrible mistake.

The first time had been after she hadn't got the first job she'd been interviewed for.

Now, several job interviews later—and many more applications that had led to absolutely nothing—her initial optimism astounded her. She literally had a degree, an internship and then almost ten years of nothing.

Well—not *nothing*. But nothing she was about to put on her CV. A million followers and a charitable foundation that she'd established herself could possibly sound impressive to *some* HR departments. But they weren't relevant to the environmental officer roles she was applying for.

And, just as importantly, they would reveal her real name. And she just couldn't do that.

Although it was tempting at times. Like tonight. How easy it would be to still be April Molyneux and organise the reissue of one of the many credit cards linked to her insane fortune? By this time tomorrow she could be eating all the Thai green curry she wanted.

She could even upgrade to a far more impressive flat.

April pushed herself up and off the couch, to search for something to eat in her lovely kitchen.

Her fridge was stocked only with expensive Australian Riesling, sparkling designer water—also expensive—a partially eaten wheel of camembert cheese—expensive—and the organic un-homogenised milk that she'd bought because she'd liked the pretty glass bottle it came in—probably also more expensive than it needed to be.

April felt sick.

Was she really so disconnected from the reality of what things cost?

Her whole life she'd known she was rich. But she'd thought she still had *some* sense of the reality of living in the real world: without a trust fund, without the mansion your mum had bought for you.

She'd liked to think she'd projected some sort of 'everywoman' persona to her Instagram and Facebook followers. That despite the good fortune of her birth that she was really just like everybody else.

She poured herself a bowl of probably overpriced granola and used up the rest of her fancy milk, then sat back in front of her laptop.

Earlier today, before heading to the gym, she'd scheduled the next couple of days' worth of social media posts.

April *Spencer* might be in London, but April Molyneux—to her followers, anyway—was still in Perth, effortlessly adjusting to her new single life.

Before she'd dyed her hair she'd made sure she'd honoured every single product placement agreement she'd signed, and had posed for months' worth of photos. She'd taken even more selfies, with all manner of random backgrounds—she'd come up with something to caption them with as she needed to.

Plus she still took random photos while here in London—the habit was too ingrained for her to give it up completely. She just made sure her hair and anything identifiably London wasn't in any of the photos. So the book she was reading... the shade she'd painted her toenails...that kind of stuff. All was still documented, still shared, interwoven with her blonde April photos and carefully coordinated with her assistant back home—thankfully still paid for by the Molyneux Foundation.

So her social media life carried on. Her followers continued to grow.

And what were they seeing?

She scrolled down the page, taking in her last few years of photos in a colourful blur.

A blur of international holidays, secluded luxury Outback retreats, designer shoes, amazing jewellery, beautiful clothes, a gorgeous husband and attractive—wealthy—friends.

They were seeing an unbelievably privileged woman who had absolutely no idea what it was like to exist in the real world.

April slapped her laptop screen shut, suddenly disgusted with herself.

And ashamed.

The whole point of all this—the move to London, her quest for a job, living alone for the first time in her life—had been about finding herself. Defining who she was if she wasn't Evan's wife. Or one of the Molyneux heiresses.

But so far all she'd achieved was a self-indulgent month during which she'd patted herself on the back for 'living like a normal person' but achieved absolutely nothing other than a new, reasonably priced wardrobe.

She knew her mum, Ivy and Mila all assumed this was just a bit of a game to her. They assumed that once she did eventually get a job she'd supplement her income with Molyneux money. On reflection, no one had pointed out the now damned obvious fact that she couldn't afford this apartment.

And, unlike April, they would know. Mila had never used her Molyneux fortune: she knew exactly how far a dollar or a pound could stretch. And Ivy had dedicated her life to building up the Molyneux fortune—so she knew, too.

She couldn't even be annoyed with them. Up until tonight, and that stupid, sad 'declined' beep at the cash register, they'd been right.

They'd been right to think that their pampered middle sister couldn't cut it in the real world.

And, if she was brutally honest, she hadn't even been trying. She'd *thought* she had, but people in the real world didn't have no income for a month—and no savings—and then casually take their time applying for some mythical perfect job while living in a luxury apartment.

She flipped her laptop open again.

She needed to find a job. Immediately.

CHAPTER TWO

SHE HAD A nice voice, Hugh thought.

Unquestionably Australian. Warm. Professional.

She didn't sound nervous, although she did laugh every now and again—which was possibly nerves. Or possibly not. Her laugh was natural. Also warm. Pretty.

Hugh's lips quirked. How whimsical of him. How unlike him.

Currently, April…he glanced down at the printed CV before him…April *Spencer* was answering the last of his four interview questions.

Rather well, actually.

He leant back in his chair, listening carefully as her voice filled the room, projected by the speakers hooked up to his laptop.

This was the third interview his recruitment consultant had organised, although the other two applicants had been quite different from April. One an art curator, another an antique specialist.

Both complete overkill for the position. He'd been clear with the consultant, Caro, that his mother's collections were not of any monetary value—although Caro *had* made some valid points that knowledge of antiques and curation skills might still be of use.

But still… He felt as if employing either skill-set would be pretending that all those boxes were something more than they actually were. Which was a hoard. A hoard he wanted out of his life.

'…so I feel my experience working for the Molyneux Foundation demonstrates my understanding of the importance of client privacy,' April said as she continued her answer. 'I regularly dealt with donors who requested their names remain absolutely confidential. At other times donors wished for their donation—whether it be product, service or otherwise—to be announced at a date or time suitable to their company. In both scenarios complete discretion was essential.'

'But your role at the foundation, Ms Spencer, was as social media coordinator,' Hugh prompted, scanning her CV. 'Why would you have access to such sensitive information?'

There was the briefest pause. 'It's quite a small foundation,' April said, her tone confident. 'And I worked closely with the managing director. It was my job to schedule posts and monitor comments—I needed to know what to announce, and also what comments to remove in case anyone gave one of our generous benefactors away.'

From the notes Caro had provided, it seemed April's work with the Molyneux Foundation had been the reason she'd been put forward. Hugh had made it clear that a proven ability to maintain strict confidentiality was essential for this position.

'And you're available immediately?' he asked.

'Yes,' April said.

Hugh nodded at the phone. 'Right—thank you, Ms Spencer,' he said. 'A decision will be made shortly.'

Then he ended the call.

After the interview April left the small meeting room and returned to the recruiter's office.

It had all been rather bizarre. She'd come in this morning expecting to be assigned to an interview for something similar to her two jobs so far—both short-term entry level social media roles to cover unexpected leave—and yet she'd been put forward for a job unpacking boxes, with a phone interview to take place almost immediately.

Across from her, at her large, impressive desk, sat Caroline Zhu, the senior recruiter at the agency April had been working for since her supermarket debacle three weeks earlier.

'I'm sorry,' April said. 'I don't think the interview went particularly well.'

Terribly, actually. She felt she'd answered the questions well enough, but Hugh Bennell had barely said a word. Certainly not a word of encouragement, anyway.

'Possibly,' Caro said, in the no-nonsense voice that matched her jet-black no-nonsense ponytail. 'But unlikely. It's been several years since Mr Bennell has required my services, but I'm certain his interview technique has not changed. He is not one for superfluous conversation.'

April nodded. Yes, she'd got that.

It fitted, she supposed—her frantic internet searching in the short period of time she'd had before her interview had revealed little about Hugh Bennell. She knew of Precise, of course—practically everyone with a smartphone would have at least one app from the company. April, in fact, had about six, all related to scheduling, analytics and online collaboration. But, unlike other international tech companies that were synonymous with their founders, Hugh Bennell was no more than a name on the company website—and the subject of several newspaper articles in which a string of journalists had attempted to discover the man behind such a massive self-made fortune.

But all had failed.

All April had learnt from those quickly skimmed articles was that Hugh had grown up in council housing in London, the only child of a single, hard-working mother. As soon as he'd left university it had been as if he'd wiped all trace of himself from public record—she'd found no photos of him, and his Wikipedia entry was incredibly brief.

It was strikingly unusual in this share-everything world.

Mysterious, even.

Intriguing, actually.

'You'll know soon enough,' Caroline continued. 'In my experience, Mr Bennell makes extremely swift decisions.'

'Are you able to tell me a bit more about the position?'

Caroline raised an impatient eyebrow. 'As I said, the information Mr Bennell provided is limited. He has a room full of a large number of boxes that require sorting and disposal. Not antiques. Nothing dangerous. He requires someone trustworthy and hardworking who can start immediately. That's all I can tell you.'

'And you thought I was suitable because…?'

'Because you're keen to work as much as possible for as much pay as possible. You were quite clear on that when we first met.'

True. After some judicious reimagining of her work experience—she'd repositioned herself as April Spencer, Social Media Manager at the Molyneux Foundation, which was technically true—she'd turned up at the best-reviewed temp agency within walking distance of her overpriced flat at nine a.m. the Monday after her credit card had been declined.

She'd been absolutely—possibly over-zealously—clear in her goals. To work hard and earn as much money as she could. In fact, she'd even found a night job, stacking shelves at a supermarket near her new home.

She needed her credit card debt cleared *pronto*. She needed money *yesterday*.

Fortunately Caroline Zhu had seemed to consider her desperation-tinged enthusiasm a positive.

The phone rang in pretty musical tones.

'Ah, here we go,' Caroline said, raising her eyebrows at April. She picked up the phone, had the briefest of conversations that ended with, 'Excellent news, Mr Bennell. I'll let the successful applicant know.'

She hung up and turned back to April.

'Just as I thought,' Caroline said. 'I'm rarely wrong on such things. Mr Bennell has selected you as his preferred candidate. You start immediately.'

'Unpacking boxes?'

'For a mouthwatering sum an hour.'

'I'm in,' April said with a grin.

Caroline might have let slip the slightest of smiles. 'You already are. Here's the address.'

Hugh Bennell's house was beautiful.

It felt familiar, actually—she'd stayed with her mum and sisters at a similar house for Christmas, many years ago. It was the year she and her sisters had campaigned for a white

Christmas and, like so many things in her childhood and adult life, it had just happened.

She straightened her shoulders, then knocked on the front door.

She'd been told Hugh Bennell would be meeting her—which had surprised her. Surely the boss of a company like Precise had staff to deal with a lowly employee like herself?

But then, she'd supposed he also had staff to *interview* lowly employees like herself—and he'd already done that himself.

If anything, it just added to the general sense of mystery: mysterious boxes for her to unpack, complete with a mysterious billionaire CEO who was mysteriously hands-on with the recruitment of unskilled labour.

It was late morning now. She hadn't had time to change, so she still wore what she now considered her 'interview suit'. Her shoes were freshly polished, and her hair was looped in an elegant low bun that she was rather proud of. Her stylist back in Perth would be impressed.

The liquorice-black door opened.

And revealed a man.

A tall man. With dark hair, dark stubble. Dark eyes.

Dark eyes that met her own directly. *Very* directly.

Momentarily April felt frozen beneath that gaze.

So this is what a mysterious tech billionaire looks like.

Jaw-droppingly handsome.

She blinked. 'Good morning,' she said, well practised from years of socialising at every event anyone could imagine. 'I'm April Spencer. Are you Mr Bennell?'

He nodded. 'You got here quickly.'

'I did,' she said. 'The agency emphasised the urgency of this placement.'

Silence. But, despite her usually sparkling conversational skills, April didn't rush to fill it. Instead she simply stood still beneath Hugh Bennell's gaze.

He was still looking at her. Unreadably but intensely. It was a strange and unfamiliar sensation.

But not entirely uncomfortable.

There was something about him—the way he stood, maybe—that created a sense of calm. And of time.

Time to take a handful of moments to study the man before her—to take in the contrast of his black hair and olive skin. To admire the thick slashes of his eyebrows, the sharpness of his cheekbones, the elegance of his mouth.

He was more interesting than gorgeous, she realised, with a slightly crooked nose and an angular chin. His too-long hair and his stubble—forgotten, she was sure, rather than fashionable.

But it was that sum of those imperfect parts that made a darkly, devastatingly attractive whole.

And definitely not what she'd been expecting.

Whatever she'd thought a mysterious billionaire who deliberately shunned the spotlight would look like, *this* was not it.

He was also *nothing* like Evan.

That realisation came from left field, shocking her.

April blinked again. *What was she doing?*

'Please come in,' Hugh Bennell said. As naturally as if only a beat of time had passed.

Maybe it had?

April felt flustered and confused—and seriously annoyed with herself.

She'd just met her new boss. She needed to pull herself together.

She was probably just tired from the long hours she'd been working.

But did tiredness explain the way her gaze documented the breadth of her new boss's shoulders as she stepped inside?

Nope.

There was no way she could pretend she didn't know what the fireworks in her belly meant. It had just been a *long* time since they'd been associated with anyone but her husband.

And a pretty long time since she'd associated them with Evan.

She squeezed her eyes shut for a second.

No. No. No, no, *no.*

She had not flown halfway around the world to turn into a puddle over a man. Over her *boss*. No matter how mysterious.

That certainly wasn't why she was working two jobs and sharing a room in a truly awful shared house.

She'd come to London to live independently. Without her mother's money for the first time in her life and without Evan for the first time since she was seventeen.

And she needed this job. She certainly needed the very generous hourly rate.

She *didn't* need fireworks, or the heat that had pooled in her belly.

'Miss Spencer?'

April's eyes snapped open. 'Sorry, Mr Bennell.'

'Are you okay?' he asked.

He did have gorgeous eyes. Thoughtful eyes that looked as if a million things were happening within them.

'Of course,' she said with a deliberate smile.

He inclined his chin, somewhat sceptically. 'I was just saying that we'll run through your responsibilities in the kitchen.'

She nodded, then followed him down the narrow hall beside the rather grand if dusty staircase.

As they walked April did her absolute best to shove all thoughts of fireworks or heat firmly out of her mind—and her body. Frustratingly, Hugh's well-worn, perfectly fitted jeans did nothing to help this endeavour.

Neither did the unwanted realisation that—for the first time since Evan had told her he didn't love her and her sparkling life had been dulled—she felt truly alive.

April Spencer was beautiful.

Objectively beautiful. As if she'd stepped off the pages of a catalogue and into his mother's house.

For a while he'd stood and just *looked* at her, because he'd felt helpless to do anything but.

He'd looked at her chocolate-brown hair, at her porcelain skin and her crystal blue eyes. At her lips—pink, and shining with something glossy. At her fitted clothes and the long coat cinched in tight at her waist.

He'd expected a backpacker. Someone younger, really. Someone he could actually imagine lifting and shifting boxes.

This woman was not it.

This woman was poised and utterly together. Everything about her exuded strength and confidence. As if she was used to commanding a room. Or a corporation.

Not rummaging through boxes.

It just didn't fit.

He'd let her in, but then he had turned to face her—to question her.

He needed to know who she was and what she was doing here.

But when he'd turned her eyes had been closed.

He'd watched her for a second as she'd taken deep breaths. In through her nose. Out through her mouth. And it was in that moment—while that knowledgeable gaze had been hidden— that he'd sensed vulnerability. A vulnerability that had been completely disguised by her polish and her smile.

And so, instead of interrogating her, he'd asked her if she was okay.

And instead of calling the agency back, asking for someone more suitable, he'd led her into the kitchen and handed her a confidentiality agreement to sign.

That moment of vulnerability had long gone now, and the woman in his mother's kitchen revealed nothing of whatever he'd seen.

But he *had* seen it. And he of all people knew that people were rarely what they first appeared. He'd spent most his life hiding all but what people absolutely needed to know.

So for now he wasn't going to question April Spencer.

But he *did* acknowledge her incongruity, and he didn't like that this project to clear his mother's house already felt more complicated than he wanted it to.

April laid his pen on top of the signed paperwork. 'All done, Mr Bennell,' she said with a smile.

'Call me Hugh,' he said firmly.

'April,' she said, with eyes that sparkled.

He was again struck by her beauty, but forced himself to disregard it. The attractiveness of his employees was none of his concern.

He nodded briskly, and didn't return her smile. 'You'll be working alone,' he said, getting straight to the point, 'and I've provided guidelines for how I want items sorted. It should be self-explanatory: paperwork containing personal details is to be saved, all other papers to be shredded and recycled. Junk is to be disposed of. Anything of value should be separated for donation. I've provided the details of local charities you can contact to organise collection.'

April nodded, her gaze on the printed notes he'd left for her.

'Is there anything other than papers you want kept?' she asked.

'No,' he said.

Maybe louder than he'd intended, as her head jerked upwards.

'Okay,' she said carefully. 'And how do I contact you if I have any questions?'

'You don't,' he said. 'I'm not to be disturbed.'

Her glossy lips formed a straight line. 'So who *can* I contact?'

He shrugged dismissively. 'You won't need to contact anybody. It's all made very clear in my instructions. Just send me an email at the end of each day with details of your progress.'

'So you *know* what's in the boxes? Caroline implied that you didn't, which is why you need me to sort through them.'

Hugh shook his head. 'It doesn't matter.'

April met his gaze. 'So you trust me to go through a whole room of boxes and make all the decisions myself?'

'Yes,' he said. 'It's all junk. You aren't going to stumble across a hidden fortune, I promise you.'

She looked unconvinced.

'And besides—it's not a room. It's the whole house.'

Her eyes widened. 'Pardon me?'

He ran a hand through his hair. He just wanted this conversation to be over and to be out of this place. This stuffed full, oppressive house which this woman only complicated further.

'Yes,' he said. 'Three floors. Leave any furniture where it is. Don't lift anything too heavy. I've left you a key and the security code. I expect you to work an eight-hour day.' He stopped, mentally running through any further extraneous details he should mention. 'If there's an emergency—*only* an emergency—you can call me. My number is listed in the documentation.'

'That's it?' she said.

'That's it,' he said.

'Great,' she said. 'Where do I start?'

'I'll show you,' he said.

Minutes later they stood before a wall built with pale brown cardboard.

'Wow,' April said. 'I've never seen anything like this before.'

Hugh had.

'Did you buy the place like this?' she asked.

'Something like that,' he said, needing to leave. Not wanting to explain.

She'd work it out soon enough.

'I'll get this sorted for you,' April said, catching his gaze.

He already had one foot in the foyer.

She spoke with assurance—*reassurance?*—and with questions in her eyes.

But Hugh didn't want to be reassured, and he certainly didn't want her questions. He hated the way this woman, this stranger—*his employee*—thought he needed to be somehow comforted.

He'd barely said a word since they'd entered this room— what had he revealed?

'That's what you're here for,' he said firmly.

Nothing more.

Now he could finally escape from the boxes, and his breath came steadily again only as he closed the front door behind him.

CHAPTER THREE

Two days later April sat cross-legged amongst a lot of boxes and a lot of dust.

She was dressed in jeans, sneakers and a floppy T-shirt—her jumper having been quickly removed thanks to the excellent heating and the many boxes she'd already shifted today—and yet another box lay ready for her attention. Her hair was piled up on top of her head, and the local radio station filled the room via her phone and a set of small speakers she'd purchased before she'd realised she had absolutely no money.

But she was glad for her previous financial frivolity. This massive house was creaky and echoey, and she'd hated how empty it had felt on her first day, when she'd been sorting through boxes wearing a pencil skirt, heels and a blouse with a bow—in total silence.

Bizarre how such an overflowing house could feel so empty, but it did.

Music helped. A little.

Now, on day three of her new job, already many boxes lay flattened in the foyer. The shredder had disposed of old takeaway menus and shoe catalogues and local newspapers. And she'd labelled a handful of empty boxes for donations. Several were already full with books and random bits and pieces: a man's silk tie, a mass-produced ceramic vase, eleven tea towels from the Edinburgh Military Tattoo—and so much more. It was nearly impossible to categorise the items, although she'd tried.

But much of the boxes' content was, as Hugh had told her, junk. The packaging for electronic items, without the items themselves. Gossip magazines from ten years ago, with British reality TV stars she didn't recognise on the covers. Sugar and salt packets. Pens that didn't work. Dried-out mascara and nail polish bottles.

It was all so random.

Initially she'd approached each box with enthusiasm. What was she going to learn about the person who'd packed all these boxes from *this* box?

But each box gave little away.

There was no theme, there were no logical groupings or collections, and so far there was absolutely nothing personal. Not even one scribble on a takeaway menu.

Hugh hadn't given anything away, either.

It was hard in this house, with all its mysterious boxes, not to think about the rather interesting and mysterious man who owned them all.

Were they *his* boxes?

April didn't think so. That morning in the kitchen, those clear but sparse directions and neat instructions had not indicated a man who collected such clutter. There was something terribly structured about the man: he exuded organisation and an almost regimented calm.

But that had changed when he'd shown her this room. The instant he'd opened the door he'd become tense. His body, his words. His gaze.

It had been obvious he'd wanted to leave, and he had as soon as humanly possible.

So, no, the boxes weren't his.

But they didn't belong to a stranger, either—because the boxes meant *something* to Hugh Bennell.

Her guess was that they belonged to a woman. The magazines, toiletries... But who?

His wife? Ex-wife? Mother? Sister? Friend?

So—with enthusiasm—April had decided to solve the mystery of the boxes.

But with box after box the mystery steadfastly remained and her enthusiasm rapidly waned.

On the radio, a newsreader read the ten o'clock news in a lovely, clipped British accent.

Only ten a.m.?

Her self-determined noon lunchbreak felt a lifetime away.

April sighed and straightened her shoulders, then carefully sliced open the brown packing tape of her next box.

On top lay empty wooden photo frames, one with a crack through the glass. And beneath that lay two phone books—the thick, heavy type that had used to be delivered before everyone had started searching for numbers online.

The unbroken wooden frames would go to the 'donate' box, and the phone books into the recycling. But as she walked out into the foyer, to add the books to the already mountainous recycling pile, a piece of card slipped out from between the pages.

April knelt to pick it up. It was an old and yellowed homemade bookmark, decorated with a child's red thumbprints in the shape of lopsided hearts.

Happy Mothering Sunday!
Love Hugh

The letters were in neat, thick black marker—the work of a school or kindergarten teacher.

And just like that she'd solved the mystery.

She started a new category: *Hugh*.

She wasn't making a decision on that bookmark, no matter what he said.

She'd let him know in her summarising email that evening.

The email pinged into Hugh's inbox shortly before five p.m. As it had the previous two days at approximately the same time, with the same subject line and the day's date. Exactly as he'd specified—which he appreciated.

She did insist on prefacing her emails with a bit of chatter, but she'd stuck to his guidelines for updating him on her progress.

Which was slower than he'd hoped. Although he didn't think that was April's fault—more his own desire for the house to be magically emptied as rapidly as possible.

That option still existed, of course. He'd researched a business that would come and collect all his mother's boxes and take them away. It would probably only take a day.

But he just couldn't bring himself to do that.

He hated those boxes—hated that stuff. Hated that his mother had been so consumed by it.

Despite it being junk, despite the way the boxes weighed so heavily upon him—both literally and figuratively—it just felt...

As if it would be disrespectful.

Hi Hugh,
I've found a bookmark today—photo attached—and I've put it aside for you. If I find anything similar I'll let you know.

Otherwise all going well. About two thirds through this room...

Hugh didn't read the rest. Instead he clicked open the attachment.

A minute later his boots thumped heavily against the steps up to his mother's front door. It was freezing in the evening darkness—he hadn't bothered to grab a coat for the very short journey—but the foyer was definitely a welcome relief as he let himself in.

April was still in the kitchen, her coat halfway on, obviously about to leave.

'Don't panic—I didn't throw it out,' she said.

'Throw what out?' he asked.

He hadn't seen her since that first morning, and she looked different in jeans and jumper—younger, actually. Her cheek was smudged with dust, her hair not entirely contained in the knot on top of her head.

'The bookmark,' she said. 'I'll just go grab it for you.'

'No,' he said. 'Don't.'

She'd already taken a handful of steps, and now stood only an arm's length before him.

'Okay,' she said. She inclined her chin in a direction over his shoulder. 'It's in a box out there. I've labelled it "Hugh".

I'll just chuck anything in there that I think you should have a look at.'

'No,' he said again. 'Don't.'

Now she seemed to realise what he was saying. Or at least she was no longer wilfully ignoring him. He knew how clear he'd been: with the exception of any paperwork that included personal details, April was to donate or trash *everything*.

'Are you sure?'

Hugh shrugged. 'It's just a badly painted bookmark.'

Up until a few minutes ago he'd had no recollection of that piece of well-intentioned crafting, so his life would definitely be no lesser with it gone.

'I wasn't just talking about the bookmark,' April said. 'I meant anything like that. I'm sure more sentimental bits and pieces are going to turn up. And what about photos? I found some photo frames today, so I expect eventually I'll find—'

'Photos can go in the bin,' he said.

Hugh shoved his hands in his jeans pockets. Again, he just wanted to be out of this place. But he didn't leave.

April was watching him carefully, concern in her clear blue gaze. He was shifting his weight from foot to foot. Fidgeting. He *never* fidgeted.

He wasn't himself in this house. With all this stuff. Now that the boxes had necessarily flowed into the foyer behind him the clutter was *everywhere*.

April had left an empty coffee mug on the kitchen sink.

Now he skirted around her, making his way to the other side of the counter, grabbed the mug and opened the dishwasher. It was empty.

'I've just been hand-washing,' April said. 'I can wash that before I go—don't worry about it.'

Hugh ignored her, stuck the plug in the sink and turned on the hot water. Beneath the sink he found dishwashing liquid, and squirted it into the steaming water.

As the suds multiplied he was somewhat aware of April shrugging off her coat. He had no idea why it was so important for him to clean this mug, but it was.

'You can go,' he said, cleaning out the coffee marks from inside the mug. He realised it wasn't one of his mother's—it was printed with the logo of a Fremantle sporting team he didn't recognise and had a chip in the handle. It was April's.

He rinsed the mug in hot water and placed it on the dish rack.

Immediately it was picked up again—by April.

She was standing right beside him, tea towel in hand, busily drying the mug.

He hadn't noticed her move so close.

She didn't look at him, her concentration focused on her task. Her head was bent, and a long tendril of dark hair curled down to her nape.

This close, he could see the dust decorating her hair, a darker smudge creating a streak across her cheekbone.

She turned, looking directly at him.

She was tall, he realised, even without her heels.

Today her lips weren't glossy, and he realised she probably wasn't wearing make-up. Her eyelashes were no longer the blackest black; her skin wasn't magazine-perfect.

She didn't look better—or worse. Just different. And it was that difference he liked.

That she'd surprised him.

He hadn't been able to imagine her unpacking boxes—but she looked just as comfortable today as she had in her sharp suit. And her gaze was just as strong, just as direct.

He realised he liked that, too.

It should have been an uncomfortable and unwanted realisation. Maybe it was—or it would be later. When his brain wasn't cluttered with boxes and forgotten bookmarks and had room for logic and common sense…and remembering who he was. Who *she* was.

Boss. Employee…

For now, he simply looked at the surprising woman beside him.

'I know this is your mum's house,' she said. 'I get that this must be difficult for you.'

Her words were soft and gentle. They still cut deep.

But they shouldn't—and his instinct was to disagree. *They're just boxes. It's just stuff. It's not difficult in any way at all.*

He said nothing.

'Do you want me to come back tomorrow?'

Had she thought he might fire her over the bookmark?

He nodded sharply, without hesitation. Despite how uncomfortable her kind words had made him. Despite how unlike himself she made him. How aware he was of her presence in this room and in this house. How aware he was of how close she stood to him.

'Okay,' she said. 'I'll leave my mug, then.'

He didn't look at her as she stepped around him and put the coffee mug into an overhead cupboard.

By the time she'd shrugged back into her coat, and arranged her letterbox-red knitted scarf he'd pulled himself together.

'See you tomorrow,' she said, with a smile that was bright.

And then she was gone, leaving Hugh alone with a sink full of disappearing bubbles.

April's roommate was asleep when she got home from stacking shelves at the supermarket, so she went into the communal living room to call her mum.

For once the room was empty—usually the Shoreditch shared house tended to have random people dotted all over the place.

Evidence of the crowd of backpackers who lived here—three from Australia and two from South Africa—was scattered everywhere, though. Empty beer bottles on the cheap glass coffee table, along with a bowl of now stale chips—crisps, they were called here—and a variety of dirty plastic plates and cups. One of the other Aussie girls had had a friend dossing on the couch, and his sheets and blankets still lay tangled and shoved into a corner, waiting for someone magically to wash them and put them away.

Which would happen—eventually. April had learnt that

someone would get sick of the mess, and then do a mad tidy-up—loudly and passive-aggressively.

On a couple of occasions in the two weeks she'd been here it had been her—a lifetime of a weekly house-cleaning service meant she definitely preferred things clean, even though she'd had to look up how to clean a shower on the internet. She'd then realised that her relatively advanced age—she was the oldest of the group by six years—meant that everyone expected her to be the responsible, tidy one who'd clean up after everyone else.

And that wasn't going to happen.

She was too busy working her two jobs and trying to stay on top of her April Molyneux social media world to add unpaid cleaner to the mix. So she'd coordinated the group, they'd all agreed on a roster...and sometimes it was followed.

So April ignored the mess, cleared a spot on the couch and scrolled to her mum's number on her phone.

'Darling!'

It was eight a.m. in Perth, but her mum was always up early. She'd finally retired only recently, with April's eldest sister Ivy taking over the reins at Molyneux Mining. But so far her mother's retirement had seemed to involve several new roles on company boards and a more hands-on role in the investments of the Molyneux Trust.

So basically not a whole lot of retirement was going on for Irene Molyneux. Which did not come as a surprise to anyone.

'Hi, Mum,' April said. 'How's things?'

'Nate is speaking so well!' Irene said. 'Yesterday he said "Can I have a biscuit, please?" Isn't that amazing?'

Irene was also embracing the chance to spend more time with her two-year-old grandson. After five minutes of Nate stories, her mum asked April how she was doing.

'Good,' she said automatically. And then, 'Okay, I guess...'

'What's wrong?'

And so April told her about the bookmark, and her new boss's crystal-clear directive. She didn't mention the details, though—like the sadness she'd seen in Hugh's eyes in the kitchen. His obvious pain.

Her mother was typically no-nonsense. 'If he isn't sentimental, it isn't your role to be.'

But that was the thing—she wasn't convinced he didn't care. Not even close.

'I don't know. It just doesn't feel right.'

'Mmm…' her mother said. 'You can always quit.'

But… 'It pays almost double what I was earning at my last placement.'

'I know,' Irene said.

Her mum didn't say anything further—but April knew what she was thinking. She was torn between supporting April in her goal to pay off her credit card and live independently—a goal she'd supported once she'd been reassured April wasn't going to end up homeless—and solving all her problems. With money.

Which was understandable, really. Her mother had, after all, financially supported April her entire life. And April honestly had never questioned it. She was rich—it was just who she was. Her bottomless credit cards had just come with the territory.

But, really, the only thing she'd ever done that really deserved any payment was her work for the Molyneux Foundation. And besides a few meetings she'd probably spent maybe an hour or two a day working for the foundation—with a big chunk of that time focused on making sure she looked picture-perfect as possible in photos.

It had been a cringe-worthy, shamefully spoiled existence.

'You understand why I need to do this, right? All of this: living here, living on *my* money, living without the Molyneux name?'

'Yes,' Irene said. 'And you know I admire what you're doing. And I'm a little ashamed of myself for being so worried about you.'

This was cringe-worthy too—how little her family expected of her. Her fault as well, of course.

'But that's my job,' Irene continued. 'I'm your mum. I'm supposed to worry. And I'm supposed to want to fix things. But, if I put that aside, here's my non-mum advice—keep the job. Keep working hard, pay off your debt and move out of that awful shared house. It'll make me feel better once you're living in your own place.'

'Yes, Mum,' April said, smiling. 'I'll do my best.'

And then she remembered something she'd been thinking about earlier.

'Hey, Mum, did *you* keep that type of stuff? Stuff that we all made at school—you know, gifts for Mother's Day? Finger paintings? That sort of stuff?'

Irene laughed. 'No! I'm probably a terrible person, but I remember smuggling all that stuff out to the bin under cover of darkness.'

They talked for a while longer, but later, when April had ended the call and gone to bed, her thoughts wandered back to that faded little bookmark Hugh had once given to his mother.

Was she just being sentimental? She wasn't sure how she felt about her mum not keeping any of her childhood art—but then, had it bothered her until now? She hadn't even noticed. Maybe Hugh was right—maybe it *was* just a badly painted bookmark.

But that was the thing—the way Hugh had reacted…the way he'd raced to see her immediately, and the way he'd washed her Dockers mug as if the weight of the world had been on his shoulders…

It felt like so much more.

CHAPTER FOUR

'Hugh?'

'We must've lost him.'

'Should we reschedule? We can't make a decision without him.'

Belatedly Hugh registered what the conference call voices were saying.

He'd tuned out at some point. In fact, he could barely remember what the meeting was about. He glanced at his laptop screen.

Ah. App bug fixes. And something about the latest iOS upgrade.

Not critically important to his business, but important enough that he should be paying attention.

He *always* paid attention.

The meeting ended with his presumed disappearance, and his flat was silent.

He pushed back his chair and headed for the kitchen, leaning against the counter as his kettle boiled busily.

He'd left his tea mug in the sink, as he always did. He reused it throughout the day, and chucked it in the dishwasher each night.

Why had he cared about April's mug?

He was neat. He knew that. Extremely neat. The perfect contrast to his mother and her overwhelming messiness.

Although, to be fair, his mother hadn't always been like that.

At first it had just been clutter. It had only been later that the dishes had begun to pile in the sink and mounds of clothes had remained unwashed. And by then he'd been old enough to help. So he'd taken over—diligently cleaning around all his mum's things: her 'treasures' and her 'we might need it one days', her flotsam and jetsam and her 'there's a useful article/recipe/tip in that' magazines, newspapers and books.

But he wasn't obsessive—at least not to the level of compulsively cleaning an employee's coffee mug.

It had been odd. For him and for April.

He didn't feel good about that.

He didn't know this woman at all.

That had been deliberate. He hadn't wanted to use the Precise HR Department, or reach out to his team for recommendations of casual workers, university students or backpackers—he hadn't wanted anyone he knew or worked with to know about what was he was doing.

But the fact was someone needed to know what he was doing in order to actually do it—and that person was April Spencer.

And so she knew about his mother's hoard and would know it better than anyone ever had. Even him.

That sat uncomfortably. Hugh had spent much of his life hiding his mother's hoard. It didn't feel right to invite somebody in. Literally to lay it all out to be seen—to be judged.

His mum had loved him, had worked so hard, and had provided him with all she could and more on a minimal wage and without any support from his father. She didn't deserve to be judged as anything less than she had been: a great mum. A great woman.

Her hoard had not defined her, but if people had known of it…

The kettle had boiled and Hugh made his tea, leaving the teabag hanging over the edge of his cup.

April had offered to leave yesterday.

But he'd rejected her offer without consideration, and now, even with time, he knew it had been the right decision.

If it wasn't April it would be someone else. At least April wasn't connected to his work or anyone he knew. Anyone who'd known his mother.

She was a temporary worker—travelling, probably. She'd soon be back in Australia, or off to her next working holiday somewhere sunnier than London, and she'd take her knowledge of his mother's secret hoard with her.

His phone buzzed—a text message.

Drinks after work at The Saint?

It was a group message to the cyclists he often rode with a few mornings a week. He liked them. They were dedicated, quick, and they pushed him to get stronger, and faster.

He replied.

Sorry, can't make it.

He always declined the group's social invitations. He liked riding with them, but he didn't do pubs and clubs. Or any place there was likely to be an unpredictable crowd—he never had, and in fact he'd never been able to—not even as a child. He avoided any crowd, but enclosed crowds—exactly as one might find in a pub—made him feel about as comfortable as a room full of his mother's boxes.

He actually wasn't sure which had come first: Had he inherited his crowd-related anxiety from his compulsive hoarder mother, or had his hatred of bustling crowds stemmed from the nightmares he'd once had of being suffocated beneath an avalanche of boxes?

It didn't really matter—the outcome was the same: Hugh Bennell wasn't exactly a party animal.

Fortunately Hugh's repeated refusals to socialise didn't seem to bother his cycling group. He was aware, however, that they all thought he was a bit weird.

But that wasn't an unfamiliar sensation for him—he'd been the weird kid at school too. After all, it hadn't been as if he could ever invite anybody over to his place to play.

Want to come over and see my mum's hoard?

Yeah. That had never happened. He'd never allowed it to happen.

His doorbell rang.

Hugh glanced at his watch. It was early afternoon—not even close to the time when packages were usually delivered. And he certainly wasn't expecting anybody.

Tea still in hand, he headed for the door. It could only be a charity collector, or somebody distributing religious pamphlets.

Instead it was April.

She stood in her coat and scarf, carrying a box.

A box labelled '*Hugh*'.

Hugh's eyes narrowed when he saw her.

April knew she wasn't supposed to be down here, but she just hadn't been able to simply send an email.

He wore a T-shirt, black jeans and an unzipped hoodie, and he held a cup of tea in one hand. He was barefoot and his hair, as she'd come to expect, was scruffy—as if he'd woken up and simply run a hand through it. Yesterday he'd been smooth-shaven, but today the stubble was back—and, as she'd also come to expect, she really rather liked it.

Hugh Bennell seemed to be in a permanent state of sexy dishevelment, and she'd put money on it—if she had any—that he had no idea.

But now was not the time to be pondering any of this.

'Ms Spencer?' he prompted.

Ms Spencer—not April. He definitely wasn't impressed.

She swallowed. 'I'm resigning,' she said. 'I didn't just want to put it in an email.'

A gust of wind whipped down from the street and through the doorway. Despite her coat, April shivered.

Hugh noticed.

He stepped back and gestured for her to come inside.

April blinked—she hadn't expected him to do that. She had a suspicion *he* hadn't either, although his gaze remained unreadable.

Somehow as she stepped past Hugh, slightly awkwardly with the large box, she managed to brush against him—just her upper arm, briefly against his chest. It was the most minimal of touches—made minuscule once combined with her heavy wool coat and Hugh's combination of T-shirt and hoodie. And yet she blushed.

April felt her cheeks go hot and her skin—despite all the layers—prickled with awareness.

How ridiculous. Really only their clothing had touched. Nothing more.

She forced her attention to her surroundings, not looking anywhere near Hugh.

His basement flat was compact and immaculate. Two bikes hung neatly on a far wall, but otherwise the walls were completely empty. In fact the whole place felt empty—there wasn't a trinket or a throw cushion in sight. The only evidence of occupation was the desk, pushed right up against the front window, and its few scattered papers, sticky note pads and pens were oddly reassuring in their imperfection.

They were standing near his taupe-coloured couches, but Hugh didn't sit so neither did she.

Her blush had faded, so she could finally look at him again. Even if it was more in the direction of his shoulder rather than at his eyes. His *knowing* eyes?

She refused to consider it.

'Anyway,' April said, deliberately brisk, 'I found some more things today. A couple of photos of you and your mum and a birthday card.'

She shook her head sharply when Hugh went to speak. She didn't want to hear his spiel again.

'And, look…maybe I should've chucked them out, as you've insisted. But then I found one of those old plastic photo negative barrels—you know? And it had a lock of baby's hair in it.'

She met his gaze.

'*A lock of hair*, Hugh. Yours, I think. And then I was done. I'm not throwing *that* out. That's not my responsibility, and it's definitely not my decision.'

She carefully put the box on Hugh's coffee table.

'So there's the box with your things in it. You can throw it straight in the skip if you want, but *I* couldn't.' She turned around as she straightened, meeting Hugh's gaze again. He gave nothing away. 'I've finished that first reception room, and I've organised for the charity donations to be collected tomorrow.'

Still in her coat and scarf, she felt uncomfortably warm—and not entirely because of the central heating.

'I'd better get going.'

'No notice?' Hugh asked.

His tone was calm and measured. *He* definitely wasn't blushing, or paying any attention when April did.

She was being ridiculous.

'No,' April said. 'I didn't see the point. Clearly I'm unsuitable for the position.'

'What if I made the position suitable?' he said, not missing a beat.

'Pardon me?'

'What if I said you didn't have to make all the decisions any more?' He spoke with perfect calm.

'So I can have a "Hugh" box?'

He nodded. 'Yes.'

'And you'll come sort through it each day?'

Now he shook his head. 'No. I'll come and throw it in the skip each day. But at least *you* wouldn't have to.'

No. That still didn't feel right. April wasn't sure she could let that happen...

Wait. It wasn't her call. It *so* wasn't her call.

And that was all she'd asked for—not to be the decision-maker.

The job paid well. And it wasn't very difficult—now Hugh had removed the requirement to throw out intensely personal items.

And she still had her credit card debt, still had a manky shared house to move out of.

It was a no-brainer.

And yet she hesitated.

The reason stood in front of her. Making her belly heat and her skin warm simply with his presence.

His *oblivious* presence, it would seem.

In which case…what was she worried about?

She knew she didn't want to walk straight from Evan and into another relationship, and that certainly didn't seem to be on offer here.

Hugh was looking at her with his compelling eyes, waiting not entirely patiently for a response. He did *not* look like a man who enjoyed waiting.

April smiled.

It had been fifteen years since she'd been single. It was probably normal that her hormones were being slightly over the top in the vicinity of a demonstrably handsome man.

It was nothing more.

'Deal,' she said.

She had nothing to worry about.

But then Hugh smiled back—and it was the first time she'd seen him smile both with his divine mouth and with his remarkable eyes.

Probably nothing.

On the following day there was nothing to put into the 'Hugh' box.

So April emailed Hugh with her daily update, put on her coat, went home to her still messy shared house and ate soup that had come out of a can while her housemates drank wine that came out of a box. Later, when her housemates headed out to a bar, April walked around the corner to her local supermarket and stacked more cans of soup—and lots of other things—until the early hours of the morning.

The next day, at the Islington end-of-terrace house, April brewed a strong coffee in her Dockers mug, running her thumb across the chip on the handle as she always did. She then placed it on the marble benchtop just where the light hit it, artistically—or as artistically as a coffee mug could be placed—and took a photo.

Really need this today! #workinghard #ilovecaffeine #tooearly

Then she scheduled the post for shortly after Perth would be waking up.

She knew she'd get lots of questions about what she was working so hard on—which was the point. And she'd be vague, and everyone would assume it was something super-exotic—like a fundraising gala event or a photo shoot.

Not unpacking boxes in a grand old dusty house in London.

April smiled.

Part of her wanted to tell her followers *exactly* what she was doing. To tell them that she actually *hadn't* been doing totally fine after Evan had left her, that she'd run away from everyone who loved her and for the first time in her life had realised how privileged she actually was.

But the rest of her knew she had commitments. Knew that the Molyneux Foundation's sponsors hadn't signed up for her to have an early midlife crisis.

And mostly she knew that she wasn't ready to make any big decisions just yet.

She still hadn't really got her head around the fact that she was single.

Of course she'd looked at other men since she'd starting going out with Evan. She'd even had men flirt with her—quite often, really. Possibly because of her sparkling personality—more likely because of all the dollar signs she represented.

But, regardless whether she'd thought some guy was hot, or if some guy had thought *she* was hot—or just rich—it hadn't mattered. She'd been with Evan. So she'd been able to acknowledge a handsome man objectively and then efficiently deflect any flirting that veered beyond harmless.

Because she'd always had Evan.

She'd always loved Evan.

And now that she *didn't* have Evan, meeting another man wasn't on April's radar. It hadn't even been on her radar as something *not* to do—she hadn't even thought about it. It had been too impossible.

Until she'd met Hugh. And then it hadn't. It hadn't felt impossible at all.

But it still *was*, of course.

Totally impossible. As she'd reminded herself in Hugh's flat, she wasn't going to walk from a fifteen-year relationship into another. And—and this scenario felt far more likely— she *definitely* wasn't going to walk from one rejection straight into another one.

There were lots of things she had learnt she could cope with: having no money, working two jobs—two *labour intensive* jobs, no less—living in a shared house at age thirty-two and having her family on the other side of the world.

But she knew utterly and completely that she couldn't cope with another man rejecting her.

I don't love you.

How could those words still hurt so much?

She didn't miss Evan. She understood that their relationship had reached its inevitable conclusion. She definitely didn't want to be with him any more.

But… *I don't love you.*

And he never had.

That pain didn't just go away.

Hugh was already boiling the kettle in his mother's kitchen when April arrived the next morning.

Her gaze flicked over him as she walked into the room, her bag slung over her long coat, her scarf in shades of green today.

'Good morning,' she said, in that polished, friendly tone he was becoming familiar with. She was good at sounding comfortable even when she wasn't.

He could see the questions in her gaze and the instant tension in her stride as she walked towards the bar stools tucked beneath the marble counter.

'Morning,' Hugh said as she dumped her bag on a chair and then shrugged out of her coat. 'I thought I'd help move those heavy boxes.'

Her email last night had explained that she'd found some boxes that would need two people to lift them. He'd considered contacting the temp agency to recruit someone, and then had realised that to do so would be preposterous. He was thirty-six, fit and he lived ten metres away. *He* could move the damn boxes. They were, no matter how much he seemed needlessly to over-complicate them, just boxes. He didn't have to deal with any of the stuff inside them.

She nodded. 'Great!' she said, although he couldn't tell if she meant it. 'I thought you'd just organise someone to come and help me.'

'I did,' he said, then pointed towards his chest. 'Me.'

Her smile now was genuine. And lovely. He'd thought that every time he'd seen her smile. It was another reason he'd considered calling the temp office. But similarly—just as the boxes were only boxes—a smile was only a smile. It, and his admiration of it, meant nothing more.

'It shouldn't take long. I could probably do it myself, but I'd hate to drop one of the boxes and break something.'

The kettle clicked as it finished boiling.

'Doesn't matter if you do,' Hugh said. 'But still—ask me to help move anything heavy, regardless. I don't want you to hurt yourself.'

April blinked as if he'd said something unexpected. 'Okay,' she said.

They took their coffee into the second reception room.

As always, the cluttered space made Hugh feel stiff and antsy—as if he could run a marathon on the adrenalin that shot through his veins.

So far April had cleared only a small section of this room. Once it had been his mum and Len's TV room. They'd sat on the large, plush couch, their legs propped on matching otto-mans, dinner balanced on their laps.

The couch was still there—one arm visible amongst the bevy of boxes.

The heavy boxes were near the window. They were much bigger than the boxes that had filled the first room—probably five or more times their size—and stacked only two high.

It was the top boxes that April wanted to be lifted down.

Coffee placed carefully on the floor, it was easy for the pair of them to lift the boxes: one, two...

For the third, they both had to reach awkwardly around it, tucked away as it was between the heavy curtains and another wall of boxes.

In doing so their fingers brushed against each other, along the far side of the box.

Only for a second—or not even that long.

Barely long enough to be noticed—but Hugh did.

Her hand felt cool and soft. Her nails glossy and smooth beneath his palm.

His gaze darted to April's, but she was too busy lifting the box to pay any attention at all.

Or too busy deliberately looking busy.

He suspected the latter. He'd noticed her reaction in his flat when she'd so briefly brushed against him. Her cheeks had blushed pink in an instant.

He'd reacted, too.

It was strange, really, for his blood to heat like that from such an innocent touch.

He hadn't expected it.

Not that he hadn't continued to notice April's attractiveness. It would be impossible not to. She was beautiful in a classic, non-negotiable way—but beauty was not something Hugh should be paying much attention to when it came to a woman working for him.

So he'd made sure he hadn't.

Except for when she'd stood beside him at the sink a few nights ago, when his thoughts had been jumbled and unfocused. Then the shape of her neck, of her jaw, the profile of her nose and chin...

Yes, he'd noticed.

But, more, he'd noticed her empathy. And her sympathy. Even if he had welcomed neither.

Nor welcomed his attraction to her.

He didn't want complications. Right now—getting this house cleaned out—or ever.

His lifestyle was planned and structured to avoid complications.

Even when he dated women it was only ever for the briefest of times—brevity, he'd discovered, avoided the complications that were impossible for him: commitment, cohabiting, planning a future together...

Relationships were all about complications, and to Hugh complications were clutter.

And he was determined to live a clutter-free life.

But today contact with April's skin had again made his blood heat and his belly tighten.

He should go.

They'd moved the box to where April had directed, so Hugh headed for the door.

'Don't forget your coffee,' April said.

He turned and saw she held the two mugs in her hands—the one for him printed with agapanthus.

He should go—he could make his own coffee downstairs. There was nothing to be gained by staying, and as always he had so much on his to-do list today.

But he realised, surprised, that the boxes that surrounded him weren't compelling him to leave. At some point the tension that had been driving him from this house had abated.

It was still there, but no longer overpowering. Nor, it seemed, was it insurmountable.

So he found himself accepting his mug from April. A woman who, with no more than her smile and against all his better judgement, had somehow compelled him to stay.

He hadn't been supposed to stay.

April had honestly expected Hugh to take his coffee and head on down to his basement apartment.

But instead he'd taken his mug and approached the first box she'd planned to go through—its top already sliced open, the flaps flipped back against the thick cardboard sides.

For a moment it had looked as if he was going to start looking through the box. He'd stepped right up beside it, his spare hand extended, and then he had simply let it fall back against his jean-clad thigh.

Now he brought his mug to his lips, his gaze, as usual, impossible to interpret.

'You really don't like these boxes,' April said. Her words were possibly unwise—but they'd just slipped out.

Hugh Bennell intrigued her. And not just his looks—or his touch, however accidental. But who he was and what all these boxes meant to him.

The boxes, of course, intrigued her too.

He shot a look in her direction, raising an eyebrow. 'No.'

And that was that. No elaboration.

So April simply got to work.

Hugh walked a few steps away, propping his backside against the only available arm of the sofa. Boxes were stacked neatly on the seat cushions beside him.

This box was full of clothes. A woman's. April hadn't come across women's clothes before, and the discovery of the brightly coloured silks and satins made her smile and piqued her interest.

She held a top against herself: a cream sheer blouse with thick black velvet ribbon tied into a bow at the neck. It was too small for April—smaller even than the sample size clothing she'd used to have sent to her by designers before she'd given up on starving herself.

'Was this your mum's?' April asked, twisting to face Hugh.

She absolutely knew it wasn't her place to ask him, but she just couldn't *not*.

It was too weird to be standing in this room with Hugh, in silence, surrounded by all this stuff that meant something to him but absolutely nothing to her. And *she* was the one sorting through it.

Hugh didn't even blink. 'All clothing is to be donated,' he said.

'That wasn't why I was asking,' April said.

She tossed the shirt into the 'donate' box in the centre of the room. Soon after followed a deep pink shift dress, a lovely linen shawl and a variety of printed T-shirts. Next April discovered a man's leather bomber jacket that was absolutely amazing but about a hundred sizes too big.

Regardless, April tried it on. Felt compelled to.

Was it disrespectful to try it on?

Possibly. Probably.

But Hugh was about to donate it all, anyway. *He* was the one who insisted it was all junk, all worthless.

Maybe this was how she could trigger a reaction from this tall, silent man?

It was unequivocally a bad idea, but she spent her days unpacking boxes and her evenings stacking shelves. Mostly in silence.

Maybe she was going stir crazy, but she needed to see what Hugh would do.

She just didn't buy it that he didn't care about this stuff. So far his measured indifference had felt decidedly unconvincing.

She *had* to call his bluff.

'I'm not paying you to play dress-up,' Hugh pointed out from behind her.

His tone was neutral.

She spun around to show him the oversized jacket. 'Spoilsport,' she said with a deliberate grin, catching his gaze.

If he was just going to stand there she couldn't cope with all this silence and gloom. Her sisters had always told her she was the *sunny* sister. That she could walk into a room and brighten it with her smile.

It had always sounded rather lame—and to be honest part of her *had* wondered what that said about her in comparison to *clever* Ivy or *artistic* Mila. Was it really such an achievement to be good at smiling?

It had been a moot point in the months since Evan had left, anyway.

Until now. Now, this darkly moody man felt like a challenge for sunny April.

Acutely aware that this might all backfire horribly, but in-

capable of stopping herself in the awkward silence, she playfully tossed her hair in the way of a supermodel.

'What do you think?'

What would he do? Smile? Shout? Leave?

Fire her?

Hugh's shake of the head was barely perceptible.

But…was that a quirk to his lips?

Yes. It was definitely there.

April's smile broadened.

'Fair enough,' she said, shrugging her shoulders and then
tossing the jacket into the 'donate' box. 'How about this?' she
asked, randomly grabbing the next item of clothing in the box.

A boat-neck blouse, in a shiny fabric with blue and white
stripes. But too small. Which April realised…too late.

Hands stuck up in the air, fabric bunched around her shoulders on top of her T-shirt, April went completely still.

'Dammit!' she muttered.

She hadn't been entirely sure of her plan, but becoming
trapped in cheap satin fabric was definitely not part of it.

She wiggled again, trying to dislodge the blouse, but it
didn't shift.

Her T-shirt had ridden up at least a little. April could feel
cool air against a strip of skin above the waistband of her
jeans.

Mortified, she struggled again, twisting away from where
she knew Hugh stood, feeling unbelievably silly and exposed.

'Stay still,' he said, suddenly impossibly close. Behind her.

April froze. She was blindfolded by the stupid top but she
could sense his proximity. His height. His width.

His fingers hooked under the striped fabric, right at her
shoulders. He was incredibly careful, gently moving the fabric
upwards. Her arms were still trapped. It was almost unbearable: the touch of his fingers, his closeness, her vulnerability.

She wanted him to just yank it off over her head. To get
this over with.

No, she didn't.

The fabric had cleared her shoulders now, and he moved

closer still to help tug it over her arms, where the top was still wrapped tightly.

Now his fingers brushed against the bare skin of her arms. Only as much as necessary—and that didn't feel like anywhere near enough.

He was so close behind her that if she shifted backwards even the slightest amount she would be pressed right up against him. Back to chest.

It seemed a delicious possibility.

It seemed, momentarily, as she was wrapped in the temporary dark, a viable option.

And then the blouse was pulled free.

April gasped as the room came back into focus. Directly in front of her were heavy navy curtains, closed, obscured by an obstacle course of cardboard boxes.

She spun around.

'Thank you—' she began.

Then stopped.

Hugh was still so close. Closer than he'd ever been before. Tall enough and near enough that he needed to look down at her and she needed to tilt her chin up.

She explored his face. The sharpness of his nose, the thick slash of his eyebrows, the strength of his jaw. This close she could see delicate lines bracketing his lips, a freckle on his cheek, a rogue grey hair amongst the stubble.

He was studying her, too. His gaze took in her eyes, her cheeks, her nose. Her lips.

There it was.

Not subtle now, or easily dismissed as imagination as it had been down in his basement apartment. Or every other time they'd been in the same room together.

But it *had* been there, she realised. Since the first time they'd met.

That focus. That...intent.

That *heat*.

Between them. Within her.

It made her pulse race and caused her to become lost in his gaze when he finally wrenched his away from her lips.

Since they'd met his eyes had revealed little. Enough for her to know, deep in her heart, that he wasn't as hard and unfeeling as he so steadfastly attempted to be. It was why she'd known she couldn't be responsible for the disposal of his mother's memories.

And maybe that was what had obscured what she saw so clearly now. Or at least had allowed her to question it.

Electricity practically crackled between them. It seemed ludicrous that she hadn't known before. That she'd ever doubted it.

Hugh Bennell *wanted* her.

And she wanted him. In a way that left her far more exposed than her displaced T-shirt.

But then he stepped back. His gaze was shuttered again.

'You okay?' he asked, his voice deep and gravelly.

No.

'Yes,' she said, belatedly realising he was referring to the stripy top and not to what had just happened between them.

Way too late she tugged down her T-shirt, and blushed when his gaze briefly followed the movement of her hands. Then it shifted away.

Not swiftly, as if he'd been caught out or was embarrassed. Just away.

He didn't look at her again as he went over to the box April had been emptying.

Without hesitation he reached in, grabbing a large handful of clothing and directly deposited it into the 'donate' box. Then, with brisk efficiency, he went through the remainder of the box: ancient yellow newspapers to the recycling pile, a toaster with a severed electrical cord to the bin, encyclopaedias with blue covers and gold-edged pages on top of the clothing in the donation box.

April had been boxing books separately, but she didn't say a word.

The donation box was now full, already packed with yesterday's miscellanea, and Hugh lifted it effortlessly.

April followed him into the foyer and directed him to where she'd like the box left, ready for the next visit by the red-and-white charity collection truck.

'Thank you,' she said.

He shrugged. 'I just want this stuff gone.'

She nodded. 'I'd better get back to work, then.'

Finally her temporary inertia had lifted, and reality—the most obvious being that it was her job to empty these boxes, not Hugh's—had reasserted itself.

Although amidst that reality the crackling tension between them still remained.

April didn't know what to do with it.

Hugh seemed unaffected, but April knew for certain that he wasn't unaware.

'These clothes aren't my mum's,' he said suddenly. 'I have no idea who they belong to. I have no idea what most of this stuff is, or why the hell my mum needed to keep it all so badly.'

April nodded again. His tone had hardened as he spoke, frustration fracturing his controlled facade.

'She was more than all this stuff. Much more.' He shook his head. 'Why couldn't she see that?'

Hugh met her gaze again, but April knew he'd asked the most rhetorical of questions.

'I'll get this stuff out of your house,' she said. She promised.

'*Her* house,' he clarified.

And then, without another word, he was gone.

CHAPTER FIVE

HUGH HADN'T SLEPT WELL.

He'd woken late, so he'd been too late to join the group he normally rode with on a Wednesday, so instead he'd headed out alone. Today that was his preference anyway.

Because it was later, traffic was heavier.

It was also extremely cold, and the roads were slick with overnight rain.

London could be dangerous for a cyclist, and Hugh understood and respected this.

It was partly why he often chose to ride in groups, despite his general preference for solitude. Harried drivers were forced to give pairs or long lines of bikes room on the road, and were less likely to scrape past mere millimetres from Hugh's handlebars.

But other times—like this morning—his need to be alone trumped the safety of numbers.

Today he didn't want the buzz of conversation to surround him. Or for other cyclists to share some random anecdote or to espouse the awesomeness of their new carbon fibre wheels.

When he rode alone it was the beat of his own pulse that filled his ears, alongside the cadence of his breathing and the whir of the wheels.

Around him the cacophony of noise that was early-morning London simply receded.

It was just him and his bike and the road.

Hugh rode hard—hard enough to keep his mind blank and his focus only on the next stroke of the pedals.

Soon he was out of inner London, riding down the A24 against the flow of commuter traffic. He was warm with exertion, but the wind was still icy against his cheeks. The rest of his body was cloaked in jet-black full-length cycling pants, a long-sleeved jersey, gilet and gloves.

Usually by now the group would have begun to loop back, but today Hugh just kept on riding and riding, heading from busy roads to country lanes, losing track of time. Eventually he reached the Surrey Hills and their punishing inclines, relishing the burning of his lungs and the satisfying ache of his thighs and calves.

But midway up Box Hill, with his brain full of no more than his own thundering heartbeat, he stopped. On a whim, abruptly he violently twisted his cleats out of his pedals and yanked hard on the brakes until his bike was still. Then, standing beside his bike, he surveyed the rolling green patchwork of the Dorking valley as it stretched towards the South Downs beneath a clear blue sky. Out here, amongst woodland and sheep-dotted fields, London was thirty miles and a world away.

What was he doing?

He didn't have to check his watch to know he'd missed his morning teleconference. He'd miss his early-afternoon meetings too, given it would take him another two and a half hours to get home again.

Reception would be patchy up here, he knew, but still, he should at least try to email his assistant—who worked remotely from Lewisham—and ask her to clear his calendar for the rest of the day.

But he didn't.

He hadn't planned to ride this far, but he'd needed to. He'd needed to do something to ease the discontent that had kept him awake half the night—much of it spent pacing his lounge room floor.

Hugh didn't like how he felt. All agitated and uncertain.

He usually lived his life with such definition: he knew what he was doing, why he was doing it, and he always knew it was the right thing to do. Hugh made it his business to plan and prepare and analyse *everything*. It was why his business was so successful. He didn't make mistakes...he didn't get distracted.

His mother's house had always been the exception.

When she'd died he'd considered selling it. He'd been living in his own place in Primrose Hill, not far away.

But back then—as now—he just hadn't been able to.

For a man who prided himself on being the antithesis of his mother—on being a man who saw no value in objects and who ruthlessly protected his life from clutter—his attachment to the house was an embarrassing contradiction.

But he knew how much that house had meant to his mum. He knew exactly what it had represented.

For his mother it had been a place of love, after so many years of searching.

And for Hugh it had been where his mother had finally lived a life free of clutter—a life he had been sure she'd lost for ever. For more than a decade she'd been happy there, her hoard no more than a distant memory.

And so he'd kept it.

He'd ended up hoarding his mother's hoard. There was no other way to explain his three-year refusal to dispose of all that junk.

Even now, as April Spencer attempted to clean out his mother's house, he couldn't let it go.

A stranger—April—had seen that.

Why else would she be going to such lengths to save sentimental crap unless she'd sensed that he wasn't really ready to relinquish it?

And she was right. The original 'Hugh' box still remained as April had left it, cluttering up his coffee table in all its ironic glory.

He just hadn't been able to walk to the skip behind the house and throw it all away. It had felt impossible.

How pathetic.

Yesterday he'd helped April move those boxes in an effort to normalise the situation: to prove to himself that his visceral reaction to them could be overcome. Except he hadn't considered April. He hadn't considered his visceral reaction to *her*.

He hadn't considered that, while he might be able to dismiss his attraction to her as nothing when he spent only short periods of time with her, more time together might not be so manageable.

Because more time with her meant he'd seen another side of her: a mischievous forthrightness that really shouldn't have surprised him, given her refusal to follow his original instructions.

And he liked it. *A lot.*

He'd also liked it—a lot—when she'd got tangled up in that shirt.

He'd liked being so very close to her—close enough to smell her shampoo and admire the Australian tan revealed below her bunched up T-shirt. Close enough to feel her shiver beneath his touch. To hear the acceleration of her breathing.

In those long moments after he'd helped her out of the blouse it had been as intimate as if he'd actually undressed her.

It had felt raw and naked—and incredibly intense. As if, had he touched her, they would've both lost control completely. And for those long moments he'd wanted nothing more than to lose control with April Spencer.

But Hugh Bennell *never* lost control.

And so he hadn't. He'd taken a step back, even though it had been harder than he would've liked.

He'd assessed the situation: April worked for him.

His priority was cleaning out his mother's house, not fraternising with his employees.

Besides, he suspected his reaction to April was somehow tangled up with his reaction to the boxes. Because it wasn't normal for him to have such a magnetic pull towards a woman. He was generally far more measured when he met a woman he liked. In fact he always 'met' the women he dated online.

It allowed for a certain level of...well, of *control*, really. He could set his expectations, as could the woman he was speaking too. There was never any confusion or miscommunication, or the risk of having anything misconstrued.

It was incredibly efficient.

But starting with physical attraction...*no.*

Although it had been difficult to remind himself why as he'd paced his parquet floor at three a.m.

His mind had been as full with thoughts of April as with his continued frustration over the house and all its boxes.

Mostly with April, actually.

The softness of her skin. The way her lips had parted infinitesimally as they'd gazed into each other's eyes. And that urge to lean forward and take what he knew she'd been offering had been so compelling it had felt inevitable...

No.

And so his bike ride. A bike ride to clear his mind of the clutter his mother's hoard and April were creating.

It had been a good plan, Hugh thought as he got back on his bike.

A total fail, though, in practice, with his brain still unable to let go of memories of warm skin and knowing blue eyes as he rode back down the hill, alongside the song of a skylark caught up in the breeze.

Mila: OMG Gorgeous!

April: That's one to save for his twenty-first! :)

April typed her instant messaging response to Ivy's gorgeous photo of her son, Nate, covered in bubbles in the bathtub. It felt like for ever since she'd spoken to both her sisters together.

April: How are sales going, Mila?

Mila had recently started mass-producing some of her ceramic work to keep up with sales at her small boutique pottery business.

Mila: Pretty good. I've experimented with pricing a bit. I'm still not sure how much people value handmade. So far it seems that the hand-glazing is the key, because...

Mila went into quite a lot of detail—as Mila always did when it came to her business—and then posted some photos she'd taken in her workshop.

April had always been proud of Mila—of both her sisters. She'd always admired how Mila had been so adamant that she'd build her business without the financial support of their mother, but until now April had never really had an issue with spending her family's money herself.

In fact it had taken her until her mid-twenties before she'd realised she should be doing a lot more with her good fortune than attending parties and buying everything she liked on every fashion festival catwalk.

And so she'd started the Molyneux Foundation.

She'd deliberately chosen not to be the face of the foundation because it wasn't about her. In fact she'd asked her mother to be the patron. But there was no question that it was April driving the foundation. It had become *her* project and, along with a small team, she'd made sure the foundation had continued to grow—and for every dollar donated to the foundation Molyneux Mining matched it twice over.

April had experimented with a few different ideas for the foundation—a website, later a blog—and by the time Instagram had gained popularity April had known exactly how to monetise it best to help the foundation. She'd had her team reaching out to any company that sold a product she could include in a photo, and she'd carefully curated the images to ensure that she mixed promotional pictures seamlessly in with those that were just her own.

And it had worked. She didn't think her mum had expected it to take off the way it had when April had talked her into the two-to-one deal, but it was certainly too late now!

She was incredibly proud of all the foundation had achieved, and of her role in that. But she'd still really just considered it a little side project. She was as hands-on as needed, but it was hardly a full-time job. She'd still had plenty of time to shop and socialise—and until Evan had left her it had never occurred to her to live without the Molyneux money.

The Molyneux money to which *she* had contributed in absolutely no way at all.

And the brittleness of all that—the fact that without the Molyneux money she had literally nothing…no means to support herself…not one thing she'd bought with money she'd actually earned herself—was quite frightening.

Ivy: How's the new job going?

April: Good. Mostly. Lots of boxes.

She'd love to post a photo to show the magnitude of the hoard to her sisters, but photography was one of the many things expressly forbidden by the confidentiality agreement she'd signed. Along with any discussion of the contents of the boxes.

April: My boss is interesting.

She'd typed that before she'd really thought about what she was doing.

Ivy: Oooh! Interesting-interesting? Or INTERESTING-interesting? ;-) ;-) ;-)

April: Both.

She'd never been good at keeping secrets from her sisters.

Mila: Photo?

April: No. I can't even tell you his name. But he's tall. Dark hair, dark eyes. Stubble. What do you call it…? Swarthy?

Mila: I've always liked that word

April: But he's my boss.

Ivy: From an HR point of view, that's not really a problem unless there is any question of a power imbalance. And I doubt nepotism is an issue in your current role.

Mila: It's handy having a CEO in the family.

April: I'm not going to do anything about it, anyway.

Mila: WHY NOT?

Ivy: WHY?

April: It's not the right time. I need to be single for a while. Right? Isn't that what you're supposed to do when your husband walks out on you?

Mila: I don't have a husband ;-)

Mila *did* have a very handsome, very successful boyfriend who adored her, however. Everyone knew they'd get married eventually.

April: Not helpful.

Mila: Sorry. Too soon?

Too soon to be teased about her situation?

April: No. I'm not curled up in the corner sobbing or anything.

She welcomed a bit of levity—she had right from the day that Evan had left her.

Plus, she was well past that now. Now she slept easily—no thoughts of Evan whatsoever. Working fourteen-hour days possibly also helped.

Ivy: I think being single for a while is a good idea.

Ivy was always good for keeping things on topic.

Mila: But you can still be single and do interesting things with an interesting man ;-) ;-)

Ivy: Exactly.

There was a long pause as her sisters clearly awaited her response.

This was not what she'd expected. She'd expected words of caution. Now the possibilities had short-circuited her brain.

Mila: April?

April: I don't know what to do.

Ivy: But you know WHO to do!

Mila: Ha-ha-ha!

April: Can you post some more photos of Nate?

Mila: Boo. You're no fun.

Ivy had taken the bait, though, and bombarded them with three adorable photos in quick succession. The conversation swiftly moved on, for which April was extremely grateful.

But that night it was Hugh Bennell who crowded her dreams.

April was almost finished for the day when Hugh opened the front door. The charity truck had just left, taking away the latest boxes full of donated things.

It had left the foyer almost empty, with only a neat stack

of flattened boxes near the door and the 'Hugh' box sitting
on the bottom step of the grand stairway.

'Hello!' April said, smiling as he stepped inside. She hadn't
seen him since the stripy blouse debacle, but had already determined her approach: regardless of her sisters' opinion, she
was going to remain strictly professional.

Even *considering* another approach made her...

Well. It didn't matter. It was too soon after Evan, and Hugh
was her boss. These were compelling supporting arguments
for professionalism.

No matter how compelling Hugh himself might be, simply
by walking through the glossy black door.

April had just sent him her summary email, but was doing
a quick sweep-up of the dirt that the charity man had tracked
inside before going home.

'Hi,' he said, shooting only the briefest glance in her direction before striding for his box. It was the first day since
that afternoon in his basement that she'd had anything to add
to it, and of course she'd let him know.

Hugh picked up the box in the swiftest of motions and then
immediately headed down the hallway—which led through
the kitchen, the utility room and then outside to the skip.

April had assumed he'd come and check the box after she'd
gone for the day, so she wasn't really prepared for this.

'Wait!' she said, before she could stop herself.

He stopped, but didn't turn. 'Yes?' he asked. His tone was
impatient.

She knew she shouldn't have said anything.

'Nothing—sorry,' she said.

There. Professional.

Then, somehow, she was jogging up the hallway. 'Wait...
please.'

Again he stopped immediately at the sound of her voice.

This time he turned to face her.

She'd run up right behind him, so he was really close, with
only the open box between them.

She reached inside. She'd found a lot of sentimental things

across two boxes today: a large pile of ancient finger paintings and children's drawings—all labelled 'Hugh' with a date
in the mid-nineteen-eighties—and all of his school reports,
from preschool through to Year Thirteen.

But it was some photos that she picked up now, in a messy
pile she'd attempted to make neat. But that had been impossible with the collection of different-sized photos: some round-
edged, others standard photo-sized, some cut out small and
weathered, as if they'd been kept in someone's purse.

'These are from your first days of school,' she said.

Hugh didn't even look at them. He shrugged. 'I don't care.'

But he wasn't meeting her gaze, he was just looking—April
thought—determinedly uninterested.

'I don't believe you.'

That got his attention.

'I beg your pardon?' he said, sounding as British as April
had ever heard him.

'I don't believe you don't care,' she said, slowly and clearly.
As if there was any chance he'd misunderstand.

His gaze was locked on hers now. 'I don't see how that
matters.'

April fanned the photos out as if they were a deck of cards.
'Look,' she said, giving them a shake. 'These are photos of
you in your school uniform. For each year there's a photo by
yourself, with your school bag. And another with your mum.
These are *special*.'

'They're not,' he said. He nodded at the box. 'Please put
them back.'

April shook her head. 'No.'

'No?'

'No,' she said firmly, her gaze remaining steady.

It would seem she'd thrown her professionalism out of the
window.

She'd get extra shifts at the supermarket if he fired her and
the temp agency blacklisted her. Or clean toilets. Whatever.
She just couldn't pretend that she agreed with this.

'You're making a mistake.'

His eyes narrowed. His voice was rough. 'You've got no idea what you're talking about.' He turned away from her and continued down the hallway. 'I'll just throw them out tomorrow.'

'Do you hate her?' April blurted out the words to his rapidly retreating back.

Faster than she'd thought possible he was back in front of her. *Right* in front of her. He'd dropped the box at some point and there was now no barrier between them.

His presence crowded her, but she didn't take a step back.

'*No!*' he said. Not loudly, but with bite. Then he blinked, and belatedly added, 'That is none of your business.'

His words were calm now, but—again—deliberately so.

'I know,' she said, because of course it was true. But she just couldn't stop. 'You know, I don't have any photos of myself with my mum like this,' she said conversationally. 'I know that because my sisters went through all Mum's old photos when I had my thirtieth birthday party, for one of those photo-board things.' She swallowed, ignoring Hugh's glower. 'I have a couple from my first day of school in Year One, but that's about it. And I have hardly any photos of myself as a kid with my mum. It was different twenty-five years ago—people didn't take as many photos. And it was usually Mum who *took* the photos anyway, rather than being in them.'

Hugh didn't say anything.

'I'd love photos of me like this with my mum. In fact I have more photos of me as a kid with my dad—again, because Mum was the photographer. And I don't even *like* him. But I love my mum.' She knew she was rambling, but didn't stop. 'So it's all backwards, really.'

'You don't like your dad?' Hugh asked.

April blinked. 'No. He left when I was five. I hardly saw him, growing up, and I have nothing to do with him now.'

Hugh nodded. 'My father did something similar,' he said. 'I never saw him again.'

He didn't elaborate further.

'That sucks,' she said.

His lips quirked. 'Yeah.'

'But your mum obviously loved you?'

She could see his jaw tense—but then relax. 'Yes,' he said. 'She did.'

'That's why she took all these photos.'

The tension was instantly back. 'The number of photos my mother took—and, trust me, within this house there are *thousands*—is not a reflection of how much she loved me, April. I'd still know she loved me if she hadn't taken even one. They're just *things*.'

April shook her head vigorously. 'No. They're not. They're memories. They're irreplaceable. What if you ever have kids? Won't you want to—?'

'I'm never having kids. And that is *definitely* none of your business.'

She didn't understand. She didn't understand any of this.

But he'd turned, retrieved the box from the floor. He faced her again, gesturing with the box for April to dump the photos inside.

But she couldn't. *She could not.*

'Why are you doing this?' she asked, still holding the photos tight.

For the first time the steady, unreadable gaze he'd trained on her began to slip. In his gaze—just briefly—there flashed emotion. Flashed pain.

'I don't have to explain anything to you, Ms Spencer. All I want is for you to empty this house. That's it. Empty the house. I don't require any commentary or concern or—'

'You want an empty house?' April interrupted, grasping forcefully on to a faint possibility.

He sighed with exasperation. 'Yes,' he said.

'Well, then,' she said, with a smile she could tell surprised him. 'I can work with that.'

'Work with what?' His expression was wary.

'Getting this stuff out of your mother's house.' A pause. 'Just not into a skip.'

'A storage unit solves nothing. This isn't about relocating the hoard. I want it gone.'

Again she smiled, still disbelieving, and now she was certain she was right. 'You're the CEO of an international software company, right?' she said.

His eyes narrowed, but he didn't respond.

'So why didn't you think to just scan all this? You could even put it all in the cloud, so you don't even have a physical hard drive or anything left behind. It would be all gone, the house would be empty, and...'

And you won't do something you'll regret for the rest of your life.

But she didn't say that. Instinctively she knew she couldn't. She couldn't give him something to argue with—that he could refute with, *You've got no idea what you're talking about.*

Which would be true. Or *should* be true. But it wasn't. And, no matter how weird that was, and how little she knew about this man, she was certain she was right.

When she looked at Hugh Bennell—or at least when he *really* looked at *her*, and didn't obscure himself behind that indecipherable gaze—she saw so much emotion. So much... *more*. More than she'd see if he didn't care.

She was sure there were people out there who truly didn't care about photos and old school report cards and badly drawn houses with the sun a quarter crescent in the corner.

But one of those people was definitely not standing before her.

His gaze wasn't shuttered now. In fact she could sense he was formulating all manner of responses from disdain, to anger, to plans for her immediate dismissal.

As every second ticked by April began to realise that she was about to be fired.

But that was okay. At least she'd—

'That is a possibility,' he said suddenly. As if he was as surprised by his words as she was.

April grabbed on to them before he could change his mind. 'Awesome! I can even do it for you—it won't add much time...

especially if you can get one of those scanners you can just feed a whole heap of stuff into at once. And maybe I can take photos of other stuff? Like if I find—'

'I'll organise the equipment you need.'

He stepped around April, carrying the box back into the foyer. He dropped it onto the bottom step and April added the pile of photos on top.

She wanted to say something, but couldn't work out what.

'Hugh—'

'It's late,' he said. 'You should go home. See you tomorrow.'

Then, just like that, he left.

CHAPTER SIX

THE NEXT AFTERNOON Hugh set up the scanner on the marble kitchen benchtop.

April was just finishing up the second reception room. He could hear the sound of the radio station she listened to above the rustle and thud of items being sorted.

When he'd interrupted her earlier to announce his presence she'd been singing—rather badly—to a song that he remembered being popular when he was back at high school.

She'd blushed when she'd seen him. The pinkening of her cheeks had been subtle—but then, he'd been looking for it, familiar now with the way she seemed to react to him.

He reacted too. As he always did around her. Even when she'd been standing before him, hands on hips, acting as self-designated saviour of old photos, evidence of his lack of artistic ability and irrelevant school reports.

Even then—as he'd struggled with the reality that the distance down that hallway to the skip had been traversed on feet that had felt weighted to the ground with lead—and *hated* himself for it—he'd reacted to her.

He'd reacted to the shape of her lips, to the way she managed to look so appealing while her hair escaped from its knot atop her head, and to the shape of her waist and hip as she leant against that broom...

And then he'd reacted to her imperious words, admiring her assertiveness even as he'd briefly hated her for delaying him. He'd needed to get that stuff out of the house. Quickly. Immediately. Before he succumbed to inertia like with the other box, which—while no longer on his coffee table—still taunted him from the back of the cupboard in his otherwise spotless spare room.

But then he had succumbed to April's alternative. At least temporarily.

If it keeps a good employee happy, then what's the problem? I can just delete it all once she finishes.

That was the conclusion he'd decided he'd come to.

He finished hooking up the scanner to the laptop he'd previously provided for April, then waited as the software was installed.

Footsteps drew his gaze away from the laptop screen.

April stood across from the kitchen bench, smiling again. *Sans* blush.

She looked confident and capable and in control—as she always did in all but those moments between them he refused to let himself think about.

Again, questions flickered in his brain. Who was she, really? How had she ended up working here?

But that didn't matter. Their relationship was purely professional.

Really?

He mentally shook his head.

It was.

Belatedly he realised she was holding those damn photos.

'Shall we get started?' she asked.

This was when he should go. From her CV, he knew April was computer savvy—she'd work it out.

Instead, he held out his hand. 'Here, let me show you.'

They sat together, side by side at the kitchen bench, on pale wooden bar stools, scanning the photographs together.

They'd quickly fallen into a rhythm—Hugh fed the photos through the scanner and then April saved and filed them.

Initially she'd attempted to categorise the photos, but Hugh wouldn't have any of that. So April simply checked the quality of the scan, deleted any duplicates and saved them into one big messy folder.

Based on the decor of his flat, April would bet that Hugh usually carefully curated his digital photos. He'd give them meaningful file names, he'd file them into sensibly organised folders, and he'd never keep anything blurry or any accidental photos of the sky.

But she got why he wasn't doing that today: he was telling himself he was just going to delete them all one day, anyway.

Was it weird that she could read an almost-stranger so easily? Especially when he was so deliberately attempting to reveal nothing.

Possibly.

Or possibly she was just spending too much time with young backpackers she had nothing in common with, pallets of groceries that needed to be stacked and walls of cardboard boxes? And now she was just constructing a connection with this man because in London she had no connections, and she wasn't very good at dealing with that?

That seemed more likely.

But, even so, she *liked* sitting this close to him. Liked the way their shoulders occasionally bumped, when they'd both act as if nothing had happened.

Or at least April did.

What was the reason she'd given her sisters for not...*doing* anything with Hugh?

Ah. That was right. She was still technically married.

And what would she do anyway? She'd had *one* boyfriend. *Ever.* She'd kissed one boy—slept with one man. Evan. That was it. Plus, Evan had pursued *her.* In the way of high school kids. With rumours that had spread through English Lit that Evan *liked* April. Like, *liked*, liked her.

She was ill-equipped to pursue a darkly handsome, intriguing, damaged man.

But what if she turned to him? Right now? And said his name? Softly...the way she really wanted too? And what if he kissed her? How would his lips feel against hers? What would it be like to kiss another man? To be pressed up tight against another man...?

'April?'

She jumped, making her bar stool wobble.

'You okay?'

She put her hands on the benchtop to steady herself. 'Yes, of course.'

He looked at her curiously. Not anything like the way he had that day of the stripy top.

Another of those damn blushes heated her cheeks. It was ridiculous—she was never normally one to blush.

'In my first day-at-school photos, from Year One, I'm always with my sisters. I'm the middle child. That means I'm supposed to have issues, right?'

She was rambling—needing to fill the tense silence. In addition to never blushing, she *never* rambled. She had sparkling, meaningless conversation down to an art—she'd been to enough charity functions/opening nights/award galas to learn how to speak to *anyone*. Intelligently, even.

Not with Hugh.

'My big sister is a typical first child. *Such* an over-achiever. I get exhausted just thinking about all she does. Although my baby sister has never really felt like the baby. She's kind of wise beyond her years—she always has been. But that fits with something I read about third-born children—they're supposed to be risk-takers, and creative, which totally fits her.'

She paused, but couldn't stop.

'You know what middle children are supposed to be? Like, their defining characteristic? *Peacemakers*. I mean, come on? How boring is *that*?'

She was staring at the laptop screen and all the photos of cherubic child-sized Hugh.

'You're not boring,' he said.

April blinked, hardly believing he'd been paying attention.

'Thank you,' she said. She rotated the latest photo on the screen and dragged it over to the folder she'd created.

'I can see the peacemaker thing, too. Just not when it comes to my old school photos.'

April grinned. 'Nope,' she said. 'Especially when I wish *I* had photos like this. My mum worked really hard when we were growing up. She was often already at work when it was time for us to go to school.'

'What did she do?' Hugh asked.

She swallowed. 'She worked in an office in the city,' she

said vaguely. *As CEO of Australia's largest mining company.* The words remained unsaid.

Thankfully, Hugh just nodded. 'My mum had lots of different jobs when I was growing up. We didn't have a lot of money, so she often juggled a couple of jobs—you know, waitressing, receptionist…she even stacked shelves at a supermarket for a while, when I was old enough to be alone for a few hours at night.'

This was the longest conversation they'd ever had.

'*I* do that!' April exclaimed. 'After I get home from this job.'

'Really?' he asked. 'Why?'

April shrugged. 'So I can get out of the awful shared house I live in in Shoreditch.'

His gaze flicked over her—ever so quickly. April ignored the way her body shivered.

'Aren't you a bit old to live in a shared house?'

She narrowed her eyes in mock affront. 'Well, yeah,' she said. 'I'm thirty-two. But I made some dumb decisions with a credit card and I need to pay it off.'

She was choosing her words carefully, keen to keep everything she told him truthful, even if she wasn't being truly honest with him.

But then, her family's billions really shouldn't be relevant. That, after all, was the whole point of this London 'adventure'. Even if it *had* made a dodgy flatshare detour.

'What kind of dumb decisions?' he asked.

The question surprised her. She hadn't expected him to be interested. 'Clothes. Eating out. Rent I couldn't afford. No job. That kind of thing.'

He nodded. 'When I first moved out of home I rented this ridiculous place in Camden. It was way bigger than what a brand-new graduate needed, and my mum thought I was nuts.'

'So you racked up lots of debt, too?'

'No. I'd just sold a piece of software I'd developed for detecting plagiarism in uni assignments for two hundred and fifty thousand pounds, so the rent wasn't a problem,' Hugh replied. 'But I did move out because all that space was really echoey.'

April laughed out loud.

'And—let me guess—you didn't move into a shared house?'

His lips quirked upwards. 'No. I can't think of anything worse.'

'You *do* realise your story has nothing in common with mine, right?'

He shrugged. 'Hey, we both made poor housing choices.'

'Nope. No comparison. One of my housemates inexplicably collects every hair that falls out of her head in the shower. Like, in a little container that she leaves on the windowsill. I…'

'I'll pay off all your credit card debt if you stop your sentimental junk crusade.'

It wasn't a throwaway line. He said it with deadly seriousness.

April tilted her head as she studied him. 'I know—and you know—that if you really wanted this stuff gone it would already be gone. Some random Aussie girl nagging you about it wouldn't make any difference.'

He slid off his stool, then walked around to the other side of the kitchen bench. She watched as he filled the kettle, then plonked it without much care onto its base. But he didn't flick the lever that would turn it on.

He grabbed April's mug from the sink, and another from the overhead cupboard, then put both cups side by side, near the stone-cold kettle.

'Do you want to talk about it?' she asked. She could only guess at whatever was swirling about in his brain. His attention was seemingly focused on the marble swirls of the benchtop.

His head shot up and their gazes locked.

'*No.*'

'Cool,' April said with a shrug. 'I don't need to know.'

Although she realised she *wanted* to know. Really wanted to.

April slid off her stool, too. She skirted around the bench, terribly aware of Hugh's gaze following her. She didn't *quite* meet his gaze. She couldn't. Even as thoughts of discovering what was really going on in Hugh's head zipped through her mind, other thoughts distracted her. About discovering how Hugh might feel if his lovely, strong body—hot as hell, even in jeans and jumper—was pressed against hers. If, say, he kissed her against the pantry door just beside him...

Stop.

This was Ivy and Mila's influence, scrambling her common sense. It wasn't how she really felt. She'd *never* felt like this.

She reached past him, incredibly careful not to brush against him, and switched on the kettle.

She sensed rather than saw him smile—her gaze was on the kettle, not him.

'Let me help you,' she said. 'Stop trying to convince yourself you want something you don't actually want. At all. Stop pretending.'

Too late, she realised the error of her 'help him with the kettle the way she'd help him with his stuff' metaphor. She'd ended up less than a foot away from him.

Or maybe it hadn't been an error at all.

'Okay,' he said. His voice was deep. Velvety.

April looked up and their gazes locked.

It was like the stripy blouse moment all over again. But more, even.

She was suddenly unbelievably aware of her own breathing—the rise and fall of her chest was shallow, fast. And the way her belly clenched, the way her nails were digging into her palms to prevent herself from touching him.

'I'll stop pretending,' he said.

His gaze slid to her lips.

She closed her eyes. She had to, or she couldn't think.

The way Hugh was looking at her...

'April...?' he said, so soft.

Was that his breath against her lips? Had he moved closer so he could kiss her?

She refused to find out.

Instead, she stepped away. Two steps...three.

'Good!' she said. 'Great! Let's make time to go through the stuff I find each couple of days, okay?'

Hugh wasn't thinking about the boxes. 'What?'

April nodded sharply. 'Okay, I can finish up here. Thanks for your help.'

He was gone a minute later—just as the kettle whistled to say that it had boiled.

Later, as she walked to the supermarket, all rugged up in scarf and coat, Hugh's words echoed in her brain.

I'll stop pretending.

But *she* wouldn't stop pretending. She couldn't.

For now she was April Spencer, not April Molyneux.

The thing was she had no idea what was pretend any more.

Hugh sat at his desk, typing a message to an old friend from university.

Ryan had completed the same computer science qualification that Hugh had, although he'd made his money in a completely different field—internet dating. Ryan's innovative compatibility matching algorithm had been game-changing at the time. But his friend had long since sold the empire he'd built, and now ran an extremely discreet, exclusive online dating agency, using a new—Ryan said better—matching algorithm.

This had come in handy for Hugh.

Ryan's system was cutting-edge, and Hugh honestly couldn't fault it. He'd liked every woman he'd met through Ryan's system—even if he hadn't been attracted to them all. Or them to him.

After all—there still wasn't an app that could guarantee that.

He didn't date often, but when he did he was very specific. He liked to meet at quiet, private restaurants where it was easy to converse without distraction. He'd go to the movies, or to a show. He didn't go to bars or pubs—there was too little order and too many people talking. He couldn't think.

If things went well, after a few dates he might sleep over at his date's place. But he never lingered long the morning after. Or stayed for breakfast.

Usually, at some point later, he'd be invited to a party, or to a family event.

He always said no.

At such events he would become 'the boyfriend'. And he didn't want that.

Understandably, usually things ended then.

A couple of times he'd met women equally happy to avoid a relationship. Those arrangements had lasted longer, until eventually they'd run their course too.

Of course he was always clear that he wasn't after a relationship, and he was never matched with anybody who specifically wanted to settle down. However, it would seem that the 'wanting a relationship' and 'not wanting a relationship' continuum was not linear. And everyone's definition of where they stood along that line varied. Wildly.

So a woman who started off not wanting a relationship might actually want a bit of clarity around her relationship with Hugh. Or an agreement of exclusivity.

And exclusivity, to Hugh, was an indicator of a relationship—not that he had ever dated more than one woman at once, however casually.

So at that point he was out.

He got it that he was weird when it came to relationships. Women always eventually asked him about his stance. But it wasn't easy for him to define.

He knew, intellectually, that it originated from his mother's serial dating. She had been quite openly on a quest to find her Mr Right after the disappearance of his deadbeat father. He'd become used to the cycle of hope and despair that each new boyfriend would bring, and he'd decided he had no wish to experience that for himself.

But—and this had been his original theory—the risk of a relationship ending in despair was surely reduced if you approached dating with comprehensive data on your side. If you were matched appropriately—your values, your interests, your goals—then surely you minimised risk.

And this, in his experience, was true. He had never experienced the euphoric highs or the devastating lows of his mother's relationships. When he dated it was...*uncomplicated*.

But that was where his stance on relationships became much more about *him*. Because, despite all this data-matching and uncomplicated dating, he still didn't want a relationship.

It was a visceral thing. When he woke up in a woman's bed—he never invited them to *his* place—his urge to leave was not dissimilar from the way the bloody boxes that filled his mother's house made him feel.

Trapped.

It all came back to the same thing: to Hugh, relationships were clutter.

Ryan: I'll send you the link to our latest questionnaire—we've tweaked things a little so you'll need to answer a few more compatibility questions.

Hugh: No problem.

Ryan: Then the system will automatically send you a short-list. Same as always—if the women you say yes for also say yes then you're set.

Hugh: Great. Thanks.

But it was weird... He'd been keen to talk to Ryan, but now he was losing enthusiasm. He'd been so sure that it was the six or more months since his last date that had triggered his interest in April. And today he'd almost kissed her.

Hugh: What's your current success rate with your matching algorithm?

Ryan wouldn't need time to look this up—he knew his company inside out.

Ryan: Almost one hundred per cent. We rarely have a customer receive no matches.

That wasn't what Hugh had meant.

Hugh: So one hundred per cent go on at least one date?

Ryan: Yes. And over ninety per cent of users rate their first date experience with a score of eight or above. We're very proud of that stat.

Hugh: Second date?

Ryan: We don't track activity beyond the first date.

Hugh: Long-term relationships? Engagements? Marriages?

Ryan: Lots. There are many testimonials available.

He pasted a link, but Hugh didn't click on it.

Hugh: Percentages?

Ryan: We don't have that data.

Hugh: Could you guess?

He could just imagine Ryan sighing at his laptop screen.

Ryan: Low. Easily under ten per cent. Under five per cent, probably. Which makes sense when you consider that each user gets matched with multiple people. But anyway our job is the introduction. The rest is up to the couple. But, mate, why the interest? Do we need to update your profile to 'Seeking a long-term relationship'?

Hugh: No. Just—

He stopped typing.

Just *what*?

Why was he suddenly questioning the method he'd been following for ten years? Especially when he'd contacted Ryan today to follow that exact method again. Nothing different. No changes.

He finished the sentence:

Hugh: No. Just wondering.

If Ryan had been a close friend—the kind of mate who knew when you were talking out of your backside—he would've questioned that. But he wasn't a close friend. Hugh didn't have close friends. The habits of his childhood—of keeping people at a distance, and certainly away from his home—had never abated.

Hugh asked Ryan a few more questions—just being social now. About his new house, his new baby...

After several baby photos, Ryan wrote: We should catch up for a beer. Somewhere quiet, of course.

Hugh: Sure.

And maybe they *would* organise it. But, in reality, ninety-five per cent of their friendship was conducted via video-conference or instant message. And that suited Hugh just fine.

Later, he answered the new compatibility questions.

He hesitated before submitting them.

Why?

Because his subconscious was cluttered with thoughts of April Spencer.

Particularly the way she'd looked at him that afternoon in the kitchen. Particularly the way her lips had parted when she'd closed her eyes.

But Ryan's algorithm would never match him with April.

April was vivacious and definitely sociable. She had an easy sunniness to her—he found it difficult to imagine that many people would dislike April. He imagined her surrounded by an ever-expanding horde of friends and family, living somewhere eclectic and noisy.

While he— Well, he had a handful of friends like Ryan. A handful he felt no need to expand. No family.

She was a traveller…an adventurer. She must be to be her age and working at this job in London. Meanwhile, he'd lived nowhere but North London. And he rarely travelled—save for those essential meetings when he'd first expanded his company internationally. Now he insisted all such meetings took place via video-conference.

He was intensely private, and unused to having his decisions questioned.

She questioned him boldly, and she'd told him about her family and her absent father without the slightest hesitation.

And somehow he'd revealed more to her than to anyone he could remember.

So, no, they wouldn't have been matched.

Apart from the added complication of her working for him, their obvious incompatibility could not be ignored.

He was attracted to her—that was inarguably apparent. She was beautiful. It was natural, but it didn't mean anything. April Spencer was all complications. He didn't *do* complicated.

What he needed was a date with a woman who knew exactly what he was offering and vice versa. And who was like him: quiet, private, solitary. No ambiguity. No confusion. Just harmless, uncomplicated fun.

He clicked '*Submit*'.

A minute later he received an email confirmation that his responses had been received.

Now he just needed to wait to be matched.

CHAPTER SEVEN

APRIL SAT CROSS-LEGGED in bed. It was Sunday, and her room-mate had headed out for brunch, taking advantage of an unseasonably warm winter's day.

Loving my new nails! So pretty. What's your go-to shade for summer? #diymanicure #mint #glam #THEnailpolish

April studied her nails after she'd scheduled her post to appear at about this time the next day, Perth time—eight hours away. She'd painted them the lovely minty green that THE had supplied, along with their generous Molyneux Foundation donation. Her assistant, Carly, had priority-mailed the bottle overnight all the way to London—at a ridiculous cost that April planned to pay back to the Molyneux Foundation. But it had had to be done.

It was getting increasingly complicated as each week went by to be both April Molyneux and April Spencer. To be truthful, she hadn't really planned this far ahead, and while her absences at social events had so far been attributed to her marriage breakdown, that excuse wouldn't last for ever.

So far her Instagram account had supported the narrative of a fragile divorcee-to-be with carefully curated images. Yesterday she'd posted one of the photos she'd taken with Carly just before she'd flown to London. In that image—despite her blow-dried hair and designer-sponsored dress, apparently going for dinner with her sisters—she fitted the brief well.

She *had* looked fragile. Because she had been.

When that photo had been taken she'd been barely a month on from that devastating evening at the beach.

At the time, April hadn't seen it. Maybe because she'd become used to seeing herself like that in the mirror: her gaze flat, her smile not quite convincing.

She'd been wearing heaps of make-up to hide the shadows beneath her eyes, to give colour to her cheeks. Without it she'd looked like death. And not in an edgy, model-like way. But really crap. Like, *my husband has just left me* crap.

She didn't, she realised, look like that now.

When had that happened?

She dismissed the thought. It was more important that it had—that Evan and all he represented no longer dominated her psyche.

She wiggled her nails, liking the way the sun that poured through the windows made them sparkle. She'd flung open the curtains both for better light for her photos and to revel in experiencing actual sun in London.

Her sponsors were also tricky. But Carly was doing well: scheduling long into the future, where possible, and being creative with everything else. After all, it wasn't essential that April appeared in every photo. She'd even roped Mila into one—with her sister admirably hamming up her mock-serious pose as she'd modelled long strands of stunning Broome pearls. This nail polish was the first product that had definitely required April to model it. It had been speci-fied by the company, and her hands had featured in too many photos to risk that an eagle-eyed follower wouldn't notice a substitution. Not that she would have considered it anyway...

But April knew that this couldn't continue for ever.

The thing was, she'd assumed she'd have everything worked out already.

She'd imagined writing an inspirational post—maybe at her desk at her Fabulous Job In London. She'd talk about over-coming life's challenges. About realising that she needed to stand on her own two feet and chase her dreams.

And she'd write that she'd done it all by herself, without using her family name to leap to the front of the queue.

Ugh.

That would've been rather sickening, wouldn't it? As if someone as privileged as her was in any position to present herself as poster girl for grit and determination.

Well, she certainly couldn't post a little snapshot of her life right now. It had been an effort to photograph her hands without accidentally including a glimpse of the peeling walls, or the cheap laminate floor, or the battered beds and bedside tables. She'd actually ended up using a pretty plum velvet cushion she'd retrieved from one of Hugh's 'donate' boxes to lay her manicured fingers artistically across—after asking permission from Hugh via email, of course.

Take anything you want, he'd said.

Hugh...

He hadn't come up to the main house on Friday. There'd been no need with nothing for him to sort through.

Which was for the best, she'd told herself. Firmly.

And yet her realisation that there was no need for her to see Hugh that day had been tinged with both relief and disappointment.

She'd finished up in the front reception room and was now up the stairs, working on the front guest bedroom. It wasn't quite as packed with boxes as the first two rooms, although it was definitely a marginal thing. The first few boxes had been full of beautiful manchester—a word she'd discovered was actually a term for bedlinen used only in Australia and New Zealand when she'd provided her summary to Hugh and subsequently confused him.

See? She was learning so much from her move to London. April grinned. Just not exactly what she'd expected.

Sitting, as she was, on the cheapest doona—*duvet*, she'd learnt, in the UK—she'd been able to find at her local supermarket, she questioned her decision not to take one of the beautiful, soft vintage white linen covers she'd found on Friday.

But she couldn't. As hard as she was trying to live as if she wasn't, she *was* an heiress—with a mammoth trust fund. Someone shopping at the local charity shop deserved an expensive doona cover far more than she did.

What was she doing?

In London? Living in this dodgy shared house? Working for Hugh?

Based on her current progress, in another month she would have paid off her credit card. Only another month of two jobs, rice, beans, two-minute noodles and tins of soup.

And then what?

Would she quit her night job? Start applying for jobs back in her own field—or at least her field of study? Eventually move out of this place to some place on her own?

She didn't know.

If she did that she'd definitely need to shut down her social media profiles. There was no way she could continue to use them for the Molyneux Foundation all the way over here.

The idea felt unexpectedly uncomfortable.

Because, surely, her social media profile represented all that had been excessive in her life? Shouldn't she be glad to be rid of it? Glad that she'd be leaving that version of herself behind?

But...

It also represented how successful she'd been—how well she'd connected with her followers and how seamlessly she'd incorporated her sponsors. It represented how much money she'd raised for the foundation by being social media savvy and putting all that Molyneux privilege to good use.

She had over a million followers, and she'd worked hard for every single one of them.

It was only logical reasoning to suppose that those followers were unlikely to care about her new, unglamorous life, but that didn't make the idea of deleting her accounts seem any more appealing.

She wasn't entirely sure what it said about her, but she wasn't ready to give her followers up.

Not yet, anyway.

On Tuesday, April found more photos to add to the 'Hugh' box.

This time it was a bunch of birthday photos, all stuffed

into a large white envelope that had become deeply creased and soft with years of handling.

She carried it downstairs to the kitchen, leaving it on the kitchen bench while she turned on the kettle for her morning tea break.

The photos she'd scanned with Hugh still remained in the 'Hugh' box, atop the benchtop. They hadn't worked out the finer details after he'd left so abruptly, and she hadn't seen him since. Was she supposed to keep on scanning the photos she found? Or would he? Or would he not even bother now and just keep the photos…?

She should just put them into the box and let Hugh decide.

Instead she found herself pulling up one of the bar stools and settling down with both her coffee and the envelope before her.

Even as she slid the photos out she questioned what she was doing. There was no need to *look* at the photos, really. And so to do so felt…not quite right. But that was silly, really. It was her *job*, after all, to go through everything in this house. That was what she was doing.

And so she did look.

Like the images from Hugh's first days at school, these birthday shots were across all of Hugh's birthdays. The envelope was chock-full of them—several from every year. The classic 'blowing out the candles' shot, breakfast in bed with unwrapped presents and always a photo of Hugh with his mum. The very early ones also featured his father.

His mum, of course, had been stunning. April had thought so when she'd first seen her in those school photos. She'd had dark hair and eyes, like Hugh, but her face had been rounder and her eyes and lips had looked as if they always smiled, not just in photos. She'd worn her long hair mostly loose, and had alternated year to year from having a fringe and growing it out.

These photos were different from the school ones, though, which had all been taken outside Hugh's kindergarten or primary school. These were taken indoors. And not all in *this* house, which surprised April.

For some reason she'd assumed this was the house where Hugh had grown up, but the photos showed she was wrong. Silly of her, really, given she'd known his mum hadn't had much money, and Islington was decidedly posh.

April took a sip from her coffee, and then shuffled back to the beginning again.

Outside, it had started raining, and the occasional fat droplet slapped against the kitchen window.

The first photo had a chubby Hugh sitting on his mother's lap, reaching out with both hands for a birthday cake in the shape of a lime-green number one. Standing at his mother's shoulder was—April assumed—his father. A tall man, but narrower in the shoulders than Hugh, he had dark blond hair. He was handsome, but his smile looked uncomfortable.

They sat at a dining table with a mid-nineteen-eighties swirly beige laminate top. Behind them was a sideboard with shelving above it, neatly filled with books, trinkets and brass-framed photographs.

For Hugh's second birthday the cake photo was again taken at the same table. This time Hugh looked as if he was deliberately avoiding the camera, his gaze focused on something out of the picture. Again, he was with his mum and dad. There were more things now, on the shelves behind Hugh and his parents: more brass-framed photographs, more books. But still neat.

For his third birthday Hugh had had a cake in the shape of a lion, with skinny, long pieces of liquorice creating its eyes, nose and whiskers. There was no dad in this one, and while the table and sideboard were still the same the paint on the walls was now blue, not beige. There was less on the shelves—only a few photos. A new house? Or new paint?

April checked the other photos from his third birthday— yes, definitely a new house. His breakfast in bed was no longer beside a lovely double sash window, but instead one with a cheap-looking frame, probably aluminium.

His mum, though, still smiled her luminous smile.

When Hugh had turned four, the birthday parties had clearly begun.

There was Hugh playing pass the parcel, sitting on top of an oriental-style rug with his friends. Or playing pin the tail on the donkey. This photo was a wider shot, showing Hugh from the side, blindfolded and with his arm outstretched. Beyond him was a small kitchen, where a row of parents stood, some observing their kids, others chatting to each other.

The room was very neat, the kitchen bench clear but for trays of party food. In fact in all these early photos every room was tidy. April knew that careful angle selection could make the messiest room appear tidy, but she didn't believe that was the case here. There wasn't one cardboard box, or any pile of useless random things to put inside one, anywhere to be seen.

When had it started?

April flipped ahead through the photos, trying to work it out.

In the end it was that sideboard behind the dining table that told the story.

In front of that blue-painted wall it gained items year on year. At first neatly. More books, more photos, more trinkets, a small vase, a snow globe. But each item had definitely been carefully placed.

By the time Hugh had reached age seven the shelves were stuffed full. So many books jammed in horizontally and vertically. Photos in mismatched frames along the top. A few more trinkets...fat ivory candles. A carved wooden horse.

But still neat. *Organised* chaos.

By Hugh's ninth birthday it was just chaos.

Books were randomly stacked with pages outwards. The vase had been knocked over and damaged, but it still remained on its side in multiple pieces. Paper had now appeared on the shelves: envelopes with plastic windows, sheets of paperwork...piles of magazines.

In the background of a blurry photo of kids dancing—musical statues?—April spotted a cardboard box. Just one.

Beside it was a stack of newspapers, and beside that a stack of books.

But in the photo of Hugh and his mum together she was still smiling. Her hair was still lovely, her eyes sparkling. Hugh was smiling too, looking up at his mum.

April's throat felt tight and prickly.

It seemed impossible, given she'd now spent weeks surrounded by the hoard, but until now she hadn't really thought about the actual compulsive hoarding that must have occurred for this house to be in this state.

Maybe because the house was very neat—for a house full of boxes. And April associated hoarding with those unfortunate people you saw on television documentaries, with rotting food and mountains of rubbish. Vermin. This place wasn't like that.

But that didn't mean accumulating all this junk was normal.

April went back to the photos. For Hugh's tenth birthday there had been no party. Possibly he just hadn't wanted to have one, but April doubted it.

There weren't any party photos the year after, or any of the years after that.

Instead it was just pictures of Hugh and his mum and—in the background—more and more boxes...

'Boxes suck as party decorations.'

Hugh's voice made April jump.

Her stool wobbled dramatically, and his hand landed firmly at her waist, steadying her.

She was wearing a chunky knitted jumper with a wide neck. The wool was soft against his fingers and the shape of her waist a perfect fit against his palm. But he made sure his hand dropped away the instant the chair was still.

A moment after that April practically leapt from her seat, turning to face him.

'I didn't hear you,' she said, unnecessarily.

Her gaze roamed over him—just briefly. He was wearing

his normal uniform of sorts: jeans, T-shirt, hoodie, trainers. Completely unremarkable.

And yet he sensed April's appreciation. She liked how he looked.

Although hadn't he known that since he'd helped her out of that stripy top? He'd certainly appreciated how April looked from the moment he'd first seen her.

Today was no different.

She wore light-washed jeans, and her jumper was pale lemon, oversized and slouchy, revealing much of her golden shoulders and a thin silver chain at her neck. Her dark hair was scraped back from her face in a high ponytail. It was neater than normal—probably because it was early in the day, and all those rogue strands hadn't had the opportunity to escape.

He gave himself a mental shake. It wasn't important. Wasn't he supposed to be annoyed with her?

That was what he'd meant to do when he'd walked into the kitchen to find April so absorbed in those photos that she hadn't heard his approach. He'd meant to ask her, *What the hell are you doing?*

Although, he reflected, that *would* have been a dumb question.

She was looking at photos. *Duh.*

But why? There was no need any more. The photos were *his* responsibility now. And something about having her look through them felt…almost intimate. Crazy when a few days ago she'd done the same thing with his school photos and he hadn't cared.

Or at least hadn't *let* himself care. He'd still been telling himself the photos were worthless and meaningless to him, after all.

But that hadn't been true.

So maybe that was why his instinctive reaction was anger—anger that she'd been looking at images he now accepted meant something to him. Just what they meant he could work out later. They were his, and they were private photos. None of her business.

But by the time he'd gone to speak he hadn't been angry at all.

Boxes suck as party decorations.

'You stopped having birthday parties,' April said, reading his mind.

'Yeah,' Hugh said.

He stepped closer to the bench, picking up a bundle of the photos she'd been studying with such concentration. He'd dump them in the box to take down to his flat. He would go through the photos later. It had been nice of April to offer to help him, but it wasn't necessary.

'I didn't notice at first,' he said. 'You know...all the clutter, I mean. I was a kid. It was just my house. When I was old enough to tidy I kept my room pretty neat, but the rest of the house... I don't know. Like I said, it was just my house.'

Hugh hadn't intended to continue the conversation. *At all.* And yet—he continued.

'The other kids didn't notice either. Why would they? Their parents may have, but I wouldn't have known, and Mum never would've cared.'

'Really?' April asked with raised eyebrows.

Hugh shook his head. 'No. At first it wasn't that bad, and my mum had always been pretty forthright about people accepting each other for who they were. She figured if the house was a bit untidy what was the big deal?'

'But you didn't like it?'

'No,' he said. 'And it just got worse. And as kids get older they notice things. I had a friend over one day after school, before it got really bad, and he had a box fall on him while we were playing. He was fine, but I remember his mum talking to my mum in this really low, concerned voice, asking if she was okay and if she'd like some help. My mum didn't like that. She laughed, I remember, and said she'd just had a busy week and really needed to get all the stuff to the charity shop.'

He was flipping through the photos, but not looking at them.

'That was a lie. I knew she was never going to do that. Although I suppose maybe she was telling herself that she would one day. I don't know. But—anyway—my mum never lied. Ever. And that combined with the other mum obviously thinking something was wrong... Well, then I knew something was wrong. So I didn't have anyone over again.'

April hadn't moved from where she stood. She just watched him, letting him speak.

'Things got worse after that. Mum was always really sociable. I remember when I was really little that she'd have these elaborate dinner parties where she'd always try something fancy out of this fat hardcover cookbook she'd get from the library. But they stopped, too. She'd still go out and see her friends—we had a nice neighbour and I'd go and stay with her and watch TV—but the house was just for us. Us and the damn boxes.'

'That must have been hard,' April said.

Her words were soft. Kind. That was the *last* thing he wanted. Kindness. Pity. He didn't know her. Why was he telling her this?

'I was fine,' he said, his words hard-edged. 'I managed.'

She stepped close to him now and reached out her hand, resting it just below his elbow.

Instinctively he shook his arm free. 'What are you doing?'

She looked surprised—at her action or his, he couldn't be sure.

April swallowed. 'Sorry. I...' There was a pause, then she straightened her shoulders. 'I wanted to touch you,' she said. 'I thought it might help.'

He shook his head. 'It was a long time ago,' he said. 'I'm fine.'

'A long time ago?' she prompted, her forehead wrinkled.

Hugh ran a hand through his hair. 'I mean since I had to live like that. Mum—' He hadn't intended to explain, but he couldn't stop himself. 'When she met Len I was in the Lower Sixth, and she got better. She got the help she needed—did this cognitive behavioural therapy stuff, got in a professional organiser—and then, when she married Len, we moved here.

She was good for a long time. It only started again when Len died, and—honestly—I did all I could. *Everything* I could think of to stop it happening again, to stop her filling the emptiness she felt after my father left and Len died with *stuff*. Objects she could cling on to for ever, that would never leave her—'

Her hand was on his arm again. His gaze shot downwards, staring at it. Immediately she removed her touch.

'I'm sorry, I—'

'It's okay,' he said. 'I don't mind. It felt good.'

She placed her hand on his arm again.

Her touch through the fabric of his hoodie was light against his skin. Her fingers didn't grip...they were just there.

'I'm a hugger,' April explained, her gaze also trained on her hand. 'I can't help it. I hug everybody. Happy, sad, indifferent. Hug, hug, hug.' She sighed. 'It's sucked, really, not having anyone to hug since I've been in London.'

'You want a hug?' he asked, confused.

Her head shot up and she grinned. 'No!' she said. 'I was just explaining.' She nodded at their hands. 'The touching thing. Because I'm guessing you're not a hugger.'

A rough laugh burst from his throat. 'No,' he said. 'I'm not a hugger.'

Her lips curved upwards again. 'I thought so.'

He rarely touched anyone except by accident. When would he? He had no family. A handful of friends. He worked remotely. He was resolutely single. And when he dated touch was about sex. Not this—not reassurance or comfort. This was touch without expectations.

It should be strange, really, to find comfort in the touch of a woman he was attracted to. The few times they'd touched before had been fleeting, but charged with electricity. And, yes, that current was still there. Of course it was.

But what she was offering was straightforward: her touch was simply to help him calm his thoughts and to acknowledge the uncomfortable memories he'd just shared.

It was working, too.

His gaze drifted from her hand to the photos he still grasped. On top was a photo taken of him in bed the morning of his tenth birthday. He'd just unwrapped his present: a large toy robot that he'd coveted for months. His mum had used the timer on her camera, propping it on his dresser, and she sat beside him, her arm around him, his superhero pillows askew behind them.

He and his mum were both smiling in the photo, and Hugh smiled now. A proper smile at a happy memory.

'Thank you,' he said.

For making him keep the photographs. For listening.

'My pleasure,' said April.

Then she squeezed his arm and her touch fell away.

'Wait,' he said.

CHAPTER EIGHT

HUGH'S VOICE WAS LOW. Different from before.

April went still. Her hand fell back against her thigh, already missing his warmth.

He stepped towards her, close enough that she needed to tilt her chin up, just slightly, to meet his gaze.

He studied her intently. 'Why did you leave behind all the people you used to hug?' he asked.

Her gaze wavered.

She put on a smile. 'Early midlife crisis,' she said.

Best to keep it simple.

'No,' he said. 'Why are you here? Why are you working for me?'

She shrugged. 'I told you the other day. Credit card debt.'

He looked her dead in the eye. 'I don't believe you.'

Ah. He was echoing her own words…the way she'd been challenging him.

She hadn't expected the tables to turn.

She twisted her fingers in the too-long sleeves of her jumper…the fabric was all nubbly beneath her fingertips.

She wasn't used to being secretive. She did, after all, document her life for millions of strangers. But this was different.

Hugh didn't talk the way he just had about his past very often. Ever, maybe. April knew that—was sure of it. She understood what he'd revealed to her. How big a deal it was for him. So he deserved her honesty—she knew that.

But her reticence wasn't just about hiding April Molyneux from a man who thought her to be April Spencer—it was more than that. There was something about Hugh—something between them that was just so different. So intense.

Until today they'd only teased the very edges of that intensity, and neither had taken it any further.

They'd both resisted temptation. The temptation to touch. To kiss.

Right now—with these questions, this conversation—it wasn't as primal as before, although all that continued to simmer below the surface. But it was still a connection. And it still felt raw. As if sharing any part of herself, even her past, was only the start of a slippery slope.

It would lead to more. Much more.

And that was as tempting as it was frightening.

Frightening?

What was she scared of?

She didn't answer her own question. It didn't matter. Because she hadn't come all the way to London to be scared of anything.

'My husband left me,' she said.

Silence.

She'd expected him to recoil. Because surely *this* wasn't the conversation Hugh Bennell wanted to have with her?

Instead, he nodded. 'Are you okay?' he asked simply.

She smiled. Genuinely this time. 'Yes,' she said with confidence. 'Now. Sucked for a bit, though.'

He smiled too.

'I needed a change. So here I am. Unpacking your boxes and stacking supermarket shelves. Trust me, it's not as glamorous a midlife crisis as I'd expected.'

'What happened?' he asked. Gently.

'We fell out of love,' she said. 'Him first, but me too. I just hadn't realised it. So I'm okay. Not heartbroken or anything. But it was still sad.'

'Not heartbroken?' he prompted.

Her gaze had travelled downwards, along his jaw and chin. Now it flew upwards, locking with his.

'What do *you* think?' she asked.

Her gaze was heated. Hot. Deliberately so.

Nope. Definitely not scared any more.

'No,' he said, his voice deliciously low. 'I don't think you are.'

And just like that weeks of tension, of attraction, of *con-*

nection were just—*there*. No glancing away, no changing the subject, no pretending it didn't exist.

It was *there*. Unequivocally.

Oh, God.

His eyes were dark, and intensely focused on her. He'd moved closer again, so that only centimetres separated them, and there was no question about what he wanted to do next.

He leant closer. Close enough that his breath was hot against her cheek and then her ear.

'I want to kiss you,' he said, and the low rawness of his voice made her shiver.

How did he know? April thought. That she needed that? That she needed a moment? That despite the crackling tension between them doubts still tugged at her?

Could she trust her instincts after what had happened to her marriage? She'd got it all so very wrong. And, even more than that, could she actually kiss another man?

It had been so long—so very, very long...

'Kiss me,' she said, because she couldn't wait another moment.

Although it turned out she had to.

His lips were at her ear, and he didn't move them far. Instead he pressed his mouth to the sensitive skin of her neck, at the edge of her jaw. Suddenly her knees were like jelly, but strong hands at her waist steadied her.

The sensation of his lips against her neck and his hands against her body was *so good*, and April's eyes slid shut as a sigh escaped from her mouth.

Her fingers untangled themselves from the sleeves of her jumper and reached for Hugh blindly, hitting the solid wall of his stomach and sliding up and around to the breadth of his back.

Hugh dotted her jaw with kisses that were firm but soft. And glorious. But not even close to enough. More than almost anything, she wanted to turn her head to meet his mouth with hers—but she didn't. Because, even more than she wanted that, she wanted this anticipation to last for ever. This promise of Hugh's kiss that, she realised, had been growing from the moment they'd met.

But he was definitely going to kiss her now—this mysterious man who was so different to anyone she'd ever met—and the wonder of that she wanted to hold on to. Just a few seconds longer.

By the time his mouth reached hers April felt about as solid as air. His hands pressed her closer, and then her own hands drew his chest against her breasts.

His mouth was hot against hers, and confident.

If she'd been tentative, or if her brain had been capable of worrying about her kissing technique or other such nonsense, his assuredness would have erased it all.

But, as it was, April didn't feel at all unsure. In fact, Hugh made her feel that this kiss was about as right as anything could get.

His tongue brushed a question against her bottom lip and her own tongue was her crystal-clear answer. Her hands slid up his chest to entwine behind his neck and in his hair, tugging him even closer.

Their kiss was as intense as every moment between them, and as volatile. He kissed her hard, and soft, and voraciously. As if he could kiss her for ever, and as if they had all the time in the world.

But April was impatient.

She took the lead now, kissing him with everything she had and more. More than she'd thought she was capable of: with more passion, less control.

This was raw and passionate and…near desperate.

April wanted to be as close as she could be to him. She wanted him pressed up hard against her. She wanted to feel his solidity and his strength.

She wanted to feel his *skin*.

Her hands drifted down his back, skimming wide shoulder blades and the indentations of his spine. And then they slid beneath jacket and T-shirt to land at the small of his back. Against smooth, gorgeous, hot skin.

His hands followed a similar path, and his touch made her sigh into his mouth as it moved against her back, her stomach, and then upwards—against her ribs to the underside of her—

Something vibrated and Hugh went still.

He broke his lips away from hers, but not far. She could feel him breathe against her mouth as he spoke.

'My phone,' he said. 'I'm sorry.'

'Me too,' she said, all husky.

His smile was crooked. 'Yeah…'

Then he stepped away, and her skin felt bereft without his touch.

He fished his phone out of the back pocket of his jeans. It appeared to have been a notification vibration, not a call, and he turned slightly to scroll through his phone.

When he turned back to her, he just looked at her for long moments. At her still slightly askew jumper, at her lips that felt swollen, at her eyes that she knew were inviting him to pick up exactly where they'd just finished.

But he didn't.

Instead, he said, 'That probably shouldn't have happened.'

April blinked, her brain still foggy. 'Why?'

'Because you work for me. And your husband just left you.'

She shrugged. 'You definitely didn't take advantage of me,' she said. 'And the husband thing—that's my problem, not yours. Nothing about what just happened was a problem for me.'

Mila and Ivy's encouragement fuelled her. For all her misgivings up until their kiss, she didn't regret it one bit now. She felt amazing: alive, and strong, and sexy and feminine…

'I don't want a relationship with you, April.'

Ouch.

It shouldn't have hurt, but it did.

'And you thought the desperate divorcee must be keen to jump straight into another relationship?' Her tone was tart. She didn't give him time to respond. 'And also, that if I did, I'd want a relationship with *you*? That's rather presumptuous.'

April crossed her arms.

His forehead crinkled as he considered her words. 'I suppose it is,' he said. 'I apologise.'

April nodded sharply. 'Just to be clear—the *last* thing I want is a relationship. I was with my ex for a long time—I need to just be me for a while. That being said, I really liked what we just did. I'd like to do it again.'

She didn't know where this bravado came from. She was practically propositioning Hugh Bennell. In fact, she definitely was. She was *propositioning* him.

Because that kiss… She'd never experienced anything like it. She'd never felt like this before and heat continued to traverse through her veins simply from the memory of his mouth against hers. His body against hers.

'I'd like to do it again, too,' he said. His gaze was steady and his words measured—as if he'd carefully considered her proposal before constructing his answer. 'But, I'd also like to be clear. I date, but that's it. I never take it further. I'm never anyone's boyfriend. I'll never be someone's husband. You need to be aware of that before this goes any further.'

April found herself fighting a smile in response to his seriousness. 'That seems a bit extreme,' she said. '*Never?* Really?'

'Really,' he said.

He didn't elaborate. He still looked at her with a determinedly serious expression.

'Well,' April said, smiling now, 'I must say my experience of marriage wasn't ultimately positive, so maybe you're onto something.'

His lips quirked now. 'It would seem so.'

'Okay,' she said. 'I can deal with that. No relationships. *Deal.*'

As she'd told Hugh, it was exactly the right thing for her. Quite honestly, the last thing she wanted was to leap from one relationship into another. But for some silly reason, Hugh's rejection of anything more with her still stung.

There was another noisy buzz as his phone, now on the kitchen bench, vibrated again.

'I need to go,' he said. 'I have a meeting. Can we do dinner? Tonight? I can email you the details?'

He was in business mode now, as efficient as his instructions and his emails.

'Sure,' she said. 'But I only have a few hours before my second job.'

He paused, looking up from his phone. 'How much extra would I need to pay you so you could quit that job?' he asked.

'Ah,' April said, 'that sounds like a conflict of interests. I don't think HR would approve of that.'

'I own the company,' Hugh pointed out. 'And I don't like rushing dinner.'

'Well, then, *I* don't approve,' April said firmly. 'Let's keep this professional.'

Hugh stepped closer—much closer. He leant down and spoke just millimetres from her lips. 'Sure,' he said, 'except for making out in the kitchen.'

Long minutes later they came up for air, and April lifted her fingers to her thoroughly kissed lips as Hugh finally walked away.

'Agreed,' she said, as the front door clicked shut.

The conference call was endless.

Hugh sat back in his chair, letting the wheels roll him back a small distance from his desk.

He'd docked his laptop, so the other attendees' faces were displayed on the large slender screen before him. Everybody else allowed their faces to be shown, so Hugh could see each of them: the red-headed product manager in Ireland, his gaze focused on his keyboard, the dark-haired user experience manager in Sydney, her attention focused on the slides that the senior developer, also in London, was showing them...

The developer was talking directly into his camera as he discussed some of the technical difficulties his team was currently encountering, his purple dreadlocks draped over his shoulders.

Of course, Hugh's face didn't appear.

Hugh still insisted upon that, despite the recommendations of the digital collaboration expert he'd engaged to improve the effectiveness of his widely dispersed team. Yes, he could see how a video feed might—as the consultant had advised—improve both rapport and communication, but no matter how large his company became he was still in charge. Hence—no cameras. For him, anyway.Even now, so many years later, old habits died hard. Because, of course, it wasn't about *him*. He didn't care if his colleagues saw him and his slightly too long hair and three-day-old beard.

It was about his *house*. Everyone on the conference call was in their home. This meeting had a backdrop of contrasting wallpapers and paint colours, of artwork and photographs, of bookcases and blinds and curtains.

Hugh wasn't going to contribute his home to that landscape. He didn't let anyone into his home. In any way. Ever.

Except April.

It seemed April had become the exception to several things. Such as his structured approach to dating.

It had been timely that he'd received an alert from Ryan's dating app mid-kiss with April. It should've been a reminder that he already had a tried and true approach to meeting women. And that kissing an employee in his mother's kitchen was *not* his modus operandi.

Instead, he hadn't even bothered to open the profile of the woman he'd been so carefully matched to.

After all, he'd just experienced a kiss that made his pulse beat fast and his body tighten simply by the act of thinking about it. It had been all-consuming: a hot, intense phenomenon of a kiss. Which was, after all, the point. He dated. He liked women. He wanted to meet women who liked him. And he definitely wanted that spark of attraction. April ticked each and every one of those boxes. Except the spark was more like a bonfire.

So—why not?

If the parameters were made as clear to April Spencer as he always made sure they were with other women, what was the problem?

Logically, none.

Although somewhere right at the edge of his subconscious doubts did twinge.

But they were easily overcome. At the time he'd simply had to look at April to forget anything but his need to touch her again. Now he just needed to recall the shape of her waist and the heat of her skin beneath his palms.

When he did that there was no need to analyse it further.

CHAPTER NINE

APRIL HAD NEVER been more grateful for an unexpected delivery in her life. But she only had a minute to photograph her new peep-toe, sky-high ankle boots before heading out through the door.

Taking these lovelies out to dinner! #highheels #peeptoes #CovetMyShoesCo

She had hardly anything to wear, what with her nonexistent social life since arriving in London, but her new shoes teamed with black jeans and her dressiest shirt made her look marginally more glamorous than she did when unpacking cardboard boxes.

At least she'd recoloured her hair the week before, so there was no hint of her blonde roots. And she'd left her hair down, although there had been hardly any time for her to attempt some loose curls with her straightening iron. Back in Perth, she put more effort into getting ready to go to the supermarket.

Part of her was a little disappointed that she didn't have the time—or the money—to really go all out for Hugh. A lot disappointed, actually. But then—did it matter? Hugh hadn't seem bothered by her dusty, messy-haired *dishabille* that morning.

Plus, it wasn't as if she needed to impress him. They'd both been pretty clear about what they wanted: each other. For a short time.

That was it. No complications. No relationship.

It should be…freeing.

But it wasn't. Instead this felt very much like a first date to her. A first date full of nerves and anticipation and possibilities.

April knew she couldn't think like that. It wasn't what Hugh was offering, and it wasn't what April wanted.

It wasn't.

She meant that with every cell in her body—except for that little chunk of her heart that had ached when Hugh had so summarily rejected her.

She supposed *I don't want a relationship with you, April* had too many echoes of Evan's *I don't love you* rejection not to hurt, at least just a little bit. She wouldn't be human if it didn't. Surely?

So it didn't mean anything.

She was strong and independent and single—and she had a date with Hugh Bennell.

April grabbed her scarf and coat, and headed for the Tube.

Hugh had booked the same table he always booked.

He figured that while April might not have been matched with him by any computer algorithm, really tonight was no different from any other date.

Except for the fact she was his employee, and that he'd already kissed her...

No, he told himself firmly. There was nothing different or special *whatsoever* about tonight.

It was just a date.

And so they were at his favourite restaurant. A very nice restaurant, with white linen tablecloths and an epic wine list. Importantly, it valued the privacy of its customers, and kept tables well-spaced and the lighting intimate. He'd had many very pleasant dates here, with great food and robust conversation.

'This is lovely,' April said from across the table. She held a glass of sparkling water in her hand, and her long hair cascaded over one shoulder in chocolate waves. 'I wish I had more time to enjoy it properly. To be honest, I just thought we'd go to a pub.'

She started work at nine p.m., so they didn't even have two hours before she had to leave.

'I don't like pubs,' he said truthfully.

'Really? But London does them so well. There's a pub near your place I've been wanting to try for ages. But I'm such a Nigel now, I haven't had the opportunity.'

'Nigel?' Hugh asked.

'No Friends. You know? Nigel No Friends? Or is that another Australianism I didn't realise was one?'

Hugh grinned. 'Like Billy No Mates?' he prompted.

'Exactly,' April said, looking pleased. 'Seems being a loser is universal.'

He laughed out loud. 'I don't believe for a second that you don't have friends,' he said.

'Well, I *do* have friends,' April said. 'Just not here. And I've been working too much to meet anyone. Not that I particularly wanted to—especially at first. I just wanted to be on my mopey lonesome.'

'Not any more?'

'No,' she said firmly. 'I guess I'm a pretty social person usually. I'm always out—catching up with friends for coffee or lunch. Going to parties or—'

Her voice broke off, and he raised an eyebrow in question.

'Or…ah…the movies, or a bar, or whatever.'

Her gaze had slid downwards, was now focused on her bread and the untouched gold-wrapped pat of butter. She seemed suddenly uncomfortable.

But then she was refocusing on him, and the moment was gone as if it had never happened. 'So, once I get rid of this night-job nightmare, I'm hoping to finally get to explore London. So at the moment you're basically my only friend, as my housemates seem convinced I'm bordering on elderly at my advanced age—'

'I don't like pubs,' he repeated.

April blinked. 'Really?' she asked again, only now seeming to realise that he hadn't elaborated on that. 'Why?'

He shrugged. 'I don't like people. And pubs are full of them.'

'No,' April said simply. 'Not true.'

'It *is* true,' Hugh said, with deliberate patience and the hint of a smile. 'They *are* full with *lots* of people.'

She shook her head. 'No, the bit about you not liking people. You like me.'

'You're not everyone,' he said.

His gaze slid over her as he reminded himself exactly how *not everyone* April Spencer was. She'd apologised when she'd arrived for her—as she'd described them—'casual clothes'. But personally Hugh thought she looked incredible, in skinny jeans that highlighted the curve of her hips and a colourfully abstract printed silk blouse that skimmed her breasts and revealed her lovely neck and collarbones. She'd painted her lips a classic red and her eyes were smoky and...

Narrowed.

Hugh sighed. 'Okay. I don't like people I don't know. Or hanging out with people I don't know in one, dark cramped place.'

'Okay,' she said. 'Then how do you meet people?'

'Women?' he clarified.

She might have blushed, but the lighting meant he couldn't be absolutely certain.

'Sure,' she said. 'Or men. Anyone. Just people.'

'Women—except you—I meet online. I prefer to set my expectations up-front, and there is no better way than in writing. And as for new mates—well, I've got friends from uni I'm still in touch with. That's enough. And I cycle with a group that lives locally, but that's not a social thing.'

'I *like* meeting new people,' April said, not surprising Hugh at all. 'Everyone has a story to tell, you know? Although I'm close to my sisters, so I've never really gone out of my way to find new *close* friends.'

She paused, looking thoughtful.

'I hadn't thought about dating yet—or online dating, I mean. When I met Evan we communicated with folded-up notes via our schoolfriends—not smartphones. But, yes, I can see the appeal of online. Seems very efficient for identifying deal-breakers. Although,' she said, leaning forward slightly,

'I've always kind of liked the idea of meeting someone random at a bar or in a pub. You know—the intrigue of it. Discovering little bits and pieces about them, revealing little bits about you, working out if you actually like each other or not. I never got to do that because I was with Evan since high school.'

'But it could be a total waste of everyone's time,' Hugh said. 'The odds aren't high that you'll meet the person of your dreams one random night at a random pub.'

'Why not?' April said as their meals were served. April had ordered gnocchi, garnished with thin slices of parmesan. In front of Hugh was placed a steak. 'Don't you believe that some people are destined to meet?'

'No,' he said firmly. 'If you want to meet Mr Perfect and you find him at the pub, that's great. But it's just luck—not destiny. Online dating takes the luck out of it.'

April looked sceptical. 'I don't know about that. Perfect on paper is different to perfect in person. You can't guarantee chemistry.'

Hugh sliced off a small piece of steak, smothering it in mashed potato and mushroom sauce. 'In my experience the matching algorithm of the app I use does a pretty good job. And it also means that when there *is* chemistry it's with someone who wants the same things as you. There isn't much point having great chemistry if you both want completely different things.'

There was a long pause as they both ate, and April's concentration was aimed at her dinner plate.

'And you don't want a relationship ever? Why?' she asked.

He swallowed, barely tasting the delicious food. 'Isn't that a bit personal for a first date?'

April glanced up and looked determined. 'I told you that my husband left me because he didn't love me enough. We've been plenty personal.'

'"Enough"?'

She hadn't mentioned that word before, and he watched as she winced—but quickly hid it—when he repeated it.

She shrugged and put on a smile. 'Our love wasn't like in

movies and books, apparently. I didn't elicit that level of emotion in him, it would seem. He met someone else who did.'

Her words were light, but he could see it still hurt her to say them.

'What a—' Hugh began, but then stopped. What was he going to say? *What a tosser?* For not loving April more?

He couldn't say that. After all, he was no better. He wasn't offering her anything: not a relationship, and certainly not love.

If her ex-husband was an idiot, what was *he*?

A realist. Not someone caught up in imaginary stories and Hollywood fairytales.

But he knew he didn't want to hurt April. So she deserved the truth.

'I'm happier on my own,' he said. 'I don't feel any urge to share my life with anyone.'

'But you date?' she prompted. 'You just said that you meet women online.'

He nodded and reached for his bourbon. 'That has absolutely nothing to do with sharing my life.'

'Ah,' April said. 'So it's just about the sex.'

Hugh coughed on his drink. But her directness made him smile. 'Well, I also just *like* women, and spending time in the company of women.'

'Just not in pubs, and you never share any of your life with them?'

'Yes,' he said. 'That pretty much sums it up.'

April tilted her head, studying him carefully. Her gaze drifted across his hair, his nose, his lips, then downwards across his off-white open-necked shirt, along the shape of his arms to his wrist and his heavy, stainless steel watch.

She met his gaze again. 'You're weird,' she said.

Hugh laughed. 'I've been told that before.' He shrugged now. 'But it's who I am. Take it or leave it.'

He'd said that casually, with no real intent. But he could see April turning it over in her mind. Really *he* should be turning it over in *his* mind. She was clearly emotionally vulnerable, for all her brave words.

He believed her when she said she wasn't ready for a relationship. But she definitely wasn't ready to be hurt again.

And he'd hurt women before, despite all his signposting and expectation-setting. With those women he'd reconciled the situation with an almost 'buyer beware' lack of emotion. Although of course he hadn't *liked* it that he'd caused anyone pain. In his quest to avoid the complications of relationships the last thing he wanted was to cause the kind of despair he'd observed in his mother's many failed relationships.

But with April—he'd kissed her before telling her any of this. He'd invited her out for dinner before she'd had a chance to catch her breath after that crazy hot kiss in the kitchen.

She'd be smart to walk away. *He* should walk away. This was already far more complicated than any other date he'd been on.

But he didn't.

And she didn't.

'Tell me about your company,' she said, 'What's actually involved in creating a new app? I've always wondered...'

And so they changed the subject, and the conversation became as pleasant and robust as on every other date he'd had at this restaurant.

For a short while.

Then it became easy and rambling, as April told him about a camping trip to northern Western Australia with her sisters as a child, and he told her about how he'd discovered cycling a few years ago and now had seen more of the UK on his bike than he'd ever thought possible. They talked about nothing serious—certainly nothing as serious as divorce or relationships.

As their desserts arrived, and April started to tell him about an amazing frozen dessert she'd had once in a food court in Singapore, she realised the time.

'Oh, crap—I'm late,' she said urgently.

And then she was up, her bag slung over her shoulder and

her coat over her arm, leaving her half-eaten dessert. She was a few steps away from the table before he knew what was happening.

A moment later his hand was on her elbow, slowing her.

Then he kissed her.

It was supposed to be quick—he knew she was late. But it wasn't.

They both lingered. It wasn't a passionate kiss—they were standing in the middle of a restaurant and he hadn't forgotten that. But his lips tasted hers for long moments, and then their gazes tangled wordlessly after their mouths had parted.

'I need to go,' she whispered.

So Hugh returned to his table to eat his parfait alone.

The next day was Saturday.

April had slept in, and the late-rising December sun had already been in the sky for at least an hour.

Her roommate lay curled up in a multi-coloured duvet bundle on her bed, her slow, deep breathing indicating she was still sound asleep.

Quietly April retrieved her phone from where it was charging, and propped herself up in bed to scroll through her Instagram and Facebook feeds.

The ankle boots had been a hit, and she had hundreds of 'likes' and comments. She replied to a few before opening up her instant messenging account, which had a little red circle on it indicating she'd missed a heap of messages.

All from her sisters.

They'd caught up for lunch in Perth while she'd been sleeping, and had sent a photo of them both—and baby Nate—sitting cross-legged on a patchwork quilt at King's Park, towering trees and a playground in the background.

Mila: Wish you were here!

Neither of her sisters was currently online, but April typed a reply anyway:

April: I miss you all so much!

Her roommate rolled over in bed. April had nothing against Fiona personally, but she *hated* not having her own space.

She started a new message.

April: I have so much to tell you. Something happened with Mr Mysterious...

But then she stopped and deleted everything she'd just written.

It felt...too soon.

For what?

She put her phone down and headed for the bathroom before the rest of her late-rising housemates woke up.

Under the sting of hot water she closed her eyes, remembering that kiss in the restaurant.

She'd spent a lot of time remembering it as she'd unloaded pallets at the supermarket and stacked shelves until one a.m.

For some reason it was that last kiss that she kept replaying. It hadn't been as sexy as their first kiss but it had been... Unexpected. And differently unexpected from that first remarkable unexpected kiss in the kitchen.

Because she knew how intensely private Hugh was. Yet he'd kissed her in a room full of strangers.

What did it mean?

Nothing.

She squeezed face-wash onto her palm and scrubbed her face much harder than necessary.

No. He'd explained that when he dated he was clear about what he wanted. That was all it was.

A few minutes later, with a towel wrapped around her, she made a phone call. After all, she could be clear about what she wanted, too.

'Hugh Bennell,' he answered, in his amazing low and sexy voice.

'I know that I was only supposed to use this number in an

emergency,' April said, remembering his instructions on the day they'd met. 'But this *is* an emergency.'

'What's wrong?' he asked, sharply.

'I need someone to have all-day breakfast with me at the best all-day breakfast place in London.'

She could sense his smile. 'And where is that?'

'I don't know,' she said. 'I'll look it up and let you know where to meet me?'

'Done,' he said. 'See you soon.'

April was smiling as she typed *Best all-day breakfast London* into her phone.

Based on reviews, and reasonable proximity to where they both lived, April had chosen a simple corner café in Clerkenwell that had red gingham curtains on the windows and white-tiled walls inside covered with black-framed old newspaper articles.

She ordered coffee while she was waiting for Hugh, and spent way too much time trying to select a table—*where to sit if your date doesn't like random people?*—before just grabbing a table by the window. She still felt very much like a tourist, and welcomed the opportunity to overlook a classic London streetscape. Hugh could always suggest they move if he wasn't comfortable.

While she waited she scrolled through the remaining photos from her shoot back in Perth, trying to work out which to use next. She only had five more left, so if she really stretched it out maybe five weeks before she needed to sort out what she was doing.

Or at the very least reveal her new hair colour.

Although even now she was losing followers—and definitely losing engagement. Her research had shown that optimum post frequency for follower growth was, on average, around one point five posts a day. Since her move to London she was down to about a post every two days. And, as she was rationing the shoot photos, very few had her physically *in* them—or at least all of her—and she knew that photos of her coffee, or her feet, or her fingernails, or the book she was reading, or shots of the sunset—*thanks, Carly*—were never going to be high-performing posts.

It wasn't great. Not for her 'April Molyneux brand'—for want of a better phrase—and certainly not for the foundation. Her follower numbers were critical when it came to enticing brands to work with her. She couldn't afford for those numbers to continue to drop.

'Blonde?'

It was Hugh—behind her. Absorbed in her phone, and her thoughts, April hadn't heard him approach.

'Oh!' she said, automatically pushing the button to make her phone screen black. 'Hi! Is this table okay? I know there are people around, but it's such a nice view…'

She was talking fast, mentally kicking herself for letting him see the photos.

'It's fine,' he said, pulling out a chair. 'It's just crowded places that I don't like. This is fine.' He gestured towards her phone. 'Can I have a look? I can't imagine you blonde.'

April couldn't think of any plausible reason not to show Hugh. Reluctantly, she handed the phone to him. 'It was just a silly photo shoot that a friend did with me. It was supposed to make me feel better after Evan.'

That excuse worked, as the photos had been taken in different outfits, and all over Perth.

Hugh nodded as he flicked through the images, and April prayed that she wouldn't receive a message or an email or notification—because if he inadvertently opened up an app her real name would be plastered all over her social media accounts.

But thankfully he simply handed her phone back after what was probably less than a minute.

'Blonde is nice,' he said, 'but I like you brunette.'

So did April. Colouring her hair had been more symbolic than a fashion statement, but she was so glad she'd done it. Her natural hair colour was a pale brownish blonde, but she'd been highlighting it for years. The dark chocolate colour she had now was flattering—and strikingly different. But then, wasn't *she*? Sitting here, in this café, watching London pass by, she didn't feel anything like the woman she'd been before Evan left her.

'Thank you,' she said, and slid a menu across the table towards him.

She already knew what she was going to order, and she needed a moment to think.

She'd just lied to Hugh. A white lie, possibly—because, technically, it *had* been a photo shoot. Just not only for herself. But for her million followers.

Did it matter?

Last night at dinner, despite a few near misses, it hadn't been too difficult to avoid revealing who she was. Because, really, her family's fortune wasn't relevant first date conversation.

And it wasn't as if she was hiding the important stuff: he knew she was getting divorced, he knew a bit about her family—skimming over the details—and now he knew she'd happily eat breakfast for every meal.

And—really—did she owe him any more than that? In this relationshipless, life-sharing no-go zone, did her billion-dollar trust fund, million social media followers and socialite lifestyle make any difference? Especially when he thought she was a penniless backpacker?

Yes, said her gut.

No, reasoned her brain.

'I know what I want,' Hugh said, nodding at his menu.

In the midday sun that streamed through the window he squinted a little. He even did that attractively, somehow. And with his stubble-less jaw—he'd clearly shaved—he looked so darkly handsome that April's heart skipped a beat.

'Do you?' he asked.

'Mmm…' she said. Then blinked, and swallowed. 'Yes,' she said more firmly. 'I do.'

He went to stand, but April put her hand on his arm. 'No,' she said. 'I'll order. This is my treat.'

So she went to the counter to order breakfast that she really couldn't afford, waiting in line behind a couple. They were older than April, and looked blissfully happy: the man's hand was wrapped loosely around the woman's waist, his thumb hooked into her belt loop.

April glanced back at their table and went still when she realised Hugh was watching her. His gaze was intense. And appreciative. It made her feel hot and liquid inside.

A sharp but low-pitched word drew April's attention. The happy couple were arguing about something in harsh staccato whispers that continued as they walked back to their table.

Now, *that* looked complicated.

Relationships *were* complicated.

So why complicate things by revealing the truth?

She ordered their breakfast and walked back to Hugh, table number in her hand.

He smiled at her, and she smiled back.

Yes. She definitely knew what she wanted.

Hugh.

Without complications.

CHAPTER TEN

AFTER LUNCH HUGH played tour guide as he and April spent the afternoon walking through London. They chatted as they ambled the mile from Clerkenwell to St Paul's Cathedral, then headed across the Millennium Bridge and along the Thames. Beside the river they stopped occasionally to lean against the stone and iron barrier and watch the boats float by, for April to take photos of the sparkling silver skyscraper skyline beyond Canary Wharf, or for April to ask questions about the height of The Shard or how often Tower Bridge opened to allow ships through.

This wasn't his usual Saturday.

He'd gone for his early-morning group cycle ride as normal, and had been reading the newspaper at his dining table when April had called.

Usually he'd spend the rest of his Saturday maybe lifting weights in his spare room, or binge-watching something that looked interesting. Later, he'd work. He always did at the weekend.

So, nothing critical.

But still... After he'd agreed to meet April so readily he'd felt uneasy. Maybe because it hadn't even occurred to him to say no.

He'd told April he liked spending time with women, which of course he did. But at dinner. At night. On a date.

Not casually. Not wearing jeans and trainers and without an actual plan.

So he'd decided he'd just have breakfast with April, then go home. That would be okay—no different from the night before.

Instead here he was. Willingly being her tour guide after she'd asked him so sweetly—with a big smile and those gorgeous eyes. And he was in no hurry to get home.

In fact he was having fun.

And having fun with April was so easy. He only felt uneasy when he reminded himself that he should be. Which was crazy, right? April had said he was weird, and he knew he was. But he wasn't a masochist.

He was having fun, and he and April were on exactly the same page. He needed to get over it—and himself—and just go with the flow.

He reached out, grabbing her fingers as she walked beside him. He tugged at her hand, pulling her to the side of the footpath and then pulling her towards him.

Hugh kissed her thoroughly, his hands at her back and her waist and hers tangled in his hair.

'Wow,' she said when they came up for air.

He murmured against her ear. 'I realised I hadn't kissed you today,' he said.

That he'd waited so long seemed impossible.

He felt her smile as he kissed her jaw. 'Where did you learn to kiss like that?' she asked on a sigh.

'Rachael Potter in the Upper Sixth asked if she could practise on me,' Hugh said, grinning against the skin of her cheek. 'She was a year older than me—an older woman. At the time it was the most thrilling moment of my life. Although I wasn't to tell a soul, of course.'

April stepped back, still meeting his gaze. 'Why not?'

'Because—as we determined last night—I'm weird. As an adult, I'm fortunate that people just consider me a little idiosyncratic. In high school I was just plain strange.'

'But why would people think that?'

Hugh shrugged and started walking again, his hands stuffed into his coat pockets.

'It's like I told you—I didn't want anyone to know about the house. As a young kid it was just easier to not have any friends. It wasn't until uni—you know, when playdates aren't really expected—that I had friends again.'

'That's sad,' April said. 'I'm sure most kids wouldn't have cared.'

Hugh raised his eyebrows. 'I was already the nerdy computer kid. I wasn't about to sign up as the kid with the crazy mother. And I definitely wasn't going to let my mum be thought of like that.'

They kept on walking. Around them it was dusk, and the trees that lined the Thames were beginning to twinkle with hundreds of blue lights that grew brighter as the sun retreated.

'Not that it made any difference,' Hugh said, minutes later. 'Kids still whispered about my mum. And about me. Maybe some kids would've been fine with it, but I didn't let anyone close enough to find out. I was moody—and resentful that I had to look after my mum.'

'Look after her?' April asked.

They were still walking, and Hugh kept his gaze on the concrete footpath.

'Yeah,' he said. 'Eventually it was more than just *stuff* that Mum was collecting. There were piles of rubbish. Piles of dirty laundry. I had to create a safe passage for her to get to bed each night. I had to make sure her bed was clear of crap and her sheets were clean. I did all the shopping…the cooking. I remembered to do my homework. I packed my own lunches.'

'She wasn't well,' April said.

'No,' Hugh said with a humourless laugh. 'And I was too young to really understand that. I'd researched hoarding at the library, and I'd tried to help—but even though I kind of got that it must be some sort of anxiety disorder, I wasn't really sympathetic. All I saw was that she managed to go to work each day. She managed to socialise, to continue her quest to find the perfect man, and yet we lived in this absolute horror story of a house that *I* had to keep liveable even as she brought more and more crap inside it.'

April remained silent, letting him speak.

He stopped again. They stood beneath a cast-iron lamp-post with dolphins twined around its base—one of many that lit the South Bank.

'So, yeah…' Hugh said. 'Rachael Potter didn't want anyone to know she was kissing the weird, friendless geek with the crazy mother.'

April reached out and held his hand. 'What happened to her?' she asked. 'To your mum?'

He'd known this question was coming.

He swallowed, angry that his throat was tight and that his heart ached and felt heavy.

'Cancer,' he said. 'I always thought her hoarding would kill her, but I was wrong. It was unexpected—quick and brutal— and she told me in the hospital that she wanted to come home to die. I thought that was bizarre—that she would want to be in the house that represented all she'd lost when Len had died, illustrated with box after box. But she did, so I organised to have her room cleared, to make it safe for a hospital bed to be delivered.'

He swallowed, staring at their joined hands.

'But it was already too late. Before the first box was moved she died.'

Suddenly April's arms were around him.

She was hugging him, her arms looped around his neck, her cheek pressed against his shoulder. She hugged him as he stood there, stiff and wooden, his hands firm by his sides.

She hugged him for long minutes until—eventually—he hugged her back. Tight and hard, with her body pressed tight against him.

He wasn't a hugger—he'd told her that. Even if he was, he'd had no one to hug when his mother had died. At the time it hadn't mattered. It hadn't even occurred to him that he might need or want someone to hug, to grieve with.

As always, it had just been him.

Eventually they broke apart. He turned from April, wiping at the tears that had threatened, but thankfully hadn't been shed.

When he caught April's gaze again, her own gaze travelled across his face in the lamplight, but she said nothing.

He didn't want to be standing here any longer.

'Want a drink?' he asked.

April blinked, but nodded. 'Let's go.'

* * *

They headed up a series of narrow cobblestoned lanes, Hugh still holding April's hand. His strides were long, and April had to hurry to keep pace with him.

He hadn't said a word, and April wasn't really sure what to say.

Then he stopped in front of a small bar. Beyond black-framed windows April could see exposed brick walls and vintage velvet couches.

'Want to try here?' Hugh asked.

She was confused. 'You don't like bars.'

He grinned. 'I don't like *people*. It's still early—hardly anyone's here.'

She followed Hugh inside. The bar's warmth was a welcome relief. It wasn't entirely empty, but only two other customers were there: two women in deep conversation, cocktails in hand.

At the bar, April ordered red wine and Hugh bourbon. April chose one of the smaller couches, towards the rear of the rectangular space, and ran her fingers aimlessly over the faded gold fabric as Hugh sat down. With Hugh seated the couch seemed significantly smaller—their knees bumped, in fact, his dark blue denim against her faded grey.

Not that April minded.

'So,' Hugh said, 'tell me about *your* first kiss.'

His tone was light, and the pain she'd glimpsed in his eyes beneath the lamppost had disappeared.

'Well,' she said, 'I was six. Rory Crothers. Kiss-chasey.' She sighed expansively. 'It was *amazing*!'

Hugh's lips quirked. 'Doesn't count,' he said.

She widened her eyes. 'You mean Rachael Potter *didn't* just give you a kiss on the cheek?'

'No,' he said. Straight-faced.

'Ah…' April said. 'So we're talking *tongue* kissing, then?'

Hugh gave a burst of laughter. 'Yeah,' he said. 'Definitely tongue kissing.'

The look in his eyes was smouldering—and April knew it had *nothing* to do with young Miss Potter.

Something suddenly occurred to her, and she leant forward, resting her hand on Hugh's thigh. 'Am I flirting with a guy in a pub?' she asked.

He grinned, obviously remembering their conversation from the night before. 'Just like you always wanted.'

She smiled. 'This is just as fun as I'd imagined.'

Hugh's eyes flicked downwards to her hand on his thigh. 'Yep,' he said.

Someone had turned up the music, and the beat reverberated around them. As they'd been talking a handful of customers had walked in, were now standing in a group only a few metres away from them.

She nodded in their direction. 'Still okay?' she asked.

He nodded.

'Well,' April said, returning to his original question, 'this is going to sound really sad, but if we're only counting tongue kissing, then Evan was it. I was sixteen, and he kissed me on my front doorstep when I was his date for his high school ball.'

'So I'm only the second guy you've kissed?'

She nodded.

He took a long drink of his bourbon. 'I know you said you met in high school, but I hadn't really considered what that actually meant.'

April tilted her head quizzically. 'It means I met him in high school.'

'You were with him half your life. You grew from teenager to adult with him. That's a really big deal.'

'None of this is news to me,' she said dryly, then sipped her wine.

'And he left *you*?'

April blinked. 'What is this? Remind-April-Of-Crap-Stuff-That's-Happened Day?'

She sounded hurt and defensive, which she didn't like.

Hugh was silent, and she knew she didn't have to answer

his question if she didn't want to. He'd be okay about it. But for some reason she started talking.

'He left me,' she began, 'and I've been telling people I didn't see it coming, but that's a lie.'

April paused, this time taking a long drink of her wine.

'We were having problems for years—even before we got married. It's probably why we took more than ten years to get married, actually. But it was nothing serious—just issues with communicating. Different expectations about stuff—when we'd have kids...that type of thing. So we went to counselling and we tried talking about it. I guess for me, after such a long time, ending it just didn't feel like an option. Evan had been part of my entire adult life, and I couldn't imagine life without him. So I didn't. But obviously Evan had no issues with imagining his life without *me*.'

April watched her fingers as she drew lines in the velvet of the couch.

'I was really keen to have a baby, and we started trying pretty much as soon as we got married—three years ago. But that was all my idea. Evan just went along with it. Maybe that's when he started wondering if things could be different—I don't know.'

Her hair had fallen forward and she tucked the long strands behind her ears as she looked back up at Hugh. Over his shoulder, she saw that more people had entered the bar, and now more couches were occupied than empty.

'I thought he was the love of my life right until the end. I mean, relationships are *supposed* to be hard at times, so I didn't see any red flags when we were having problems. I probably should have. But, yeah, Evan was right. We didn't have that epic, all-consuming love that you see in movies.' She looked at her glass, swirling the deep red liquid but not drinking. 'Although,' she said, 'I think now I realise that I always loved him more than he loved me.'

That last bit had come from nowhere, and April went still as she realised the truth of what she'd said. A truth she hadn't allowed herself to acknowledge before.

'Do you still love him?'

Her gaze flew from her glass to meet Hugh's. He was look-ing at her with...*concern*? With *pity*?

She sat up, removing her hand from his leg.

'Why?' she asked. 'Would you prefer it that I still do?'

'That wasn't why I was asking,' he said.

April didn't understand why she'd reacted this way, but anger out of nowhere shot through her veins. 'If I still loved him you wouldn't have to worry about the poor, rejected di-vorcee getting too attached to you, would you? That would keep things neater.'

'April—' he began.

But she wasn't ready to listen. The still raw pain of Evan's rejection was colliding with Hugh's pity. Pity from yet another man who didn't want a relationship with her.

'Why do you care, anyway? What do you know about love, Mr Never-Had-A-Relationship?'

'I care,' he said.

But that was just too much.

She put her glass down on a low table, then stood up and headed for the door.

After a few steps she realised just how crowded the bar had become. There was no clear path for her to take.

She turned back to Hugh, who—as she'd known he would—had followed her. He was only a step behind her. As she watched, a heavy-set bloke turned and accidentally banged his beer against Hugh's arm, spilling the liquid down Hugh's jacket. The man apologised profusely, and a moment later April was at Hugh's side as he reassured the other man and waved him away.

April was standing right in front of Hugh now. They were surrounded—a big group must have entered the bar together—and suddenly the space had gone from busy to absolutely packed. The air was heavy with the smell of aftershave and beer.

Hugh's jaw was tense beneath the bar's muted lighting.

'Are you okay?' she asked.

Hugh's expression was dismissive. 'I'll get it dry-cleaned. It was just an accident.'

'No, not that,' she said. 'I mean—you know—all the people?'

'It doesn't matter. Why did you walk away?'

Someone tapped on April's shoulder and asked to squeeze past, which moved April closer to Hugh.

She lifted her chin. 'I don't want you feeling sorry for me,' she said. 'I'm fine. I don't need your pity.'

'I don't *pity* you, April,' he said, low and harsh in her ear. 'But you've been hurt badly. This might not be a good idea.'

He meant *them*.

'You want to end it?'

'No.' He said it roughly. Firmly. His gaze told her he still felt every bit of the sizzling connection between them. 'But I should.'

'Ah…' April said, nodding slowly. 'You're being *noble*.'

'Well—'

She cut him off. 'Thanks, but no thanks. I didn't sign up for you to be my knight in shining armour, Hugh. I get to make my own decisions. And, if necessary, my own mistakes.'

'You also didn't sign up for my relationship quirks.'

'You mean all your relationship rules and expectations? I get that you don't like it that I haven't followed your rules, but you've been crystal-clear. No relationship. I get it, Hugh, and I'm going to be okay. I'm not fragile. You're not going to break me.'

Or her heart.

She wouldn't allow it.

Another clumsy patron bumped into April's back, pushing her into Hugh's chest. Her forearms landed flush against him, her hands splayed across his shoulders.

According to Hugh, she had a choice here: one was to push her arms against him and walk away. But that wasn't an option for April.

She'd spent months in a fog, questioning so much about her life and all that she'd once taken for granted. Everything was different for her now: her present *and* her future. Her life would not unfold the way she'd always expected it to.

But she didn't question this.

She knew now why she'd reacted so strongly to Hugh's concern, and to what she'd perceived as his pity. She *never* wanted someone to be with her unless she was the person they most *wanted* to be with. Her marriage hadn't been perfect, but she'd still not wanted anyone but Evan. And Evan had aspired to something more.

God, that *hurt*.

So she didn't want Hugh to feel sorry for her. She wanted him to *want* her.

And he did.

Right now he wanted to be with no one more than her. She believed that with every cell of her body: with every cell in her body that was now hot and liquid, thanks to the way his chest, belly and legs were pressed so close against hers. So what if he only wanted her *right now* and not for longer?

It didn't matter—because she *knew* that right at this moment she didn't need to worry about not being 'enough', or to worry if the man she was with was wondering if there was something—someone—*more* out there for him.

Right now Hugh wanted *her*. Just her. No one else.

It might not be about love or relationships or a future together, but it still felt good. Great. The best, even. It still felt like exactly what she needed. And, yeah, she definitely wanted Hugh more than anyone. She could barely think with him this close to her.

Her hands relaxed and shifted, one moving up to his hair. Her body softened against him. She loved how hard and solid every inch of him was. His hands, which had been at his sides, now moved. They slid across her hips to her back.

April stood on tiptoes to murmur against his lips. 'You know, there's something else I've always wanted to do in a pub,' she said. 'Kiss a hot—'

He silenced her with his mouth, kissing her thoroughly—with lips *and* tongue.

Yes, this was a *proper* kiss: sexy and playful, deep and soft and hard.

When her eyes slid shut April forgot about where they stood, forgot about the crowd, and she couldn't hear the music or the blur of conversation around them. It was just her and Hugh—the hot stranger she'd always wanted to kiss in a bar.

Although after today he didn't feel like a stranger. They'd had some big conversations. They'd shared each other's pain. Surely *that* didn't follow Hugh's rules...

But beneath Hugh's mouth, his teeth, his tongue, her ability for coherent analysis no longer existed. Instead she just got to feel—the strength of his shoulders, the heat of his mouth. And to react as she took her turn to lead their kiss, to explore his mouth and to lose herself in delicious sensation.

And then, just as Hugh's hand slid beneath her shirt and jacket, the heat of his touch shocking against the cool skin of her waist, yet another person bumped into them.

Hugh dragged his mouth from hers to speak into her ear. 'Can we get out of here?'

'Please,' she said.

And, holding Hugh's hand, April navigated them through the sea of bodies and noisy conversations finally to spill out onto the cobblestones outside.

Hugh tugged her a few metres away from the doorway into the shadows of a neighbouring shopfront, the shop now closed in the evening darkness.

'Still hate pubs?' April asked, breathless as he backed her up against the wooden door.

'Intensely,' he said, his breath hot against her skin. 'But I really like this.'

And then he kissed her again.

CHAPTER ELEVEN

'Do you think it's a form of claustrophobia?' April asked as they were driven through London in the back seat of a black cab.

'The pub thing?' Hugh said, relaxing into his seat.

Streetlights intermittently lit the car's interior as they drove, painting April in light and shadow.

'No,' he continued. 'If anything it would be ochlophobia, which is a fear of crowds. But "fear" is too strong a word. Intolerance of crowds is more accurate.'

He'd researched his dislike of bustling, enclosed spaces, much as he'd researched his mother's hoarding. It hadn't been much of a leap to realise that if his mother had an anxiety-related disorder then possibly he did too.

But the label wasn't a comfortable fit. And certainly his issues were nowhere near as extreme as his mother's.

Tonight, for instance.

He *never* would've walked into that bar if it had been busy when they'd arrived. And, truthfully, while he'd been aware of the small space filling and people growing rowdier, the longer he and April had talked, the less it had bothered him.

His focus has been on April. Solely on April.

Later, as the crowds had buffeted them both, the familiar cloak of tension had wrapped around him. He had definitely wanted out of that bar, as rapidly as possible. But then April had asked if he was okay. And then it had become about *her* again—about his clearly unwanted concern for her—and then, soon after, about his need to touch her.

When he'd kissed her he wouldn't have cared if he'd been surrounded by a million people—he wouldn't have noticed. He'd been entirely and completely focused on April and on kissing her.

Surely if he truly had a phobia he wouldn't have been able to just forget about it like that? Just for a kiss?

In the rare times he'd found himself in a crowded space in the past fifteen years he certainly wouldn't have expected a kiss to have distracted him from the way his throat would tighten and his heart would race. But a kiss *had*.

Or maybe it was April?

He didn't let himself spend any time considering that.

'It isn't even crowds in general,' Hugh said, talking to silence his brain. 'I can go to the movies, to the theatre, without much problem. I generally go outside during intermissions, and I never wait around in the foyer before a show, but once I'm in my seat I'm fine, because it's an ordered, organised crowd. Also, I generally have a date if I'm going somewhere like that, so I'm not expected to converse with random people. Something else I don't enjoy. That's why the café today was fine—there wasn't a mass of people and I was there with you.'

'So you need white space?' April said.

He hadn't thought of it quite like that before, but the analogy worked.

'Like in your flat,' she said. 'That's like one big ocean of white space.'

His lips quirked. 'Yes,' he said. 'I suppose it is.'

The antithesis of the home he grew up in.

The cab slowed to a stop outside an uninspiring town house with a collection of dead weeds in a planter box at the front window. They'd arrived at April's place—a destination they'd chosen after having had a group of passing teenagers wolf-whistle as they'd been mid-kiss within that shop doorway and April had whispered, 'I should go home.'

He still felt the stab of disappointment at those words. But she was right to slow things down—even if it was the last thing he wanted to do.

He asked the cab driver to wait as he escorted April to the door. A sensor light flicked on and then almost immediately fizzled out, leaving April to search around in her handbag for keys in almost pitch-darkness.

'I hate this house,' April said when she eventually slid the key into the lock. 'Like, with a deep and abiding passionate hatred, you know?'

'So you're not going to invite me in?' he asked with a smile.

'No,' April said. 'Because I am certain two-day-old pizza remains on the coffee table and the fridge stinks like something died in it. And because I have a roommate—literally. And also because I'm trying to be sensible.'

But it seemed whenever Hugh was this close to April, being sensible just didn't feel like an option. So he kissed her again.

She kissed him back in a way that confirmed what he already knew—that April didn't want to be particularly sensible either.

'Do you want to—?' he began.

Come back to my place.

What was he *doing*?

'Do I want to what?' April asked. Her words were a husky whisper.

'Nothing,' he said firmly, stepping away. 'Nothing.'

He *never* invited a woman back to his place. It was, as April had so accurately said, his white space. Unadulterated with clutter or complications. *Any* complications.

He was halfway back to the cab before he'd even realised he was retreating.

'Hugh?'

'Bye, April,' he said, knowing he should say more, but unable to work out what.

He didn't give her a chance to respond and slid into the back seat of the cab, then watched her step into the townhouse, turn on the light and close the front door behind her.

Hugh knew he'd just reacted poorly. That he was being weird. But then, that was what he did. It was who he was.

He didn't have unexpected, amorphous day-long dates with women who worked for him. All of today had been exceedingly weird for him. It just hadn't felt weird at the time. At all, really—even now.

Being with April had felt natural. Inviting her to his place—*almost*—had felt natural, too.

But as the cab whisked him home he felt more comfortable with his decision with every passing mile. He'd been right to halt his rebellious tongue and his rebellious libido.

This thing with April was definitely breaking *some* of his rules. But not the important ones: No sleepovers at his house. No relationships.

Those rules were non-negotiable.

And those rules would never be broken.

April: I have some news.

Mila: Yes?

Ivy wasn't online, but April messaged both her sisters so Ivy could comment later if she wanted. She needed their advice.

It was Sunday morning, her roommate was once again sleeping in and this wasn't a conversation she wanted to have in the kitchen, with her other housemates listening in. So instant messaging it was.

She snuggled under her doona and typed out a brief summary of the past forty-eight hours. It seemed completely impossible that it had been less than two days since Hugh had kissed her—it felt like for ever ago.

She closed her eyes as the memory of his lips at the sensitive skin beneath her ear made her shiver.

April: So what do you think?

She'd just described the way Hugh had practically run from her front doorstep after she'd been certain he intended to invite her back to his place.

Mila: I think he was just following your lead. You slowed things down, so he did too.

Mila's interpretation seemed logical, but April wasn't so sure.

April: I didn't want to slow things down. But it seemed the right thing to do.

Honestly, until those teenagers had whistled at them, slowing things down had been the absolute last thing on her mind.

Mila: Why?

April: Because I don't know anything about dating. Isn't there some protocol about what number date you sleep with someone on?

Ivy: No.

April grinned as her sister announced her appearance. Ivy's now husband had started as a one-night stand.

Ivy: But seriously. Do whatever feels right for you. This guy has made it clear that he doesn't want commitment, so you don't owe him anything. Do what you want, when you want. Date numbers are meaningless.

April: But the way he just left made me feel like he was having second thoughts.

Mila: Maybe he is.

April: Ouch!

Mila: Just ask him if you're not sure. What do you have to lose?

April: My job, I guess.

But she didn't really think so. Hugh wouldn't fire her—
he'd just make sure their paths didn't cross.

Ivy posted a serious of furious emoticons.

April grinned.

April: No, don't worry. I'm one hundred per cent sure he
wouldn't fire me.

Ivy: Good. I didn't think your taste in men was that bad.

April: It's not bad, just limited.

To two guys—one she'd married. She felt utterly clueless.

Mila: Exactly! So just ask him if he wants to help you expand
your experience or not. Then you'll know.

Ivy: Good euphemism. And good plan. You don't want to
waste time on a guy who isn't interested.

Ivy was right. On her bad days, April already felt she'd
wasted almost half her life with Evan.

April: But what if he says no?

She paused before she sent the message.

She already knew what her sisters would say: they'd reassure that he wouldn't, or tell her that if he did it was his loss,
not hers, or that if he did he was an idiot...blah-blah-blah.

Which would be lovely of them, but it wouldn't make a
difference, would it?

Of course not.

If Hugh rejected her, then it was going to hurt. There was
no sugar-coating that.

She deleted the words, thanked her sisters for their advice
and then they chatted awhile longer.

Later, she responded to some comments on the latest post to her Instagram account—one of those blonde images from months ago.

For the first time she felt a little uncomfortable doing so. Until now her double life hadn't been impacting anyone: her family and those close to her knew exactly where she was and what she was doing. She'd felt a little guilty hiding such a big move from her followers, but she'd justified it with her confidence that they would understand when she eventually made her grand reveal. As for her suppliers and sponsors—well, she was ensuring that she was showcasing their products just as she would if she was living her life as April Molyneux, so there was no issue there.

So it was just Hugh that was making her feel this way.

You don't owe him anything.

Mila's remembered words helped April dismiss her concerns. She was over-complicating a situation that was supposed to be uncomplicated. Nothing had changed since she'd made her decision at the breakfast café.

There was no need to tell him.

On Monday, April decided to be very civilised—and, she imagined, very British—by inviting Hugh for a cup of tea. She sent him a text message practically the moment she arrived at the house:

April: Cup of tea? I'm just boiling the kettle.

Hugh's response was to simply walk in the front door a couple of minutes later.

'Good morning,' he said.

'Morning,' said April. She'd made—she hoped—a subtle effort in her appearance. She was still dressed for work, in jeans, a button-down shirt and sneakers, but she'd made a more concerted effort with her hair and make-up. Her ponytail was sleek, her make-up natural but polished.

Her intent had been to give herself a boost of confidence.

In reality it made everything feel like a very big deal. After a whole Sunday convincing herself it was anything but.

'I'm sorry about how I left,' Hugh said from across the marble countertop.

April nodded, then held out a small box full of teabags she'd found in one of the cupboards, so Hugh could select the type he wanted. April was more of a coffee girl, and she dumped a generous teaspoon of coffee granules into her Dockers mug as she waited for Hugh to elaborate.

'I panicked, I think,' he said.

April's gaze leapt to his. She didn't think that Hugh was a man who often admitted to panic—of any kind.

'Saturday was…unusual for me. You told me in the bar that you weren't following my rules, but the thing was I wasn't either. And I didn't like that. I *don't* like it, really.' He swallowed. His hands were shoved into the pockets of his jeans. 'So I'm sorry I didn't call or text yesterday. I was still panicking.'

She nodded. 'Okay.'

'The thing is, I decided on my cab ride home on Saturday that I needed to slow things down—put some space between us. By last night I'd decided that the best possible thing to do was to end this. Immediately.'

April's stomach dropped, leaving her empty inside. It turned out she *hadn't* been prepared for this possibility. Not at all.

The kettle was bubbling loudly now, steam billowing from its spout. Suddenly, though, Hugh had skirted the counter and was standing right beside her.

'But that would've been idiotic,' he said.

April continued to study the teabags, not ready to risk Hugh seeing what she could guess would be revealed in her eyes.

'And besides, I realised it was impossible the moment I received your text. I'd been kidding myself. I don't want to end this.'

'Okay,' April said again.

She did meet his gaze now, and tried to work out what he was thinking. What exactly did he mean?

His expression wasn't quite unreadable. But equally it told her little. Not like when they'd walked along the Thames. Or even at other little moments scattered throughout that Saturday as she'd told him more about her relationship with Evan, or just before they'd kissed in the centre of that crowded bar.

'Same deal, though? No relationship?'

Deliberately she'd phrased her question lightly. As if that was what she wanted, too.

Wasn't it?

'Of course,' Hugh said.

Then, before she could attempt to read anything more into his gaze or his words, he kissed her.

Softly at first, and then harder, until he lifted her off her feet to sit her on the bench. Then the kiss was something else altogether...it had intent. It was a promise of so much more.

But, wrenching her mouth away from his, April said breathlessly, 'I have to work, Hugh.'

And when he might have told her that it didn't matter, that he was her boss, he seemed to realise he shouldn't say any of that, and that it was critically important to her that he didn't.

She *was* supposed to be working. And for a woman who'd never worked a proper day in her life until recently, it was probably strange that she found that so important. But she did. Working for a living wasn't just some rich girl's fancy to April—it was real...it was her life.

She slid off the counter and walked Hugh to the front door. She stood on tiptoes and kissed him softly, sliding her hand along his jaw. His sexy stubble was back, and she loved the way it rasped beneath her fingertips.

'See you later,' she said.

And she knew she would.

CHAPTER TWELVE

THE REST OF the week was torture.

Delicious torture, but torture nonetheless.

Despite Hugh's best efforts, April was determined to be the most diligent of workers. He thought he understood—possibly—why she felt that way. While the fact that he was technically her boss was mostly irrelevant to him, April clearly felt differently. Which was admirable, really, but also...frustrating.

By Monday afternoon April had quite a collection of things in the 'Hugh' box, having hit a bit of a mother lode of potentially sentimental items in the corner of the almost completed first bedroom.

Most of it was school stuff: finger paintings, honour certificates, ribbons from school athletics competitions. Plus yet more photos—these in battered albums, and mostly of his mother as a child.

The finger paintings went to recycling, and the ribbons to the bin. One certificate in particular he kept—he remembered how, aged about eight, he'd run his thumb over the embossed gold sticker in the bottom right-hand corner with pride. The rest he chucked. He kept his mother's photo albums.

'Penmanship Award?' April asked, dropping down to kneel beside him.

She'd cleared about ninety per cent of the boxes in the bedroom, so she'd been able to open the heavy curtains. Light streamed into the room, reflecting off hundreds of dust motes floating merrily in midair.

'It was a fiercely contested award,' Hugh explained with mock seriousness. 'But in the end I won with my elegant Qs.'

'Wow!' April said. She was so close their shoulders bumped. She met his gaze, mischief twinkling in her eyes. 'I've always rather admired your Qs myself.'

'Really?' Hugh asked.

He leant closer, so their foreheads just touched. Her grin was contagious, and he found himself smiling at her like a loon.

'Yeah…' April breathed.

A beat before he kissed her, Hugh whispered, 'When have you seen my Qs?'

'Oh,' April said, 'I have a remarkable imagination.'

Hugh's eyes slid shut. 'Trust me,' he said, his words rough, 'I do too.'

Minutes later, with her lips plump from his kisses and her shirt just slightly askew, April slid from Hugh's lap and stood.

'Looks like the 'Hugh' box is sorted for the day,' she said.

'So I'm dismissed?' he said.

She shrugged, but smiled. 'Something like that. See you tomorrow.'

On Tuesday he brought lunch.

They sat on the staircase, brown paper bags torn open on their laps to catch the crumbs from crusty rolls laden with cheese, smoked meats and marinated vegetables.

'Tell me about where you live in Australia,' he asked.

And so April spoke of growing up beside a river with black swans, of camping in the Pilbara and swimming in the rock pools at Karijini. She spoke of where she lived now: in a house where she could walk to the beach—a beach with white sand that stretched for kilometres, dotted with surfers and swimmers and the occasional distant freighter.

'So why come here?' he asked.

Today it was raining, with a dreary steady mist.

'Because,' she said as she wiped her fingers with a paper napkin, 'London was far away. From Evan and my life. And it was different. I imagined a place busy where Perth was slow; and cool where Perth was hot. Perth is isolated geographically—here the world is barely hours away. I needed a change, and I needed it to be dramatic.'

She neatly rolled up her paper bag, being sure that the crumbs remained contained.

'Although,' she continued, 'I imagined walking into my dream job—which, of course, didn't happen.'

'Why not?'

She rolled her eyes. 'Because generally environmental consulting firms want experience, not just a thirty-something with a degree from a decade ago.'

'Why didn't you use your degree?' Hugh asked, confused. 'If that was your dream job?'

'Because...' she began, then paused. She started folding her rolled-up paper bag into itself, her gaze focused on her task. 'Because I travelled a lot,' she said quickly. 'And maybe it wasn't my dream job, after all.'

She stood up and offered her hand for Hugh's paper bag. He handed it to her, and followed her into the kitchen, where she shook the crumbs out into the bin before adding the paper bags to the recycling.

'You okay?' he asked.

She nodded, and then his phone vibrated in his jeans pocket: a reminder he'd set for a meeting he needed to attend.

'I need to go,' he said, and then kissed her, briefly but firmly, on the lips.

'Bye, Hugh,' she said.

On Wednesday Hugh took her to the British Museum.

Initially she'd said no.

'Consider it a team building day,' Hugh said, firmly. 'It's a sanctioned work event, okay?'

She wanted to argue. After all, she'd been playing the professional card hard—and consistently—all week.

'It's great there on a weekday,' Hugh said. 'Not too busy. And it's such a big place that even school groups and tourists don't make it feel crowded.'

Crowds didn't bother her. It was still a no...

'I liked playing tour guide the other day. Let me do it again.'

Oh.

That got her—his reference to their day together...a day she knew he'd both enjoyed and felt uncomfortable about.

Those damn rules. Yet he wanted to do it again.

'Okay,' she said.

On the way, as they sat in the back of another black cab, she wondered—yet again—what exactly she was doing.

She was fully aware that her determined professionalism was something of a cover. Yes, it was important to her to complete the job she'd been hired to do, and to actually *earn* the money that Hugh was paying her. She wasn't going to slack off just because she got to kiss her boss during her tea breaks. Tempting as that was. But also her professionalism was giving her time.

After work she had only a few hours before her job at the supermarket started—and, as their truncated dinner had proved, that wasn't enough time to do much.

It certainly wasn't enough time to do anything more than kiss Hugh. Well, technically it was, but it seemed by unspoken agreement that both she and Hugh were waiting until the weekend before taking things further. When they would have all the time in the world.

The tension this delay was creating was near unbearable. Every touch and every kiss was so weighted with promise that the weekend felt eons away—an impossible goal.

But waiting was good, too. It gave April time to think. To process what was happening.

To process who she was now.

When she'd decided to move to London she'd wanted to discover who she was without Evan. She hadn't worked that out yet, but she did know that she didn't ever want her identity so tied up with a man again.

Not that that was what was happening with Hugh. This thing with Hugh would never be more than what it was— which was fleeting. A fling. And even if it wasn't—even if Hugh *had* wanted more—April knew she couldn't lose herself in 'Hugh and April' the way she had in 'Evan and April'.

Not that it was Evan's fault that had happened. It had been

a product of youth and inexperience and an utter lack of independence—and maybe confusing independence with wealth.

It had been *her* fault—*her* error. And she couldn't make it again.

She was different now. As April Spencer she'd proved to herself that she could live alone, and survive without her family's money. Without Evan.

But the way she was around Hugh…that pull she felt towards him…that intensity of attraction and the way it overwhelmed her when he touched her, when he kissed her…

She needed to adjust to this sensation, and she needed time to acknowledge it for what it was: hormones and chemical attraction. Nothing more.

And definitely nothing that she would or could lose herself within.

She would not allow it.

The cab came to a stop beneath a London plane tree, sparse with leaves in gold and yellow. As Hugh paid the driver April slid out onto the footpath. She stood beside the fence that surrounded the museum—an impressive, elaborate cast-iron barrier—through which she could see tourists milling in the museum forecourt. A brisk breeze fluttered the leaves above her, and April hugged her coat tight around herself.

Then Hugh was in front of her, looking both enthusiastic and just slightly concerned, as if he wasn't sure he'd made the right decision to bring her here.

But April smiled. 'Lead on, tour guide!' she said with a grin.

Hugh smiled right back—with his mouth and with his eyes.

Damn, he was gorgeous.

She definitely hadn't got used to that.

Side by side they entered the forecourt, and as April's gaze was drawn to the mammoth Greek-style columns and the triangular pediment above, she shoved everything else from her mind.

This thing with Hugh—each day with Hugh—was not

complicated. It was about fun and attraction. *Only.* She had nothing to worry about.

In that spirit, she grabbed his hand as they were halfway up the steps to the museum's entrance. He stopped, and on tiptoes she kissed him.

'This is fun,' she said. Because it was, and because it was a useful reminder. 'Thank you.'

He grinned and tugged her up the remaining steps.

Yes. Fun and nothing more.

It ended up being rather a long lunchbreak.

After they'd wandered through artefacts from the Iron Age, and then lingered amongst the Ancient Egyptians, Hugh now stood alone in the Great Court—the centre of the museum—which had a soaring glass roof constructed of thousands of abutted steel triangles. April had darted into the gift shop for postcards for her mother and sisters.

Hugh's phone vibrated in his back pocket, but a quick glance had him sliding it back into his jeans. It was just work, and for once he wasn't making it his priority.

With April no longer by his side it was easier for his brain to prod him with a familiar question: *Why had he brought April here?*

But his answer was simple. Just as April had said on the museum steps: because it was fun. There was no need to overthink it.

He'd wanted to get April out of that dusty, cluttered house and into the London that he loved. He'd been to this museum a hundred times—he loved it here. Even as a teenager he'd come. He'd been attracted to its scope and its space, and to the way people spoke in low voices. Plus, of course, all the exhibitions. It was such a simple pleasure to lose a day discovering relics from a different time and place.

'Can we get a selfie?' April asked, appearing again by his side.

Her bag was slung over her shoulder, and she was digging about within the tan leather for—he assumed—her phone.

She retrieved it with a triumphant grin, and he watched as she opened the camera app.

'No,' he said.

'Pardon me?' she asked, her gaze flying to his.

But before he could respond her phone clattered to the floor, finishing near his left foot.

'Dammit,' she said, and crouched to reach it.

But Hugh had already done the same, and now held the phone in his hand. In its fall, the phone had somehow navigated itself to April's photo gallery, and the screen was full of colourful thumbnails: April's hands, shoes that looked vaguely familiar, even a photo of the dinner she'd had with him last week.

'When did you take that?' he asked, pointing at the picture of her meal.

They were both sitting on their heels. April had her hand outstretched for her phone.

'Can I have my phone back, please?' she asked, and her tone was quite sharp.

Hugh met her gaze as he handed it back. 'Of course,' he said.

'Thank you,' she said, her eyes darting to her phone, her fingers tapping on its screen.

He'd only had her phone a few seconds, and it was hardly as if he'd been scrolling through its contents. He'd simply looked at what it was displaying—nothing more. But April seemed uncomfortable, her shoulders hunched and defensive.

'Are you okay?' he asked.

But she ignored him. 'I took it when you went to the bathroom,' she said, answering his original question.

Now she looked up at him and smiled, and the moment of awkwardness passed.

'I wouldn't have picked you as one of those people who takes photos of their food,' he said.

'One of *those* people?' she teased. 'Who are *those*?'

He shrugged. 'You know—the people who feel compelled to document every tedious moment of their existence.'

'Well,' she said, 'sorry to disappoint you, but sometimes I *do* take photos of my food. Or of my shoes, my outfit, or the view, or whatever I'm doing. Like now.' She grinned, waving her phone. 'So I guess I am one of *those*. *Can* we take that selfie?'

'Hmm…' he said.

She moved closer, bumping his upper arm with her shoulder. 'Come on,' she said. 'They're just photos. They aren't hurting anybody. Why do you care if I or anyone else likes taking photos?'

'I don't,' he said.

'You just disapprove?'

He looked down at her. She was smiling up at him, her face upturned, her hair scraped back neatly from her lovely cheeks.

'No,' he said. 'I just don't get it. Why bother?'

Now it was April's turn to shrug. 'Why not? It's just sharing happy moments with other people, I guess. Or unhappy moments, I suppose.'

A shadow crossed her face—so quickly that he decided he'd imagined it.

'So it's not a narcissistic obsession with self or a compulsive need to elicit praise and garner acceptance from others?' he asked, but he was teasing her now.

'Nope,' April said with a smile. 'It's just sharing a whole heap of photos.'

Sharing.

An echo from their first dinner together seemed to reverberate between them:

I don't feel any urge to share my life with anyone.

'Hugh,' April said, seriously now, 'I want to take a photo of us together. But just for me. I'm not going to post it on social media anywhere. I'm not going to share it with anyone.'

His instinct was still to ask why and to continue to resist. He'd never taken a selfie in his life, and had never intended to.

But he already had his answer. April wanted it for herself. It was a happy moment she wanted to document.

'Okay,' he said.

He'd surprised her, but then she smiled brilliantly and wrapped one arm around him quickly, holding the phone aloft, as if she was concerned he'd change his mind.

'Smile!' she said, and he did as he was told, looking at the image of April and himself reflected back in the phone's screen.

She took a handful of photos, and then held her phone in front of them both as she scrolled through them. One was the clear winner—they both wore broad smiles, their heads were tilted towards each other, *just* touching. The sun that poured through the glass roof lit their skin with a golden glow, and behind them the staircase that wrapped its way around the circular reading room at the centre of the Great Court served as an identifier for where they were.

'Perfect,' April said.

'Can you send me a copy?' Hugh said, although he'd had absolutely no intention of asking.

April blinked and smiled, looking as surprised as he felt. 'Of course,' she said.

Hugh cleared his throat. 'We'd better go,' he said.

April nodded, and together they left the museum.

On Thursday Hugh didn't come up to the main house.

He sent her a text, just before lunch, explaining that he had back-to-back meetings—something about bug fixes and an upcoming software release.

Not that the details mattered. The key point was that she wasn't going to see him that day.

April set her phone back in place, returned it to the radio station she liked to listen to and got back to her boxes. She was in a new room now—Hugh's mother's, she suspected, but she hadn't asked.

Why doesn't he want to see me today?

April shook her head to banish such a pointless question. He needed to work—that was all. There'd been no expectation that they were to meet each day.

Far from it.

Later that night, after she'd got home from the supermarket, April approved Carly's planned schedule of posts for the following week. Carly had also noted how low they were on blonde-haired April Molyneux photos, and had asked, gently, if April had made any plans for once they'd run out.

No.

But she knew she needed to.

She was now more than halfway through cleaning out Hugh's house and her credit card debt was nearly paid off. Decisions definitely loomed: What job next? And where? London? Perth? Somewhere else entirely?

And what would she do? Because, as she'd told Hugh, she now knew her heart wasn't in what she'd thought would be a magnificent environmental consulting career.

And what about Hugh?

Again April shook her head, frustrated with herself.

There was no *What about Hugh?*

Hugh was not part of her decision-making, and he was not part of her future.

On Friday Hugh brought lunch again.

Although it grew cold, forgotten on the kitchen counter, as April and Hugh made up for lost time.

Later, Hugh closed his eyes, breathing heavily, his cheek resting against the top of April's head. April, pressed up against the closed pantry door, was taking in long swallows of air, her breath hot against his neck. His hands lay against the luscious skin beneath her shirt…her hands had shoved his T-shirt upwards to explore his back and chest.

'What, exactly,' he managed, his voice gravelly, 'are we waiting for?'

'Time,' April replied, and he sensed her smile. 'Tomorrow.'

He groaned.

'Tomorrow,' she repeated, pushing gently against his chest. 'I need to get back to—'

'Work,' he finished for her. 'I know.'

* * *

Finally it was Saturday.

A cab was arriving at three p.m. to collect April.

Hugh was once again playing tour guide—but a mysterious one today, having only hinted at their destination with a dress code: a bit fancy…no jeans.

Another package had arrived from Perth from one of her suppliers: stunning hand-painted silk dresses that would have been perfect if it hadn't been December in London.

So April had spent the morning searching for a more season-appropriate dress along the High Street and at the many vintage clothing shops that Shoreditch had to offer. In the end she'd chosen a mix of modern and vintage—a new dress with a retro feel, in a medium-weight navy blue fabric with a full skirt, short sleeves and a pretty peekaboo neckline.

She'd also bought new stockings and heels, and spent more money than she had in weeks. Although she realised, as she walked out of the store, bags swinging from her fingertips, that this was the first outfit she'd ever bought with money she'd earned herself.

The realisation was both a little embarrassing and also incredibly satisfying.

Right on time, Hugh and his cab arrived.

She rushed to the door with her coat slung over her arm and swung it open.

Hugh was wearing a suit of charcoal-grey and a tie—something she'd never imagined him wearing. He looked *amazing*—his jaw freshly shaven, his hair still just too long and swept back from his face. His eyes were dark, and he was silent as his gaze slid over her from her hair—which she'd curled with her roommate's curling wand—to her red-painted lips, and finally down to her dress and the curves it skimmed.

He stepped forward and kissed her—hard. 'You are stunning,' he said against her ear.

April shivered beneath his touch.

Twenty minutes later they arrived at The Ritz Hotel. The

building was beautiful, but imposing, stretching a long way down Piccadilly and up at least five or six storeys.

Inside, Hugh led her into the Palm Court—a room with soaring ceilings decorated in sumptuous shades of cream and gold. Tables dotted the space, each surrounded by gilded Louis XVI oval-backed chairs, and everywhere April looked there were chandeliers, or mirrors, or flowers, or marble. It was opulent and lavish and utterly frivolous.

'What do you think?' Hugh asked.

'I *love* it,' she said.

Hugh smiled.

They were seated at a corner table. Around them other tables' occupants murmured in conversation to the soundtrack of a string quintet.

'I thought you might like to experience a traditional British afternoon tea,' Hugh said.

A waiter poured them champagne.

'You thought correctly,' April said. 'Although I wouldn't have thought this was really your thing.'

'It's not,' Hugh said. 'So this is a first for me, too.'

'Really?' April said, quite liking the idea that this was new to them both.

Hugh nodded. 'Surprisingly, a reclusive computer science nerd doesn't take himself to afternoon tea at The Ritz.'

April took a sip from her champagne. 'I wouldn't say you're a total recluse,' she said. 'You have to interact with people to run your company, even if not face-to-face. You spend time with me. And with the other women you date.'

Her gaze shifted downwards, to study the clotted-cream-coloured fabric of the tablecloth.

'Selectively reclusive, then,' he said. 'Generally I prefer my own company.'

'So I'm an exception?' April said, unable to stop the words tumbling from her mouth. What was she even *asking*?

'Yes,' he said simply.

But before he could elaborate the three tiers of plates housing their afternoon tea arrived, and the moment was lost. Or at least April decided it was best not to pursue her line of questioning as she didn't like what it revealed. Not so much about Hugh, but about her.

She didn't need to be special, she reminded herself. *This isn't about special. It's about fun. Special is irrelevant.*

Afternoon tea was lovely.

They ate delicate sandwiches that didn't have crusts; scones with raisins and scones without—both with jam and cream, of course—and pretty cakes and pastries with chocolate and lemon and flaky pastry.

They talked easily, as they always seemed to now, in a way that made their first kiss seem so much longer than eight days ago.

Today their conversation veered into travel. April had, of course, done a lot—Hugh very little.

April buried uncomfortable feelings as she deftly edited the stories she told him. She didn't lie, but rather didn't mention details—like the fact that she'd often travelled in the Moly-neux private jet, or that her grandfather had once owned his own private island in the Caribbean. Instead she told him only about the experiences: the Staten Island Ferry, the junks in Halong Bay, a cycling tour through the French countryside. Which were the important bits, really, anyway.

She took a long drink of her champagne.

'Why haven't *you* travelled more?' she asked. He'd travelled to the US—Silicon Valley—and that was about it.

'I run my business entirely remotely, so I don't need to interact with people or leave my house,' he said. 'If I did travel the world, wouldn't that seem more surprising?'

April studied Hugh as he drank his champagne. The isolated man he described did not align with the man she'd shared the week with.

'But you love the museum,' she said. 'And that's all about learning and discovering new things. You brought us here today. And you ride your bike. Don't you ever ride somewhere new?'

He nodded. 'Of course I do.'

'So are you *sure* you wouldn't enjoy travelling? You just need to avoid crowds—but that wouldn't be too hard with a bit of planning. There are these amazing villas in Bali…' She paused a split second before she said *where I've stayed*. 'That I've heard of where you have your own private beach. It would be totally private. You'd love it.'

'Would I?' he asked, raising an eyebrow.

'I think so,' April said. 'We could explore the nearby villages and swim in—'

Too late she realised what she'd said, and her cheeks became red-hot. She'd done it again—mistakenly stumbled into a fanciful world where she was special to Hugh—where with her he broke the shackles of the insular world she suspected his mother's hoard had created.

'I mean, *you* could. Of course.'

'Of course,' he said, and when he met her gaze his expression was as frustratingly unreadable as it had been when they'd first met.

The tension between them had shifted from charged to awkward, and April rushed to fix it.

'I can't wait to travel again,' she said, possibly slightly too loudly. 'My credit card is almost paid off, so once I finish working for you I'm going to start saving for my next adventure. I've never been to Cambodia, and I've heard that Angkor Wat is really amazing.' She was talking too quickly. 'Plus, accommodation is really cheap, which is good. And I've heard the food is fantastic. A friend of mine was telling me about Pub Street, which is literally a street full of restaurants and pubs, so you'd probably hate it, but I—'

She talked for a few more minutes, grasping at random remembered anecdotes from her friends and things that she'd read online. She didn't really care what she said—she just wanted to fill the silence.

'So you've got it all sorted?' Hugh asked, and his gaze was piercing now. 'Your plans after you stop working for me?'

'Yes—' she began, and then she took a deep breath. She was sick of all these half-truths. 'No,' she said. 'I have no idea. I have no idea where I'll work or what I'll do. And if I travel—who knows when?—I am as likely to go to Siem Reap as Wollongong or Timbuktu.'

She swallowed, her gaze now as direct as Hugh's. She couldn't tell what he was thinking, but he was studying her with intent.

'In fact,' she continued, 'about all I know right now is that I'm sitting here with you, the hot, charmingly odd British guy I met at work, who is absolutely perfect as my rebound guy. I know that you make me laugh, and I know that you love to show me London as much as I love you showing me.'

She lowered her voice now, leaning closer. Her hand rested on the tablecloth. Hugh's was only inches away.

'And I absolutely know that I *really* like kissing you,' she said. 'I also know exactly where this night is headed. So... um...' Here her bravado faltered, just slightly. 'I'd really like to just focus on the things I know tonight. If that's okay with you?'

Hugh's hand covered hers, his thumb drawing squiggles on her palm.

'Do with this information as you wish,' he said, his voice low, 'but *I* know that I have a key card in my pocket for a suite upstairs.'

His words were so unexpected that April laughed out loud in surprise. But it was perfect. As simple and uncomplicated as their non-relationship was supposed to be. It was what they both wanted—right now and tonight.

Tomorrow, or after she'd finished working with him, or after Hugh had walked out of her life—in fact *anything* in the future—she had absolutely no clue about. But that didn't matter—at least, not right now. As she sat here in this remarkable room, with this remarkable man.

'Let's go,' she said, lacing her fingers with his.

CHAPTER THIRTEEN

IT WAS DARK when Hugh awoke, although a quick check of his phone showed that was due to the heavy brocade curtains rather than the hour. In fact, it was midmorning. Usually by now he'd already be home from his Sunday morning bike ride, showered and about halfway through the newspaper, and probably his second cup of tea.

Right now he had no urge to be doing any of those things.

April lay sleeping beside him, her back to him. His eyes had adjusted to the darkness and now he could see the curve of her shoulder, waist and hip in silhouette beneath the duvet. She was breathing slowly and steadily, fast asleep.

He sat up so he could observe her profile and the way her dark hair cascaded across the pillow. She was beautiful. He'd always thought that, but she seemed particularly so right in this moment.

It was tempting to touch her—to kiss the naked shoulder bared above the sheets and to wake her. But they'd already kept each other awake for most of the night, and she needed her sleep. She was working two jobs, after all.

It had actually been her job stacking supermarket shelves that had inspired him to choose The Ritz. He'd already known he'd need to book a hotel room—April's house was clearly not an option and his definitely was not. A hotel had been the obvious solution for where they'd spend the night together. Clearly he would always have selected somewhere nice. *Very* nice. But The Ritz—The Ritz was a whole other level.

And he'd liked the idea of choosing somewhere so grand and iconic, to give April a London experience she otherwise wouldn't have experienced on a box-emptying, supermarket-shelf-stacking income. Something to remember after all this had ended.

Afternoon tea had been offered by the reservations office

when he'd rung to book, and he'd known instantly that April would love the idea. He'd surprised himself by very much enjoying himself too, getting as caught up in the pomp and ceremony as April had.

Hugh's stomach rumbled—a reminder that they'd skipped dinner. Although he certainly hadn't minded the trade-off. He wouldn't have passed on one touch or one sensation for literally anything last night.

It had been nothing like he'd ever experienced. More than just sex. And, considering sex had always just been sex to him, that was...

Unexpected, Hugh supposed.

Although really had anything that had happened between Hugh and April in the past week or so in any way indicated that when they made love it would be anything but raw and intense and intimate?

No.

He'd told himself as he'd driven in that cab to collect her that tonight would be it: one night with April and then they'd go their separate ways. It would be simpler that way, he'd decided. He'd simply give April his word that he would keep out of her way at work.

But that had been just as big a lie as telling himself that making love to April would just be sex.

April stirred, maybe under the relentless stare of Hugh's attention, and rolled onto her back. But she didn't wake. Now she was just simply closer to him, an outflung hand only centimetres from his hip.

In her sleep, she smiled.

April was always smiling, he'd discovered, and when he was with her he smiled too.

He wanted more than one night.

He needed it.

Hugh had never watched a woman sleep before. His usual protocol was a swift exit the morning after, and he'd always done so with ease. He'd never simply enjoyed lying in bed with a woman, watching her sleep: he'd never felt compelled to.

And *compelled* was the right word when it came to April. In fact since he'd met April so much of what had happened had felt almost inevitable—and certainly impossible to resist.

Not that he was complaining.

But if he wanted another night with April—in fact, many nights—what did that mean?

Did he want a relationship with her?

As he considered that question he waited for the familiar claustrophobic sensation he'd always associated with the concept of relationships: that visceral, suffocating tightening of his throat and the racing of his heart. Similar to the way he felt in pubs, or bustling crowds, or when he was surrounded by his mother's hoard. As if he was trapped.

But it didn't come.

April stirred again, reaching towards him. Her hand hit the bare skin of his belly and then crept upwards, tracing over the muscles of his stomach and chest with deliberate languor.

'Good morning,' she said softly, and he could hear that smile she'd worn in her sleep. 'Please don't tell me we need to check out anytime soon.'

'We have until two p.m.,' he said. 'Hours. But we should probably eat.'

Her hair rustled on her pillow as she shook her head. 'Later,' she said firmly as she sat up, and then she pushed against his shoulders so he was lying beneath her.

As her hair fell forward over her shoulders to tickle his jaw and she slid her naked body over his he said, 'That works for me.'

'I thought it might,' she said, smiling against his lips.

And then she kissed him in a way that sent all thoughts of anything at all far, far from his mind.

He wanted April. Now, and for more than one night.

The details he'd work out later.

April discovered that walking out onto Piccadilly after check-out, wearing the dress she'd worn the day before and with a biting wind whipping down the street, worked as a seriously effective reality check.

She wrapped her arms around herself, rocking back and forth slightly on her heels.

What now?

Hugh stood beside her. He hadn't shaved today, and she'd already decided that the way he looked right now was her favourite: the perfect amount of stubble, dishevelled hair and bedroom eyes.

They'd left their hotel room for the first time that day when they'd walked to the reception desk to pay. In fact it had been Hugh reaching for his wallet that had been the first fissure in their little 'April and Hugh' bubble of lust.

'Oh—' she'd said, with no idea what she'd actually planned to say next.

He'd looked at her reassuringly: *he had this.* Which of course he did—he was wealthy. A billionaire.

But she wasn't used to a man paying for her. Yes, Hugh had bought her dinner and lunch before, but April had bought him breakfast, and had insisted on paying for their lunch at the British Museum. It had felt as if they were equals.

It was just that she knew how much hotels like this cost per night—she'd stayed at many of them. Not The Ritz, for which she was immensely grateful—she couldn't have stomached pretending if she had. And she'd paid for many of those rooms. With Molyneux money, of course, not her own. Evan had never paid—it would have been crazy. His income was a mere drop within the Molyneux Mining money ocean.

For the first time she wondered if that had been problematic for Evan. Maybe it had? She'd refused to let him pay whenever he'd tried...

Well, there was her answer.

Anyway, April thought she understood money now. Or at least appreciated it more. So Hugh paying thousands of pounds for a night with her made her in equal parts thrilled and flattered and terribly uncomfortable.

He didn't even know her real name.

But then he'd leant forward and kissed her cheek before murmuring in her ear, 'I had a wonderful time last night.'

And that had been such an understatement—and his lips against her skin such a distraction—that worries about money or her name had just drifted away.

Until she'd been hit by the bracing cold outside.

She turned to Hugh. He was already looking down at her. Was he about to say something?

She could guess what it would be: something to reiterate the insubstantiality of their non-relationship, to re-establish this supposedly uncomplicated thing or fling they were doing or having.

Then later—maybe in a few days—he'd end it. He'd finally wake up to the fact that he was, in fact, doing what he'd so clearly told her he didn't want: he was sharing his life with April.

She mentally braced herself for it, simultaneously telling herself it would be for the best anyway. No point imagining their incredible evening had been anything but sex. Even though it had felt like so much more.

But what would *she* know, anyway? She hadn't even realised that her husband didn't love her any more. She hadn't even realised that he hadn't loved her enough *ever*.

Hugh didn't say anything. He was just looking at her with a gaze that seemed to search her very soul.

'So what happens now?' she blurted out, unable to stand not knowing for a moment longer.

'Well,' he said, 'I thought we might go past your flat so you can pick up a change of clothes. Then, if it's all right with you, we could go and grab some groceries for dinner. At my place.'

That was about the last thing April had expected Hugh to say, and it took her a minute to comprehend it.

Another gust of wind made her shiver. She saw Hugh reach towards her—as if to somehow protect her from the cold— but then he stopped and his hand fell back against his side.

Her gaze went to his. He was studying her carefully. Waiting.

It hadn't, she realised, been a throwaway casual invitation.

While she might not know, or *want* to know, exactly how his rule-defined dating worked with other women, she knew absolutely that what he was doing now was outside that scope.

How far, she couldn't be sure. But it was far enough that April glimpsed just a hint of vulnerability in his gaze.

He didn't even know her real name.

She needed to tell him.

But as swiftly as she'd considered it Mila's words thrust their way into her brain to override it: *You don't owe him anything.*

'April?' Hugh asked.

She was taking far too long to answer a simple question.

'That sounds great,' she said eventually. She managed a smile. 'So does that mean you're cooking me dinner?'

Hugh's lips quirked as he waved down a cab, but he didn't answer her question. He probably was. Why else would he need groceries for their meal?

You don't owe him anything.

But of course she did.

She owed him her honesty.

But if she told him, this would be over.

They climbed into the back seat of the London cab and immediately Hugh reached for her hand. He drew little circles and shapes on it again, like he had during afternoon tea. And again his touch made her shiver and her blood run hot.

It also made her heart ache.

She needed to tell him.

Just not now.

She wasn't ready to give him up, or to give up how he made her feel.

Not just yet.

He did make her dinner.

It was nothing fancy—just a stir fry with vegetables, cashews and strips of chicken. But April seemed to like it, which was good, given he hadn't cooked for anyone other than himself since he'd moved out of home. He didn't mind cooking, actually—it was a skill he'd learnt by necessity when his mother had been at particularly low points, and had been cultivated when his curiosity for varied cuisine had been hampered by his reluctance to socialise much or to have takeaway delivered to his home.

But, anyway, it hadn't really been about cooking the meal, had it? It had been about inviting April into his home. To sleep over, no less.

Not that April was aware of the significance.

After dinner, she asked for a tour of his flat.

As he opened each bedroom door he felt that familiar tension—as if he was worried that behind the door would be a hoard he'd somehow forgotten about.

Of course each room was spotlessly tidy.

April didn't comment on his severe minimalism: there was nothing on the walls, there were no photo frames or shelves… no trinkets. Had she guessed why?

Probably. It wasn't too difficult to work out why the child of a compulsive hoarder might loathe anything hinting at clutter.

The last room he showed her was his bedroom.

Right at the rear of his flat, it had French doors that led into a small garden courtyard, although currently pale grey curtains covered them. The room wasn't large, but there was ample space around his bed, and a narrow door led to the en-suite bathroom.

It was as unexciting as every other room he'd shown her, with nothing personal or special about it. But still…bringing April into *this* room felt different. More than the anxiety he'd felt at each door. Those moments had passed. *This* sensation persisted.

This room—generic as it might be—was unquestionably his private space. He wanted April here—he knew that. But it was still difficult for him. He'd been so intensely private for so long that to be showing April his house and his room—it was a big deal. He felt exposed. He felt vulnerable.

Again he wondered if April realised how he was feeling. She'd walked a few steps into the room and now turned to face him. She'd changed at her place, and now wore jeans, a T-shirt and an oversized cardigan. Her hair was still loose, though, all tumbling and wild. He could see something like concern in her gaze.

'Hugh—' she began.

But he crossed the space between them, and silenced her with a kiss. He didn't want questions or concern or worry right now: hers *or* his. April was here, in his bedroom. And he was kissing her.

That was all that mattered.

CHAPTER FOURTEEN

APRIL WOKE UP before Hugh on Monday morning.

He lay flat on his back, one arm on his pillow, hooked above his head. The other rested on his chest, occasionally shifting against his lovely pectoral muscles as he slept.

She should have told him.

On Piccadilly…outside The Ritz. Or probably the first time he'd kissed her, actually. Definitely last night, when he'd walked her into this room and she'd suddenly realised what a massive deal it was to Hugh. It had been written all over his face: a mix of determination and alarm and hope that had made it clear that *this* was most definitely not in the scope of his non-relationship rules.

But he'd wanted her enough to break his own rules. He'd *trusted* her enough to allow her into the sanctuary of his home. She'd realised, too late, that the young boy who'd never invited his friends over to play had grown up into a man who never had overnight guests. Who never let people into his house or into his life.

It seemed obvious now—from the eccentricity of the confidentiality agreement she'd signed to the way he'd insisted on only email communication when she'd started work—even though he lived only metres away. And his aggravation when she'd turned up at his doorstep in her aborted attempt to resign.

Somehow he'd let her beyond all his barriers—both tangible and otherwise.

Yet she'd been lying to him the whole time.

Hugh was smiling now. He'd woken, caught her staring at him. He captured her hand to tug her towards him, but she didn't move.

Belatedly he seemed to realise she was dressed. His gaze

scanned her jeans and shirt, her hair tied up in a loose, long ponytail.

He sat up abruptly. 'What's going on, April?' he asked.

'Do you want to get dressed?' she asked.

It felt wrong that she was clothed while he was naked.

His eyes narrowed. 'No,' he said.

Where did she begin?

'Can I ask you a question?' she asked.

'What's going on, April?' he said again, this time with steel in his tone.

'I just need to know something. Just one thing and then I promise I'll tell you.' She didn't wait for any acknowledgment from Hugh, certain she wouldn't receive it anyway. 'I just want to know the last time you had a woman sleep over.'

He blinked, and his expression was momentarily raw: she'd hit a nerve. That, in itself, was all the answer she needed. But she could practically see him thinking, determining how he would answer her or if he would answer her at all.

Then—heartbreakingly—she realised he'd decided to be honest.

'Never,' he said. 'I've never wanted a woman to sleep over before.'

Hugh wasn't trying to be unreadable now. He'd clearly made a decision to cut through the pretence that had overlaid their relationship. And why wouldn't he? For Hugh, inviting her into his home—and therefore into his life—was the point of no return. He probably felt he now no longer had anything to hide.

And yet she'd been hiding all this time.

'Okay,' she said, struggling to force any words out and hating herself more with every passing second.

'Is that what this is about?' he asked. 'About what we're doing?' His mouth curved upwards. 'I know I've talked about rules and no relationships, but you, April…with you, maybe—'

'Stop, Hugh,' she said. She couldn't bear to hear him say anything like that: words that would tell her she was special and words that she wanted so desperately to be true.

She'd been so caught up in her lies that she hadn't allowed herself to think how she'd feel if Hugh actually *wanted* to be with her. If he had feelings for her. Like she had feelings for *him*.

What feelings?

She shook her head—at Hugh and at herself. None of this mattered because none of it would be an option once she'd told him the truth.

April took a deep breath. 'Hugh,' she said finally, 'I need to tell you something. Something I should've told you at the beginning but thought it was okay not to, I thought it was okay to keep it secret because we weren't actually *in* a relationship, you know? It was just kissing, or sex, or just dinner, or the museum, or afternoon tea… Which, I suppose, when you say them all together, sounds pretty much like a relationship, right?'

Her smile was humourless. But she needed to say this now, because she knew instinctively she wouldn't get to explain later.

Hugh just watched her. He sat there motionless, tension in his jaw and shoulders, but otherwise perfect and glorious in his nonchalant nakedness—the sheets puddled around his waist, the light from the bedside lamp making his skin glow golden.

He said nothing. Just waited.

She swallowed. 'The name on my passport is April Spencer, but for as long as I can remember I've gone by April Molyneux. I'm the second eldest daughter of Irene Molyneux, and I'm an heiress to the Molyneux Mining fortune.'

Hugh recognised her mother's name—she could see it on his face. Most people did…she was one of the richest people in the world.

'When Evan left me I realised that I've never been truly independent. That I've never been single, never had a real job and that I've never lived off anything but Molyneux money. So I got on a plane with practically nothing and came to London to—'

'To play a patronising, offensive, poor-little-rich-girl game.' He finished the sentence for her.

'Hugh—'

But he ignored her, ticking his words off on his fingers as he spoke. 'Live in a shared house, work on minimum wage and pretend to live in the real world. I get it. Then, once you're tired of living like an actual real person, walk away. Feel fleetingly sorry for all those genuine poor people who don't get that choice as you fly home in your private jet. I'm sure you have one, right?'

'That's not what I'm going to do at all—' she began.

But he wasn't prepared to listen. 'So I was just part of the fantasy? A story to share with all your friends when you got home, along with humorous anecdotes about life in the real world. That was what that selfie was for, right?'

April shook her head vehemently. 'No. I didn't plan any of this,' she said. 'How could I? I never expected to kiss my boss. I certainly never expected this week…then this weekend. Hugh, these past two nights with you—they are like *nothing* I've ever experienced. Please understand that. There was nothing false about that—'

'Except the person I thought you were doesn't exist,' he said.

'Of *course* she does, Hugh. The woman you've been with is *me*, regardless of my surname or my family's money. These past few months I think I've been more me than I ever have in my life. *Especially* with you.'

Now Hugh shook his head. 'I'm *so* pleased I was such a helpful, if unwitting assistant in your journey of self-discovery, April.' His tone was pancake-flat.

He turned from her as he slid out of bed. She watched as he retrieved his boxer shorts and pulled them on, and then his jeans. She probably shouldn't have been watching him, but she couldn't stop herself.

Maybe she'd been secretly desperately hoping that this would somehow all be okay—that he'd brush off the specifics of her past and accept her for the woman she'd been with him.

Yeah, right.

Now she knew for certain. Knew that this was it—this was her last few minutes with Hugh…at least like this. He wasn't going to invite her into his room, and more importantly into his life, ever again.

So she looked. She admired the breadth of his back, the curve of his backside, the muscular thighs and calves honed from thousands of cycled kilometres. When he pulled his T-shirt over his head she admired the way his muscles flexed beneath his skin. And then she closed her eyes as if to capture the memory of a naked Hugh she would never see again.

'Who *are* you, April? What do you *actually* do if you're not a backpacking traveller?'

Her gaze dropped to her fingers. They were tangled in the hem of her untucked shirt, twisting the fabric between them. She still sat on his bed, reluctant to move and take that first physical step towards walking away.

'I…ah—' she began, then stopped her repentant tone. *No.* She was *not* going to apologise for who she was—or who she had been. She didn't know which just yet. 'I have a heavy social media presence,' she said.

Hugh rolled his eyes, but she ignored him.

'I use my public persona as a wealthy jet-setting socialite to gather followers—currently I have just a little over one point two million, although that has dipped a little since I've been here.'

She met his gaze steadily.

'I use my platform to attract suppliers and companies that I respect and admire to offer product placement opportunities in exchange for donations to the Molyneux Foundation, which is a charitable organisation that I founded. Last year the foundation made significant contributions to domestic violence and mental health organisations, and while since I've left Perth I've realised that there is far more that I could be doing, I'm still incredibly proud of what I've achieved so far.'

If Hugh was in any way moved by what she'd said he didn't reveal it.

'I'm not some vacuous socialite. At one stage I was—and I own that. And until recently I had no comprehension of the value of a dollar, or pound, or whatever. But I've learnt a lot and I've changed. I'm never going to take my good fortune or my privileged existence for granted ever again.'

Hugh's hands were shoved into the front pockets of his jeans. If she didn't know him she'd think his pose casual, or indifferent. But she did know him, and she knew that he was anything but calm.

'I've been poor, April,' Hugh said, his voice low and harsh. 'After my father left we were on benefits, on and off, for most of my childhood. We were okay...we always had heat and food...but it wasn't easy for my mum. She struggled—you've seen her house. *She struggled.* It wasn't a game.'

'It was never my intention to trivialise another's experiences, Hugh.'

'But you *did*, April. Can't you see that?'

April was getting frustrated now. 'What would you have preferred? That I continued to live off my mother's money for the rest of my life?'

'No,' he said, and his tone was different now. Flat and resigned, as if he'd lost all interest in arguing. 'But I also would've preferred you'd told me your name.'

It was a fair comment, but even so April couldn't bite her tongue. 'But why *would* I? You were offering me absolutely nothing, Hugh. A kiss, sex, but absolutely not a relationship. You may scoff at my so-called journey of self-discovery, but I needed it. Desperately. For *me*. Why would I jeopardise that for a man who couldn't even stomach the idea of officially dating me? I'm so sorry I lied, Hugh, but this wasn't just about you.'

'So I'm just collateral damage?'

April slid off the bed, unable to be still any longer. 'No, of course not, Hugh. You are *so* much more.'

'More?' Hugh prompted. 'What does *that* mean?'

April blinked. She hadn't answered her own question what felt like hours earlier: *What feelings?*

'What would I know, Hugh?' she said honestly. 'I've been with one other man before you and I totally got that one wrong. All I know is that for you to invite me into your home, and for me to be telling you my real name, there *must* be more. More than either of us expected.'

She was standing right in front of him now. If they both reached out their hands would touch. But that wouldn't be happening.

'It doesn't matter,' Hugh said. 'Not now.'

'No,' April said. 'I know.'

For a while they both stood together in silence.

Finally April stepped forward. On tiptoes, she pressed a kiss to Hugh's cheek.

'I'm sorry,' she whispered in his ear, just as he'd murmured so intimately to her on so many other occasions. 'But I promise you I meant what I said. I was more *me* with you than I've ever been. In that way I never lied to you.'

Then she collected her packed overnight bag from a side table and headed for the door.

'Just finish up today,' he said, sounding as if it was an afterthought. 'I'll pay you your two weeks' notice. Donate it to the Molyneux Foundation—I don't care. But I don't want to see you again.'

April nodded, but didn't turn around.

Tears stung her eyes. Pain ravaged her heart.

Oh. *Finally* she recognised those feelings.

What they represented. Only they were different this time. Amplified by something she couldn't define, but distinctly new, distinctly *more* than she'd experienced before.

What she was feeling was love.

CHAPTER FIFTEEN

One week later

HUGH SAT DOWN at his desk and set his first tea of the day carefully onto a coaster.

It was raining, and the people walking along the footpath above him were rushing across the wet pavement.

As always, he checked his to-do list, which he'd prepared the night before.

Except—he hadn't.

The notepad instead listed yesterday's tasks. Mostly they were ticked off, but the remainder had definitely not been transcribed into a new list for today. There was a scrawl in the corner which he'd scribbled down during yesterday's late-afternoon conference call…but it was indecipherable now that he'd forgotten its context.

Also, surely he'd received an email about something he needed to action today? He *always* added such tasks to his list. He liked everything to be in one place.

He opened up his email, searching for that half-forgotten message in his inbox. Unusually, the screen was full of emails—many unread. Time had got away from him yesterday, so he spent a few minutes now, filing and then responding to the emails that had been delivered overnight.

Just as he remembered he was supposed to be looking for the email with information about today's action, a little reminder box popped up in the right-hand corner of his screen: he had a conference call in five minutes.

He had a moment of panic as he wondered what was expected of him at this meeting—he was completely unprepared—but then he remembered. It was a pitch for a totally new app concept—something he would need to approve before it could begin formal analysis, research and requirements-gathering.

So he was fine. He hadn't forgotten to prepare because he hadn't needed to.

He took a long, deep breath.

What was wrong with him?

He was all over the place: an impossibility for Hugh Bennell. He was always structured, always organised, always in control.

Except when he wasn't.

Hugh dismissed the errant thought. He *was* in control. He was just…temporarily out of sorts. His mother's house was still half full of her hoard, following the termination of April's employment. The weight that had lifted as he'd watched the hoard being dismantled and exiting the house had returned. Oppressive and persistent.

The termination of April's employment.

As if that was really what had happened.

Again the little reminder box popped up—this one prompting him to enter the meeting. He clicked the 'Join' button and immediately voices filled the air around him as people greeted each other, punctuated by electronic beeps as each attendee entered the virtual meeting room.

As always, everyone in the meeting appeared in a little window to the right of his screen. Some were talking, some had their eyes on their computers, a few were looking at their phones. Of course there was, as usual, a generic grey silhouette labelled 'Hugh Bennell' in place of the live video feed of himself.

He wasn't chairing this meeting, so he sat back as the group was called to order and the agenda introduced. First up was a staff member he didn't recognise: a junior member of the research and development team.

She was young, looked fresh out of uni, with jet-black hair and stylishly thick-rimmed glasses.

She was also nervous.

She was attempting to be confident, but a nervous quiver

underscored her words. She was sharing her screen with the group, showcasing mock-ups and statistics along with competitors' offerings that didn't cover the opportunity she suggested *they* could capture. But she was still visible in a smaller window, deliberately glancing to her camera as she spoke, as if she was attempting to make eye contact with the group.

Or with the *rest* of the group. She couldn't meet Hugh's gaze, because black electrical tape still covered his camera lens. But of course *he* was the one she was presenting to. He was the one who had the power to approve or reject her idea. He'd listen to the other heads of department to gather their thoughts, but ultimately it was up to him.

The woman presenting knew that, too.

And she was presenting to a faceless grey blob.

He reached forward and peeled the tape off the camera. A moment later he clicked the little video camera icon that would connect his camera feed to the rest of the meeting.

A second later, the presenter stopped talking.

She was just looking at him, jaw agape.

The rest of the group seemed equally flummoxed.

Hugh shrugged, then smiled. 'I'm nodding as you speak,' he said, 'because you're doing a good job. I thought it would help if you could see that.'

'Yes,' she said, immediately. 'It definitely does. Thank you.'

Then she started talking again, her voice noticeably stronger and more confident.

Later, once he'd approved the new app concept and wrangled his email inbox and to-do list back into order, he headed into the kitchen for another cup of tea.

Why, after so many years, had he turned on his camera?

Why today? And—more importantly—why was he okay about it? It should have felt significant. Or scary, even. After all, he'd been hiding behind that tape for so very long.

Instead it just felt like exactly the right thing to do.

He had nothing to hide. He wasn't about to invite all his

staff over to his place for Friday night drinks or anything—ever—but still...

Revealing himself to his team, even in this small way, had to be a good thing. Revealing himself *and* his house.

It felt good, actually. Great, really. As if part of that weight on his shoulders had lifted.

Because nothing had happened. Nothing bad, anyway. Something good, definitely. The vibe of the meeting had shifted with his appearance—there'd been more questions and more discussion. It had felt collaborative, not directive as he'd so often felt in his role.

The risk had been worth it.

Unlike other risks he'd taken recently.

The kettle whistled as it boiled and he left his teabag to brew while he headed for the spare room, so he could cross off that forgotten emailed task he'd eventually added to his to-do list. It hadn't even been work-related in the end—it had just been a reminder to check if he still had the original pedals from his mountain bike, as one of the guys from his cycling group needed some.

However, it wasn't the container of bike parts his gaze was drawn to when he opened the cupboard door, but the simple cardboard box that sat, forgotten, on the floor.

The original 'Hugh' box. Complete with two faded photos of him with his mother, a crumpled birthday card, an old film canister and that awful finger-painted bookmark he'd made in nursery.

He picked up the bookmark and turned it over and over aimlessly with his fingers. It was just a bookmark. It wasn't anything special. He didn't remember his mother using it, but she would have—just as she'd used or displayed all of his primitive artwork and sculptures when he was growing up.

The bookmark didn't stand out as special, or different. Or worth keeping, really.

But April had asked the question anyway. Despite his clear directions, despite his prickliness and impatience when it came to the hoard he'd so long refused to deal with. And by asking the question April had confronted him with the hoard. She'd forced him to engage and to make decisions.

She'd sensed that he needed to. That if he sat by passively as the hoard disappeared he would be left with a lifetime of regret.

And she'd been right.

He wouldn't keep everything. He might not even keep the bookmark. But he realised now that he needed to make choices. That he needed to pay attention to his mother's treasures and identify his own.

Because there *were* some there. Reminders and mementos of the mother he'd loved with all his heart. And without April they would have been gone for ever.

He bent down and picked up the box. He carried it back into the kitchen, placing it on the benchtop as he fished the teabag out of his mug. He sat on one of the bar stools, staring at the box, thinking as he drank.

He'd spent the week angry because the one woman he'd ever let into his life didn't actually exist. April Spencer had been a fraud, and no more than a facade for a spoiled, rich, selfish woman who enjoyed playing games with people's lives.

But that wasn't true. That wasn't even close to true.

Yes, she'd lied. And it still hurt that the one woman he'd ever trusted could have treated him that way.

But—as she'd asked him—what other choice had she had?

He'd been up-front with all his rules and regulations, and with his immovable view on relationships. And, given he'd spent so much of his life building up barriers between himself and the world, was it fair to be surprised that April hadn't immediately torn down her own?

He recognised what she was doing with her April Spencer persona now: she was being an authentic, independent version of herself, without the context of her wealth or her family which he realised must colour every interaction in her life.

They weren't so different, really. They were both hiding a version of themselves.

April had been hiding the *old* version of herself—the

moneyed, privileged socialite, out of touch with reality. Yet he'd met the *real* April: the woman who'd challenged him, who'd made him laugh, and who had made him want to get out of his house and into the real world just so he could share it with her.

The woman who'd cared enough about a still grieving, complicated stranger to save a child's bookmark when it would have been so much easier to throw it away.

Yes, she'd hidden her old self—but she couldn't have been more honest when it counted.

He, however, had been hiding for a lot longer than April. Hiding in his house, in seclusion, behind self-imposed rules and regulations and the piece of tape obscuring his camera.

He'd been hiding his true self until April came along.

He realised now—too late—that everything important in their relationship remained unchanged despite April's disclosure. April Molyneux or April Spencer—she was still the same woman.

The woman he loved.

He picked up his phone.

The interview had felt as if it would never end.

April sat at a narrow table that looked out over the Heathrow runway, her boots hooked into the footrest of the tall stool she sat upon.

Her impatience wasn't the interviewer's fault, however.

'Thank you,' April said, briskly. 'I look forward to reading it.'

'It' being the glossy magazine that was included in Perth's Saturday newspaper. This was a great opportunity for the Molyneux Foundation—she needed to remember that.

The interviewer thanked her again, and then finally hung up.

Phone still in hand, April rubbed her temples. She felt about a hundred years old—as if this week, like the interview, would never, ever end.

But of course it would. No matter how hard each day was,

inevitably it eventually faded into night and a new day would begin. She'd learnt that when Evan had left her.

She'd learnt it again now that…

She closed her eyes. God, how could she possibly compare *one week* with Hugh to fifteen years with Evan? It shouldn't be possible.

And yet she hurt. Badly.

On that awful Monday she'd been a zombie as she'd finished up as well as she could upstairs, sorting through half-finished boxes, leaving detailed hand-over notes for whoever Hugh hired next.

She hadn't cried then. She'd thought maybe she shouldn't. After all, it had only been a week. Surely it wasn't appropriate to cry after such a short period of time?

April had no idea if there were rules about such things.

But in the end, she *had* cried. Silently, curled up in her single bed under her cheap doona, horrified at the prospect that her roommate would hear her.

Crying hadn't really helped, but she was still glad she had.

The next day—before she'd told her sisters what had happened—she'd gone for a walk. She'd walked to the supermarket where she'd stacked shelves even that very night before and resigned.

Then, outside the shopfront, with the large red-and-blue supermarket logo in the frame, she'd taken a selfie.

And uploaded it to Instagram.

I have so much to tell you! #london #newjob #newhair #new-beginnings

And so she'd taken control of her account, sharing with her million-odd followers over the next forty-eight hours what she'd *really* been doing these past few months.

She'd caught the Tube to take a photo of the glitzy apartment she'd originally rented, she'd printed out all her polite 'we regret to inform you that you weren't our preferred candidate' emails and asked a random person on the street to take her photo as she waved them in the air. She'd shared the balance of her embarrassing credit card debt, and then she'd taken a photo of her scratchy, terrible bedlinen, and shared a recipe for a tomato soup and pasta 'meal' that had helped her spend as little as possible on food.

She'd shared how it had felt to be rejected for so many jobs—how it had felt not to have the red carpet laid out for her as it had been so often in her life. She'd shared her shame at her lack of understanding in her privileged life, and the satisfaction she had felt from earning her very first pay-cheque.

She'd posted about being lonely—being *alone*—for the first time in her life. About learning how to clean a shower, and discovering muscles she'd thought she never had as she'd stacked supermarket shelves.

And she had apologised for not telling her followers any of this earlier, and written that she hoped they would understand. She had told them that she had needed to do this—had needed to be April without the power of her surname carrying her through her life. That she had needed to do it on her own.

What she hadn't shared was Hugh.

She placed her phone back on the table, belatedly noticing a missed call notification.

Hugh had called her.

The realisation hit her like a lightning bolt.

But why?

He must have called during her hour-long phone interview, but he hadn't left a message.

Should she call him?

She twisted in her seat to check the flight information screen.

There was no time. Her flight was boarding soon—she needed to head for the gate.

As she strode through the terminal she wondered why he would have called. It had been a week since she'd last seen him, and they'd spoken not a word. Why would they? Hugh couldn't have made it any clearer: *I don't want to see you again.*

So why call?

A silly little hopeful part of her imagined he'd changed his mind, but she immediately erased that suggestion.

Hadn't she learnt anything? She'd already worked it out that first night, as she'd wrapped herself in her doona, that it was just like with Evan. Hugh simply hadn't loved or even *wanted* her enough to see beyond her past and her good fortune in being born into one of the wealthiest families in the world. To see who she actually was—the woman she had been with *him*.

She arrived at the gate.

Boarding hadn't yet started, and other passengers filled nearly all the available seats. With surely only a few minutes before boarding, April didn't bother searching for a seat. Instead she opened up Instagram, intending to respond to some of her latest comments. This past week her followers' 'likes' and comments had exploded. It would seem that her riches-to-rags experience had struck a chord. Of course now she needed to harness that engagement and monetise it for the foundation. Hence the interview and—

'April,' said a low, delicious voice behind her.

She spun round, unable to believe her eyes.

'What are you doing here?' April asked Hugh.

He shrugged. 'I needed to talk to you. When you didn't answer your phone I came here. Thanks to that selfie you posted I knew where to find you. Had to buy a ticket I won't use, though, to get to the gate—which was annoying.'

'*You* follow my feed?'

He shook his head. 'No. Not my thing. But it came in useful today.'

April needed a moment to wrap her head around his unexpected appearance. She used that moment simply to look at Hugh. At his still too long dark hair, his at least two-day-old stubble, his hoodie, jeans and sneakers.

He looked as he had nearly every time April had ever seen him.

He also looked utterly gorgeous.

She'd missed him.

'What are you doing here, Hugh?' she asked again, wariness in her tone.

'I'm here,' he said, capturing her gaze, 'to apologise for my behaviour.'

April took a deep breath, attempting to process what he was saying.

Over the PA system, a call was made for all business class passengers to board.

'Is that you?' Hugh asked. 'Because I'll get on that plane if I need to. I can't let you leave like this.'

April shook her head. 'No,' she said. 'I can only afford economy seats on my new income. I've got a few minutes.'

'New income?' he prompted.

'Yes,' she said dismissively. 'I'm Chief Executive Officer of the Molyneux Foundation. It's about time I took it seriously, I figure. Fortunately the board agreed.' She paused. These details didn't matter right now. 'Hugh, what exactly are you apologising for?'

'For overreacting,' he said. 'You may not have told me your name from the start, but now I know you were always the real April with me. I guess—'

His gaze broke away from hers and drifted towards the pale, glossy floor.

'I was upset, of course. I trusted you, and that was a big deal for me. When you told me your real name I felt like that trust was shattered. As if you'd been laughing at me the whole time—as if it had been a game.'

'None of this was ever a game for me,' she said quietly.

Hugh was looking at her again now, searching her face. His lips curved upwards. 'I know,' he said. 'I was the one with the rules—not you.'

He was holding his phone in one hand, and he absently traced its edges with his thumb as he spoke.

'I think maybe,' he said, 'I was looking for a reason to justify my lifelong stance on relationships. I've always hated the idea of being trapped within one, of being controlled by one. My mother's hoarding began after my father left her, and I watched her search for love over and over. But she chose the wrong men and they left. That's when she started keeping everything—surrounding herself with things while she was unable to keep the one thing she desperately wanted. Love.'

He swallowed.

'I didn't want to be like her...to *feel* like her. All that pain... all that disappointment. It was all clutter to me, making life more difficult and more complicated. Without love I was in control of my life. And if I walked away from you then I'd be back in control. I would've been right all along.'

Around them people were beginning to line up for the gate, responding to a call that April hadn't heard, with her focus entirely on the man before her.

'But of course,' Hugh said, 'it turns out I was wrong.'

Finally April smiled. Until now she hadn't dared to believe where this was heading.

'This week I *haven't* been in control. I've been a right mess, actually. Life hasn't gone back to normal—or if it has it isn't a "normal" that's enough for me any more. Not even close. Not without you.'

April closed her eyes.

'April, I want to share my life with you.'

Her eyes popped open and for a minute they stood in silence. Around them the terminal bustled. A small child dragging a bright yellow suitcase bumped into Hugh as he hurried past, sending Hugh a furtive glance in apology.

Very late, April realised they were surrounded by a jostling crowd of people.

'Are you okay Hugh?' she asked, suddenly concerned. 'With all these people?'

'Seriously...?' he said. 'I can deal with any crowd when I'm with you.'

But April saw the way he gritted his teeth as the passengers swarmed around them.

'Nice try, Hugh,' she said, grabbing his hand. 'Very romantic. But we're in the way, anyway.'

She tugged him several metres away, so they stood before the floor-to-ceiling windows that looked out onto the runway. The plane that would take April home to Perth sat waiting patiently.

'April?' he said.

She readjusted her handbag on her shoulder, trying to work out what to say. Joy was bubbling up inside her now, and she was desperate to launch herself into Hugh's arms. But instead she dropped his hand.

'April?' he prompted again, raw emotion in his eyes.

'I want to share my life with you, too, Hugh,' she said. A beat passed. 'I think.'

'You *think*?'

April nodded. 'In fact,' she said, 'I'm pretty sure I'm falling in love with you. But the thing is how can I be sure? We were together little more than a week.'

'*I'm* sure,' he said, with no hesitation.

He loves me, April realised—and that realisation almost derailed her resolve.

He meant it too. It was obvious in the way he was looking at her—as if right now nobody else in the world existed.

It was an intoxicating sensation.

'I'm not,' she said firmly. 'And I want *so* badly to believe that you are, but I won't allow myself to. Not yet.'

She registered, absently, the final call for her flight.

'I was with one man for fifteen years, Hugh. I loved him and I thought he loved me. But I was wrong. Love is... complicated for me right now. I really don't know what I'm doing, and I definitely don't trust my judgement. I think I need time to work that out—to be just April for a while, and make sure that I'm not leaping from one relationship to another simply because being in a relationship is what I'm familiar with.'

To Hugh's credit, he seemed to take no offence at that.

'So you just need time?' he said. His gaze was determined.

Ah, April realised. He was confident—not offended.

She smiled.

'Yes,' she said. She searched her brain for a time frame—for a number that felt right to her. 'Six months.'

He nodded immediately, and April would have loved him a little more just for that—if she'd been allowing love to enter the equation, of course.

'Okay. I can work with that. Gives me enough time to sort out the house and work out any logistical issues.'

April's eyes widened. 'Logistical issues?'

He grinned. 'So I'm ready to move, should you decide you still want me. You know I like to be prepared.'

'You do,' she said, and she was smiling now.

'Are there any rules and regulations?' he asked, teasing her, but he was serious too.

God, there was so much of Hugh in that moment—his rigidity and sense of fun intersecting.

'Of course,' April said. 'Loads. I'll work them out and email them to you.'

She knew he'd like that.

'A question,' he said, as they both heard April's name being called over the PA and both flatly ignored it. 'Are there rules about kissing?'

'Most definitely,' April said, 'but they don't start until I get on that plane.'

And just like that he was kissing her. Her arms were tight behind his neck...his arms were an iron band around her body. It was a kiss that told of their week apart, of mistakes and regrets and hope and...

Hugh broke their mouths apart to trail tiny kisses along her jaw to her ear.

'I *know* I love you, April,' he said, his words hot and husky and heartfelt.

I love you too, April thought. But she wasn't even close to ready to say the words.

Instead she kissed him again.

Then, when she heard her name being called one last time, she said goodbye.

EPILOGUE

One year later

APRIL'S BARE TOES mingled with the coarse beach sand, and she felt the January sun hot against her skin.

Before her stood her sister Mila and her partner, Seb. Mila's *husband*, Seb, actually—as of about thirty seconds ago. Her sister wore a bright red dress and the most beautiful smile as she stared up at the man April knew Mila had loved for most of her life.

The sun just touched the edge of the blue horizon as the small group watched the celebrant say a final few words. The beach was otherwise deserted—the small, isolated cove surrounded by towering limestone cliffs, and with oversized granite rocks interrupting the white-tipped waves.

It was a tiny wedding: just Mila and Seb; Seb's parents; Irene Molyneux; Ivy and her husband, Angus; and their son, Nate.

And April and Hugh.

Hugh wrapped his arm around April and kissed her temple. She could feel his lips curve into a smile against her skin.

The ceremony over, the group headed for picnic blankets laden with hors d'oeuvres and bottles of champagne. Candlelit lanterns dotted the space, waiting for dusk and the opportunity to flicker in the dark.

April hung back and looked up at Hugh as the sun continued to descend beyond them.

The last beach wedding she'd attended had been her own—to Evan. It had been in Bali, with hundreds of guests—so very different from the wedding they were attending today.

But still today had triggered memories.

Not of Evan, but of how she'd felt that day. Her joy and anticipation at marrying Evan. And her love for him.

She *had* loved her ex-husband. On that day on that beach in Nusa Dua she had thought it impossible to love anybody more.

But she'd been wrong.

And on that night in London a year ago, at Heathrow Airport, she'd found it impossible to trust her judgement when it came to love. After months of berating herself for not realising that her husband hadn't loved her, love had seemed to her like a complex, complicated and impossible concept. A concept she hadn't yet been equipped to handle.

And she'd been right. She had needed those six months. To heal after the end of her marriage. To establish herself in her new role at the Molyneux Foundation. And to live independently of both any man and of her fortune.

She'd also needed the time to work through what she'd learnt while she'd lived in London about her life of excessive privilege and her ignorance of the reality of the world—despite all the charity events her socialite self had attended.

Really, it had taken those six months to love *herself* again. To be proud of what she'd achieved and continued to achieve at the Molyneux Foundation. To let go of the shame of her years of excess.

And to forgive herself for loving a man for fifteen years when he hadn't loved her the same way.

Because she'd realised that love existed even if it wasn't returned. Her love for Evan had been valid, regardless of his feelings. And that love would remain important and special— a love she couldn't regret.

She'd also realised that love grown over a week could be even more powerful than love cultivated over half a lifetime. And that she *could* trust in that love. That she could believe in it and that it could be real and true.

Her rules and regulations for Hugh regarding those six months had been simple: there was to be no contact.

None at all.

It had been hard, and it had felt impossible, but it had been necessary.

Her week-old love for Hugh had been just as strong—

stronger, actually—after all that time, when she'd woken on the morning of her six-month deadline to an email from Hugh.

He was in Perth, and he would be having all-day breakfast at a café on Cottesloe Beach at lunchtime that day. He would love her to join him. If not he would continue his Australian holiday alone, and wish her well.

And so she'd taken herself and her love for Hugh to breakfast.

And his love had been waiting for her. No pressure, no expectations.

'I love you,' April said now, on this beach, as the setting sun painted the sky in reds and purples.

'I love you too,' Hugh said, and kissed her again.

When they broke apart his gaze darted to the rapidly setting sun.

'You'd better hurry with that photo,' he pointed out. 'The light is about to go.'

April grinned. Hugh might not participate in any of her photos, but she now had his full support and understanding of the business of social media.

Today she wore black South Sea pearl drop earrings, and a generous donation from the company that made them was awaiting after a suitably glamorous photo.

She fished her phone out of her clutch and handed it to Hugh. A sea-breeze made the silk of her dress cling to her belly and her legs, and she fiddled with the fabric as she planned her pose. She needed to be careful—

But then Hugh was standing beside her again, holding the phone aloft to take a selfie of them both.

'Hugh…?' she asked, confused.

He grinned. 'I figure a close-up might be easier. That wind doesn't seem to realise you've got a bump to hide.'

Only for a few more weeks. And at the moment her followers were more likely to think her a bit plumper than usual, not pregnant, but even so…

'But with you?'

Another smile. 'It's about time I become more than the

"mysterious new boyfriend" people are talking about, don't you think?'

'Are you sure?'

He nodded. 'I've got nothing to hide, April. Not since I've met you.'

And so, as the sun made the ocean glitter and the breeze cooled their summer-warm skin, Hugh took the photo. A photo of the two of them on a beach—and of the earrings, of course—but mostly of their love. For each other and for the baby they'd created together.

It was a love that April knew was more real than any love she'd ever experienced. A love for the man she loved more than she'd thought possible, and a love for her that had taught her she would always be enough—and more—for the man she loved.

Later, after the sun had set and they were sitting together on the beach in the candlelight, April posted the photo to her followers.

There's someone I'd like you to meet... #love #romance #happilyeverafter

* * * * *

BEHIND
BOARDROOM
DOORS

JENNIFER LEWIS

For Pippa, international pony of mystery and
cherished member of our family

One

"There is one good thing about this situation." RJ Kincaid slammed his phone down on the conference table, his voice cracking with fury.

"What's that?" Brooke Nichols stared at her boss. She failed to see a bright side.

"Now we know things cannot possibly get any worse." His eyes flashed and he leaned forward in his chair. The other staff in the meeting sat like statues. "My calls to the prosecutor's office, the police, the courts, the state senator—have all been ignored."

He stood and marched around the table. "The Kincaid family is under siege and they're firing on us from all angles." Tall and imposing at the best of times, with bold features, dark hair and smoky slate-blue eyes, RJ now looked like a general striding into battle. "And my mother, Elizabeth Winthrop Kincaid, the finest woman in Charleston, will be spending tonight behind bars like a common criminal."

He let out a string of curses that made Brooke shrink into her chair. She'd worked for RJ for five years and she'd never seen him like this. Normally he was the most easygoing man you could meet, never rattled by even the most intense negotiations, with time for everyone and a nonchalant approach to life.

Of course that was before his father's murder and the revelation that his privileged and entitled existence was founded on lies.

RJ walked over to his brother Matthew. "You're the director of new business—is there any new business?"

Matthew inhaled. They both knew the answer. Even some of their most stalwart clients had fled the company in the aftermath of the scandal. "There is the Larrimore account."

"Yes, I suppose we do have one new account to hang our hopes on. Greg, how are the books looking?" RJ strode around to the CFO and for a moment she thought he was going to collar him.

Mild-mannered Greg shrank into his chair. "As you know, we're experiencing challenges—"

"Challenges!" RJ cut him off, raising his hands in the air in a dramatic gesture. "That's one way of looking at it. A challenge is an opportunity for growth, a time to rise up and seize opportunity, to embrace change."

He turned and walked back across the room. Everyone sat rigid in their chairs, probably praying he wouldn't accost them.

"But what I see here is a company on the brink of going under." RJ shoved a hand through his thick, dark hair. His handsome features were hard with anger. "And all of you are just sitting in your chairs taking notes as if we're at some garden party. Get up and get out there and do something, for Chrissakes!"

No one moved an inch. Brooke rose from her chair, unable to stop herself. "Um…" She had to get him out of here. He was acting like a jerk and if he continued like this he'd do himself permanent harm in the company.

"Yes, Brooke?" He turned to face her, and lifted an eyebrow. His eyes met hers and a jolt of energy surged in her blood.

"I need to speak to you outside." She picked up her laptop and headed for the door, heart pounding. He could probably fire her on the spot in his current mood, but she wasn't doing her job if she let him insult and harangue employees who were already under a lot of pressure and stress through no fault of their own.

"I'm sure it can wait." He frowned and gestured to the gathered meeting.

"Just for a moment. Please." She continued toward the door, hoping he'd follow.

"Apparently my assistant's need to consult with me in private is more urgent than the imminent collapse of The Kincaid Group, and the imprisonment of my mother. Since it's the end of the day I'm sure you also have better places to be. Meeting dismissed."

RJ moved to the door in time to hold it open for her. A wave of heat and adrenaline rose inside her as she passed him, her arm almost brushing against his. He closed the door and followed her out. In the hush of the carpeted hallway Brooke almost lost her nerve. "In your office, please."

"I don't have time to loll about in my office. My mother's in the county jail in case you hadn't noticed."

Brooke reminded herself his rudeness was the result of extreme stress. "Trust me. It's important." Her own firm tone surprised her. She walked ahead into the spacious corner office with views of the Charleston waterfront. The sunset cast a warm amber glow over the water reflected on the walls in moving patterns. "Come on in."

RJ sauntered into the room, then crossed his arms. "Happy now?"

"Sit down." She closed the door and locked it.

"What?"

Her resolve faltered as her boss glared at her.

"On the couch." She pointed to it, in case he'd forgotten where it was. She almost blushed at the way it sounded as she said it. What a lovelorn secretary's fantasy! But this situation was serious. "I'm going to pour you a whiskey and you're going to drink it."

He didn't move. "Have you lost your mind?"

"No, but you're beginning to lose yours and you need to step back and take a deep breath before you damage your reputation. You can't talk to employees like that, no matter what the circumstances. Now sit." She pointed at the sofa again.

A stunned RJ lowered himself onto it.

Brooke poured three fingers of whisky into a crystal tumbler with shaking hands. Everything really did seem to be going to hell in a handbasket for RJ. Until now he'd faced each disaster with composure, but apparently he'd reached his breaking point.

Their fingers touched as she handed him the glass, and she cursed the subtle buzz of awareness that always haunted her around RJ. "Here, this will settle your nerves."

"My nerves are just fine." He took a sip. "It's everything else that's screwed up. The police can't really believe my mother killed my father!"

He took a long swig, which made Brooke wince. She bit her lip. The pained expression on his handsome face tugged at her heart. "We both know it's impossible, and they'll figure that out."

"Will they?" RJ raised a dark brow and peered up at her. "What if they don't? What if this is the first of many long nights in jail for her?" He shuddered visibly and took another swig. "It kills me that I can't protect her from this."

"I know. And you're still grieving the death of your father."

"Not just his literal death." RJ stared at the floor. "The death of everything I thought I knew about him."

She and RJ had never discussed the scandalous revelations about the Kincaid family, but they were both aware she knew all the details—along with everyone else in Charleston. They'd been splashed all over the local media every day since his father's murder on December 30th. It was now March.

"Another family." He growled the words like a curse. "Another son, born before me." He shook his head. "All my life I was Reginald Kincaid, Jr. Proud son and heir and all I wanted to do was follow in my father's footsteps. Little did I know they'd been wandering off into some other woman's house, to sleep with her and raise her children, too."

He glanced up, and his pain-filled gaze stole her

breath. It killed her to see him suffering like this. If only she could soothe his hurt and anger.

"I'm so sorry." It was all she could manage. What could she say? "I'm sure he loved you. You could see it in his face when he looked at you." She swallowed. "I bet he wished things were different, and that he could have at least told you before he died."

"He had plenty of time to tell me. I'm thirty-six years old, for Chrissakes. Was he waiting until I hit fifty?" RJ rose to his feet and crossed the room, whiskey splashing in the glass. "That's what hurts the most. That he didn't confide in me. All the time we spent together, all those long hours fishing or hunting, walking through the woods with guns. We talked about everything under the sun—except that he was living a lie."

RJ tugged at his tie with a finger and loosened his collar. Recent events had given him an air of gravitas that he'd never had before. The strain hardened his noble features and gave his broad shoulders the appearance of carrying the weight of the world.

Brooke longed to take him in her arms and give him a reassuring hug. But that would *not* be a good idea. "You're doing a great job of keeping the family together and the company afloat."

"Afloat!" RJ let out a harsh laugh. "It would be a real problem for a shipping company if it couldn't stay afloat." His eyes twinkled with humor for a split second. "But at the rate we're losing clients we'll be belly up in the bay before the year is out if I don't turn things around. For every new client Matthew brings in, we're losing two old ones. And I don't even have a free hand to guide the company. My father—in his infinite wisdom—saw fit to give his illegitimate son forty-five percent of the company and only leave me a measly nine percent."

Brooke grimaced. That did seem the cruelest act of all. RJ had devoted his entire working life to The Kincaid Group. He'd been executive vice president almost since he left college, and everyone—including him—assumed he'd one day be president and CEO. Until his father had all but left the company to a son no one knew about. "I suppose he did that because he felt guilty about keeping Jack secret all these years."

"As well he might." RJ marched back across the room and took another swig of whiskey. "Except he didn't seem to think about how much it would hurt the rest of us. Even all five of us Kincaids together don't have a majority vote. Ten percent of the stock is owned by some mystery person we can't seem to find. If Jack Sinclair gains control over the missing ten percent he'll get to decide how to run The Kincaid Group and the rest of us have to go along with it or ship out. I'm seriously considering doing the latter."

"Leaving the company?" She couldn't believe it. Selfish thoughts about her own job disappearing almost toppled her concern for RJ.

"Why not? It's not mine to run. I'm just another cog in the machine. That's not what my dad groomed me for or what I want for myself." He slammed the empty glass down on a table. "Maybe I'll leave Charleston for good."

"Calm down, RJ." Brooke poured another three fingers of pungent whiskey into the glass. Right now it seemed a good idea to get him too drunk to go anywhere at all. "It's early days yet. Nothing will be decided about the company until the shareholders' meeting and, until then, everyone's counting on you to steer the ship through these rough waters."

"I love all your nautical lingo." He flashed a wry grin as he took the glass. "I knew there was a good reason I hired you."

"That and my excellent typing skills."

"Typing—pah. You could run this company if you put your mind to it. You're not just organized and efficient, you're good with people. You've managed to talk me back off the ledge today, and I thank you for it." He took another sip. The whiskey was certainly doing its job. Already the hard edge of despair and anger had softened.

Now was not the time to mention that she had applied for a management job, and been turned down. She didn't know if RJ was behind that, or if he even knew.

"I didn't want you to upset people any more than they already are." She pushed a hand through her hair. "Everyone's temper is running high and we need to work together. The last thing you want is for key employees to quit and make things worse in the run-up to the shareholders' meeting."

"You're right, as usual, my lovely Brooke."

Her eyes widened. Obviously the whiskey was going straight to his head. Still, she couldn't help the funny warm feeling his words generated inside her, almost like a shot of whiskey to her core.

"The most important thing right now is to find your dad's murderer." She tried to distract herself from RJ's melting gaze. "Then your mom won't be under suspicion."

"I've hired a private investigator." RJ peered into

his glass. "I told him I'll pay for twenty-four hours in the day and he shouldn't stop until he finds the truth." He looked up at her. "Of course I told him to start with the Sinclair brothers."

Brooke nodded. Jack Sinclair sounded like a man with an ax to grind, though her vision could be skewed by the fact that he'd inherited her boss's birthright. She hadn't met Jack or his half brother Alan. "They must be angry your dad kept them secret all these years."

"Yup. Resentment." RJ sat down on the sofa again. "I'm beginning to know what that feels like."

"Very understandable." Her chest ached with emotion. She wished she could bear some of the burden for him. "This whole situation came out of nowhere for you."

"Not to mention my mom." He shook his head. "Though sometimes I wonder if she knew. She didn't seem as surprised as the rest of us."

Brooke swallowed. Elizabeth Kincaid would have had at least some motivation for the murder if she'd known about her husband's adultery. And she had seen her in the office on the night of the murder. She shook the thought from her brain. There was no way such a quiet and gentle person could fire a bullet at another human, even her cheating husband. "Let me pour you some more."

She brought the bottle over to the sofa and leaned down to fill RJ's glass. The whiskey sloshed in the bottle as he stuck out a strong arm and pulled her roughly onto the sofa with him. She let out a tiny shriek as her hips settled into the soft leather next to his.

"I appreciate the company, Brooke. I guess I needed someone to talk to." His arm had now settled across her shoulders, his big hand wrapped around her upper arm. She could hardly breathe. And when she did his warm, masculine scent assaulted her senses and raised her blood pressure.

RJ settled into the sofa a little, caressing her shoulder with his hand. Heat bloomed under his fingers, through her thin blouse. She still held the whiskey bottle and wondered if she should pour from it, or if he'd had enough. He answered the question by taking it from her with his free hand, and putting it on the floor along with his glass. His hand then settled on her thigh, where she could feel the warmth of his palm through her smart gray skirt. Her heart quickened when he turned to look at her.

RJ's expression was one of intense concentration. He seemed to be examining her face like she was a table of container ship sailings. "I never noticed how green your eyes are."

Brooke had a sudden urge to roll those eyes. How many women had he used that line on? RJ was famous throughout the Southeast as a Most Eligible Bachelor and had enjoyed his single status as long as she'd known him. "Some people would call them gray." Was she really sitting almost in RJ's lap talking about her eyes, or was this some kind of manic dream?

"They'd be wrong." Again his expression was deadly serious. "But lately I'm learning that people are wrong a lot of the time." His gaze fell to her mouth. Her lips parted slightly and she pressed them back together. "I'm having to question a lot of my assumptions about the world."

"Sometimes that's good." She spoke softly, wondering if she'd said the wrong thing. Sitting this close to

RJ was dangerous. Arousal already crept through her limbs and strange parts of her were starting to tingle.

"I suppose so." RJ frowned. "Though it doesn't make life any easier."

Poor RJ. He was used to being the golden child, his entire life mapped out at birth and his every need taken care of before he could even voice it.

"Sometimes challenges can make us stronger." It was hard to form sensible thoughts with his arm around her shoulder and his other hand on her knee. She could feel the power of his sturdy body right through her clothes. Part of her wanted to stand up and go organize the papers on his desk. The other part wanted to wrap her arms around his neck and...

RJ's lips crushed over hers in a hot, whiskey-scented kiss that banished all thought. Her body melted against his and she felt her fingers do what they'd wanted all along—roam into his stiff white shirt and the hard, hot muscle beneath.

His hands caressed her, making her skin hum with arousal. Her nipples thickened and a powerful wave of heat rose in her belly. RJ's raw hunger for affection— for help—gave urgency to his touch. She could feel how badly he needed her, right now, here in his arms.

She kissed him back with equal force, affection for him overpowering any more sensible urges. She wanted to heal his hurt, to make him feel better, and right now she almost felt that was within her power. Emotions surged within her. She'd adored RJ almost since the day she met him and his strength under adversity only made her admire him more. She'd never dared imagine for a single second that he'd return her feelings.

Their kiss deepened and heated and for a moment she thought they'd fuse and become one, then RJ pulled back gently. "Brooke, you're an amazing woman."

His soft sigh contained a thick aroma of all those fingers of whiskey she'd poured him. Would he regret this in the morning? Still, hearing him call her an amazing woman stirred something powerful inside her. Was this the beginning of a totally new phase in their relationship? Maybe they'd start dating and she'd be able to help him negotiate the minefield of his life and come happily out the other side with him—arm in arm. His arms felt fabulous around her right now.

Or would she remember this as the moment she destroyed her hard-earned career at The Kincaid Group and permanently alienated her boss by getting him drunk and compromising their professional relationship? A ball of fear burst open like a mold spore inside her.

What was she doing? She'd gotten him drunk, then let him kiss her. It was all her fault, even she could see that.

RJ stroked her cheek and she fought a sudden urge to nuzzle against him like a cat. Was it so wrong to give him the affection and comfort he craved? Again, violins and visions of a rose-scented courtship hummed in her mind. She was strong enough to help him through this. Her own background had made her a resilient person.

RJ caressed her, taking in the curve of her breast with his fingers then trailing over her thigh. The musky scent of him filled her senses for a second as his lips met hers again and kissed her softly.

Cigar smoke clung to his suit from the long business lunch he'd hosted at a local restaurant, and mingled rather intoxicatingly with the whiskey. Everything about RJ seemed delicious to her right now. She wanted to wrap herself up in him and stay there forever.

But he withdrew again, leaving her lips stinging. Then he frowned and pushed a hand through his hair as if wondering what he was doing.

An icy finger of doubt slid down Brooke's back. Perhaps that smoky smell came from the smoldering ruin of her career and reputation. Instinct pushed her to her feet, which wasn't easy with her knees reduced to wobbly jelly. "Maybe it's time to get out of here. It's after seven."

RJ leaned his head back against the sofa, eyes closed. "I'm beat. I don't think I can take another step today."

"I'll call you a cab." She certainly didn't want him driving with all that whiskey in him. He didn't live far away, but driving or walking him home didn't seem like such a great idea, either. If he invited her in, she wasn't sure she could say no, and she knew she'd regret being that easy.

"Don't worry about me, Brooke. I'll sleep here on the sofa. I've done it many times before. If I wake up in the middle of the night I'll go through some of the paperwork I need to read."

"You'll wake up sore."

"I'll be fine." Already he was sinking into the sofa, eyes sleepy. "Go home and rest and I'll see you in the morning."

Brooke bit her lip. Somehow it hurt to be dismissed like this after their steamy kisses. What did she expect? That he'd want her by his side every moment from now on? Maybe after so much whiskey he'd already forgotten he even kissed her.

"What about dinner?"

"Not hungry," he murmured.

"There's half a plate of sandwiches in the fridge left over from a luncheon meeting today. I could get them for you."

"Stop trying to mother me, and go home." His tone was almost curt. Brooke swallowed and turned for the door. Then she noticed RJ had sat up again, head in his hands. "I can't believe my mom is in jail. It's just so wrong. I've never felt so powerless in my life."

Brooke walked back toward him. "She's a strong woman and she'll survive. You've done all you can for now and it won't help her if you worry yourself sick over it. Get some sleep so you'll be ready to make the most of tomorrow. You've got a company to save."

He blew out a hard breath. "You're right, Brooke, as usual. Thanks for everything."

Already he'd lain down, eyes closed. A fierce pang of tenderness for him ached in her chest. So tall and strong and proud and so anxious to go immediately into battle to save his mom. RJ was the kind of man any woman would adore. And she was only one among the many who did.

She slipped out of his office and closed the door, then picked up her jacket and bag from her own desk outside it. *Thanks for everything.* Was that his way of wrapping up the evening's events—memos typed, letters filed, kisses received. All in a day's work.

"Bye, Brooke."

She startled at the sound of her name. She'd totally forgotten there might still be other employees on the floor. Usually everyone was long gone by now, but PR assistant Lucinda was donning her jacket two cubicles away. Brooke wondered if her cheeks were flushed or her lips red. Surely there must be some telltale signs that she'd locked lips with her boss.

"Bye, Luce." She hurried for the elevator, hoping no one else would see her.

When the doors opened Joe from Marketing was inside. "What a day," he exhaled, as she stepped in. "This place is coming apart at the seams."

"No, it isn't." She bristled with indignation. "We're going through tough times but a year from now this will all be forgotten and the company will be back on top again."

Joe raised a sandy brow. "Really? If old Mrs. Kincaid did it I don't think the family reputation will recover. And it's sure looking like she did. I bet she's enjoying life as the merry widow now."

"She didn't do it." Still, a sliver of doubt wedged itself into her mind. Anyone could be pushed past their breaking point, and Elizabeth Kincaid had been pushed pretty far from the sound of it. "And don't go spreading rumors that she did. You'll make things worse."

"Are you going to report me to your boss?" He shifted his bag higher on his shoulder.

"No. He's got enough problems right now. He needs all of our support."

"You're like a wife to him, so supportive and attentive to his needs." His grin was less than reassuring. "If only we could all be as lucky as RJ."

She froze. Could he know something had happened between her and RJ? The doors opened and she stepped out with relief. "I'm not his wife."

Though maybe one day I could be. Fantasies already played at the edge of her mind. Dangerous fantasies. Dreams that could explode in her face and destroy her career and reputation.

Still it was hard not to let her imagination wander just a little....

TWO

Brooke had a sleepless night. In the morning her hair was a mess and she had to whip out the curling iron to bring some life back to the limp brown locks brushing her shoulders. She applied her makeup carefully, wanting to look as beautiful as RJ had made her feel last night. Did she look different now that she'd kissed him?

Not really. At least her eyes weren't red from crying—yet. RJ would be able to blame his sudden enchantment with her on the whiskey she gave him. She, on the other hand, could blame only her years-long fascination with him. She'd fallen into his arms without a protest, and kissed him with passion that came from the heart.

She wore her smartest black suit. She'd bought it on sale at a fancy boutique, and with its well-cut designer lines it was something a rich girl would wear. She stood back and surveyed herself in the full-length mirror. Did she look like a potential girlfriend of RJ Kincaid?

She knew what her mom would say. *You have a nice figure, you should show it off more.* But that wasn't her style. Besides, the last thing she wanted was a man who only cared about her breasts and not her brain.

She donned her Burberry raincoat, a cherished consignment store find. She preferred a demure, somewhat conservative style that said, *I mean business.* She wanted people to take her seriously. She'd never flirted with RJ for a single instant, as her job meant far more to her than the prospect of a quick kiss and cuddle.

Fear licked around the edges of her brain. Would RJ be embarrassed by last night's indiscretions and find a way to shunt her aside? Her heart pounded as she walked into the Kincaid building.

Her throat dried as she stepped out of the elevator on their floor. How would she greet him? Would he be furious she'd made him drunk and landed them in a compromising position?

Maybe he wouldn't remember that he'd kissed her at all.

His office door was closed. Was RJ still in there sleeping on the sofa? She hung her coat with shaking hands and wiped sweaty palms on her skirt before approaching. She lifted her hand to knock, then hesitated.

Maybe she should wait for him to come out. He might have a major hangover he needed to sleep off. She turned and went to sit at her desk. She was always the first person in each morning. She liked to get her in-box dealt with before the phones started ringing.

Brooke checked her email, then pulled the mail from her tray and started to sort through it. But her eyes kept straying to the closed door. Was he still upset about his mom being jailed? Who wouldn't be? He could probably use a coffee and some breakfast.

She rose from her chair and approached the door again. She inhaled deeply and raised her hand—and the door opened.

The polite greeting she'd rehearsed fled her lips at the sight of RJ. She'd expected him to look rumpled and tired, but he didn't. Well groomed and wearing a perfectly pressed suit, he looked every inch the business titan his rivals feared.

"Morning, Brooke." His eyes twinkled with amusement.

"Morning." The word burst out fast and loud. Somehow he seemed even more gorgeous than usual. Maybe because she knew just how his mouth tasted in a kiss. She struggled to drag her mind back to practical matters. "Did you sleep okay?"

"I slept very well under the circumstances." He leaned against the door frame, eyes resting on her face. "It wasn't easy sleeping alone after that kiss." His deep blue eyes smoldered and his hushed tones carried more than a hint of suggestion.

Brooke bit her lip to stop a huge smile creeping across it. "For me either." Her admission was a relief. He wasn't trying to forget the kiss ever happened. "I'm glad you're feeling better this morning."

"I took your advice to heart. No sense weakening under pressure when I need all my energy to fight. Onwards and upwards, Brooke."

"That's the spirit." She let the big goofy smile widen her mouth. This was the RJ she'd grown to know and love. "What's first on the agenda this morning?"

He tilted his head slightly and lowered his voice. "The first thing on my agenda is to secure a date for tonight."

Brooke's heart almost stopped. Did he mean with her, or did he intend for her to call some strange woman and...

"Are you free after work this evening?"

"Yes," she stammered. "Yes, I am." How cool. Oh well, not like she had an image as a seductress to uphold.

"I'll make reservations and will pick you up at your place at seven-thirty."

"Great." Already her mind spun with worries about what to wear. Her cherished collection of business suits would be too stuffy for dinner and she didn't have that many—

"I'm off to a meeting and I've left a pile of items in your inbox."

"Great." Apparently that was the only word left in her vocabulary. "See you later," she called, as he swept into the elevator.

A date with RJ. Tonight. And she didn't even have to make the reservation! But she did still have to go through his correspondence and coordinate his schedule, just like any other day.

She felt as if she was stepping onto a board of chutes and ladders. Three steps forward and dinner with RJ leads up the tall ladder! What next? Would she roll a five and plunge to estrangement and unemployment at the bottom of a chute?

With no idea what kind of restaurant RJ would choose, Brooke decided to go smart-casual. She donned a floral patterned dress she'd never worn to work and a cute cashmere shrug she'd found in a boutique walking home from work one day. Her hair was shiny, her complexion clear for once and except for the heightened redness in her cheeks she looked pretty darn good!

Still, she jumped when the doorbell rang. She'd never given RJ her address, but no doubt he could just look in her personnel file. She drew in a breath as she walked across the living room to open the door.

"Hi." She felt yet another huge goofy grin spread across her face at the sight of RJ, several inches larger than life, as always, standing right there on her doorstep. "Won't you come in?" She'd spent at least an hour cleaning the place to within an inch of its life.

"Sure." He smiled, and stepped inside.

"Would you like a martini?" She knew he loved them.

"Why not?" RJ managed to look both classic and hip in a jacket that hung elegantly from his broad shoulders, and loose khakis. He often had the air of an old-time matinee idol, which perfectly matched his bold, aristocratic features and easy confidence. Right now she felt like his leading lady, since her dress had a vintage flair to it.

She mixed the martinis and poured them into long-stemmed glasses while RJ complimented her place.

"Thanks, I like it here." She'd lived in the two-bedroom condo near Colonial Lake for five years now and was proud of how she'd decorated it. A mix of timeless pieces and funky touches that reflected her personality. "I'm renting right now but I hope the owner will sell to me when the lease is up." *As long as I still have a job by then.* She smiled and handed him the drink. "Bottoms up."

RJ raised his glass. "I never know which end will be up lately." He took a sip, and nodded his head in approval. "You look gorgeous." His gaze lingered on her face, then drifted to her neck, and she became agonizingly conscious of the hint of cleavage her dress revealed.

"Thanks." She tried not to blush. "You don't look too bad, either." He'd obviously taken the time to go home and change after work, which touched her. She knew how often he headed out to dinner straight from the office.

"I clean up okay." He shot her a sultry look. "I'm glad to do something fun for a change. Lately I feel like I'm running from crisis to crisis, either in the company or in the family."

"Crisis-free here." She offered him a plate of tiny puff pastries she'd picked up on her way home. "Want something to nibble?"

"Why, sure." His eyes rested on her face for a second longer than was entirely polite. All the parts of her body that never knew how much they wanted to be nibbled by RJ started to hum and tingle. Then he took a pastry, put it in his mouth and chewed.

Brooke quickly swallowed one herself. She could see his gleaming black Porsche parked outside. She'd never ridden in it before as he used a more practical Audi sedan for work. She could imagine the neighbors whispering and peering through their miniblinds. "Where are we going for dinner?"

"A new place just off King Street. It's a grill, of

sorts, with a Low Country twist to it. A friend told me it's the best food he's eaten in ages."

"Sounds great, but isn't that kind of central? What if people see us together?" It probably wasn't the best idea for them to hang out right in the historic district. She'd assumed he'd pick somewhere discreet and out of the way.

"People see us together every day. Let them assume what they like."

Was he implying that this evening meant nothing so there was no need to worry if anyone saw?

The steady heat in his gaze suggested otherwise. If she didn't know better she'd suspect he could see right through her dress.

"I'd prefer to go somewhere more private." Her nerves jangled as she said it. He was her boss, after all, and not used to hearing her opinion on such things. "I'd hate for people to start talking."

"Let them talk. Everyone in Charleston is talking about the Kincaids right now and it hasn't killed us yet." His face darkened.

He must be thinking about his father's murder. Why was she bickering over restaurants when RJ was under so much pressure already? "All right, I'll stop worrying. We can always tell them we were testing it out as a place to hold a client party."

"Always thinking." He smiled and took another sip of his martini. "That's a damn good martini but I think we should get going. I made a reservation for eight and it's the hottest table in town right now."

Uh-oh. That meant there might be people he knew there. What if people started to gossip about them and things didn't work out? Her hands shook slightly as she put on her shrug and grabbed her purse. She was hoping for a promotion. What if people thought she was trying to sleep her way to the top? She was hardly from RJ's usual social circles. She swallowed hard. Still, it was too late to back out now. "I'm ready." She was heading out to dinner with her boss, for better or worse.

The reclined seats in his black Porsche felt every bit as decadent and inviting as she'd imagined. Excitement raced through her as RJ started the engine. She wouldn't be able to resist telling her mom about this. She'd be impressed for sure. Then again, maybe she was starting to think too much like her mom. She did not like RJ because he had a Porsche, or a large bank account—she liked him because of his intelligence and kindness.

And his washboard abs and fine backside.

"Why are you smiling?" His eyes twinkled when he glanced at her.

"I think the martini made me giddy."

"Excellent. I like you giddy."

He pulled into a parking space in the historic district, then opened her car door before she even had time to unbuckle her seat belt. He took her hand and helped her out, and she felt like royalty stepping onto King Street with RJ Kincaid. Which was funny because she'd been to restaurants here with him before— as part of a business party, of course. Now everything was different.

Her hand stayed inside RJ's, hot and aware, as they walked down a picturesque side street to a restaurant with a crisp green awning. The maître d' took them to their table on a veranda overlooking a tiny but perfect garden behind the building, where flowers climbed an old brick wall and water trickled in a lion's-head fountain. The table was set with a thick, starched tablecloth and heavy silverware, and a bright bouquet of daisies in a cut glass vase.

RJ pulled back her chair, again making her feel like a princess.

"A bottle of Moët, please," he said to the waiter.

Brooke's eyes widened. "What are we celebrating?"

"That life goes on." RJ leaned back in his chair. "And dammit, we're going to enjoy it no matter what happens."

"That's an admirable philosophy." Along with everyone else in Charleston, he must be wondering what could possibly happen next. His dad was dead and his mom was being held at the county jail under suspicion of murder. Bail had been denied as, with money and connections, she was considered a flight risk.

And there was something he didn't know.

Brooke had told the police she'd seen Mrs. Kincaid at the office that night. She hadn't mentioned this fact to RJ. In light of the arrest she wasn't sure he'd be happy she told the truth. Of course she knew Elizabeth Kincaid was innocent, but still… Guilt trickled uneasily up her spine. She really should tell him she'd seen his mom there. Just to clear the air.

"My dad would have wanted me to hold my head up and keep fighting." He watched as the waiter poured two tall glasses of sparkling champagne. "And that's what I intend to do. I spent all afternoon trying to get the D.A.'s office to agree to set bail for Mom, but they've refused. And I talked Apex International down from the ledge in between phone calls to the D.A."

"The toy importer?"

"Yup. Getting ready to jump ship to one of our competitors. I convinced them to stick with us. Told them the Kincaid Group is the most efficient, well-run, cost-effective shipper on the east coast and we intend to stay that way." He raised his glass and clinked it gently against hers. "Thanks for brightening a dark day."

His honest expression, weary but still brave and strong, touched something deep inside her. "I'm happy to help in any way I can." That sounded odd. A bit too businesslike, maybe. But it was hard to step out of her familiar role and embrace this new one, especially when she had no idea what role she'd be in tomorrow. *You know I'd do anything for you.* She managed not to say it, though she suspected he knew.

"You're helping already." That little flame of desire hovered in his pupils and sent a shiver through her. "Your loyalty means a lot to me. You've proved I can count on you in a crisis. I don't know what I would have done without you in the last few weeks."

His deep voice echoed inside her. Did she really mean that much to him? Her heart fluttered alarmingly. "I'm glad."

Further words failed her and she distracted herself by looking down at the menu, which had an array of elegant yet folksy-sounding local dishes. After some hemming and hawing, RJ chose roast pork shoulder with mustard barbeque sauce and sautéed greens. She chose a shrimp dish with a side of grits and an arugula salad.

"It occurs to me that I don't know too much about you, Brooke Nichols." RJ raised a brow. "I know you live in Charleston, but other than that you're a bit of an enigma. You don't talk about yourself much."

She inhaled slightly. "There isn't much to know." Did he really want to learn that her college quarterback father had resisted all her teenage mother's attempts to trap him into marriage, and how she'd grown up with a succession of stepfathers? "I was born in Greenville, and I went to high school in Columbia. Mom and I moved here after I graduated and we both adore it."

"Does your mom live with you?"

"No, she lives in the 'burbs." With her latest boy-friend. "I enjoy having my own place."

"Do you? I find I'm getting tired of living alone. I miss Mom's cooking." He smiled, then a shadow of pain passed over his features.

A jolt of guilt tightened her stomach. Was her police interview the reason Elizabeth Kincaid had been arrested? She really should tell RJ about that right now. *Did you know I told the police I saw your mom at the scene of the crime?* How did you say something like that without sounding accusatory? "I'm sure they'll let her out soon. They have to know she's innocent. She's the sweetest lady I've ever met." She wasn't exaggerating. And now she knew what Elizabeth Kincaid had put up with over the years. She must have suspected her husband was cheating, at least, even if she hadn't known about his second family. "I wish we could help them find the real killer."

"Me, too. Mom's always been the linchpin of the family. I'm trying to hold it together for everyone but we're all tense and anxious."

Her heart swelled. "I envy your large family. It must

be reassuring to have siblings you can turn to as well as your parents."

"Or fight with." He grinned. "I think we probably argue as much as we get along. Maybe not so much these days, but when we were kids…" He shook his head.

"I never had anybody to fight with, and I'm not sure that's a good thing. Sibling spats must teach you how to negotiate with people."

He laughed. "Are you saying I honed my business bargaining skills over the Hot Wheels set I shared with Matt?"

"Quite possibly." She sipped her champagne, a smile spreading across her lips. RJ was visibly relaxing, his features softening and the lines of worry leaving his face. "Whatever you did as children has made you close as adults. I don't think I've ever seen a family spend so much time together."

RJ sighed. "I really thought we were the perfect family, but now the entire world knows that was just an illusion."

"No family is perfect. Yours is still close-knit and loving, even after everything that's happened."

The waiter brought their appetizers, fried calamari with a green tomato salsa.

"We'll get through this. I need to focus on what makes us stronger, not what's threatening to tear us apart. And somehow you've managed to deflect the conversation off yourself again." He raised a brow. "You're a mysterious character, Brooke. What do you do when you're peacefully alone in your private palace?"

She shrugged. It would have been nice to be able

to chatter gaily about flamenco dancing sessions and cocktail parties, but she wasn't one to embroider the truth. She had friends over once or twice a month, but mostly she valued the peace and quiet of her sanctuary after a long day at work. "I read a lot." She paused to nibble a crispy piece of calamari. "Not very exciting, is it?"

"I guess that depends on how good a book you're reading." His blue gaze rested on her face, and she warmed under it. "Sometimes I think I should make more time for quiet pastimes like reading. Might improve my mind."

She laughed. "I can't see you sitting still long enough to read a book."

"Maybe that's something I need to work on." He hadn't touched his food. If anything he seemed transfixed by her, unable to take his eyes off her face. Brooke felt her breathing grow shallow under his intense stare. "I used to go out to our hunting cabin at least once a month with my dad. We'd mellow out and recharge our batteries together. I haven't been there since he died."

"Can you still go visit it?"

"It's mine now. He left it to me in his will." A shadow passed over his face. The same will that left almost half the company to Jack Sinclair. "It's been sitting empty since he died."

"Why don't you go there?"

He shrugged. "I never went there without Dad. I can't imagine going alone and I can't think of anyone I'd want to with." His expression changed and his eyes widened slightly. "You. You could come with me."

"Oh, I don't think so." She shifted in her chair. Their

first date wasn't even over yet and he was inviting her on an overnight trip? She knew his family never went there just for the day. It was probably a long drive. She'd likely be expected to share a bed with him and so far they'd only kissed once. Already her heart pounded with a mix of excitement and sheer terror.

RJ's face brightened. "We'll go this weekend. Just you and me. We'll get Frankie Deleon's to pack us some gourmet meals and we'll spend a weekend in peace."

"I don't know anything about hunting." The idea of killing things made her cringe.

"Don't worry, we don't have to really hunt. Dad and I mostly just walked around in the mountains carrying the guns as an excuse. It's so peaceful up there it seems a crime to pierce the air with a shot."

She smiled. "That's a funny image. So there aren't racks of antlers on the living room wall?"

"There's one set but we bought it at an antiques auction." His eyes twinkled. "We call him Uncle Dave. We did sometimes go fishing and eat the fish, though. Fishing was the only time I ever saw Dad sit still for more than a few minutes."

"I used to fish with my friend June's family years ago. They'd take a camper to a lake and stay there for a week every summer. I caught a huge rainbow trout once."

"Excellent. Now we know what we're doing this weekend." He rubbed his hands together with enthusiasm. "Nice to have something to look forward to as this promises to be a long week."

Brooke didn't know what to say. He'd already planned her weekend without even waiting for a response. Yes, he was her boss, but going fishing on the weekends was not part of her job description. She should be mad at his arrogance.

On the other hand, a weekend in the mountains with RJ... What girl would say no to that?

Her. "I don't think I should come. I'm sure you have other friends you could invite." Her gut was telling her to slow this whole train ride before it went off the tracks. "I have...things to do here at home."

"Are you afraid I'll take advantage of you, out there in the lonesome woods?" He tilted his head and lifted a brow.

"Yes." Her blood sizzled at the prospect.

"You're absolutely right, of course."

"I think it's a bit premature."

"Of course, we've only known each other five years." A dimple appeared in his left cheek, emphasizing his high cheekbones.

"You know what I mean."

"Sure. One amazing kiss is not enough to plan an entire weekend around."

She shrugged. "Something like that."

"How many kisses? Two, three?" He looked impatiently at the expanse of tablecloth between them. Humor twinkled in his eyes.

"Probably somewhere around five." She fought to keep a smile from her mouth.

"Five years and five kisses." He looked thoughtful. "Let's see what we can do before the night is out."

The handsome waiter whisked their appetizer plates away and settled their mains in front of them while the sommelier poured two glasses of white wine. She'd barely made a dent in her champagne. Maybe that was her problem. She needed to drink a bit more to take the edge off her inhibitions. The whiskey had certainly done wonders for RJ yesterday. On the other hand, the prospect of four more kisses before the evening ended made her light-headed.

She could see the glow of impending victory in RJ's eyes. She'd become familiar with that look in meetings right when he knew he'd clinched a big deal. RJ hated to lose, and sometimes went after quite small clients just for the satisfaction of beating the competition.

Apparently she was to be his next conquest. Her blood pressure ratcheted up a notch. RJ in motion was hard to stop. "Can you really get away for the weekend with everything that's going on right now?"

RJ raised a dark brow. "That's exactly why I need to get away." He reached out and touched her fingers gently where they sat at the base of her glass. A tiny shiver of arousal ran through her. "And you're just the distraction I need."

His voice was husky, thick with the arousal that weighted the air between them. Did he expect her to go home with him tonight? Just what had she gotten herself into here? Him calling her a "distraction" did not entirely bode well for a lifelong commitment.

Then again, she was getting way ahead of herself. And already her lips tingled in anticipation of the second kiss he'd promised. She tried to distract them with a piece of shrimp, but the sauce proved surprisingly spicy and only made things worse. "I suppose some fresh air won't do either of us any harm." That sounded lame. She should probably be making suggestive and witty comments. Soon enough RJ would realize he'd made a terrible mistake thinking she was an attractive and desirable woman.

If he even did think that. Maybe it was more of an "any port in the storm" thing. Even your assistant started to look good when your entire world was falling apart.

"What *are* you thinking about?" RJ peered into her eyes, mischief sparkling in his own blue depths.

"Just wondering where this evening is heading." The truth seemed as good a response as any other.

RJ's mouth broadened into a sensual smile. "Somewhere beautiful."

It was dark when they parked near Waterfront Park and strolled along the promenade looking out at the lights reflected on the dark water. They were dangerously close to RJ's apartment, or at least she suspected so, but he'd shown no signs of trying to take her home. He hadn't even tried to kiss her.

Her skin craved his touch and each time she hoped for it and didn't get it, the longing only grew more bone-deep. Five years of suppressed yearning were unleashed by one kiss, and if she didn't get another kiss soon she might just burst into flame.

Moonlight mingled with the streetlights to illuminate RJ's dramatic features. "So your mom is your only real family?"

"Since my Gran died five years ago, yes." RJ had been plumbing her for information all evening. Not in an unkind way. He seemed genuinely curious.

"Did you ever want siblings?"

"All the time," she admitted. "When I was little I wished for a sister to share my dolls with. Then when I was a teenager I wished I had a brother to bring home handsome friends."

He chuckled. "My sisters weren't shy about asking me to do just that. But I bet you managed fine, anyway."

He caressed her with another one of those lingering glances that made her feel like a supermodel. No need for him to know her last date had been nearly a year ago. Since her best friend got married she hadn't been out much at night and she knew better than to have an affair with someone at the office.

Until now...

He stepped toward her and slid his arms around her hips. Her breasts stirred inside her dress as he pulled her close. Her lips parted and her hands rose to the soft wool of his jacket. She ached for his kiss, a long, deep ache that rose inside her and pulled her closer into his embrace. When his lips finally met hers sensation sparkled through her. All day she'd dreamed of this moment, craved and hoped for it, despite all her misgivings. RJ's arms around her made her feel safe, protected and adored. He kissed with exquisite gentleness, touching her lips gently then pulling back, letting the very tip of his tongue touch hers, teasing and tasting her until she was in a frenzy of arousal. It took all her strength not to writhe against him in full view of the other people enjoying the breezy moonlit night.

"Yes, it's a good idea." RJ's words surprised her. "Us kissing." They'd barely pulled apart and she hadn't even had time for doubts to creep back into her consciousness. No doubt he was trying to preempt them.

"Certainly feels like one." A silly smile plastered itself across her face. A sense of euphoria suffused her entire body, and she'd only had two glasses of wine so she couldn't even blame the alcohol.

She was high on RJ.

His lips touched hers again, and again her synapses lit up like a Christmas tree. She'd never experienced such a sharp physical reaction to a simple kiss. It was a full-body experience. By the time he pulled gently back she was sure she'd broken out in a sweat.

Already her lips itched to meet his again. But if she gave him all five kisses, was she agreeing to the weekend away? "I really should get home now."

"No way." His hands held her steady. "Five years, five kisses."

"There's nothing about kisses in my employment contract." She attempted to look fierce.

"There wouldn't be, since we don't use an employment contract." That naughty dimple appeared again as he lowered his lips to hers. Brooke's lips parted instinctively, and a tantalizing tip of his tongue probed her mouth, sending a shiver of suggestion down her spine. Her knees wobbled and she was forced to hold him tighter. With her pressed against his hard chest, kiss number three was broken only by a quiet whisper. "Brooke, why did we wait so long?"

She didn't answer. Boring explanations about her long-term career prospects had no place in this electric moment. Kiss number four crept up on them and her eyes shut tight as sensation swept through her. RJ's hard chest felt like a safe foundation to lean on, so she let the world drift away and lost herself in his kiss. An hour could have passed before their lips finally pulled apart, she had no idea.

The streetlights, even the reflected glow from the

water, seemed painfully bright when she opened her eyes.

"I expect you're wondering if I'm going to ask you back to my apartment." RJ looked down at her, arms still wrapped around her, holding her close.

The thought did cross my mind. She kept her mouth closed, though. She still had no idea what she'd reply if he did ask.

"I'm not."

A tiny frisson of disappointment cascaded through her. Had this evening led him to decide he was no longer interested in her? Maybe he just liked talking to her and didn't want to take it further. Perhaps those kisses that lit her whole body on fire had simply been a series of tests that she'd failed.

"I have the utmost respect for you, Brooke." His expression was serious.

Her heart sank further. Was this the "you're too valuable an employee for me to fool around with" speech?

"I know you're a lady and would be offended if I asked you in on our first date." He moved his hands until they were over hers. "And I'm still enough of a gentleman to resist the temptation."

His fingers wove into hers and the full force of that temptation rushed through her. He was taking it slow because he respected her. Somehow that truly touched her.

He leaned in until she could inhale his enticing male scent. "But I'm not letting you go without one last kiss."

Relief swept through her as their lips pressed together. He wasn't rejecting her. She held him tight and kissed him back with passion.

"And I'm already anticipating the pleasure of an entire weekend with you, so asking for tonight as well would be greedy."

Misgivings still crept in her veins. An entire weekend was a long time. If things got out of hand there would be no turning back. Though likely it was already too late to return to their normal workaday existence. "What should I bring?" Would she need waders, or an evening gown? Or both?

"Just yourself. The house is fully stocked for entertaining guests so there's loads of extra gear there."

"Will anyone else be there?" What if other Kincaid siblings were around to witness her liaison with RJ? She cringed at the thought of them laughing behind her back, or exchanging shocked whispers.

"I certainly hope not." RJ pressed a quick kiss to her lips. "Since the house is mine now and I haven't invited anyone but you we should have the whole two hundred acres to ourselves."

Two hundred acres. It must be in the middle of nowhere. Of course that was probably the point with hunting cabins. Less chance of shooting one of the neighbors. She and RJ would have more than enough privacy to do anything they liked.

Which reminded her she was arm in arm with him in a popular spot in downtown Charleston. Did she really want coworkers or his family to see them kissing? They might think she was trying to sleep her way to a promotion. Or even take advantage of him when he was under stress. "I think it's time for me to go home. I have to work tomorrow—and so do you in case you've forgotten." It was nearly eleven last time she'd checked.

"I don't have to worry. My capable assistant handles everything for me while I take long lunches."

Brooke made a mock gasp. "I'll have to schedule some of those investor conferences you so look forward to. Perhaps some early breakfast meetings."

"Now you're scaring me. I'll do my best to roll in after a late breakfast."

His cocky attitude didn't annoy her. In fact she was proud he could count on her to keep his work life on track. He looked so relaxed and happy right now you'd never guess his family was in turmoil. Maybe she could take some credit for that, as well.

A warm sense of satisfaction bloomed inside her, along with the delicious arousal RJ had stirred. If things went well this weekend, who knew what the future might hold?

Three

"**Y**ou're going to spend the weekend in the woods with *your boss?*" Her friend Evie had been speechless for a few seconds. Now apparently she'd recovered.

Brooke moved the phone back closer to her ear again. "He's quite different than I thought. Much more sensitive."

"I don't care how sensitive he is. What will happen when he gets bored with you?"

"Ouch." Brooke walked across her apartment. "Am I that dull? You've been friends with me for nearly eight years."

"You know what I mean. Most men, especially in his position, just want to fool around and have fun, and after a few dates they're ready for someone new. Didn't you tell me yourself that he's a bit of a Casanova?"

"Sure, he used to date a lot, but this big family scandal has made him more serious." He hadn't been going out much lately. At least not that she knew of.

"So he's turned into the white picket fence type and is looking for a nice, quiet girl to settle down with."

"Maybe he is."

"You could be right, but what if he isn't? You've put five years into the company. Didn't you say something about a management position?"

"I applied to be the events coordinator but I didn't get it." Yes, it smarted a little, especially since the woman they'd hired from outside was more than a bit flaky. "I just have to keep trying."

"And you think an affair with your boss will help?"

"It's not an affair yet. All we've done is kiss."

"After a weekend in the woods it will be an affair. Do you genuinely believe he'll decide you're the girl of his dreams and ask you to marry him?"

Brooke took in a breath. "Is it a crime to dream? You're married."

"To the guy in the next cubicle, not the one at the head of the boardroom table. I care about you, Brooke, and I know how much your job at Kincaid means to you. It really is a place where you could take your career to the next level and I don't want to see you throw that away for a quick sympathy fling."

"I can always find a job somewhere else."

"In this economy? I'm being very careful with the job I have as there's not a lot out there."

"You're so supportive." Her joy had deflated. One minute she'd been swanning around the air castles of her mind as Mrs. RJ Kincaid. Then the castle went poof and she was now single again and jobless, too. "Maybe I want to have some fun."

Evie sighed. "I miss our nights out together. I know being married is no reason to stay in every night, but we have our hands full with this renovation project right now and—"

Brooke laughed. "I wasn't trying to guilt trip you into a night on the town with me. I know it sounds crazy but the roller coaster has already left the station. I can't go back to before the kiss, so I might as well enjoy the ride and hope for the best."

"My knuckles are turning white just thinking about it. And I want to hear *all* the details on Monday."

RJ left his keys and wallet on the tray and walked through the security machines at the detention center. His entire body reacted to the oppressive atmosphere of the building. A place where hardened criminals were locked up awaiting trial, and where his kind and gentle mother was forced to suffer their company.

A silent guard led him to a private interview room. His lawyer had apparently gone to great trouble to arrange a face-to-face meeting with his mom, otherwise he could only speak to her from the lobby over a video link. The guard opened the door to a small room with a metal desk and two chairs.

She looked tiny, sitting alone at the desk, dressed in the regulation jumpsuit. He walked toward her, unable to govern his features into any kind of polite greeting. "Mom." He took her in his arms and held her tight. She seemed so frail and helpless, not at all the steel magnolia he'd always proudly bragged about.

"No contact." He'd forgotten the no touching rule, and the gruff voice behind him reminded him. With great reluctance he pulled back his arms.

"I won't do it again." He turned to the guard. "Can we be alone for a few minutes?"

"I'll be standing right here, watching." The tall, older man gestured to a square of window in the door, then slipped outside.

His mom's face was pale and drawn, with tiny blue shadows under her expressive eyes. Her trademark auburn hair was slicked back in a way that only made her look more gaunt and slender.

"I'm trying everything to get you out of here."

"I know." The barest hint of a smile lit her eyes. "My lawyer says you won't even let him sleep."

"He can sleep later, once you're free. I'm going to see the D.A. again this afternoon, before I go away for the weekend."

"Are you going to the lodge?" Her eyes brightened. He nodded. "I wondered how long it would take before you went there again. I know how much you love it up in the mountains. Who's going with you?"

"Brooke." Why not tell the truth? Anticipation rose in his veins like sap in the spring. He couldn't wait to be alone with Brooke on that peaceful mountainside. He could already picture sunbeams picking out gold in her hair, and those soft green eyes gazing at the majestic views. She'd love it there. He knew she would.

"Your assistant?" His mom's shocked response drew him from his reverie. Her pale eyebrows lacked their usual flourish of pencil, but he still saw them rise.

"Yes. She and I... She's been a great help to me lately." His brain filled almost to bursting with a desire to tell his mom all about his newfound relationship with Brooke. Brooke was sweet and kind as well as beautiful and he was sure his mom would love her.

Still, he could tell his mom was shocked by the idea of him dating his own assistant and somehow it seemed premature, so he held his tongue.

She nodded. "She seems a bright girl, and very pretty. I hope you have a lovely time. You certainly deserve a break and some fresh air. I know how hard you've been working."

"Thanks, Mom." His chest tightened. How sweet she was to wish him a good weekend when she'd be stuck in here. Anger and frustration raged inside him again. "Why are they holding you? No one will explain. I can't understand why they won't let you out on bail. I had a hell of a time even coming to see you in person."

His mom glanced around the room. "Sit down, will you." She gestured politely as if inviting him to take up residence in one of her beautifully upholstered Liberty print chairs at home, not a scarred metal folding chair.

RJ sat.

She leaned toward him. "They know I was in the office on the night...the night your dad was shot." Her voice faded on the last word and he saw pain flash in her eyes.

"You were there?" He kept his voice as hushed as possible.

"I was." Her lips closed tightly for a second, draining of blood. "I brought him a plate of food as he'd said he'd be home late."

RJ frowned. "They didn't say any food had been found."

She shook her head. "He didn't want it so I took it home with me." She let out a sigh, which rippled through her body as a visible shiver. "I know it seems odd, me bringing him dinner. I only did it that night as I was worried your dad had been so distant, like he was troubled by something. I'd been short with him the night before and I wanted to show him I cared."

"Dad knew you cared about him." RJ's heart filled with red-hot rage that his dad had caused her so much pain by carrying on with another woman. "If anything, he didn't deserve you."

Her eyes filled with tears, but she managed to blink them back. "I do miss your father, even after all that's happened."

"Of course you do." He took her hands in his. They were cold and bony, and he chafed them lightly, trying to warm them. "But you bringing dinner doesn't make you a murderer."

"It makes me a murder suspect."

RJ frowned. Something was seriously off here. "But how did the police know you were there?" The front desk didn't bother logging family members or employees, who were allowed to come and go as they pleased.

"Someone saw me."

"Who?" What kind of person would finger his mom at the crime scene?

She hesitated. Looked away. "Does it really matter? I don't even remember if anyone saw me. As I said, I was there."

"The accusations still don't make sense. You have no motivation to kill Dad. For one thing, you were as much in the dark as the rest of us about Angela and her sons." The words soured in his mouth. "I wish to God none of us had ever found out."

She pulled her hands back and placed them in her lap. "I have a confession to make, RJ."

RJ's eyes widened. "What?" Was she going to admit to killing his dad? His stomach roiled.

"I did know about Angela." Her eyes were dry, her expression composed. "I'd known for some years. Ever since I found an earlier version of Reginald's will in his desk while looking for a calculator."

RJ swallowed. So his suspicion was correct. "Why didn't you say anything?"

"Your father and I had words, but he convinced me to stay with him for the sake of the family. The reputation, the company, you know how important all that was to him." She smoothed back her hair. "And to me."

He blinked, unable to process this. "So you were sitting there with us at family dinners, week after week, and you never breathed a word to anyone?"

Her head hung slightly, and lines of pain formed around her eyes. "Your father and I were married for a very long time. There was a lot of history there. Maybe too much to throw away for an affair that began so long ago."

"But that was still continuing, unless I understand wrong."

He watched his mom's throat move as she swallowed. "You're not wrong. Reginald loved Angela." It took visible effort for her gaze to meet his, and he fought the urge to take her in his arms again. Her rigid posture told him to keep his distance. "He loved me, too." A wry smile tugged at her lips. "He was a man with a lot of love to give."

"That's one way of looking at it, though I'd like the opportunity to give him a piece of my mind." He realized his hands were clenched into fists, and he released them. "I know you didn't kill him." He had to say it, because he had thought it for that split second after she announced a confession, and he needed to clear the air.

"Of course I didn't, but the police and the courts don't know that, and I don't have an alibi for the time of the murder."

"We need to find out who really did it. Do you have any suspicions?"

She shook her head. "Trust me, if I had even the slightest inkling, I'd tell everyone I know."

RJ glanced around the grim room. "This place is a nightmare." He remembered the bag he'd brought with him. "I brought you some books. Flannery O'Connor, William Faulkner. Lily said you'd want something more cheery, but I wasn't so sure. They put them through the metal detector downstairs. Apparently razor-sharp wit doesn't show up on the screen."

She smiled, and peered into the offered paper bag. "RJ, you're so thoughtful. And you're right, I feel like reading about experiences darker than my own." She sighed. "Hopefully I won't have time to read them all."

"Not if I can help it."

"I've never flown in a small plane." Brooke's hands trembled as she buckled the seat belt in the Kincaid jet. "Couldn't we drive there?" Her wide green eyes implored him.

A protective instinct surged inside RJ and he took hold of her hand. "It's almost 150 miles away, near Gatlinburg, Tennessee. We'll be fine." Strange to see ever-capable Brooke looking worried. He squeezed her trembling fingers gently to reassure her. "At least we have a professional pilot today. My dad used to fly it himself sometimes and while he claimed military flying experience, I never saw any kind of license."

"Scary!"

"Tell me about it. I even toyed with getting a license myself so I'd be able to take over in an emergency. One time we got caught in a wind shear coming out of the mountains, but Dad handled it like a pro." His chest tightened as a wave of sadness swept through him. He still couldn't believe that he'd never see his dad again. Never hear his chesty laugh or another tall tale about his days in Special Ops.

"You're not making me feel better."

"We'll be fine." He lifted his arm and placed it around her shoulder. Her soft floral scent filled his nostrils. Soon they'd be alone together in the mountains. The fresh air would lift the cares off both of their shoulders. He couldn't wait to hear her infectious laugh echo off the wooded hillsides, or see the morning sun sparkle in her lovely eyes. And then there would be the nights... He'd instructed the caretaker to put the best fresh linen on the beds—he planned to offer her one for herself, then tempt her out of it. The prospect of Brooke's lush body writhing under those sheets made his pulse quicken.

Yes, she was his assistant. Doubts did force their way to the forefront of his consciousness from time to time. Mixing business and pleasure was always risky, and in a family business it could be downright explosive. His father had warned all of them to keep their personal affairs out of the office and RJ had never had an affair with an employee before, despite considerable temptation over the years. Funnily enough he'd never seen Brooke in that way until their whiskey-flavored kiss in his office. She'd been his right-hand woman, his trusted friend, his rock—but their kiss had opened up a new world of possibilities.

Now he knew his assistant was a sensual woman, with passion flickering behind the jade of her eyes and excited breaths quickening in her lovely chest when he looked at her, the temptation was irresistible. He'd never have dreamed anything could take his mind off the hailstorm of disaster raining down on the Kincaid family over the last few months, but when he was with Brooke, all his burdens seemed lighter. It was such a relief to be with someone whom he could totally trust.

He heard Brooke's breath catch as the plane lifted off the runway, but she soon relaxed as they rose high over the Charleston suburbs, heading toward the sunset and the distant shadow of the mountains. If only they could fly away from all his troubles and worries. Those were hitchhiking along, but with Brooke by his side they'd stay in check.

"How's your mom doing?" Brooke's soft question revealed her natural empathy.

"She's hanging in there. She's a brave woman and she doesn't want us to worry. I visited her this afternoon and took her some books she wanted. I told her we're doing everything we can to get her out. The police have been pretty closemouthed so I hired a private investigator to work full-time on the case, and he's going to work with Nikki Thomas, our own corporate investigator. The lawyers are still trying to negotiate bail. They keep promising she'll be released but it gets shot down at the last moment. Apparently someone saw her in the office that night. Hey, are you okay?"

Brooke's face had turned so pale, even her lips lost color. "Sure, just a little queasy. I'll be okay."

He squeezed her hand. It was easy to dismiss your own problems, but you couldn't always help the ones you cared about. Lately that made him feel powerless, an unfamiliar experience he hated. At least he could show Brooke a glorious and relaxing weekend in the country. She deserved the best of everything and he intended to give it to her.

Brooke gripped his hand tightly during their descent into the airport at Gatlinburg, then exhaled with relief as the plane taxied to a halt.

"See? You survived."

"Only just. And my nails have probably left permanent scars on your hand."

"I'll wear them with pride."

RJ was pleased to see the caretaker had dropped the familiar black Suburban off at the airport then discreetly disappeared. The first sign that his plans were going smoothly. He'd told the caretaker he didn't need any staff on hand, as he suspected Brooke might be spooked by the presence of other people. Much better that they enjoy peace and privacy.

A now-familiar pang of grief hit him as he climbed behind the wheel. His dad usually drove, maintaining the familiar patterns of father-and-son even though RJ had been driving for nearly twenty years. "Dad loved it up here. He always said the whole world fell away if you got high enough up into the mountains."

"It's beautiful. The light is different here." That light illuminated Brooke's hair and her delicate profile as she looked out the window. For a split second he longed to press his lips to hers and lose himself in a kiss. Instead he started the engine.

"Dad wrote me a letter when he made his will." He frowned. He'd never spoken to anyone else about it. "Said he wasn't sure how much longer he'd live and he wanted to make sure the lodge would be mine."

"Oh." Brooke turned sharply, shock written on her face. "Sounds like he almost knew he was going to die."

"He never said a word to anyone." He shook his head. "His lawyers told me he redrew his will every few years, so they didn't think much of it. He included letters each time. But when he died there was one for everyone in the family...except my mom."

"Did he leave any hints of who he suspected?"

"That is odd. Nothing I could figure out. He does mention his other family that none of us knew about. Well, except Mom."

"Your mom knew about his other woman and her children?"

RJ swallowed. "Apparently so. She didn't say anything to us. She learned about them while he was writing his will. She found a copy in his desk." It was good to get that awkward truth off his chest. He knew he could trust Brooke not to tell anyone. "She didn't want any of us to know."

"Is that why police think she has motive?"

"I suppose they think she wanted revenge." He heard Brooke's intake of breath. Did she think it was possible that his mom could wield a gun against her husband of nearly four decades? "You do know she's innocent."

"Yes, of course." The color had fled her cheeks again. "It's just a shame she had to find out that way."

Brooke seemed distracted, staring hard out the window, not even noticing the bait and tackle shop and the quaint country inn he'd intended to show her.

"I brought Dad's letter with me because he mentions something in the lodge." He paused while a big truck crossed at the intersection ahead. "Something else he wanted me to have."

"An object?"

"I don't know. It's rather mysterious. He said to look in the third drawer down, but he didn't say what piece of furniture."

"Hmm. I guess you'll just have to open every third drawer down in the house, and hope for the best."

He didn't mention the other things his dad had said in the letter. For now those were between Reginald Kincaid, Sr., and his namesake, and maybe it was better that no one else knew about them.

Brooke was lost for words when they pulled up at the lodge. Then again, what had she expected, a shack with an outside toilet? This was a Kincaid residence. The vast log home rose up out of the surrounding woodlands, high gables braced with chiseled beams and walls of windows reflecting the sunset. RJ strode up the steps and unlocked the impressive double doors, then ushered her inside.

Golden sunlight illuminated the foyer from all directions. RJ put down their bags then walked through a door in the far wall. "Dad named it Great Oak Lodge. Come see why we built the house here."

Brooke followed him into another grand room, decorated in an updated, minimalist interpretation of hunting-lodge chic: pale sofas with muted plaid accents, a painting of a stag and an impressive stone fireplace. The last rays of sunlight blazing in through a wall of windows largely obscured the view, until RJ opened a pair of patio doors and she saw an endless vista of tree-cloaked hills.

She walked out and stood beside him. There were no signs of civilization at all, just peaks and valleys filled with more trees. "It feels like we're on top of the world."

"Maybe we are." He stepped behind her and slid his arms around her waist. Her belly shimmered with arousal. They hadn't kissed since their date two nights ago, and on the plane she'd been too nervous to think much about kissing. Or any of the things that might follow.

RJ bent his head and pressed his lips to her neck. "You smell sensational." Excitement trickled through her, peppered with anxiety about where this was all going. Now his hot breath warmed her ear, making her shiver with anticipation.

"Shouldn't we put our bags away?" She could hardly believe that was her voice interrupting the sensual moment.

RJ chuckled. "Trying to delay the inevitable?"

"Just being practical. That's why you hired me." Ouch. Why did she have to remind him—and herself—that she was his employee?

"Let's leave the office at the office." RJ still held her tight in his embrace, and his mouth had moved barely an inch from her skin. "Do you think any of those trees care about memos and meetings and deadlines? It's a whole different world up here. Breathe in some fresh mountain air."

"I think I am." Surely if she wasn't she'd have passed out by now. Which was a distinct possibility the way RJ was tantalizing her earlobe with his tongue and teeth.

"Mountain air is restorative. Draw it all the way to the bottom of your lungs."

She drew a breath deep down into her belly the way she'd learned in yoga class. Evening cool, scented with pine and fresh soil, the rich air filled her lungs, and she exhaled with gusto. "That does feel good."

"Standing up here restores perspective. Out here it seems like time doesn't exist—the sun rises and sets and everything stays the same except the slow change of the seasons."

"RJ, you're turning out to have more dimensions than I expected."

"And you've known me five years already. Just shows how important it is to step out of context. Now kiss me."

Before she could protest he spun her around and pressed his lips firmly to hers. Her eyes slid shut and her hands rose to his shoulders. The kiss was delicious, golden and heady as the sunset warming their skin. The slight stubble on RJ's chin tickled her and she felt his eyelashes flutter against her cheeks as he deepened the kiss.

She hugged him, enjoying the closeness she'd craved, letting go of her worries and losing herself in the powerful sensation of his strong arms around her waist, holding her tight.

When they finally pulled apart, by only a feather's depth, his eyes sparkled and she knew hers did, too.

Happiness swelled in her chest and the moment felt so perfect.

"You're a very beautiful woman, Brooke. The sunset suits you."

"Maybe I should wear it every day."

"Most definitely. And I have a feeling that sunrise will become you, as well."

"I guess we'll have to get up early and find out." A tiny blade of anxiety poked her stomach. By morning they would have slept together.

Or would they?

After they disentangled themselves from each other's arms, RJ took her to a bedroom with panoramic views and invited her to unpack. Then he disappeared. Maybe they weren't going to sleep together at all. The closet was empty, except for a few hangers and a plain white terry bathrobe. The room had an adjoining bath, with freshly unwrapped soap and tiny bottles of expensive Kiehl's shampoo and conditioner. The rustic yet elegant bentwood bed was covered with a thick, soft duvet and the whole room was decorated in neutral colors that complemented the jaw-dropping view out the window. It was like being in a very high-end hotel.

Brooke hung her few items in the cavernous closet, then changed out of her work suit into her favorite jeans and a green shirt that highlighted her eyes. The carpets were soft pure wool, so she left her feet bare to better enjoy them and show off her rather daring jade-green toenails.

She peered out into the hallway. She followed the sound of whistling and found RJ in a similarly spacious bedroom, with a large bed made of rustic planks, checking his phone. "Settled in?"

"Perfectly." There was his bag, half-unpacked, on top of a pine chest of drawers. So they were sleeping in separate bedrooms. She should be relieved, but instead she felt disappointed. Maybe she was hoping for a whirlwind romance and he just planned to cast some flies and kick back in the sunshine.

"I've never seen you in jeans before." His eyes roamed down her legs, heating her skin through the denim. "Clearly, I've been missing out."

"I've never seen you in jeans before, either." She smiled, glancing at the pair peeking out of his duffel bag.

"Mine don't hug me quite the way yours do." A dimple played in his cheek.

"Shame." A sudden vision of RJ's body flashed in her mind. Even in his suit—the jacket hung over a corner of the wardrobe door and his sleeves were rolled up—you could see he was built and muscular. He played a lot of tennis and squash and sailed competitively. No doubt his muscles were bronzed by all that time in the sun. Hopefully soon she'd get to compare her imagination to reality.

If that was really a good idea.

"Are you hungry?" RJ's expression suggested he wanted for something entirely different than food.

"I am. All that shaking with terror on the flight built up an appetite."

"Good, because I'm making dinner."

Her eyes widened. RJ Kincaid in front of a stove?

"Don't look so shocked. You should know by now that I'm a man of many talents."

"I'm impressed."

"One of my talents is delegating to skilled professionals." He strode out of the room, leaving his phone on the bed. "Frankie Deleon owns the best restaurant in town and this afternoon I had the fridge stocked with provisions." She followed him into a bright kitchen with gleaming professional quality appliances. He pulled open one door on the fridge. The inside revealed a collection of smart earthenware dishes, each labeled with a Post-it note. "Let's see, jambalaya, baby back ribs, black-eyed peas and greens—hey, those need actual cooking. Poached salmon, sesame noodles." He moved a dish aside to reach behind it. "Macaroni and cheese, rice salad, green salad, beet and goat cheese salad... Where do you want to start?"

Brooke's mouth was already watering. She could get used to this Kincaid lifestyle. "It all sounds sensational. What are you in the mood for?"

His blue gaze settled on her face and she read her answer loud and clear. A smile crept across her mouth as her nipples tightened under her green shirt.

"You decide."

A challenge. She knew RJ liked people who could think on their feet and make executive decisions. "Ribs with sesame noodles and green salad."

"I like." RJ pulled the containers from the shelves and placed them on a butcher-block island large enough to have its own sink. Brooke turned on one of the stainless steel ovens, and RJ pulled some fine china dishes from one of the cabinets. They picked a chilled white wine to sip while waiting for the ribs to bake.

"Did you check the drawers yet?"

RJ looked up from the bottle opener. "What drawers?"

"The one mentioned in your dad's letter." Maybe

that was too personal. He probably wanted to search for the item alone.

He looked back down at the bottle. "I'm not sure I'm ready yet. I still hardly believe he's gone."

"I can't imagine what a shock it must have been."

"I keep expecting him to walk around the corner and say it was all an elaborate hoax." He gestured toward a wing-backed red chair in the great room adjoining the kitchen. "That was his favorite chair. I feel like he's going to get up out of it and rib me for not catching any fish yet this year."

The cork popped out with force, almost making Brooke jump. "I know he's proud of you for how you're handling things."

RJ nodded. "He's got to be watching from somewhere."

She fought an urge to glance over her shoulder. She wasn't sure she wanted RJ's dad watching the things she hoped to get up to with him tonight. Then again, maybe she should think more about how this would look to all the other people around them. What would RJ's siblings think of her spending the weekend with him? She worked closely with his brother Matthew in the office—would she be able to look him in the eye on Monday? And what about his mom? Would she see sleeping with his assistant as somehow beneath a Kincaid?

Of course Elizabeth Kincaid had much bigger problems to worry about right now. Partly due to information that she, Brooke Nichols, had provided to the police. She really needed to get that off her chest. Maybe now was a good time. She could casually say she'd seen his mom in the building and then... No.

Better to say the police had interviewed her and she just happened to mention—

"I'm glad you're here with me." RJ's soft voice jolted her from her fevered ruminations. He handed her a cool glass of clear white wine and she took a hasty sip. The moment for telling him had passed. Now he was getting romantic and she'd ruin it all if she said anything. "I've been wanting to come up here for a while, but didn't know how I'd feel."

"How do you feel?" She squeezed her guilt back down. He wanted a relaxing weekend, not more to worry about. It was probably better if she didn't mention it until they were back in the everyday world of Charleston.

"Okay. It's as beautiful as ever, peaceful and a perfect escape from reality."

"Can you ever really escape from reality?" Somehow it kept sneaking back into her consciousness.

"Sure." He smiled. "You file it away in a drawer."

"The third drawer down, perhaps?"

"Maybe that one, maybe another. Maybe more than one." He raised a brow. "Then you lock it and lose the key until some later date."

"That does not sound like the RJ I know."

He laughed. "It doesn't, does it? Maybe I'm trying to change."

"I don't think you should change." She said it in earnest, then wondered if she'd revealed too much about herself. "You're up-front and honest. You tackle things head-on and don't beat around the bush or try to people-please."

"And you've been the victim, more often than not."

"I'd much rather have you tell me what you think than have to guess it."

"I suppose that's one thing I got from my dad." His expression darkened. "Or I thought I did. He was blunt and truthful, and I never doubted a word he said." He swirled his glass of wine and peered into its depths. "Now I can see I should have been wary of all the things he left unsaid. Maybe you can never really know anyone."

"I don't suppose you can, but most people don't have secret families, so I don't think you could have seen it coming." It was hard to know what to say without overstepping the mark.

"No? My mom knew about them, and she kept quiet, too."

"She was probably trying to protect you from pain."

"Instead, she accidentally set herself up as a possible murderer." He shook his head and took a swig from his wine. "There's no justice in this world."

Brooke's stomach clenched. She hated to see RJ sounding so bitter. He was usually the most upbeat and positive person she knew. "There will be justice, but it might take some time."

"I wish I believed you. How can there be justice in a world where the Kincaid Group, the company I've devoted my working life to, is now forty-five percent owned by a half brother—" he said the word with a growl "—that I never knew existed." He looked up at her, eyes cold. "And who despises my entire family and the company he's just been handed."

Brooke put her wineglass down on the island. "It's all very strange and hard to understand right now." How could his father have been so cruel as to take away the company RJ saw as his birthright and hand it to an unknown rival?

"You know what?" RJ's voice was low with anger. "I do want to see what's in that third drawer. I want to see exactly what Dad wrote that would help me to understand why he stopped seeing me as his eldest son and heir." He slammed open the third drawer down on one side of the kitchen island. "Napkins and napkin rings. Can you see the significance?"

Brooke swallowed. She wanted to laugh, just to ease the tension, but it wasn't funny. "Did he have a desk?"

"Yes, there's a study." He strode from the room. Brooke glanced at the oven and saw the ribs still needed a few minutes. Always the trusty assistant, she followed him.

RJ marched into a bright study with cathedral ceilings and a leather-topped desk. "Ha. Two rows of three drawers." He pulled open one bottom drawer and rifled through the interior. "Bullet casings, ballpoint pens, paper clips, a broken golf tee." He slammed it and pulled open the other. "Reginald Kincaid letterhead and matching envelopes." He lifted the papers. "What's this?" He pulled out a manila envelope. "It has his name on the front. Or my name—since according to my birth certificate I'm Reginald Kincaid, as well." The envelope was sealed. Thick too, like it had a wad of papers, or even an object. "It's heavy."

"Are you going to open it?"

RJ hesitated, weighing it in his hand. The oven timer beeped in the kitchen.

Four

"I'll go check the ribs." Brooke seemed relieved at the excuse to leave him alone. Once she'd gone, RJ glanced down at the envelope in his hands. The writing was his father's familiar script, neat and commanding. He slid a finger under the sealed flap and ripped the paper carefully, aware he was frowning.

Then he lowered the open envelope to the desktop and eased the contents out onto the desk. Papers, mostly, a pair of cuff links, a ring he'd never seen his dad wear and some old photographs.

"They're done. I'll just toss the salad," called Brooke from the kitchen.

"Great." What was this envelope of things supposed to mean? He picked up the ring and looked at the design. Gold with a flat top, it was shaped almost like a class ring. As he stared at the shield he realized it was probably from his dad's time in special forces.

He recognized the bird holding a lightning bolt. The ring was worn, the gold scratched by use, but he didn't remember ever seeing it on his dad's finger. A relic from another lifetime, the lifetime in which Angela had been the woman he loved—and unbeknownst to him, the mother of his firstborn son.

"It's ready." Brooke's voice tugged him back to the present.

There was a lovely woman waiting for him in the other room, and painful memories could wait. He pushed the items back into the envelope and slid them into the same drawer. "Coming."

Brooke looked so beautiful standing silhouetted against the last rays of light. Her lush body beckoned to him, promising an evening filled with pleasure. Much better to tuck all that other stuff away in a drawer for now.

"Looks delicious." He stared directly at her as he said it.

A pretty smile played around her pink mouth. "It sure does. Where do you want to eat?"

"There's a table on the deck." He served the ribs onto two plates, and Brooke spooned out the salad and noodles. He grabbed cutlery from a drawer, picked up the wine and glasses with one hand, and Brooke brought the plates. The last rays of sun lit the polished wood table and chairs in a fiery reddish gold. He lit the decorative hurricane lamps with the BBQ lighter, and topped up their wine.

"Okay, this really is paradise." Brooke couldn't stop staring at the view. "This must be the only house for miles around."

"There are cabins and people out there, they're just hidden by the trees."

"The trees are kind to cloak everyone in peace and privacy." Her sweet smile made his chest fill with emotion.

"They're in charge around here. Dad always said that coming up to the mountains put everything into perspective. Problems shrink away and so does the human ego."

Brooke laughed. "I can't picture your father saying that."

"He could be quite introspective when the mood caught him." He could tell Brooke was rather intrigued by the new side of him she'd seen lately. Usually he didn't think too much about the impression he made on people, but right now it pleased him to show Brooke he wasn't just a hard-partying playboy. "It's easy to see why, now we know his life was a lot more complicated than any of us imagined." He took a bite of his food.

Being out here in the mountains brought a sense of equanimity that dulled the pain of recent events. He could think and talk about his dad calmly. Brooke's peaceful presence helped. He couldn't imagine her getting upset about anything. She was always the voice of reason in the office, ready to pour oil on troubled waters. "Did I ever thank you for taking me by the scruff of the neck and getting me out of trouble the other day?"

"When I marched you to your office and plied you with liquor?" Her pretty green eyes sparkled.

"Yes, that. A wise executive move."

"More an act of desperation. Still, I'd like to be an executive one day."

"You'd be good. You have an instinct for how to deal with people—getting them to deliver weekly updates so we know where everyone stands, for example."

"I got the idea from a management video I watched."

"I had no idea such bold ambition burned in your chest." RJ took a swig of wine. Brooke probably was wasted as his assistant, much as it pained him to admit it. HR had recently informed him that she'd submitted her application for a management role in the Events department and he'd told them he couldn't spare her right now. He needed an assistant he could trust with all that was going on in the wake of his father's death. Still, holding her back for his own reasons was selfish. He'd have to look around the company for the right role for her.

Brooke's sparkle had dimmed slightly. "I hope I didn't overstep the mark. I do really enjoy working with you."

"Of course you're looking to the future. I'm glad to hear you have big plans. You have a lot to offer the business world." He was relieved to see her lips curve into a smile again. "We'll have to talk about your future when things settle down."

She nodded. He felt a twinge of guilt that he didn't want to talk about her future right now, but frankly that was too big, complicated and potentially disturbing a subject for what was supposed to be a relaxing weekend in the mountains.

They chatted more innocuously about Charleston and their favorite music while the sun set and plunged them into the familiar velvety darkness. They swept the plates and glasses back inside. "Should we wash the dishes?" Brooke glanced at them where they lay on the counter. RJ had already disappeared into the next room.

"Don't worry about them. Come relax."

Brooke shrugged and followed him into the living room. It was hard to remember she was his guest, not his assistant right now. She hated leaving loose ends but maybe that was part of becoming the kind of person who managed others, rather than one who did everything themselves. RJ had changed the conversation rather deftly after her mention that she'd like to go into management, but maybe he just didn't want to be reminded of the office when he was trying to relax.

RJ leaned over a sleek device, and suddenly the room filled with music. Ella Fitzgerald, mellow and sultry. He looked up and smiled. "I thought we should dance."

Excitement stirred in her chest, along with a flutter of nerves. "Sure."

Dancing would get them close. Closeness would get them… RJ wound his arms around her waist. She could feel the heat of his body through his thin shirt. His back muscles moved under her hands as they swayed to the music. He pulled her against him and soon the rise and fall of her breath matched his. Or was it the other way around?

The song ended and another started, while they moved slowly around the big room. Dancing this way with RJ felt oddly natural, unhurried and relaxing. Arousal crept through her like wine, making her giddy but happy. They didn't even kiss until the third song started. RJ's lips brushed hers. Their mouths melded together slowly, tongues meeting and mingling.

Her chest pressed against his, her nipples tightening

against his hard muscle. Their hips swayed in rhythm and his hands roamed over her back. By the fifth song the kiss deepened to the point where their feet stopped moving. She felt RJ's fingers tugging at the hem of her shirt, then sliding over her skin. She shivered with pleasure and let her fingers roam into his waistband.

Soon they were plucking at each other's shirt buttons and pressing bare skin to bare skin. The music wrapped around them as RJ guided her onto the sofa and together they eased off her jeans. Her body throbbed with desire that gave urgency to her movements. The zipper of his pants got stuck as she tried to undo it and she found herself struggling with desperation that would be funny if she wasn't so...desperate!

RJ took over and together they shed his pants then wrapped themselves into each other on the wide surface of the sofa. RJ's big body fit perfectly around hers. His muscled arms held her close and his strong legs and hard abs made her pulse quicken.

Was she really lying semi-naked on a sofa with RJ Kincaid? Perhaps this was one of her more elaborate fantasies getting out of hand?

But his hot breath on her neck felt so real. So did the broad fingers slipping inside her delicate panties, and the lips closing over her nipples through the lace of her bra. Brooke gasped when he sucked on her nipple and sensation shot through her. She pushed her fingers into his thick hair and gave herself over to the sensation, arching her back and pressing her pelvis against him.

They both still wore their underwear, but she could feel RJ's intense arousal through his cotton boxers, and soon found her hands pushing down the elastic waistband and reaching for his erection. She shivered when she discovered how hard he was, how ready.

"Let's go into the bedroom." RJ's voice was thick with need. Without waiting for her response he picked her up in his strong arms and carried her across the room. Supported by his strong body, Brooke felt weightless and desirable. RJ swept her into his bedroom, and laid her gently on the soft duvet.

"You're so beautiful." His gaze roamed over her body, making her skin tingle with excitement. He caressed her skin, starting at her shoulder and trailing his fingertips over her lacy bra and along her waist. When he reached her skimpy panties he hooked a finger into each side and slid them slowly over her legs, devouring her with his gaze as he pulled them down to her toes.

Excitement built in her chest as she waited for him to finish. Then he rose back over her and she leaned forward while he unhooked her bra and released her breasts. He kissed each freshly bared nipple and cooled it with a flash of his tongue. Breath coming faster, she pushed his boxers down over his thighs.

At last they were both naked. RJ climbed over her, kissing her face and murmuring how pretty her eyes were, and how soft her hair. The simple compliments made her feel like a goddess. She let her fingers roam over the thick, roping muscles of his arms and back and wished she could find words to admire them, but words deserted her as sensation overtook her body.

He entered her very gently, kissing her as he sank deep. Brooke arched against him, relishing the feel of him inside her, his powerful arms wrapped around her. The weight of his body settled over her, pushing her into the mattress as she clung to him.

"Oh, RJ." The words slipped from her mouth as she brushed his rough cheek with her lips. She'd waited years for this moment. She could feel him inside her, hard, yet so gentle as he moved with her.

A shiver of pleasure crept over her as he slid deeper, and she felt herself opening up to him. She snuck a peek at his face, and their eyes met in a single, electric moment. The expression on his face was almost pained, so intense, his blue eyes stormy with emotion.

Brooke felt her heart swell with feeling for this man. So strong and capable, he led the company with such energy and pride, and at this moment his entire being focused on her. His arms wrapped around her, enveloping her in their protective warmth, while he moved with precision and passion.

"You're an amazing woman, Brooke." His whispered words stirred something deep inside her. He shifted slightly, sending arrows of pleasure darting through her. Was she amazing? She certainly felt special right now.

Or were they both just caught up in the moment? Or in the madness that had brought her into his arms that night in his office.

A ripple of fear made her hold him tighter. "I'm not amazing." She couldn't bear for him to be making love to some imaginary woman who had nothing to do with the real Brooke Nichols. "I'm just…me."

RJ paused for a moment and their eyes met. Again that fierce gaze almost stole her breath. "You're amazing because you are just exactly you. The most beautiful, capable, sweet, organized, sexy and irresistible woman I've ever met."

A giggle rose in her chest. "That's quite a mix of adjectives."

"You're a unique person." He brushed soft kisses over her cheek and the bridge of her nose, making her smile. "And it's my very great pleasure to be sharing this bed with you." His penis stirred inside her, sparking a ripple of laughter along with a rush of erotic pleasure.

Her eyes slid closed as she kissed him on the mouth, drinking in the rich taste of him. She'd imagined moments like this, but not that she'd feel so totally swept away on a tide of intense pleasure.

RJ's strong arms eased them into a new position where she was sitting in his lap. As they moved together, the powerful penetration took her deeper into the mysterious otherworld they shared. RJ's hands on her skin, his thighs wrapped around her, his hair brushing her forehead...

Feelings raced through her. She wanted to shout, or cry. *I love him.* The thought flashed in her brain and she held him tighter. *Is it just my body talking?* Her brain grappled with powerful emotion while her body clung to his, moving with him in a thick sea of pleasure.

I love you, RJ.

She let her mind release the thought, though she didn't allow her lips to voice it. It was enough for her to know. She didn't want to throw pressure at him and ruin this beautiful moment. She'd never felt closer to anyone, and maybe she never would again.

For now, it was precious.

Her climax crept over her gradually, starting with

little waves that lapped at her fingers and toes, and ending in a big breaker that crashed over her.

RJ joined her, exploding with a gruff cry, crushing her against his chest and pressing his face to hers as they collapsed back on the bed. Overwhelmed by sensation and emotion, she lay limp in his arms.

"I don't remember the last time I felt this good." RJ cradled her, stroking her softly. "You're a miracle."

Brooke's chest, already bursting with happiness, almost exploded. Being here with RJ felt so absolutely right. It seemed odd that they hadn't come together earlier, when they were so perfect for each other. He stroked her cheek and she sighed. She'd made RJ feel good, too. Maybe that was the best part of all.

Lying here in his embrace she could imagine them living happily as a couple. They'd worked together successfully for five years, which was quite an accomplishment already. They'd always got on and never argued, and he obviously respected her opinion. "I'm glad I dragged you out of that meeting and plied you with liquor."

"Me, too. Not many people would have dared." He kissed her cheek softly and nuzzled against her. Again her chest swelled with joy. "You're a brave woman, Brooke Nichols."

She was, wasn't she? Not many women would chance a weekend away with their boss. For a moment the familiar doubts started to creep back in. How would they behave at the office? Would he be affectionate or would they go back to professional cordiality? What would she do if he kissed her in front of the other employees?

She blushed just thinking about it. She'd love it, of

course. She'd be so proud and happy to be RJ Kincaid's girlfriend. A dream come true. And here she was, living it.

They kissed, then dressed and went to enjoy more music and dancing, then undressed and made love again. This time they fell asleep together, with seductive music still throbbing away in the living room. Brooke slept deeply, totally relaxed and at ease in RJ's arms.

In the morning she awoke with an odd mix of anticipation and anxiety. They had two whole days to spend together with no interruptions.

Then again, what if they had nothing to talk about? What if he grew bored with her?

"Morning, gorgeous." RJ pressed a kiss to the back of her neck.

"Hi." A wave of pleasure lapped over her at the touch of his lips and her doubts scattered. "Did you sleep okay?"

"Never slept better in my life. You're the best medicine in the world."

She smiled. "I'm glad. Last night was fun."

He kissed her cheek. "More than fun. You're full of surprises, Brooke."

"I am?"

"I had no idea you had such a sensual side."

"I try to keep it under wraps when I'm at the office." She winked. "Might not be appropriate."

"There's a whole different Brooke that I never knew about."

"Actually I think the Brooke you know is about ninety percent of the real Brooke." She didn't want him to start thinking she was really a temptress superspy or something, and then be disappointed. "There are just a few facets of me best not viewed under fluorescent lighting."

RJ glanced down at her body and lifted the covers to reveal a peaked pink nipple. "I think you'd look amazing under any lighting."

The way he stared at her made her feel beautiful. She worked hard to keep her body in reasonably good shape, but she'd never felt ultra gorgeous—until RJ's appreciative blue gaze touched her skin.

She trailed a finger over his muscled chest. "I'm not sure what I expected under all that crisp suiting, but let's just say I can tell you work out."

"I play a lot of tennis and squash. They're a full-body workout."

"I used to play tennis in high school." She said it shyly. She'd been their team's star player, but never pursued it in college since she didn't want to take too much time away from her studies and she needed to work almost full-time.

"No kidding? We'll have to hit some balls together. We can go to the club when we get back."

The club? The ultra-exclusive country club that cost over fifty thousand dollars a year just for the privilege of membership? She swallowed. "I haven't played in years. I probably wouldn't even be able to hit the ball over the net."

"We'll have to find out, won't we? Tennis is like riding a bicycle, at least I think so. After ten minutes or so you'll feel like you never put down your racquet."

"Maybe, if you promise to take it easy on me." She slid her finger down over his hard belly, which contracted under her touch.

"I don't know. That's not really the Kincaid way."

"You're more into crushing your opponents then dancing over their shattered remains?" That was their business reputation to a certain extent. RJ looked surprised. Had she stepped over an unspoken boundary by talking about the family? "I don't mean that literally, of course. Just that I—"

RJ laughed. "Don't back down now. That's exactly what I meant. We're not able to lose gracefully. It's not in our DNA. If we were, maybe we'd be able to fit in better with crusty old Charleston society, where you need to suck up to someone whose great-great-granny came over on the *Mayflower* just so you'll get invited to their garden parties. We're constitutionally unable to do that."

"But the Kincaids are part of Charleston society."

He laughed again. "As if there was only one Charleston society. Believe me, there are plenty of people in this town who look down on the Kincaids as nouveau riche upstarts who won't be around for long." He looked thoughtful. "It's never bothered me before, but with everything that's going on lately I'm more determined than ever to prove them wrong."

"The Kincaid Group will weather this storm. So far it doesn't seem so much worse than the time we lost the Martin account."

"The Martins went out of business. This time people are leaving just because they can, and they're going to the competition."

"So, you'll have to show them what they're missing. And now's a good time to build up the company's real-estate portfolio."

"It is. We've been moving assets in that direction.

When the real estate market comes back we'll be sitting on a gold mine, especially along the Charleston waterfront. Hey, why are we lying here naked talking business?"

"Because we're that kind of people." She smiled at him.

He lifted a dark brow. "We're a lot alike."

Brooke shrugged. She wasn't sure how alike they really were. Not being accepted into the highest echelons of Charleston society had never been one of her most pressing problems. And a relationship with her would hardly boost his social standing, which apparently was a big concern for him.

"We are alike." He obviously sensed her doubts. "We're both teetering on the brink of being workaholics, we like good restaurants, we play a mean game of tennis and we're both lying in this bed."

Brooke chuckled. "When you put it like that... But you're making a lot of assumptions about my game of tennis."

"I know you well enough to know you wouldn't have mentioned it unless you were practically on the tour."

"I'll have to be careful what I tell you. You have dangerously high expectations."

"Only because you never disappoint." He said it plainly, no hint of teasing.

"Never? Surely I've made a few typos along the way."

"I sincerely doubt it, but I'm talking about you as a person, not an office appliance. Don't think I haven't noticed how brilliant you are."

Brooke beamed inside. "I enjoy a challenge."

"And I enjoy you." He nibbled her earlobe gently,

sending a rush of sensation through her. Suddenly they were kissing again, then twisted up in the duvet making mad, early morning love.

Love? No. Not that. Having crazy, wild, before-breakfast sex. She'd never had so much sex in a twenty-four-hour period, and they were barely twelve hours in. Energetic and passionate, RJ soon brought her to new heights of arousal and excitement. They climaxed together, with a lot of noise, followed by laughter as they tried to disentangle themselves from the duvet.

"I'd suggest we shower together," said RJ, once they stopped panting long enough to form a sentence. "But I'm worried we may never make it to breakfast."

"What are we doing for breakfast? I don't recall too much breakfast food in the fridge."

"That's because there's an excellent diner up the road, and I always go there. You'll love it. It's a real slice of life in the mountains. I'll shower first, then leave you with some privacy."

Brooke couldn't resist sneaking a few long, lascivious peeks as RJ rose from the bed and strode naked across the room. His body was magnificent. Broad shoulders tapered to a slim waist, and his backside... ooh la la. She would probably never be able to keep a straight face in the office again.

She fanned herself as she heard the rush of water in the shower. She'd expected RJ to be a romantic charmer, but not that he'd drive her so completely over the edge. Maybe all the years of fantasizing about him in secret made their actual coming together so intense.

She loved that he was so affectionate. He seemed to really enjoy holding and hugging her, as well as kissing and licking and all that other good stuff. And, boy, was he deft at sliding a condom on at just the right moment. He didn't even need to interrupt the flow of events. He must have had the packet ripped open before they even started.

She frowned. This should remind her that he was no innocent boy next door on his first date. RJ Kincaid had bedded a lot of women, and she wasn't likely to be the last.

Her chest tightened, then she realized how foolish it was to be thinking about the future when they still had the whole weekend ahead of them. She had no idea what the future would bring. Who could have predicted that Reginald Kincaid, one of the most vibrant men she'd ever met, would be shot dead by a mystery assailant, let alone that his wife would be accused of his murder?

Brooke let out a long sigh. If only she could figure out who else might be responsible. She was in the office on the night of the murder and left less than half an hour before it happened. The police had even interviewed her as if she was a suspect at first. Whoever killed him might have been in the building the entire time. But who?

"Why the serious face?" RJ appeared in the doorway, toweling off his spectacular bronzed body.

Already she felt a smile creep across her lips. Who could stay serious when confronted with such a vision? "What serious face?"

"Much better."

They ate an enormous breakfast in the 1950s-style diner, served by the owner who had probably been doling out grits since the 1950s. He made a big fuss of both RJ and Brooke, treating them like visiting royalty. His great-granddaughter, aged about seven, brought them flowers she'd picked in the garden and handed the bouquet to Brooke. "You're very pretty."

Brooke smiled. "You're very pretty, too. And I'm impressed with the standard of service here. You don't get flowers and compliments every day with breakfast." When the little girl had skipped back outside she whispered, "I wonder if they pay her to flatter the guests."

"It's a good strategy. Maybe The Kincaid Group should try it out on our customers." Humor twinkled in his eyes. "On the other hand, most of our clients aren't nearly as easy on the eyes so it might come across as phony."

"Oh, please." She wanted to protest that she wasn't pretty, but she didn't want to appear to be fishing for more compliments. She'd certainly never felt prettier in her life. "I hope you don't have anything too strenuous planned for this morning. I'm not sure I'll be able to move after that fantastic meal." Perfectly crisp bacon, golden scrambled eggs, freshly baked rolls and spicy fried potato. And the ubiquitous bowl of grits.

"We'll save the hike to the summit for this afternoon then. How about we stroll to the lake and pretend we're fishing?"

"Sounds good."

She had no idea how good. While they'd been relaxing in the diner, a member of staff had packed the trunk of the Suburban with an icebox of chilled beer and a packed lunch.

"I feel like elves are following close behind us waiting on us hand and foot."

"Just takes a little organizing."

Again, Brooke wondered if he did this sort of thing often. Bringing girls up to the cabin and scheming with all the locals to pamper and spoil them. Maybe right now the people in the diner were shaking their heads and clucking their tongues and discussing how long "this one" would last.

How long would it last?

RJ opened her car door, always the perfect gentleman. Right now she didn't feel like his admin at all. It was almost impossible to imagine showing up at the office on Monday and going through his in-box. On the other hand she could imagine any number of intriguing things that could happen between now and Monday.

RJ seemed like a different person than when they left. For the first time since his father's death he appeared truly relaxed, his face crinkling into smile lines rather than the frown he'd worn so much lately. His broad shoulders looked at ease, not tight with tension.

She felt different, too. Their night of passion had awakened something inside her. She was no virgin but she'd certainly never experienced pleasure like that before. This morning she'd grown into a more deeply sensual person than she was yesterday. Colors were brighter and smells sweeter and even the air tasted bright and crisp as champagne.

By Monday they'd both be different people, one way or another. Her fantasy of a relationship with RJ was coming true and happiness seemed right within her grasp.

Though if it didn't work out, if this weekend was all they had, she'd have the agony of knowing just what she was missing—for the rest of her life.

Five

A lazy morning of casting flies from a grassy river-bank, followed by their luxurious picnic, led to a relaxed walk in the woods. RJ was easy to talk to. Which was hardly a surprise given that she'd known him for years. It was odd, and wonderful, how quickly and totally their relationship had altered from being purely professional to...utterly unprofessional.

They carried a thick foam camping pad out onto the broad balcony of the cottage, and now lay on it, naked, covered only by a thin sheet swiped from the linen closet. Warm spring air caressed their skin, still damp from the exertions of a heated afternoon love-making session. RJ traced patterns on her belly with a lazy finger, stirring little rivers of sensation that made her want to giggle.

His hair, tousled at some point by her fingers, hung

down to his eyes, which shone, dark with arousal. "Maybe we shouldn't ever go back."

Brooke's stomach contracted slightly under his fingers. "Tempting as that sounds…"

"Come on. Would they really miss us?" Humor deepened his dimples. "That unpleasant Jack Sinclair can take over running the company and you and I can just live in the woods on trout."

"We didn't catch any trout." The idea held marvelous appeal. No more early morning commutes. No more taking minutes in meetings. But at heart she was a practical girl. "We didn't even see any trout."

RJ's grin was infectious. "Berries, then."

"Okay, berries. Supplemented with orders from your favorite restaurant." She played with the lock of dark hair on his forehead.

RJ planted a kiss on her stomach. "I've never contemplated any other life than the one I was born to. Lately, though, with all this madness surrounding the family and the company, I can't help thinking that there are other possibilities out there." His expression darkened somewhat. "And that in making his will my dad was giving me permission to explore them."

Was he serious? She couldn't imagine The Kincaid Group without RJ, or RJ without the company that seemed to be his lifeblood.

But she wanted to be supportive. "What would you like to do, if you could do anything?"

RJ traced the line of her thigh with his broad thumb. "I think I'm doing it." His mischievous expression teased her. "And maybe I could branch out into this." He lowered his head and licked her nipple, tightening it to a hard peak. "And this." He raised his mouth to hers and kissed her with exquisite tenderness.

Brooke's heart swelled inside a chest already very full with the wonder and excitement of their new relationship. RJ spoke as if he'd just discovered the love of his life—her.

Don't get carried away! Up here in the clouds it was easy to forget all about the real world, but sooner or later they'd have to go back to it.

After another delicious dinner from the bounty in the fridge they watched a classic Hitchcock movie together. RJ held her tight during the scary bits and Brooke loved enjoying such a normal, everyday couple activity with the man who'd once seemed wholly unobtainable. After the movie they shared a dish of caramel ice cream, then kissed with cold tongues and warm hearts.

Sunday was a lazy day. They didn't even rise from bed until nearly noon, and only then because RJ decided it was time to confront the manila envelope of memories his father had left him.

RJ brought a new sense of calm back into the study with him. He'd closed the door on Friday night determined to enjoy his weekend with Brooke. By Sunday, however, a sliver of guilt was intruding on their shared paradise. Sunday dinner was a Kincaid tradition. They all gathered in the big family home and shared a traditional roast or some other delicacy their mom had conjured up. Now she was in jail, the family tradition was temporarily suspended. How could they face each other across the table with neither the matriarch nor the patriarch of the family present?

Their dad would never sit there again. They'd stubbornly kept the tradition going at their mom's insistence in the weeks and months since his death. It was no doubt his responsibility as the eldest to gather the clan in their mom's absence, but he didn't have the heart.

He'd spent two enjoyable days here on the outskirts of his life, with the lovely Brooke for company. But he had decisions to make and avoiding them didn't sit well with him.

Brooke had cooked pancakes from a packet mix while he made coffee, and after they'd eaten she tactfully excused herself, saying she needed time to make a couple of phone calls. She went out on the terrace, where the reception was strongest, and he headed back into his father's inner sanctum with a heavy heart.

The envelope lay there in the drawer where he'd left it. He wondered if his dad had prepared it all at once in a typical flourish of brusque efficiency, or if its contents were the product of hours of thought, packing and unpacking.

Probably the former. With a swift inhale he pulled the packet from the drawer and emptied its contents on the desk in a rude clatter and rustle. Amongst the yellowed papers was a crisp, new sheet, folded in two. RJ snatched it off the desk and pulled it open. His scalp pricked with discomfort as he saw the handwritten lines. Another letter. The letter he'd opened and read so hastily after the funeral had cut a dark scar in his heart and he suspected this would only reopen and deepen the wound.

While you bear my name, you are in truth not my firstborn son.

He'd seen Angela and her sons at his father's funeral, but refused to believe the gossip about who they were. When he opened the letter, that one brief line had knocked away the foundation of his life. So swift and brutal was the blow that he'd been hard-pressed to act like himself for the rest of the day. He no longer was himself. Since birth he'd been Reginald Kincaid, Jr., chip off the old block. All he'd wanted was to be just like his dad, a proud family man, successful in business and in everything else he turned his hand to, from fighting foreign wars to scoring birdies on the club golf course.

In that letter his father had revealed he was not the man they'd all assumed him to be. Fathering a child before his marriage was one thing—and as he'd posthumously explained, he didn't know about his son Jack until years after his birth—but resuming his relationship with his son's mother and maintaining them as a second family went beyond the common accusation of adultery and into the realm of almost criminal deception.

Steeling himself, he focused on the handwritten script that covered most of two pages.

Dear Reginald,
We all make choices in life and, as you are by now well aware, I made choices that many would disapprove of. You may well be angry with me, and knowing your proud and honest spirit, I bet you are. You've had some time to think about how all this affects you, and above all I want to make you aware that you have choices, too.

RJ growled. Did his father think he was some beardless sixteen-year-old looking for a pep talk? He'd been a man himself now for a decade and a half.

My parents took away my choices when they forbid me to marry Angela, the woman I loved.

RJ suppressed a curse. How he wished he'd never heard the name of Angela Sinclair, or her accursed son.

Being an obedient son, I didn't marry her. Instead I ran away from them all, from all of their plans and hopes and dreams for me. As you know, my time in the service was a defining period in my life that shaped me like a blade in the furnace, and I look back on it with pride as well as regret. I'm enclosing the ring I wore for many years as a symbol of my commitment to my unit. It was a wedding ring of sorts, when I wore it, as I had thrown away all other allegiances. I sought to escape my former life and forge a new one all my own. I also enclose the pilot's license I earned all those years ago and that you used to tease me about. As you can see, it really does exist, along with the other, less savory, realities of my life.

Escape is an illusion. No matter how far you run, or how fast, the truths of your life—of who you are and what you've done—dog your heels over all terrain, and sooner or later you have to turn and face them. When I returned home I had to face the parents who'd waited and worried every day I was gone. This time, obeying their wishes that I take a suitable bride and start a family seemed a far more livable kind of escape, and I soon met and married your wonderful mother. My happiness was complete and

I barely thought of the lives I'd left behind, until I learned by chance that the woman I once loved had borne my child and raised him in my absence.

By this time I had children of my own with your mother and knew the force, and felt the commitment, of the paternal bond. I hope you'll one day understand that there was no way I could turn my back on my own flesh and blood. When I met Angela again, I felt the full power of our grand passion that I'd tried so hard to leave behind in my attempts to be a good son.

Don't be a good son, RJ.

RJ blinked and thrust the letter down, growling with a mix of fury and disbelief. All his life he'd been proud to fulfill his parents' goals and dreams, to now be told it was all some kind of colossal mistake? He snatched the pages up again, anxious to get to the end.

All your life you've been told where to go and what to do. Your mother and I carefully chose the best schools and groomed you for your future role in The Kincaid Group. We never asked you what you wanted. RJ, my son, I want you to take this opportunity to look inside yourself and decide what you truly want from your life.

RJ threw the letter down with another curse. How arrogant of his father to assume that he'd blindly followed along with their plans for him. He'd been successful in school and in business and everything in between because of his own hard work and dedication and because he'd wanted to. He knew plenty of men with all his advantages who'd thrown them away and run off to pursue alternate dreams. His old pal Jake ran a beach bar in Jamaica, for Chrissakes. He could have dropped out of the Caine Academy, or flunked out of Duke and opened a surf shop. He hadn't done those things because he'd chosen the life he was living. He'd fully intended to spend his entire career building The Kincaid Group until his father decided to pull the rug out from under him.

He was nearly at the end of the letter anyway. Blood boiling with a mix of anger and frustration, he focused his eyes on the neat handwriting again.

> The defining fact of my life, son, is that I loved two women.

RJ shook his head. Surely love was an act of choice. In his opinion his dad should have told his parents to shove it and married Angela. Of course he would never have been born, but right now that didn't seem like such a bad deal.

> I never claimed Angela and our son during my life as my role in society was important to me. I wanted those invitations to the black tie affairs, the yacht club memberships and the satisfaction of being a leading member of Charleston society.

RJ snorted. *Thanks for setting fire to all that and leaving us in the ashes.*

His father had always put a lot of stock in what other people thought. More than a man of his standing should have to. It likely went back to the Kincaids never being on quite the upper tier of Charleston society. His mom's family was one of the old guard. In retrospect he could see that was probably the chief reason his dad married her. And now look where marriage to Reginald Kincaid had put her.

I'm not proud of the choices I made. I've long carried the burden of keeping Angela and her sons secret. In making my will I tried to redress some of the wrongs I committed against Jack. He grew up on the sidelines of society, as the child of a single mother, and without many of the advantages you enjoyed. In giving him a majority share in The Kincaid Group I aimed to give him the opportunities he was denied as a boy. I realize this may seem unfair to you, but I also know you're wise enough to understand my reasoning and strong enough to forge ahead and make a success of your life, either in the company or outside it. If you're reading this letter it's because I'm dead, of natural causes or otherwise. I wrote it to explain myself to you after you'd had some time to reflect on the terms of the will, since knowing you as I do I suspect you tore up my first letter and threw it on the fire.
I love you, RJ, and I'm proud of you.
Dad.

RJ sank into the chair. His anger had evaporated, replaced by a wounding sorrow. Apparently his dad hadn't known him as well as he'd thought. Far from tearing up his first letter, he'd carried it with him since the day he received it. Maybe his dad really hadn't known how much he'd loved him? They'd never been much for words or hugs.

Angry as he was at the choices—no, the stupid mistakes—his father had made, he'd give almost anything to see him just one more time.

But life—and death—didn't work like that.

He folded the letter and thrust the ring, the license, the photos and other stray bits of paper that commemorated milestones in his dad's life, back into the envelope.

His dad had given him permission, perhaps encouragement, to leave The Kincaid Group if he wanted to. He could move away, start a new life in a different city.

A cold shiver ran through him at the limitless possibilities, the many routes his life could take. Right now the only thing he wanted was to see Brooke's lovely smile again.

"Brooke! You promised you'd tell me everything!" Evie's voice rose with exasperation.

Brooke moved the phone further from her ear. "I'm trying. The weekend's not even over yet. I'm sitting on a balcony with a ridiculous view over what must be the entire range of the Great Smoky Mountains." The morning "smoke" or fog had evaporated, leaving a crystal-clear vista of wooded slopes and sapphire blue sky. How could she even describe what she'd experienced over the last two days? "It's just a romantic weekend. You know what that's like." She wanted to downplay the whole thing. It was their first weekend together. Yes, it was fantastic. More than fantastic. But it didn't mean RJ would be shopping for a ring later.

"You had sex with him?"

"No, we meditated together."

"Oh, stop! Okay, that was a bit crude. You slept together."

"We did that, too. He's a very heavy sleeper, who makes this adorable purring noise right before he's about to wake up." A vision of his powerful chest rising and falling filled her brain. She'd watched him for over an hour, afraid that if she moved she'd wake him and spoil the pleasure of watching him sleep in her arms. He'd looked both powerful and vulnerable at the same time. Irresistible.

"Aw, like a big kitty. So when are you seeing him again?"

"I imagine I'll see him first thing tomorrow when I give him his mail." She swallowed. Would she be able to maintain her usual professional demeanor now that she knew exactly what he looked like beneath those elegant pin-striped suits? Now that he knew exactly what she looked like beneath her tailored skirts and blouses.

Her nipples pricked to attention as she remembered his blue gaze raking over her skin, drinking her in like a long, tall glass of water in the desert.

"Hmm, mad passionate love on the office desk, papers sliding forgotten to the floor while the phone rings."

"Definitely not." Brooke blushed at the vivid image her friend had conjured.

"Never say never. Would you have thought a week ago that you'd be locking lips in his office?"

"Not in a million years. I won't say I didn't fantasize about it, but I never thought it would happen."

"See? Anything could happen. Before the year is out you could be Mrs. Brooke Kincaid."

"I very much doubt it. The Kincaids are apparently obsessed with their social standing in Charleston. In addition to being illegitimate, I don't have a drop of blue blood in my veins. RJ's father didn't marry his mistress because she wasn't from the right social class, and from the sound of it not much has changed since then."

"Don't be silly. RJ's crazy about you, and he's far too self-assured to worry about other people's opinions of his lovely bride."

"Stop! I thought you were the one warning me to go slow in case it all ends in tears."

"The way I see it, you're in over your head already. Might as well enjoy it and worry about the tears later. Did you ever figure out what to get your mom for her birthday?"

Brooke gasped. "I can't believe it. I totally forgot! And it's tomorrow. No, it's today, Sunday! I haven't even called her. I'm supposed to be at her place for dinner."

Becoming involved with RJ had totally derailed her brain. She hung up and called her mom to confirm they were still on. As she was speaking, she heard the sliding door to the balcony whisper open, and RJ stepped out. She waved hi and finished the conversation, telling her mom to book a table wherever she wanted.

"I missed you." RJ's deep voice wrapped around her at the same time his arms did.

"We weren't apart more than twenty minutes."

"Felt like an eternity." He nuzzled her neck, then rested his head on her shoulder for a moment.

"Are you okay? Did you read the letter?"

She felt his chest rise as he sucked in a breath. "I read the letter. My dad apparently gives me permission to abandon all my responsibilities and seize a new life by the…" He looked up and his gaze met hers with blistering force. "All I can say is thank heaven for you being here in my arms right now."

"Don't let it get to you. Maybe we should go for a walk in the woods to blow off steam."

A sparkle of mischief crept into his eyes. "I can think of another way to blow off steam."

Brooke wasn't at all nervous on the flight back. Hand in hand with RJ, she felt they could stride across the world together and nothing could harm them.

Back in her condo, she shrugged out of the chic "country attire" she'd bought for her weekend in the woods, showered and dressed in something her mom would approve of. "You have such a nice body. You should let people see it." By people, she meant men. Barbara Nichols's life revolved around men and the chance of being admired by them.

She stopped by a mall and picked up the most expensive tennis bracelet she could find. Expensive was always good as her mom would know exactly how much it cost. When she arrived at 14 Pine Grove, as usual her mom was dressed for a night on the town. "Oh sweetheart, you shouldn't have!" The sparkly bracelet hit its mark, and was immediately added to the collection of bling on her thin wrist.

"Where's Timmy?" Her mom's boyfriend had been a regular fixture around the house for nearly two years.

"Moved to Charlotte."

"Why?"

"His job transferred him to their plant there." She shrugged as if she couldn't care less. Brooke could see the lines in her face had deepened.

"Oh, Mom, I know you two got along well. Did you talk at all about going to join him?"

Her mom's pale blue eyes had a hollow look. "He said he thought it was better if we made a clean break. He started talking about kids and you know how that goes." She swatted the air dismissively with her manicured hand. Timmy was at least fifteen years younger than her. This had happened before.

"I'm sorry to hear that, because I thought he was nice." Not interesting, or funny, or charming or gorgeous, like RJ, but he treated her mom well.

"Yeah, well. Sooner or later it's time to move on. Maybe we'll meet Mr. Right tonight. I booked us a table at Dashers, it's a new place just up the road."

Brooke's heart sank. The prospect of sitting at a bar booth, eyeing potentially eligible males with her mother, was enough to suck every last breath of wind from her sails. Again, this had happened before. Still, it was her birthday.

Twenty minutes later they sat in the shiny black booth, which looked just as Brooke had imagined it. Her mom's sculpted legs were artfully draped outside the booth where they could catch the eye of any passing males. "How about you, sweetheart? Are you still spending the weekends holed up in your apartment practicing yoga or do you ever go out into the world?"

All of Brooke's better judgment told her to keep quiet about RJ. "Actually I'm seeing someone." Apparently her better judgment had disappeared with her first sip of Frascati.

Her mom's mouth and eyes widened. "Who? Someone from work?"

Brooke gulped. "Um, yes, actually."

"Did you finally catch that gorgeous boss of yours?" She leaned in conspiratorially. "I'm always telling you you're beautiful enough for even the richest man in Charleston, if you'd just shine a light on your assets." She glanced approvingly at the cleavage revealed by her blouse. "You do have a glow about you, now I'm looking closer." Her penciled brow lifted. "Well, don't sit there in silence. Tell me more!"

Brooke took another sip of her wine. "It is my boss." She said it quietly. "RJ. He's been through a lot lately and I think I've been a shoulder to cry on for him."

"Oh God, not a crier! I can't stand them and they usually drink like fish, too."

Brooke laughed. Her mom had a way of disarming anyone's inhibitions. "Not literally. He's just been going through a lot. I'm sure you've seen the stories in the papers."

"About his mom killing his dad." She grimaced. "Nasty stuff."

"Mrs. Kincaid didn't do it, I'm sure of that."

"Papers said they have evidence that she was at the scene of the crime around the time that it happened. That sounds pretty guilty to me."

Brooke's back stiffened. Was her admission to the police that she'd seen Elizabeth Kincaid in the building shortly before the murder the entire reason RJ's mother had been arrested? She'd yet to hear of anything more concrete.

"She came to bring him his dinner or something. Probably, I mean. I don't know for sure." She didn't want anyone to know she was involved in the investigation. At least not until she'd found a chance to tell RJ. If only she could take back her words and tell the police she hadn't seen or heard anything. "She's a really nice lady. Very quiet and sweet."

Her mom clucked her tongue. "Those quiet ones. There's always more to them than meets the eye. You don't work in my business for more than thirty years without learning a thing or two about people." As a waitress, she claimed to have gained astonishing insight into the human psyche. "She probably smiled her way through decades of marriage, being the good little wife, then when the revelations about his second family came out, she snapped." She clapped her hands together and Brooke jumped in her seat.

"I'm sure it must have been someone else. But the problem is no one else has a real motive."

"What about that newly discovered son who inherited a whole lot of money?"

Brooke nodded. "He seems to have gained the most by Reginald's death. And I hear he's not very nice, either." She drew in a breath. "Don't tell anyone I said that, okay?" Her mom loved to gossip with the customers. "He is part of the family, after all. Or at least sort of."

"Bitter." Her mom puckered up her lips and took a sip of her Manhattan without leaving any lipstick on the glass. A skill she was proud of. "I bet you anything it was him that did it. But we seem to have gotten off track here." Her lips widened back into a smile. "Are you getting serious with Reginald Kincaid, Jr.?"

Brooke laughed. "It's RJ. No one calls him Reginald."

"Well, don't you let him get away. You won't get many opportunities like that in a lifetime."

"I don't know where it will lead, but I really like him."

"Don't let him treat you badly because he's a rich boy. Not that you would. My Brooke has a good head on her shoulders." Their plate of nachos arrived and her mom took one and crunched it. "I never got my big break. Not yet, anyway." She winked. "But it sounds like you'll soon be living in fine style."

"Mom!" Suddenly Brooke could picture her bragging to her customers about how her little Brooke was dating one of those big-shot Kincaids that were all over the papers. "Will you do me a huge favor and keep it to yourself, at least for a while?"

"And spoil all the fun of bragging about you? Aww." She pouted. "I'll do my best. You'd better get engaged quick, though, as I'm not sure I'll be able to hold my tongue for long."

"I have no idea if we'll ever get engaged. We only started dating this week."

"You could always try telling him you're pregnant." Her mom lifted a brow.

Brooke stiffened. "If that had worked for you we'd still be living with my father. As it is, I've never even met him."

Her mom drew in a breath. "You're right. I forgot. Now why did I ever tell you about that?"

"Because I kept asking until you broke down." Brooke smiled. "And you knew it was better for me to finally hear the truth rather than all those crazy stories about a traveling salesman who'd be back from the Far East any day now."

"Well, it sounded more exciting than a balding ex-quarterback who owns a shoe store in Fayetteville. I looked him up on Facebook and let me tell you he's not aging well. He sure was handsome in his day, though."

"And maybe he did us both a favor by letting you go." Her mom had tearfully admitted that he'd left town—for good—the day after she'd happily told him about her surprise pregnancy.

"We'd been dating for six months. I thought it was a sure thing." She shrugged her slim shoulders inside her silky dress. "But you never know what people are made of until their feet are to the fire."

"Well, RJ's feet are in several different fires right now, and I'm doing my best to be the water that cools them."

"Just make sure you don't get left to run down the drain when the fire's been put out. And you don't want to lose your job over him, either. One thing I've always prided myself on is keeping my job. Men come and go, but work will put food on the table if they're there or not, and don't you forget it."

"Don't worry." Brooke picked up a nacho and nibbled it thoughtfully. "I won't."

Six

"You took Brooke to the cabin?" RJ's brother Matt stared at him. They were alone in RJ's office with the door closed. "Things aren't so desperate that you need to work on weekends. I did score the new Larrimore Industries account after all, and that should start bringing in revenue as early as—"

"Matt! I didn't bring her there to type my memos."

He watched while understanding dawned in his brother's green eyes. "You and Brooke... Oh, RJ, are you sure that was a good idea? She's such a key member of the company and you know how you are with women."

RJ bristled. "Exactly how am I with women?"

"Enthusiastic."

"So now I'm enthusiastic about Brooke. She's beautiful, intelligent, kind and she gives great hugs." He couldn't stop a smile creeping across his mouth. Even thinking about Brooke gave him a warm glow. "There's quite a different side to her than the one we see at the office."

"I bet she's saying the same thing about you." Matt raised an eyebrow. "Are you going to be kissing in meetings and sneaking off for afternoon trysts?"

RJ fought a grin. "Appealing as that sounds, I think we'll both have enough self-control to maintain a semblance of professional decorum."

"And what happens when you get tired of her?"

"Unimaginable."

"Maybe I have a more vivid imagination than you. I know what it's like when a relationship starts to sour. You do realize she could sue you for sexual harassment and win?"

RJ frowned. "Brooke would never do that."

"Let's hope not. We can't afford another scandal right now. I guess you'll just have to marry her." There was not the slightest glimmer of humor in his brother's steady gaze.

RJ's stomach tightened. "Let's not get too carried away. We haven't even been dating for a full week, yet."

"See? That's the RJ I know. You're crazy about them for a while, then something better comes along."

"These days I never know what's going to happen next, so I'm going to seize the moment. Did you guys visit Mom over the weekend?"

"Both days, just like we promised. She says she's doing fine but she's looking rather thin and drawn. We've got to get her out of there."

"I've been on the phone to the D.A.'s office every day. Three times today already. If they have evidence they need to produce it. You can't keep someone behind bars without a trial in this country. It's not like she's accused of an act of terrorism." He felt his hackles rising again. "The assistant D.A. said something about a witness at the scene, but then she clammed up. I know there wasn't an eyewitness to the murder or we'd have heard about it. If there was, we'd know what the hell happened and Mom would be home where she belongs. The private detective I hired is trying to break down the blue wall of silence that is our local police department right now, but no luck so far."

"Lily's going to visit her again this afternoon."

"I'm going, too, after the meeting. I bought some of her favorite chocolates." He shook his head. "Though I'm sure even Ghirardelli doesn't taste all that great when you're locked up in a tiny cell sleeping next to a toilet. It makes me sick."

"I know, RJ. Honestly, I understand about the Brooke thing. This nightmare is hard on all of us and I can see the temptation to fall into the nearest pair of soft arms." He clapped RJ on the shoulder. "Let me know if you hear anything new from the police or the D.A.'s office, okay?"

"Will do."

Brooke darted away from RJ's office door and back to her desk, heart pounding, before Matthew emerged.

He looked right at her and smiled, and she managed to stammer a greeting, sure her face was red as fire. She'd been unable to resist listening in on RJ's conversation with Matt—horribly unprofessional, not to mention totally uncool, but she couldn't help herself. She'd pretended to rearrange some files in the tall cabinet next to his door, but every nerve in her brain and body was fine-tuned to pick up all sound from inside.

Her heart had soared as RJ said such sweet things about her, then crashed when Matt muttered about lawsuits and accused him of falling into the nearest pair of soft arms. That rang painfully true. None of them knew where this was going, and it could be heading to a lot of very dark places.

The door was now wide open, and she glanced inside to see RJ, head bent over some papers on his desk. He looked up. "Are you going to sue me for sexual harassment?"

"Never." She said it too fast and too loud. Did he know she'd been listening?

"Never say never." RJ raised a brow. "You could, you know."

She walked into his office and closed the door gently behind her. "What happened between us was entirely mutual." She kept her voice composed and professional, though her heart was hammering. How typical of RJ to come right out and say what anyone else would want to brush under the carpet. Right now she adored him more than ever. "I don't regret it."

Though maybe I will one day.

RJ rose and came around the desk. In his dark suit he looked imposing and elegant. Different from the rugged charm of the RJ she'd enjoyed all weekend, but every bit as irresistible. He wrapped his arms gently around her waist and pulled her close for a kiss. Her insides bubbled with pleasure and she let her hands slide under his suit jacket and caress his back through his cotton shirt.

"This is fun." RJ's breath heated her neck.

"It feels naughty."

"It is naughty." He squeezed her backside gently. "And I could think of even naughtier things we could do."

She giggled. "Don't you have a ten o'clock?"

"I'm the executive vice president. I can cancel it." His deadly serious expression only made her want to laugh harder.

"It's with a potential new client." She ran a finger along his shirt buttons. "A large manufacturing company with factories in China."

"Hmm. You're making this all very confusing and difficult for me."

"Then as your personal assistant I'll have to insist that you go to the meeting."

"Can you do that?"

"Apparently I just did." She kissed his dimple. "Though only time will tell if you listen." She could hardly believe she was being so bold. The chemistry between them must be affecting her brain.

"I'll only go if you'll come, too." Humor sparkled in his eyes. She would have been at this meeting anyway.

"If you put it that way, how can I refuse?" Her lips tingled as he feathered one last kiss over them. She pulled herself away, slightly breathless, opened the door and went to get her laptop.

Everyone on the floor must know something by now. Or they'd figure it out from her burning cheeks. Or the loopy expression on her face.

And RJ had come right out and told Matthew! Did he plan to tell the entire family they were seeing each other? Surely the others would also worry about lawsuits. It hadn't occurred to her that she'd have a case against him, but her friend Evie had told her about a woman at her company who sued her boss when he dumped her. She'd won, even though it was consensual, because he was her direct boss and should not have embarked on a relationship with her.

It was easy to forget about all the pitfalls when she was in RJ's arms, or even gazing at his handsome face. The moment she moved away she felt exposed again to the chill winds of reality.

Brooke sat next to RJ during the meeting, which was normal since she sometimes needed to show him correspondence or data on her laptop. Opposite her, a tall blonde with a very large mouth was representing the Xingha Corporation, a manufacturer of children's toys that did a lot of business with U.S. supermarkets. Three non-English-speaking Chinese men in gray suits sat further along the table, and occasionally she turned to repeat something to them in Chinese.

"Oh, RJ, you must come to Beijing again soon. You'll love what they've done with your favorite hotel. Hot tubs in every room." Her dark eyes clashed with her blond hair, and gave her face a sense of drama that really annoyed Brooke. Already she found herself anxiously casting her mind back to RJ's trips to Beijing—had he even been to Beijing?—and wondering and worrying how intimate he'd been with Ms. Claudia Daring.

"I'm sure I'll be in Beijing sometime soon, but right now we have a lot happening here."

"I've heard." She leaned forward, and reached out to clasp his hands. "It's terrible. If there's anything I can do...anything at all."

Brooke barely managed not to roll her eyes, but

inside her stomach was churning. RJ and this woman had obviously had an affair.

She tried to glance sideways at RJ without moving her head. Were his eyes lighting up at the sight of Claudia's smile? He leaned back in his chair so she couldn't get a good look at him.

Matt sat farther down the table. What was he thinking about right now? Was he laughing at RJ being confronted with his own woman-loving ways at the first meeting of the day? She wished she could slide under the table and hide.

She was just the latest in a long line of Kincaid conquests. She knew that. You didn't work for RJ for five years and not realize that he enjoyed the company of women every bit as much as James Bond.

"You'll recall that we moved our account to Danmar Shipping in 2009 over pricing issues." Claudia lifted her rather pointy chin. "We understand you might be in a position to offer a more competitive price." One slender brow lifted slightly.

"Yes." Matthew chimed in from far down the table, although Claudia had addressed RJ. "We'd like to bring the Xingha Corporation back to The Kincaid Group, and we can provide some strong incentives. We understand that some of your new products are temperature sensitive and we can provide climate controlled..."

He continued speaking but Brooke no longer heard a word he said. She was staring directly at Claudia, who never took her eyes off RJ. Her breath caught as Claudia's tongue sneaked out and flicked over her upper lip. Probably supposed to look sensual, but it made Brooke think of a lizard.

Her eyes flew to RJ's face, and horror crept over her as she saw his familiar dimples deepen.

"Excuse me." She rose from her chair and hurried for the door, unable to contain herself for a single second longer. Once outside the meeting she walked quickly to the ladies' room. RJ was flirting with that woman, in front of everyone, when he'd slept with Brooke only yesterday!

And despite the fact that his brother knew about their affair and had taunted RJ for his womanizing ways not half an hour earlier.

Her breathing was rushed and unsteady and she wasn't surprised to see her face looking pale, except for a nasty flush spreading across her neck. That only happened when she was really embarrassed. How could she survive this meeting? If RJ had coolly rebuffed Ms. Daring, and perhaps said, "I'd love to come to Beijing, with my fiancée, Brooke Nichols," and gestured proudly toward her, she'd feel quite different.

"Ugh!" She said it aloud. This is what happened when you let your imagination run away with you. Even after RJ's conversation with Matt, she'd focused on the moment when he said it was unimaginable that he should tire of her, not the part where he had a new woman every week. Within an hour his dimples were deepening over some scrawny executive with an account to dangle.

Still, she had to go back. A bathroom break was one thing, ditching the meeting was another. And her laptop was still in there. She drew in an unsteady breath, patted cold water on her hot cheeks and dried it with a paper towel. *You're a professional and you can do this. You actually want The Kincaid Group to get*

*this account because you care more about the future
of the company than your future as RJ's latest female
conquest.*

It wasn't working. Nevertheless, she gritted her teeth
and strode out the door.

She plastered a smile on her face as she entered the
meeting and sat down.

RJ turned to her. "Brooke, we came to an arrangement with Xingha, and we're going out for a celebration lunch. Can you book us a table at Montepeliano?"

"Sure." She maintained her stiff smile and picked
up her phone. "How many people?" Was she invited
or was she merely making reservations for RJ and his
new bilingual playmate? She cursed the angry flames
of jealousy that licked inside her. How had a few days
of intimacy with RJ turned her into an irrational, emotional wreck?

"All of us." He glanced around the table. "Nine." A
quick count revealed that did include her.

"Will do." She made the reservation in hushed tones.
Great, now she had to sit through lunch watching Ms.
Daring make eyes at RJ. And vice-versa. The restaurant was a short walk from the offices, and a favorite
for business lunches.

"Do excuse us." RJ spoke to Claudia. "My assistant
and I need a moment." He glanced at Brooke, and her
heart jumped. Was he going to scold her for running
out of the meeting? She was there to take minutes and
she'd obviously missed the most important part—the
deal. Of course Matt or RJ could fill her in on the details, but it was unprofessional of her to just vanish.

She followed him out of the room, and he gestured
for her to come around the corner toward an empty

conference room. Once inside, he closed the door. He looked at her and a tiny line appeared between his eyebrows.

"I'm sorry I left like that, I…" The rest of her words were lost when his mouth crushed over hers. His broad hands settled on her hips, and she shuddered, once, as his tongue slipped into her mouth.

Brooke heard a tiny moan leave her as the kiss deepened. Relief and the shock of excitement stirred her blood. Her nails scratched at RJ's strong back through his shirt, and she got a sudden urge to pull off his stiff suit jacket and feel his warm skin.

"Whoa, there." RJ pulled back, dimples deeper than ever. "Let's not get too carried away. The door's not even closed."

Brooke flushed. "Whoops."

"We'll use up all that energy later, and that's a promise." His blue eyes shone with dark fire. "Though it'll be hard to keep my hands off you for the rest of the afternoon. I guess this is why they say office romance is a bad idea."

"Just one of the reasons why it's a bad idea." A naughty smile crept across her mouth. "Makes it hard to stay focused in meetings, too."

"Or does the desire to get out of the meeting sharpen one's focus enough to make a deal in record time?"

"Yes, how did everything happen while I was in the washroom?"

RJ raised a brow. "I guess you'll never know." He gestured for her to leave the room before him, and she felt his fingers trail across her rear end as she turned to go. That sparked a little ripple of laughter. What did she care how they made the deal so fast? RJ had let her know he wanted her, not their glamorous client.

She walked to the restaurant on a cloud of joy. She didn't even mind RJ chatting with Claudia Daring. Now she had the perspective to see him using his charm to build the business, not to lure another woman into his bed. Her earlier flash of jealousy seemed petty and foolish.

She noticed Matthew casting wary glances at his brother. Was Matt worried she or RJ would somehow reveal their clandestine relationship? She knew the company couldn't afford even a wisp of scandal, so she made sure to sit at the far end of the table and did her best to make conversation with the Chinese men who had about twelve words of English among them.

That night she and RJ stayed at his place. His large, modern apartment had stunning views of the Charleston waterfront. They ordered in Thai curries and played a game of strip Go Fish then made lazy, intoxicating love on his oversize bed. After midnight they called a cab so she could go home, sleep and get ready for work.

By Thursday, at RJ's suggestion, she'd left a robe and a spare dress there, to avoid having to rush home. She took to carrying extra makeup and hair implements in her purse, because she now spent more time at his house than her own.

Her clothes looked strange hanging in the spare closet next to his off-season clothes. Of course if they lived together here, this would be her closet.

"I've decided to reinstitute a family tradition this week. Sunday gatherings at the old homestead."

"Your mom's house?"

She turned to see RJ frowning at the phone. "Yes. It may seem strange for us to go there when she's not in it, but she insists she wants us to get together and she'll be there in spirit. We've met for dinner nearly every Sunday since we were kids, and it doesn't feel right to drop the ball because everything's a mess right now. Besides, it'll be nice for you to meet the whole gang."

Her eyes widened. "Me? I don't know. Your family has a lot to talk about. And I don't want to scandalize them. They're sure to think it's odd that you're dating your assistant." Her stomach clenched as she immediately regretted the use of the word dating. That sounded so…serious, and RJ had plainly told Matt he had no idea where things were headed.

"Matt knows already."

She didn't plan to admit she'd heard Matt's reaction. "I don't want to be in the way."

"You won't be. My sister Lily will bring her new fiancé, Daniel, and Laurel—who you know—will bring her fiancé, Eli. Kara is planning both of their weddings. Then you already know Matt and you've probably met his fiancée, Susannah."

"Yes, I met her when she brought Flynn in to meet him for lunch." Flynn was Matt's toddler son, who'd recently scared everyone by getting some rare disease that had the family hovering over his bedside around the clock.

"Did you know Susannah is Flynn's mom?"

"But I thought Matt was married when… I mean, I know his wife passed away, but…" She felt her face heat. Matt's wife, Grace, had died in a small plane crash a year or so ago. Flynn must be just three, or thereabouts.

RJ laughed. "Matt didn't cheat on his wife. They'd hired her as a surrogate since Grace couldn't carry a child. What Grace and Matt never told us is that they used Susannah's egg, so Flynn was actually Susannah's biological child. She came back to Charleston in case he needed a compatible bone marrow donor when he was ill, and she and Matt fell in love. Pretty crazy, huh?"

"It's wonderful. For both of them and for Flynn."

"Romance is in the air amongst the Kincaids lately. It only seems fair that they get to know you, too."

"It would be nice to get to know your sisters. Sure, I'd love to come." Already caterpillars crawled in her stomach at the idea of them all looking at her. No doubt they would wonder why their brother was interested in someone ordinary like her.

"They'll love you." RJ crossed the bedroom and rested his hands on her hips. Her belly swirled with arousal. "And I know you'll love them, too."

I sure hope so. She sank into his embrace and enjoyed the warm, protected feeling of his arms around her. She was getting far too attached to RJ. Now she knew he was thoughtful, passionate and sexy as well as smart and gorgeous....

Brooke let out a small sigh. Everything was going so well. Somehow she'd climbed the tallest ladder on the chutes and ladders board and was sunning herself on a lofty square near the top. Why did she feel like a long chute was just around the corner?

Seven

Brooke agonized over what to bring to the meal, especially since she wasn't sure who the host was in Elizabeth Kincaid's absence. She didn't want to bring flowers and have them die alone in an empty house. She settled on a bottle of champagne and a hand-painted ceramic bowl filled with gourmet fudge.

She'd agreed to meet RJ there, and she felt a growing sense of trepidation as she walked past the other large, elegant mansions on tree-lined Montagu Street. As she approached the imposing Kincaid residence, she heard muffled voices through an open, lace-curtained window.

"You're kidding me!" A woman's voice. "Who invited him?"

"I did." Another female. "He's making a big effort to be a member of the family."

Brooke paused on the brick walkway to the front

door. Both voices were raised. She didn't want to enter into a scene.

"He's not even related to us. Alan is from Angela's second marriage."

"I invited Jack, too, but he didn't reply. Maybe he'll come anyway."

"Jesus, Kara. Why did you invite either of them? I just wanted a quiet family dinner, like we used to have." RJ's voice. His sister must have invited the sons of Reginald Kincaid's second family.

"I think we should give Alan a chance. He's been perfectly pleasant. He even seems interested in working for The Kincaid Group. Why not get to know him?" Brooke couldn't tell his sisters apart by their voices. She still hovered outside on the path, pretending to look for something in her purse.

"You always were too nice for your own good." RJ again. "At least Alan didn't inherit part of the company. He isn't even a relative. He's just an innocent bystander as far as this whole situation is concerned."

"Exactly. So let's welcome him into our midst. Anyone bring champagne?"

Brooke decided this was her cue, and she marched up the front steps and rang the bell. RJ greeted her with a warm kiss on the cheek and summoned her into a large, airy room with high ceilings and comfortable sofas. Everyone exclaimed over the champagne and fudge and she heaved a sigh of relief that she'd gotten off to a good start.

"This is my sister Lily." He gestured to a pretty woman with red-gold hair cascading over her shoulders. Her blue eyes were bright as she shook Brooke's hand.

"We've run into each other a few times at the office. Sometimes I hang around just to annoy RJ and Matt."

Matt, seated on a sofa with his toddler son on his lap, waved a cheery hello. She tried not to blush at the recollection of him discussing her with RJ.

"Daniel is Lily's fiancé," continued RJ. Brooke shook hands with a tall blond man with a warm smile. "And this is Kara. She's the event planner in the family."

"And right now I'm being blamed for overplanning this event." Her green eyes sparkled. "Trust me, people, I know what I'm doing."

RJ continued, "Of course you know Laurel." A striking beauty with long, auburn hair, Laurel Kincaid worked for the company as public relations director. She stepped forward and gave Brooke a kiss on the cheek, and introduced her fiancé, Eli, a tall, handsome man who Brooke knew owned a respected resort chain.

"We're glad you could come. It's nice to see RJ more relaxed lately." Laurel gave her brother a quick nudge.

"Brooke is definitely helping me keep things in perspective."

The doorbell rang again. The siblings looked at each other. "That must be Alan," whispered Laurel.

"I'll get it." Kara smiled and marched for the door. Brooke hadn't met either of the Sinclair men. She couldn't help a spark of curiosity at what the sons of Reginald Kincaid's former mistress would be like. All eyes swiveled to the door as Kara returned with a blondish man of medium height, smartly dressed in a wool jacket and pants.

RJ introduced her, and Alan Sinclair smiled and shook hands—firmly, Brooke noted—with everyone.

"Delighted to be here. So kind of you to invite me. What a stunning room!" He marveled over the crisp, Federal-era plasterwork.

Brooke had a feeling she'd seen him somewhere before. Maybe he'd come to the office for one reason or another. His hair curled just over his collar and gave him a raffish air, like a professor who slept with his students.

Now, now. You're as bad as the rest of them. Give him a chance. She didn't even know this man. She just knew RJ didn't want him here.

"Actually a lot of the details have been restored," Lily chimed in. "The house was a wreck when the family bought it. Dad's mother insisted on buying it and she spent years bringing back all the original features and furnishing it in period style."

"Which is why it looks more like a museum than a real house," murmured RJ.

"It is a museum, of sorts," Laurel spoke up. "A monument to an era that Grandma loved. She always wished she'd lived back in the 1800s, so she could swan around in long dresses and spend entire afternoons playing whist."

"She pretty much did that anyway," teased RJ. "Mom likes to have card parties, too. Mint juleps and cutthroat bridge."

There was a moment of silence, while they no doubt all thought of poor Elizabeth Kincaid sitting in the county jail.

Alan cleared his throat. "The house is obviously a labor of love. I don't suppose one of you would give me a tour?"

Laurel said, "Of course, I'd be happy to. Lily, is the meal under control?"

"Almost. Pamela should go away for the weekend more often. I love having the kitchen house to myself."

"Let me come help in the kitchen." Brooke was eager to make herself useful. In truth she was much happier working at an event rather than trying to make small talk, especially when they all must be wondering exactly why she was there.

She followed Lily outside into the manicured garden, and along a small brick walkway to the large, bright kitchen house. The building was a relic from the days when servants and their steamy labors could be kept separate from elegant family life, but had been renovated into a chef's kitchen with marble work tops and tall painted cabinets. Something delicious simmered in three pots on the stove and salad fixings sat, still bagged, on a long wooden table in the middle of the room. "Shall I make the salad?"

"That would be great. I'll just toast the garlic bread." Lily ripped off a hunk of French bread from one of three loaves and popped it in her mouth. "I'm in the second trimester of my pregnancy right now, and I'm absolutely ravenous."

"How exciting. Do you know if it's a boy or a girl?"

She pulled romaine lettuce from its bag and started to peel leaves off into a colander. "Not yet. We can't decide whether to find out. I know it's easier to know the gender because you can decorate the room, but I've also heard people can get really stressed about picking family names and creating expectations before the kid is even born. We went through a lot of drama just getting to this point, and I just want to enjoy our pregnancy without stirring up any more excitement."

Brooke rinsed the lettuce under a high, arched tap. "Having a baby must be one of the biggest adventures there is. You're bringing a brand-new person into your family, who you'll be spending the rest of your life with. It's magical, really."

Lily turned to her, eyes bright. "That's exactly how I feel. I admit I didn't intend to get pregnant, but it's brought Daniel and me closer than we would have dared become otherwise." She lowered her voice. "So are you and RJ...an item?"

"I guess we are." Brooke felt a little thrill of nerves. "Just since two weeks ago. I never intended for anything to happen, but..." She shrugged.

Lily's face turned more serious and her blue eyes looked steadily at Brooke. "Do be careful."

"What do you mean?" Brooke swallowed hard.

"Emotions are running high right now and the media's watching us all very closely."

Brooke's hands grew cold. "I'm not sure what you're saying."

Lily leaned in close. The lettuce dripped water onto the marble sideboard. "In case things don't work out between you, you know, it's important not to stir up any bad press."

"You think he'll break up with me and I'll go to the media?" First Matthew, now Lily. No doubt all the Kincaids suspected she'd betray the family. What would they say if they knew she'd told the police about their mom? Suddenly she felt like an intruder at their family gathering. If only she'd told RJ about it right away. Now there was so much water under the bridge she could hardly come out and admit her involvement. The deception by omission ate at her insides.

"No! None of us expects you to cause trouble." Lily put a hand on her arm. Her fingers felt soft, not accusatory. "I just want you to be prepared for anything and to handle it calmly. RJ's a smart, fun guy and a stand-up brother, but he's always sworn he'd never marry or have children." She gave a wry expression.

Brooke's stomach clenched. He'd actually said that? His own sister would know. And she was warning her to be careful not to get her heart broken. Brooke took the lettuce back to the wood table, and started to tear the leaves with shaking hands.

"I'd never deliberately stir up any trouble for the family," she said quietly. "I care very much about RJ, and about The Kincaid Group."

"I'm sure you do." Lily came close again. "I can see RJ looks different lately. More like his old self before Dad died. I'm sure that's attributable to you. I hope everything works out well."

Brooke heard the doubt in her voice. Brooke knew herself that RJ changed girlfriends like most men changed ringtones. She should be grateful for the wake-up call.

She and Lily chatted innocuously about a recent music festival, and Brooke prepared the rest of the salad, then they heard Alan's house tour coming toward the kitchen house.

"Stunning plasterwork in the archways." Alan's confident voice boomed outside the doorway. "She must have hired craftsmen from Italy."

"She did." Kara accompanied him into the room.

"Only the best for Grandma Kincaid. Do you ladies need some help with the food?"

"It's all ready." Lily smiled. "Perhaps you could both help us carry it into the dining room?"

The long mahogany table gleamed under its load of antique porcelain and sterling silver flatware. Obviously someone was polishing and dusting in Elizabeth Kincaid's absence. Not that she would clean things herself even if she was here.

Alan picked up one of the crystal glasses and peered underneath. "I knew it. Penrose Waterford. The original Waterford crystal." He beamed at the gathered group, taking their chairs. "It's a privilege to be surrounded by such treasures."

"It's fun to meet someone who appreciates them so much," said Laurel. "We tend to take everything for granted since we've seen all these things since we were babies." Little Flynn had picked up a scrolled silver spoon and raised it, ready to bang it down on the burnished wood surface before his father caught his hand with a laugh. "See! No appreciation for the finer things."

Alan laughed, showing even white teeth. "Born with a silver spoon in his mouth, lucky little devil. And surrounded by such a warm and loving family, too." He beamed at the gathered crowd.

Brooke shrank into her chair. He seemed perfectly comfortable here. She felt they were all watching her, wondering what would happen when RJ dumped her. RJ made such a handsome head of the family, carving the big roast and passing plates around. She helped herself to minted potatoes and steamed asparagus and raised her glass in a toast to the family and the fervent hope that Elizabeth Kincaid would be at next Sunday's gathering.

"What I want to know," said Matthew, "is who gave the police the information that led to Mom's arrest. They won't even say what the information is. The investigator RJ hired says someone saw Mom in the building, but the police aren't confirming."

Brooke's fingers tightened around her glass of white wine. She put it down carefully.

"Damn, but I wish I was there that night." RJ looked up. "I went out to a dinner across town and left around six, so I didn't see a thing."

Brooke swallowed, and stared at her asparagus. She'd been there until shortly after seven, finishing a report and PowerPoint presentation for one of RJ's upcoming meetings. That's when she'd joined Elizabeth Kincaid on the elevator and exited the building with her. Had RJ's mother been so upset because she'd found Reginald dead…or worse…killed him? No, no she couldn't believe it of her. Maybe she should just say something right now. She hadn't done anything wrong in speaking to the police, but sitting here in silence felt terrible. Perhaps she could just—

"If an employee told the police they saw Mom, they should be fired," RJ spoke loudly.

Brooke's knife rattled against her plate, and she cleared her throat and busied herself cutting some meat. Speaking up right now was not a good idea. She'd definitely have to tell RJ alone, not surprise him in front of his family. If only she could pluck up the courage.

"Be fair, RJ," Laurel said. "If they were just speaking the truth they've committed no crime. Mom did say she was there that night, bringing Dad's dinner."

"No way. It's a police investigation and they should have pled the fifth. It's a simple matter of company loyalty."

"Maybe they had no idea what was going on?" Lily peered at RJ over her glass of sparkling water.

"Hardly. The police were crawling all over the office for weeks investigating the murder. No one could have thought they were simply making casual conversation. Someone out there is responsible for our mother being behind bars right now, with a bunch of real hard cases and nut jobs, and that's not something I can forgive."

Brooke's breathing had become so shallow she started to feel faint. RJ would surely find out it was her who spoke to the police. Part of her wanted to confess right now and get it over with. Have them all shout at her and blame her and throw her out of the house. She silently twisted her napkin in her lap.

No, apparently she was too weak to speak up and face the music. And worst of all, she couldn't bear to hurt RJ.

And there was her job. And the rent to pay. And her dream of buying her little condo. She should probably start looking for another job, since they'd fire her for sure once they found out and it was bound to happen sooner or later.

"Brooke, are you okay? You look pale?" Kara turned to her.

"Sure, fine!" Her voice came out loud and forced. "Delicious dinner." Her lame comment echoed down the table.

"Marvelous." Alan smiled and lifted his knife.

"Quite the most succulent roast I've had this year. My congratulations to the chef."

Lily smiled. "Mom taught me everything I know. She's an amazing entertainer. Speaking of which, Laurel, she wanted to know how your wedding plans are coming along. Did you choose the dress yet?"

Laurel looked slightly startled. "Choose a dress? I can't possibly get married until Mom is out of...that place."

"She wants us to forge ahead with all our plans so she can leap right back into life once this ordeal is over. She and I spent ages poring over menu ideas for my wedding. And she thinks I should go for the Vera Wang dress I showed you."

Laurel bit her lip. "I don't know. It just seems wrong to think about dresses and cakes and reception venues at a time like this." She turned to Eli. "Don't you think?"

"Absolutely." He patted her hand. "No need to rush. We have the rest of our lives together."

"I agree with Mom and think you're being silly. Come on, Eli. Don't you think Mom would be cheered up by pictures of your lovely bride in sixty or seventy different fabulous gowns?" Eli shrugged in response to Kara's question. "I tell you, I'm more excited about this wedding than the bride or groom. If they didn't have a party planner in the family, there probably wouldn't ever be a wedding.

"I think everyone needs a party planner in the family. Come on, I'm up to three weddings right now, Lily and Daniel, Matt and Susannah, Laurel and Eli—who's next?"

Brooke felt a sudden raw flush of irrational hope in her chest. Why not her and RJ?

Well, there were any number of reasons why not. RJ didn't say anything and she forced herself not to look at him. Lily's warning reverberated in her mind.

"Alan, how about you? Have you got a blushing bride hidden somewhere?"

"Not yet, I'm afraid." He smiled around the table. "I'm still waiting for that perfect lady to enter my life." Brooke noticed his eyes skip right past her as he shone his klieg-light charm on the gathered group. He probably wasn't interested in her since she wasn't a member of the mighty Kincaid family. She was just a nobody who happened to be there. "And who knows, it could happen any day now." He let his blue eyes fall to rest on Kara, and Brooke watched the slight suggestive lift of his eyebrow.

"That's the spirit." Kara smiled. Then she clapped her hand over Eli's. "I still think you should be pushing your bride to make some decisions. One couple I helped recently had been engaged for sixteen years. They hadn't planned it that way, they just never got around to setting the date."

"Maybe they just weren't all that crazy about each other." RJ topped up the glasses of those seated on either side of him. "When people realize that they really like each other, things happen fast." His bright gaze settled on Brooke, who couldn't stop a smile rushing to her lips.

"Maybe you'll be next then, RJ?" Kara looked at him with an arch smile.

RJ laughed. "Or maybe you will, Kara?"

Brooke deflated as suddenly as she'd filled with

hope. Which was absolutely ridiculous after two measly weeks of dating. You'd think she'd never been in a relationship before.

"Since I'm not even seeing anyone right now, I'm not entirely sure how that could happen." Kara took the bottle from him and refilled the next two glasses down the table. "But I suppose you never know what life is going to bring."

"Truer words were never said." Alan beamed around the room. "I never imagined I'd find myself in the midst of such a charming family. I'm honored to be here and delighted to find that I truly feel at home among you."

Brooke wished she could say the same. But, kind as they were, she still felt like an outsider. The kind of outsider who was responsible for putting their beloved mother behind bars. And when they found out, she'd be on the outside for good.

Eight

"**I** guess Alan's not so bad after all." RJ piloted his Porsche back to his apartment. Brooke sat beside him, looking gorgeous in a green dress that gracefully hugged her curves.

"He's certainly making an effort." Brooke seemed a little tense, her pretty mouth tight and her lovely green eyes darting around a lot. He'd be sure to release all that tension with a nice, soothing massage when they got home. His fingers tingled with anticipation at the prospect.

"Was it overwhelming being surrounded by Kincaids?"

"Everyone in your family is lovely. They couldn't have been nicer."

"Still, there are a lot of us. And more all the time, it seems. The clan keeps growing." He beamed. He loved the way she'd pitched in with Sunday dinner and he could tell she'd made a positive impression on his sisters. "You fit right in." There weren't many women as intelligent and fun as his sisters, but he'd managed to find one. That she was gorgeous, too? Icing on the cake.

"Thanks. I've had practice, being in the company so long, I knew half of you already."

"But socializing is different. For one thing you look a lot hotter in that dress than in your power suits." How could he not have noticed how breathtakingly beautiful she was until recently? He must have been blind. He took the briefest of red-light opportunities to admire the way her dress draped over her slender thighs, and saw her smile out of the corner of his eye.

"Thanks."

"I can't wait to peel it off you."

"You won't have to wait long."

He pulled into the parking garage under his building and they hurried upstairs, laughing at their own eagerness. Every glance, every touch that passed between them only ratcheted the tension higher. RJ's muscles ached to wrap themselves around Brooke again. He'd made an effort not to paw her in front of the family, as he didn't want to embarrass her. He could tell she still felt a little shy and awkward, probably because she was used to having a much more formal relationship with all of them.

In the elevator, RJ seized the opportunity to steal a greedy kiss. Brooke's mouth tasted like honey and flowers, and her skin was smooth silk under his fingers. How could he have worked with her for five years and never realized such a delicious and inviting woman was right under his nose?

So much for being sensible and keeping work and play separate for five years. If it hadn't been for that one crazy whisky-fueled night he could have missed out on becoming intimate with the most appealing woman he'd ever met.

They tore into the apartment, flushed and breathless. Brooke fumbled with the buttons on his shirt while he unwrapped the complicated sash around her waist. Her nipples poked eagerly through the delicate fabric of her bra when he unzipped her dress and let it fall to the floor.

He circled her waist and held her against his chest. Brooke let out a shuddering sigh. He could tell she'd been anxious today, maybe nervous about making the right impression on his large family. Now they were alone again her reserve melted away, leaving her warm and eager in his arms.

Their kisses had a dimension he'd never experienced before. Something more than taste and touch, a thrilling quality that never failed to surprise him. Her mouth fit his so well, he could kiss her for hours and not notice the time passing.

Brooke's hand covered his erection through the pants they'd not yet managed to shed, and he released a little groan of his own.

"I feel like a teenager when you're around." He breathed in her ear and nibbled the nape of her neck. "I had a hard time keeping my hands off you today."

"Lucky thing you don't have to anymore." She stroked the hard length of him, then unzipped his pants and took him firmly in her hand. RJ arched his back at the sensation.

"I think we'd better get horizontal."

Brooke squeezed again, making him breathe harder.

"Horizontal is so...predictable." She spoke quietly. He cracked open his eyes to see her mischievous grin.

"Brooke, you never fail to surprise me." They shrugged off his pants and he lifted her onto the back of the broad leather sofa, which was just wide enough to hold her gorgeous ass while he held her steady.

It drove him crazy to see how wet and ready she was. He entered her slowly, and enjoyed her sweet moan of pleasure. Her breasts bounced gently against his chest as he rocked back and forth. He loved the feel of her hands on his back, clinging for balance as he moved with her. When she wrapped her legs around his hips and pulled him deeper, he thought he'd explode right there and then, but he pulled himself back from the brink and teased her lips with licks and kisses.

"Oh, RJ." His name on her sigh heightened his arousal. He sensed her climax growing close. Her nails dug into his skin and she moved with increasing speed and passion, legs still wrapped firmly around him. When she finally let go, he felt the force of serious relief ripping through him, and they almost toppled backwards onto the sofa together until he managed to right them.

Still in the same position, he picked her up and carried her into the bedroom, where they settled on the bed. Brooke's eyes were closed, her lashes long and thick against her rosy cheeks. Her hair splayed over the pillow and her lips were red and slightly parted.

"What a vision," he murmured.

Her eyes opened a little, a sliver of jade green glory, and he saw the spark of a smile in them. Brooke's smile did something really odd to his chest. In fact he was currently experiencing a host of unfamiliar sensations. Is this what love felt like?

He settled next to her onto the pillow. Brooke had already drifted off into a sweet sleep, and he was almost ready to do the same until he realized he'd better go remove the condom.

Which was when he realized he hadn't used one.

Brooke woke up to the first rays of lazy sunshine peeking around the heavy curtains. She'd slept like a corpse. The anxiety of the family dinner knocked her right out. Or maybe her brain was hiding from the ugly reality of the truths she had to reveal. She turned to find RJ, but his side of the bed was empty.

When she glanced at the clock it was only 6:30. Early for him to be up already.

"RJ?" How odd. He didn't seem to be in the bathroom, and the bedroom door was closed. She tried to settle her head back on the pillow, but found she couldn't relax. She climbed out of bed and pulled her robe from the wardrobe, then stepped out into the living room.

Still no RJ.

The kitchen was empty, and so was the spare bedroom. The door to his office was closed. Not exactly an early riser, RJ usually rolled out of bed at the last minute when it was time to head to work. She'd never known him to work in his study in the morning. Maybe something was going on with his mother's case?

That now-familiar knot of fear reappeared in her stomach. Had he realized it was her who spoke to the police?

"RJ, are you in there?"

She heard a rustle, and the sound of a chair being pulled back, then the door flung open. RJ's face was dark, his eyebrows lowered.

Immediately Brooke felt the blood creeping from her body. He knew. "I'm sorry, I never meant to——"

"Don't blame yourself. I screwed up, Brooke."

"What?" She was confused.

RJ shoved a hand through already disordered hair. "I've been taking responsibility for birth control, so it's my fault I forgot to use a condom."

Brooke's mouth fell open. She'd been so excited and aroused it never crossed her mind. "I didn't even think of it."

"You could be pregnant."

The words hung in the air for a moment. Her hand flew to her belly as if life was already taking shape in there. Which it might be.

"I can't believe I was so stupid." RJ's tone made it clear there was nothing positive about the possibility.

Brooke shrank back into the living room slightly. For an odd, irrational second, she'd welcomed the idea of RJ's baby. Now she could plainly see he was horrified by the possibility of having a child with her. "It was my fault, too. I should have said something."

"It's not your fault. I've taken care of it every time, so you could reasonably expect me to continue." He hesitated. "I don't suppose you're on the pill or anything, are you?"

She swallowed. "No. I should have gone to the doctor for something, but everything happened so fast…." Their whirlwind romance had seemed above prosaic matters like birth control. And the sad fact was she hadn't had a relationship in so long that she hadn't thought about contraception in ages. She had an old diaphragm buried somewhere in her bathroom cupboards, but it probably didn't even fit anymore.

RJ shook his head. "With everything that's going on, the last thing we need is more worry. And considering that our current situation was precipitated by my dad's illegitimate son, you'd think I'd be more careful." He wasn't looking at her, but right past her, into the living room.

Our child wouldn't be illegitimate if you married me. The thought penetrated her brain before she had a chance to stop it. The man right in front of her looked like he had no intention of marrying anyone, ever. Just as his sister had warned her.

"How soon will we know?" He turned his gaze back to her, where it hit her like a blow.

"Uh, I think it's at least a month." Didn't you have to miss a period, or something? She'd never been in a position to worry about it before. Her periods were as regular as tax bills. She hugged her robe about her. The mood had morphed from fevered excitement to worry and regret. "I guess I should get ready for work." Where she'd be sitting outside his office all day, knowing he was in there wishing he'd never met her and hoping and praying that she wasn't pregnant with his child.

The reality of the situation settled like a stone in her stomach.

"I'm sorry, Brooke." The pain in his blue eyes scratched a tiny hole in her soul. She wanted to say, "Don't worry about it," or something equally banal, but RJ's grim countenance made her keep her platitudes to herself. She turned and walked back to the bedroom, each footstep feeling like a mile. She managed to shower and climb into the clean suit she'd left there. Her eyes looked hollow as she brushed her teeth at RJ's sink. She'd been tiptoeing along, enjoying her romance with RJ and skirting all conflict for as long as she could. She'd finally hit that game board chute she'd worried about, and now she'd landed in a heap back at the bottom of the board, sitting on a pile of shattered dreams with an aching heart.

"Oh, Brooke, I won't say I told you so." Evie sat opposite Brooke on the sofa in her living room, sympathy in her big brown eyes and her freshly made martini sitting un-sipped in her hand. "But I had a feeling something like this would happen. I've never heard of anyone having an affair with the boss and going on to enjoy decades of happy marriage afterwards."

Brooke put her own martini down on the coffee table. Making it had been a welcome distraction, but she didn't have the heart to drink it. Besides, alcohol might make her more emotional, which was definitely not a good thing right now. And there was the possibility that she might be pregnant, which meant she shouldn't be drinking at all. "Trust me, I know! I never intended to have an affair with him. It just happened. I knew it wasn't a good idea from the moment we first kissed, but it was so…" She groped around her brain for words.

Perfect…magical…dreamy…wonderful…sensual… amazing…

She didn't feel like voicing any of those out loud right now.

"I've told you before that I see a pattern in your relationships." Evie drew her brows together slightly, the way she did when she was about to get serious.

"What relationships? I haven't had a date in over a year."

"Is it that long? Well, you did say you wanted to take a break. And I don't blame you, after the blond guy."

"Sam." Brooke grimaced slightly. "He seemed sweet at first."

"He seemed needy." Evie sipped her drink. "He was needy. I think that's why you were drawn to him. He wanted someone to tell all his problems to, a shoulder to cry on and someone to have lots of warm sympathy sex with."

Brooke chuckled. "Not lots of sex. Trust me."

"And that guy you dated in college, Ricky. He was seriously high maintenance. I'm not sure how you managed to attend your classes and hold a job while tending to his many needs."

"RJ's not needy. He's extremely capable, independent, brilliant...."

"And going through the biggest personal crisis of his life. At any other time he'd probably be a different person, but in the last few weeks he's been a strapping, muscular bag of needs, and you've been doing your best to meet them all."

"You are right about the strapping and muscular part." A tiny smile tugged at her lips. Then she wiped it away. "I was crazy about RJ for years. Long before all this latest drama. I can't believe I forgot all about contraception and gave him yet another thing to worry about. If only I could turn back the clock and—"

"Stop trying to save everybody."

"My desire to save everybody may be what makes me such a good executive assistant."

"Then stop doing it at work, too. I thought you wanted to move into management."

Brooke stared at her untouched martini. "I hope I still have a job to go to. If RJ gets tired of dating me he's not going to want to see my face every day."

"So, apply for another job before it happens. Didn't you say the HR lady thought you had potential for promotion?"

"I think she was just trying to let me down easy when I got passed over for the Events job. She did tell me to come back and try again, though. She almost hinted that RJ wasn't willing to give me up just yet."

"What?" Evie sat up. "Did you ask him about it?"

"No." Brooke sighed. "I never even told him I'd applied. I thought it would be awkward if I got rejected."

"You'd better believe he knew about it. His family owns the company." Evie raised a brow. "They'd better not try any funny business, especially if you're pregnant. Then you'll really need the job."

"I know." Brooke hugged herself. "I've heard pregnant women can't even get health insurance these days unless it's through an employer."

"Don't panic yet. You don't even know if you are pregnant." Evie leaned forwards and rested her chin on tented hands. "Would you marry him?"

Brooke shrank under her inquiring stare. "You mean if I was pregnant?"

"Yes, and he decided to be a gentleman and face up to his responsibilities."

Brooke pulled further back into her chair. "Not if it was an obligation for him." What a horrible thought.

That RJ might feel compelled to marry her out of duty. "I'd hate that."

Not that he'd seemed at all inclined to propose this morning. His grim expression still haunted her mind, and he'd managed to be out of the office most of the day in "meetings" that weren't on the calendar. They'd made no more after-work plans.

Maybe this was the end?

Perhaps he'd simply grow more distant and there'd be no more mention of kisses or weekends in the mountains. They'd go back to sharing memos and emails, rather than hugs and sly glances.

Her hands grew cold just thinking about it.

Or worse, maybe he'd want her out of sight. She might get transferred to a "crucial position" at the dockyard, or maybe even one of the overseas offices. She'd lose her job—and her health insurance—just when she needed them most.

"Don't look so grim." Evie tapped her hand, drawing her back into the present. "No one's died yet!"

"Except RJ's father."

Evie grimaced. "I forgot. Poor RJ, he really does have it coming at him from all angles. Do they still think his mom did it?"

"Apparently so. She's still being held without bail."

"I bet if you could spring her you'd make him the happiest man alive."

"I'd love to, but that would mean knowing who murdered his dad." She didn't want to admit, even to Evie, that she was the person responsible for his mom being arrested. "Apparently there's a paper log kept at the security desk of everyone who enters and leaves the building, but the page for that day is missing."

"The killer must have taken it."

"I'd imagine so." The killer had been in the building with her that night. She suppressed a shiver. "It's scary knowing there's someone out there who could kill Reginald Kincaid in cold blood."

"And no one knows why."

"That's the weirdest part. I know RJ has suspicions about Reginald's oldest son, Jack, who he left a huge stake in the company to. He keeps his distance from the rest of the family, almost as if he has something to hide."

"Sounds very guilty."

"But apparently Reginald knew, or at least suspected, that someone was out to get him. He wrote letters to all the family members, to be read in the event of his death. If he suspected his son Jack, why would he leave him almost half his company?"

"Maybe it was RJ?" Evie lifted a brow. Humor glittered in her eyes, which was enough to prevent Brooke getting upset.

"Yes, and maybe he'll kill me next so I won't sue him for sexual harassment. His brother Matthew actually warned him I might do that."

"Would you?" Evie's eyes widened.

"Never. It was utterly consensual so I'd be a real loser if I sued."

"Might be easier than winning the lottery, though."

"I'd rather take my chances with the Powerball."

"I notice how you deftly dodged my question about RJ being the murderer. Just for the sake of argument, he does have motive. Maybe he found out about his dad's second family and was so mad he wanted revenge?"

Brooke shook her head. "That's not his style. He's too smart to risk spending his life in prison, for one thing. And he really loved his dad. It's easy to see. He told me about all the time they spent together at their cabin in the woods, and how much he misses him every day." Her heart filled with emotion just thinking about the look in his eyes when he spoke of his father.

"Shame, because discovering he's a killer would really help you go off him if things turn sour."

"Maybe this crisis will help us grow together."

"See, there you go again, looking for troubled waters to pour oil on. You need to find a nice, uncomplicated guy without a care in the world," Evie said.

"Except that I'm in love with RJ." She said it aloud, needing to admit it to her best friend as well as herself. The word *love* gave her a rush as it sounded in the air of her condo. "I truly am."

"I can tell." Evie tilted her head and gave Brooke a sympathetic look. "Go on. Call him. You know you want to." She looked at Brooke's phone where it sat on the coffee table next to her keys.

A rush of adrenaline prickled Brooke's fingers and toes. Did she dare? Maybe he'd be thrilled to hear from her and tell her to come on over. Then they could spend the night making love in his big bed and share a sleepy breakfast in their robes before walking to work together.

She picked up the phone and dialed his number.

"Who?" RJ stood up violently from his chair and shoved his hand through his hair. Matt was in his office, along with Laurel and corporate investigator Nikki Thomas. Tall, with shoulder-length black hair and blunt bangs that framed intense blue eyes, Nikki had found the private investigator RJ had hired to look into the murder. Tony Ramos, a tall man with a shaved head and a way of making you feel he could read every thought in your head. "We all know someone saw Mom here on the night of the murder. She told me so herself, but who the hell was it and why won't anyone tell me?"

"Yeah, who was it?" Matt paced in front of the door. They were all on edge, as the D.A.'s office had just turned down their umpteenth request for bail.

"Brooke Nichols."

The name fell like a stone in the crowded office. All eyes swiveled to RJ.

"You're kidding me." He looked from Matt to Laurel. Everyone in the room seemed frozen to the spot. He felt his head begin to pound. "It couldn't be Brooke. She would have said something."

Laurel swallowed, and Matt looked down at the carpet.

"You got this information from the police?" Anger and confusion rose and snarled in his chest. His phone started vibrating in his pocket, and he reached in to turn it off.

Ramos nodded. "Yes. They interviewed all the employees the next day, and there were only five people in the building after seven that evening. Unfortunately security only had people sign in on a paper log, and—as we all know—it went missing. These are the people who admitted to being there, and Jimmy, the security guard who was on duty that night, said these are also the only people he remembers seeing. Alex Woods, the night shipping clerk, Reginald himself, his wife, Elizabeth, and Brooke Nichols."

RJ blew out a hard breath. Brooke, the person he trusted more than anyone else in the world, had kept this from him. "Why didn't she tell me?"

"Maybe because she was afraid you'd react like this?" Laurel raised a brow. "All she did was tell the truth, RJ. Would you have wanted her to lie?"

"None of the others saw Mom?"

"Jimmy says she waved hello. Nothing out of the ordinary. Apparently Brooke later told the investigating officer Mrs. Kincaid seemed anxious, or stressed."

"Dammit." RJ banged his fist on the desk. "Poor Mom stuck in that place with all those criminals because of a thoughtless comment. Brooke couldn't possibly suspect Mom."

"I'm sure she doesn't, RJ." Matt rubbed his eyes. "This situation is a giant quicksand swamp that everyone is getting sucked into. What we need is to find the real killer. Any news on that, Tony?"

"The police have eliminated all the other people who were here from their inquiries, and I admit I've done the same. The only possibility is an intruder no one saw."

"We have security on the desk 24/7," said RJ. "We're in a competitive business, and shipping containers can hold a lifetime's worth of trouble so we're ultra conscious of who comes and goes from this building and all our other facilities. Everyone has to come through the lobby. There's no other way into the building."

The investigator narrowed his sharp eyes. "I've checked all the windows and the former cargo doors that were sealed shut. The building is as tight as one of your container ships. The assailant could only have come through the lobby. He also must have removed the log page at some point. Jimmy says the only time the desk is left unattended is when he goes to the bathroom. He said he always bolts the lobby doors before leaving the desk, and he's sure he did so that night." Tony looked from Laurel to RJ. "But when he came back from the can and went to unlock the door, the bolt was pulled."

"So someone left the building while he was in the bathroom." Laurel's hand flew to her mouth. "And it wasn't Mom because Jimmy said she left much earlier."

"Exactly," Nikki chimed in. "The big snag is, other than Jimmy's word, there's no concrete proof of when she left the building, and even if there was proof, she came and left right around the time of the murder."

"When did Brooke leave?" RJ's gut churned. He hated that she was now involved in this mess. His fury at her deception was tempered by worry that she'd be somehow implicated.

"She left at the same time as your mother. They came down in the elevator together. Apparently Brooke got on the elevator as Mrs. Kincaid came down from visiting your dad's office."

"But Brooke isn't a suspect."

"Nope. Never was."

RJ felt a small wave of relief. Then his head started to ache again when he wondered why she'd never told him any of this. They'd been intimate in every way. He'd shared stories about his dad that he'd never told anyone, and she never mentioned that she'd said anything to the police. Her behavior was bizarre and troubling, especially since the subject had been discussed openly with her in the room, including at the family dinner. Why had she kept such crucial information from him?

And what if she was pregnant, right now, with his baby? Choosing to have a baby was a huge, lifetime responsibility that should grow from careful thought and planning, not spring from a steamy night of sex. The situation was further complicated by him being her boss. At this point, that was a nightmare. He couldn't keep a straight face while she walked in and out of his office with letters and files, acting like everything was completely normal and they'd never done more than hold hands.

"RJ, are you still with us?"

"What?" He realized Matt had been talking to him.

"Tony wants to know if he should talk to Brooke, hear exactly what she told the police."

"No. I'll talk to her myself." He'd avoided her all day, wary of the effect her big green eyes had on him, but there was no avoiding the conversation they needed to have right now.

He tried hard to tug his attention back to the reason for this meeting. "We need to find out more about the suspected intruder. Has the building been combed for fingerprints?"

Tony shrugged. "This office building is fifty years old. There are tens of thousands of fingerprints on every surface."

"Dad redecorated his office not long ago." Laurel spoke up. "And surely the killer was in there."

"The police went over the office during the initial investigation. I'll talk to them about our new theory of a separate intruder who hid in the building and see what they have." Tony typed something into his laptop.

"Jack Sinclair is still top of my list." RJ looked from Tony to Nikki. "And now apparently he's spreading the word that he plans to use his new shares to make changes in the company. Nikki, didn't you say his car was parked in a nearby lot on the night of the murder?"

"Uh, I'm not sure it was his car. The police are still looking into it."

"You can use your skills to dig into his corporate activities and see if he's been working to damage our company."

"I'm not sure why he'd do that when he's the biggest shareholder."

"Am I sensing reluctance?" RJ frowned at her. Why did she keep finding excuses not to dig up dirt on Jack?

Nikki blinked and tucked a neat lock of black hair behind her ear. "Of course not. I'll look into the situation from all my usual angles. I'll report back as soon as I find anything."

RJ nodded. "And I'll talk to Brooke and see if she remembers anything else about that night." If he knew she was there he'd have asked her earlier. Even the tiniest shred of evidence in the right direction could get his mom out of jail, which was the most important thing right now.

More important than his affair with Brooke. When he was with Brooke, everything else faded into the background. He forgot about his responsibilities and worries. He needed to pull off the rose-tinted glasses and find out exactly what was going on in that sharp mind of hers. How could she have been so thoughtless?

When the others had left his office he pulled out his

phone and saw the call he missed was from Brooke. He pressed the button to return the call, and as soon as she picked up he said, "I'm coming over."

Nine

No amount of sun salutations could calm Brooke down after RJ's brusque phone call. He'd told her he'd be there in twenty minutes, then hung up. She rolled up her yoga mat and put it in the closet, then commenced to wiping down her kitchen countertops—again—like someone with obsessive-compulsive disorder.

She jumped a good few inches when she heard a loud knock on the door.

"Coming." She tried to steady her breathing as she pulled the latch.

RJ's fierce blue gaze hit her like a blast of icy air. He walked into the room, as tall and erect as a statue.

She closed the door. *Hi, RJ. How are you doing? Did you have a good day?* Normal pleasantries stuck in her throat.

"You told the police you saw my mother on the night

of the murder." He spoke quietly, but his voice held an edge of steel.

"Yes, I did." She managed to keep her voice from shaking. "I never suspected her, but I did see her as I was leaving, and when they asked me, I simply told them."

"Your testimony is the reason she's being held without bail. You're the reason they consider her a suspect."

She felt herself shrink under his gaze. "All I said was that she was in the elevator when it stopped on our floor, carrying a large bag."

"With dinner for my dad."

"I didn't know what was in the bag."

"You said she seemed…distressed." His eyes narrowed. She fought the urge to step back, away from the force of his fury.

"She had tears in her eyes, or the beginning of tears. And she looked anxious. I think that's what I said. It's hard to remember, it was weeks ago." She felt tears rise in her own eyes. "I never imagined they'd arrest her."

"You knew the police were investigating a murder and looking for suspects." His gaze bored into her.

"Yes." She swallowed. "All I did was tell them the truth."

"Why didn't you say anything to me? We've all been wondering why they're holding Mom without bail, and it's because of your testimony."

"Why?" She blinked back the tears that still threatened. "I suppose I knew you'd be angry."

His eyes flashed with a mix of anger and confusion. "I'm not angry that you spoke the truth, but for you to keep it secret all this time, while we were together and so intimate." He shook his head. "I don't understand it and it makes me feel like I don't know you, Brooke."

She took a step back, shrinking under the force of his stare. "I'm truly sorry I didn't say anything. I wanted to but the time never seemed right and then it was weird that I hadn't already told you." She hadn't wanted to mess up their budding romance. That seemed to have gone right down the toilet. She'd better hope nothing resulted from their little mistake last night. A thick, heavy sadness descended over her.

"Why didn't you tell me my mom looked upset? Don't you think I'd want to know?"

"I didn't see you until the next day when we all arrived to the news that your dad was dead. I never got a chance to talk to you in private until after the police interviewed me." She shivered slightly, remembering that terrible day. Yellow crime scene tape in Reginald's office, swarms of investigators everywhere, press jamming the doorway to the building.

"So you were one of the last people in the building before the murder."

She nodded. "I wish I could be more help in finding out who did it."

"Maybe you can." He rubbed his temples. "Did you notice anything unusual?"

She hesitated. "Your mother being there was unusual. I don't remember her bringing him dinner too often."

His eyes narrowed. "You do suspect her, don't you?"

"No, I'm just answering your question." She lifted her chin. She'd tried to do the right thing. It didn't occur to her at the time that her few words would lead to an arrest.

"She said she and Dad had an argument the night before, and he left for work in a mood, then called saying he'd be working late, so she decided to soften him up by bringing his favorite roast beef and potatoes." RJ crossed his arms. "Not exactly suspicious."

Brooke kept her mouth closed. She could see why the police were suspicious, especially given all the information about Reginald's infidelity that came to light after his death. She hadn't known about any of that when she spoke to the police.

The corner lamp in her living room threw RJ's strong features into high relief. Why did he have to be so handsome? Her life would be so much easier if her boss was a balding, middle-aged guy with a potbelly. Even now, with tension hardening the lines of his face and darkening his blue eyes, he was stunning. And the way he leaped in to defend his mom only showed what a loyal family man he was.

Her heart ached. "I so wish I'd seen someone else, or noticed anything strange. I've gone over that evening so many times in my head, but it was just a regular day in so many ways, until we discovered what happened."

"My dad was murdered within minutes of you leaving. The killer must have been in the building."

"What does your mom say? Did she see anyone?"

He shook his head. "No one. She said she went to Dad's office and the door was closed, so she knocked. He didn't answer, so she opened the door and he was sitting at his desk. He told her to go away."

"What?" She'd never heard Reginald speak that way to anyone.

"Yup. Nice, huh? She was totally shocked. She told him she brought dinner and he said he didn't want any and for her to go home, now. She said he almost growled it at her."

"That's terrible."

"And that's her last memory of my dad. Now she's in jail for killing him. And you just *forgot* to tell me you shared the elevator with her that night."

She lowered her eyes. "I'm so sorry, RJ."

"We need to take a break from each other. I'd like you to take a paid leave of absence, starting immediately." She glanced up, to see his brows lowered in a frown. "In fact, I'll double your pay if you'll stay home until things clear up around here."

Brooke's knees went weak. Did this mean she was fired? She'd already figured out that her relationship with RJ was over.

"Tasha can take over your duties in the meantime. If there's anything personal at the office, I'll have her send it here."

She felt like she'd been slapped. RJ's pained expression tugged at her heart and she wanted to reach out to him and say she never meant to hurt his mom, but he wanted her to vanish.

"I'll get my laptop. Tasha will need it." Her voice barely rose above a whisper. She tried her best to keep tears out of her voice. She moved to her work bag, which was near the kitchen table, and fished out her laptop. Her hand trembled as she handed it to RJ. Her fingers brushed his thumb as he took it from her and she steeled herself against the jolt of energy that passed between them.

Last night she'd lain in his bed. Tonight she'd sleep here alone.

RJ was already at the door. "Your increased pay will

be wired directly into your account. You will not return to work until further notice." He avoided her gaze. He hesitated with his hand on the door handle. "But if you learn of anything...unexpected..."

Her mind flew to his reaction this morning when he realized they forgot to use a condom.

"I'll call you if anything important happens." Her voice sounded so tiny, like it was coming from far away.

RJ turned one time to look at her, eyes hooded and face set in a hard line, then he tugged open the door, stepped out and closed it firmly behind him.

Brooke collapsed onto the sofa, and the tears flowed like summer rain. This beat all the bad outcomes she'd imagined for their relationship. Obviously she hadn't been creative enough in imagining how things could go wrong. He'd literally ordered her to keep away from him, and was paying her twice her salary to stay out of his sight.

She hugged herself, suddenly cold. If only she'd told him sooner about her encounter with his mother. He might still have been annoyed that she told the police, but he could hardly blame her. Her secrecy, however—born of cowardice—was inexcusable. She knew that. His anger was justified, and seared her like a hot brand.

RJ slammed the door of his Porsche and fired up the engine. His entire body was on fire with rage and hurt. Brooke had been his port in this crazy ongoing tempest, and all the time he'd held her, and lain with her and kissed her, she'd neglected to tell him that she had identified his mom at the scene of his father's murder.

You really couldn't ever know people. His father's

untimely passing and the wake of chaos it left behind should have hammered that home. Everyone had secrets that grew and tangled like briars, snaring them in a web of deception.

He roared through the streets, wishing he could drive fast enough to blow right out of this dimension into another life where none of this was happening.

He wanted to go visit his mom, but he hadn't obtained special permission to see her in person and the thought of talking to her via a video monitor made his chest hurt. It was past visiting hours anyway.

He swung into the underground parking of his building and pulled into his space. For a moment he rested his head and hands on the wheel. How could he face going back to his empty apartment when only last night he and Brooke had shared such a joyful night? At least until he realized how his foolish mistake could have ruined everything. The last thing any of them needed at a time like this was an unexpected pregnancy.

He hauled himself out of the car and took the elevator up to his apartment. As expected the large space seemed chill and empty. He'd barely even been there without Brooke for the last couple of weeks. They'd grown so used to each other's company that it seemed stranger for them to be apart than together.

The answering machine light flashed green, so he walked over and pressed the button. "RJ, it's Lily. Mom's been released! The lobby door being unbolted from the inside late at night was enough to make her eligible for bail. She's on her way home right now. Come over and join us for a celebration."

"Yes!" RJ did a fist pump. "About time." He picked up the phone and dialed Lily. "I'll be right there."

Glad to leave the lonely space of his apartment, he almost ran back to the elevator. It was as quick to walk to the family mansion as to drive, so he set off along Charleston's familiar streets with renewed vigor. Despite everything that had happened with Brooke, his heart soared with relief that his mom was out of that grim place, back in her beloved home.

Her body felt frail and thin when he hugged her in the front hallway of her house. "I'm desperate to style my hair." She patted her dark hair self-consciously. "My gray roots were previously a secret between my hairdresser and myself. I'll have to see if he can squeeze me in first thing tomorrow." Her soft, old-Charleston lilt was music to his ears.

"I can see you have your priorities straight, Mom." Kara squeezed her again. They all crowded around her in the big family room, crackling with excited energy. "You need a lavish dinner after all that jailhouse food."

"I think I'll make my fortune by writing a book called *The Prison Diet*." She glanced down at her shrunken frame. "I thought I was slender before, but apparently there was plenty of room for improvement if you believe the old saying you can never be too rich or too thin."

"I'm glad your sense of humor survived intact," said RJ. "We Kincaids take some serious lickings."

"Where's Brooke? I heard she came for dinner on Sunday." His mom's sharp green eyes met his.

He hesitated. His mom didn't need to hear any bad news. "She's at home."

"Why don't you invite her to join us?"

RJ glanced at Matt. He knew, as did the others, that Brooke had kept her words with the police secret. Part of him yearned to pick up the phone and invite her back into their lives, but some cooler, more practical instinct told him to maintain distance. "I think it's better if we enjoy your newfound freedom as a family." He didn't comment on the fact that Susannah and Lily and Laurel's fiancés had joined them. He wasn't engaged to Brooke, after all.

"I hope my newfound freedom is permanent. And you all better hope I don't skip out on the two million dollars bail they made you post."

"Cheap at the price, Mom." Matt kissed her slim cheek.

Kara handed Elizabeth a glass of champagne she'd poured. "And if you skip you'd better take us with you. I don't think any of us could stand that kind of separation again."

"Much as I hate everything that's happened to our family in the last few months, there's no denying it's brought us closer than ever." Laurel sat on the sofa next to Eli.

"And now you guys can really start planning your wedding." Kara's eyes lit up. "Mom, Laurel wouldn't even look at invitations until you were released."

"Oh, I think we need some time for things to settle, don't we?" Laurel looked at Eli.

"Sure, yes. A lot going on right now." He patted her hand in a reassuring way. "We have the rest of our lives to plan our wedding."

"Of course you do." Elizabeth Kincaid smiled at the handsome pair. "No sense rushing into marriage. It's a big commitment and sometimes involves a good deal of sacrifice."

RJ could understand Laurel's reluctance to launch into marriage. Especially now they knew their parents' marriage wasn't quite the rosy union they'd grown up imagining.

"Mom." Lily leaned forward. "Did you really know about Dad's second family?"

She hesitated for a moment, then nodded. "Not all the time. Just the last couple of years. I didn't see any reason to burden the rest of you with the news."

"It wasn't right for you to bear it alone." Lily stroked their mom's arm.

"Maybe that's the only way I could bear it." She shrugged her shoulders. "It's a lot harder now the secret's out, and when anyone looks at me I wonder if that's what they're thinking about. Have those two boys been causing any trouble?"

"Jack's stayed out of the picture." RJ frowned at the very thought of Reginald's true oldest son. "So who knows what he's up to. If you ask me he's responsible for the murder. I still can't believe Dad gave him a controlling share of the company." He shook his head and blew out a disgusted breath.

"Alan's been lovely, though," Kara chimed in. "He's really quite sweet. I know he was devastated to hear that you'd been arrested, and he's been very supportive. He seems quite keen to become part of the family, even though he's not related by blood."

"Well, perhaps that's something good to come out of this mess. We Kincaids can always stretch to welcome a new family member." His mom's smile warmed RJ's heart. "And what a relief it is to be back in my own home, surrounded by all of you."

They took champagne glasses from a tray and raised a toast. Still, despite the bubbly and festive mood, a cold sorrow settled in RJ's gut. Brooke should be here. He still resented that she hadn't told him about her talk with the police, but she'd woven herself tightly into the fabric of his life and his arms now felt empty without her in them. He missed her with a painful ache he'd never known before. Was this love? If so it wasn't exactly a happy feeling.

"You okay, RJ?" Laurel nudged him. "You look a bit dazed."

"Overwhelmed, I guess." He took a bracing swig of champagne. "I'll be fine." Already he regretted driving Brooke away in such a cold and cruel manner. Paying her to stay away from him? His shock and anger had gotten the better of him.

And what if she was pregnant? For a single, mad instant, he had a vision of Brooke gazing, with her kind, loving expression, at their baby.

He took another swig. Everything was moving so fast and he didn't know where he'd be from one day to the next. Jack could take over the company and boot him out. The last thing he needed was to establish some kind of permanent relationship. He'd better keep his options open and his feet ready to dodge bullets.

Still, he had to apologize to her.

"Dinner's ready!" Pamela opened the door bearing a steaming dish of food. "Come into the dining room. I set the table already."

The apology would have to wait. He was needed

here for now. RJ followed the others into the elegant dining room, where the silver cloche opened to reveal their mom's favorite roast lamb and potatoes au gratin. Matt poured wine and they settled down to enjoy their first real family dinner since the arrest.

"Okay, let me get this straight." Evie's voice emerged from Brooke's phone, set on speakerphone so she could pace around her living room. "Since I was at your house—oh, two hours ago—and you were telling me you loved RJ, he's now dumped you and fired you."

Brooke inhaled an unsteady breath. She'd already cried once; surely she could keep the tears in for now. "That's pretty much it. I'm not technically fired. I'm on paid leave. In fact he was so keen to get rid of me that he's paying me more to stay home than I'd get to come to the office. He's furious with me."

"All because you neglected to mention that you shopped his mom to the cops."

"Evie! Are you my friend?"

"I'm teasing. You didn't tell him because you thought he'd dump you and fire you. Apparently you were right." She could tell Evie found this slightly funny. "I'm thinking he's not quite so fabulous as you originally told me."

"He's a very passionate, proud family man. He was raised to be head of the Kincaid family, and they come first. I admire that."

"Even when it means you come last?"

Brooke bit her lip hard. "I wish the two weren't mutually exclusive. If I could figure out a way to get his mom out of jail, he might forgive me."

"Elizabeth Kincaid is out of jail!" Evie's voice boomed out of the tiny phone. "I saw it on the news not fifteen minutes ago. She's been granted bail."

"She's out?" RJ hadn't told her. Then again, why would he? He didn't want anything to do with her. Her heart crumpled.

"They showed a video of her leaving the jail. She's one of those people who manages to look like a society matron even in that situation, polite smile at the cameras, and all that."

"That is good news." She shoved a hand through her hair. "RJ must be thrilled. I wonder if they know who the real killer is." If his mom was truly freed, he might not be so angry with her anymore.

"From what you said, it sounds like you and Elizabeth Kincaid were there right at the time the murder was committed. Did you see or hear anything odd?"

"The building was pretty much empty. But apparently the intruder hid somewhere after the murder and crept out when the guard was in the bathroom."

"So they probably snuck in well before the murder. Were there any unfamiliar people around the office?"

"I didn't notice any but it was a very crazy day. There were at least three big meetings, one of them offsite at the architects. I had a terrible time struggling back with all those blueprints." A thought struck her. She stopped pacing and stood still in the center of the room. An entire, fully formed memory sprang into her head. "My God, the blueprints. I brought them to talk with RJ about the plans for the new retail development on the waterfront. RJ went off to a meeting and I came back to the office with armfuls of blueprints. It was right before closing and pouring rain and I ran from the car park to the front door, trying not to get them wet, but I couldn't get into the revolving door."

Suddenly the whole scene was crystal clear in her mind. The fish smell of the rainstorm, her face and hair wet in the heavy shower, big drops splashing on the crucial blueprints.

And a man in a raincoat, who took half of the blueprints, opened the revolving door for her, and stepped in with her.

They'd emerged on the other side and she'd thanked him profusely as he handed back the rest of the tall cylinders of paper, then they'd walked to the bank of elevators. He didn't get in with her, and that was the last she saw of him.

But he hadn't stopped to sign in at the security desk.

"Brooke, have you been struck dumb?"

"The man, who came through the door with me. He was quite tall, but not quite as tall as RJ." Why did her thoughts spring so readily back to him? "He wore one of those felt hats, you know, the Indiana Jones kind."

"I call those jerk hats, because that's the kind of person who usually wears them. In fact my last boyfriend before—"

"Evie! This is important. His hat was dripping from the rain, and he had little round glasses, the kind with the metal rim, thick lenses, so you could barely see his eyes."

"What about his features. Did you recognize him?"

"No. He had a beard and moustache. Damn, I can't remember the color. Gray, maybe? He was an older guy. And he had a Boston accent, I remember it. You know the kind. *I pahked the cahr in Hahrvad Yahd*."

Evie laughed aloud. "He sounds very suspicious."

"He didn't stand out much at the time. The coat and hat kind of fit, with the rain. It was so wet, and dark, one of those intense, stormy days. Besides, we get quite a few characters at the office, especially since we've branched into real estate. You wouldn't believe the kind of people who just happened to own a derelict dock in North Jersey."

"Or Massachusetts."

"Exactly. I didn't really think anything of it, but since it was five everyone was leaving, security was in the middle of a shift change and he was with me so he breezed by the security desk without anyone stopping him."

"When he wasn't actually with you."

"No. Not at all."

"He could have been waiting for that opportunity."

"I suppose so." A tingle of anticipation—or was it fear—shot up Brooke's spine. "I think this is important."

"You should call RJ and tell him."

For a moment her fingers itched to hang up on Evie and dial RJ immediately. Then an awful thought occurred to her. "Do you think RJ will be happy to hear I let the killer into the building?" If anything, this made things worse.

"Since he's mad at you already, what's the harm?"

Brooke hugged herself, and stared out the window onto the dark street. "I think I should call and tell the police. I can't believe I never thought of this when I first spoke to them. Then again, maybe this guy had a reason to be there? Perhaps he's not relevant at all."

"Or maybe you've just helped to identify Reginald Kincaid's murderer. RJ will be over the moon that you've cleared his mother of all suspicion, and he'll run right over there and ask you to marry him."

Bright moonlight fell at an angle on the cars parked outside, casting long, sharp daggers of light that fell through her window and across her carpet. "I doubt it."

Ten

"Where's Brooke?" Matt appeared in RJ's office doorway, then cast a glance back at Brooke's empty desk.

RJ shoved a hand through his hair. His chest ached and his head hurt. "On a leave of absence." He said it coolly, hoping Matt would drop the subject.

"Is she sick?" His brother looked worried.

"Nope. I just thought it better if she was home for a while. Things were getting too complicated."

Matt cocked his head. "Don't say I didn't warn you."

RJ stood up from his chair and stretched. Or tried to. Every muscle in his body was tight as a bowstring. He felt Brooke's absence like a missing limb. The office seemed dark and empty without her sunny presence. "I didn't plan it. What a cliché, to have an affair with my assistant. I lost my mind."

And then I lost my heart. He cursed the unwanted

thought that sprang into his brain. Another cliché. Mom read him too much poetry when he was a kid.

Matt moved in and closed the door. "Is she making threats?"

"God, no."

"You're angry she didn't tell you she saw Mom on the night of the murder."

"I was angry. I'm still confused by it. And there's something else." Adrenaline pulsed through him. He picked up a paperweight on his desk and studied it in the light. A tiny model ship trapped in glass, sailing nowhere.

Matt raised a brow. "Care to tell me?"

"I forgot to use a condom."

His brother's eyes widened. "You think she's pregnant?"

"No idea yet, but she could be. Can you see how things were getting complicated?" His heart squeezed. Was Brooke sitting somewhere alone and worried? He cursed the violent urge to take her in his arms and comfort her.

"What a mess. Still, it's not nice to banish her when she's worrying about it, too. She didn't mean to get mom into trouble."

"We needed some space. Things were too intense." At least that's how he tried to explain the strange commotion of feelings that left him unsettled and edgy.

"You miss her, don't you?"

RJ placed the paperweight back on the desk with a thud. "I don't know how I feel. Too much happening all at once."

"I know the feeling." Matt grinned. "It all came

thick and fast between me and Susannah. I think you should go with your gut instincts."

"I'm not sure I have any." His gut was in turmoil right now, maybe because he couldn't face breakfast. Or because he couldn't face a day without Brooke in it. "Besides, we have work to do. To make Jack Sinclair richer." He attempted a wry grin.

Matt crossed his arms. "Don't change the subject."

"Why not? Isn't that what we're doing here? You'd think Jack would be here himself pitching in, since he owns forty-five percent of the company. And what's with Nikki stalling on digging into his books?" Phew. He'd managed to get off the topic of Brooke.

Matt shrugged. "I don't think she suspects him of murder as much as you do."

"Me? What about you?"

"I barely know the guy. Too soon to draw any conclusions. Things aren't always what they seem. Besides, I heard from Tony that the police have new eyewitness testimony about a strange man in the building on the day of the murder."

He sat up. "That's great. Details?"

"An older guy in a trilby, with a Boston accent." Matt shrugged. "I can't think of any clients with Boston accents, can you?"

RJ shook his head. "No, but this is great news. I'm going to call Tony for the full scoop. Hopefully they'll drop all charges against Mom and we can put that ugly chapter behind us."

"Brooke is the new eyewitness. Apparently she called the police last night after remembering the man."

RJ froze. Could Brooke have made this new suspect up? For a moment he cursed himself for the disloyal thought. But he didn't trust Brooke anymore. The realization hit him like a fist to the gut.

"Why the grim expression?" Matt shrugged off his jacket and threw it over his arm.

"Seems very convenient that she suddenly remembers a mysterious intruder, right after everyone's angry with her for surreptitiously fingering Mom."

Matt stepped forward and clapped his hand on RJ's upper arm. "Bro, you're all on edge, but Brooke is not the type to lie. That's why she told the police the truth in the first place. We've both worked with her long enough to know it."

Emotion gripped his chest like a nutcracker. He knew Matt was right. "She never did lie, she just didn't tell me the whole truth." He rubbed his forehead. "Because she was afraid the truth would upset me. If anything, it's my fault she kept silent." He blew out a hard breath. "I owe her an apology." His neurons fired with energy, spurring him forward. "I'm going over to her house."

Matt grinned. "Glad to hear it. I hope she'll forgive you for overreacting."

RJ grabbed his jacket off the back of the chair and pulled it on. "Me, too."

Brooke didn't know what to do. It was midmorning and usually she'd have sorted through a ream of mail and coordinated several schedules and possibly attended a meeting or two. This morning all she'd done was drink a cup of coffee (decaf in case she was pregnant), do some halfhearted yoga poses and dust her bookshelves. She'd be wise to start looking for another job, but she didn't have the heart.

She let out a long sigh and poured the dregs of her coffee into the kitchen sink. She felt like someone had taken a hunting knife to her chest and cut her heart right out of it. All the excitement and happiness of yesterday had crashed and burned so fast she was still too numb to even react properly. She knew pain was coming but right now she was still too shocked and dazed for it to touch her.

How quickly RJ had gone from cherishing her to despising her. He must have never really cared about her in the first place. A sharp pang of disappointment stung her. She still cared about him. She should be angry with him for dismissing her so harshly, but she couldn't blame him. He was under stress and his family came first. She knew both those things before they got involved.

It was her own stupid fault she wasn't brave enough to tell the truth about seeing his mom there that evening and telling the police. Now he'd learn that she let the killer into the building, which was hardly likely to help him forgive her.

She brought her empty coffee cup down on the sideboard with a light thunk. What a mess. Still, time to get dressed. No sense spending the day moping around in her pajamas. If she was pregnant she'd need to be strong for her child, and she might as well start now, just in case.

She'd turned on the shower and started to take off her PJs when the doorbell rang. She frowned. The mail had already been delivered and no one could expect her home at this time. She pulled her T-shirt back down again, turned off the water. Maybe it was the police. She'd spoken to a detective at the station yesterday and they said they might want to speak to her again. She grabbed a robe off the back of the door and slid her arms into it. She couldn't face those flint-eyed officers in her heart-print shorts and top.

As she slid back the chain and undid the lock she couldn't stop a massive, painful flash of hope that it might be RJ on the other side. This in no way diminished her surprise when she opened the door to his tall, imposing presence on her doorstep, dressed in a dark suit.

"May I come in?" His deep voice barely penetrated her shock. She hadn't said a word.

Her pulse now pounded hard and fast. "Yes." She stepped aside and he walked in. Didn't try to kiss her. Didn't shake hands. Still, a rush of energy crashed through her as his body passed within inches of hers.

She closed the door behind him and turned to face him, still no idea what to say. Why was he here?

His bold blue eyes met hers. "I've missed you."

"I've missed you, too." The words fell from her mouth. So much for playing it cool. "Very much." She bit her lip to stop more confessions pouring forth.

"I've come to apologize." His eyes darkened. Brooke held her breath. "Banishing you from the office was out of line. I've been on edge, upset about my mom being in jail. I overreacted to hearing that you were the eyewitness." Morning light shone through the window onto his hard profile.

"I should have told you it was me. I kept trying to pluck up the courage to tell you, but I was so afraid you'd be angry, and I only made it worse."

His expression softened. "My behavior proved you were right. I flew off the handle and it was inappropriate." He hesitated. The air thickened with tension and anticipation until Brooke felt faint. "I'm sorry."

Sorry. Her heart sank. What had she hoped for? He was sorry. For sending her home. For sleeping with her without a condom. For sleeping with her at all. For kissing her. For ever hiring her in the first place...

Her head hurt and she fought to keep herself from shaking, as RJ's tall presence filled her living room.

"Brooke." He stepped forward, and again, pathetic hope rushed through her like a burst water main. He took her hands. Her fingers tingled and heated inside his. "All these years we worked together, sitting in meetings and discussing correspondence and spending all day with each other." She held herself steady. "And all along I never realized I was working side by side with the perfect woman for me."

She blinked. The perfect woman for him? Her tongue seemed stuck in her mouth. Surely she should say something here, but no words rose from her confused and anxious brain.

"I love you, Brooke." His voice deepened as he said the words, and something dark and powerful flashed in his eyes. "I've felt empty and hollow every second I've been without you. All I could think about is coming to see you, to hold you in my arms, and beg you to forgive my cruel behavior. When I thought I might have made you pregnant I panicked about making our lives more complicated than they already are."

He hesitated, frowned slightly, and looked away. Brooke's stomach turned over. Doubts crept back into her mind. Maybe he was just here trying to "do the right thing" in case she was pregnant. Her hands grew cold inside the cocoon of his fingers.

"Brooke, I want to marry you." His eyes met hers again, with a jolt. "I want to have children with you. I want to spend the rest of my life with you." His words, spoken fast and gruff, wrapped around her and swirled through her mind. Did she imagine them? Was this some kind of crazy dream or delusion? It couldn't possibly be happening, right here in her living room, on an ordinary weekday morning.

Could it?

"Brooke, are you okay?"

"I…I don't know." She searched his face. His strong features were taut with emotion. "What did you say?" Her ears must be deceiving her.

One of his dimples appeared. "I said I want to marry you." His eyes twinkled. "You, Brooke Nichols, and me, RJ Kincaid, getting married."

She drew in a ragged breath. He wanted to marry her? Her heart soared, then her excitement screeched to a halt again. Better clear the air. "Is this because I might be pregnant?"

"Not in the least. I want to live the rest of my life with you, for better or for worse. For richer for poorer. All that stuff. How does that sound?"

"It sounds…good." Joy sparkled over her. What an insane roller coaster her life had been lately. Suddenly she'd shot up the ladder to the top of the game board again, and could hear party whistles and see streamers as she approached the final square. Images of her and RJ, walking down a church aisle hand in hand, flooded her mind. "Really good."

Then something hit her like an icy thunderbolt.

RJ didn't know that she had likely let his father's

killer into the building. That she was, in some way, responsible for his dad's death.

Her joy drained away.

"What's the matter? You've turned pale." RJ's dimples disappeared again.

"You don't know, do you?"

"Know what?"

She swallowed. Her hands tightened into cold fists inside his grasp. "I let the killer into the building."

RJ dropped her hands as if they burned. "What are you talking about?"

Pain trickled through her as his expression darkened. She inhaled a shaky breath. "I remembered, when I thought hard, that a strange man came through the revolving doors with me. I didn't think anything of it at the time, since I didn't know him. There's no record of him and no one knows who he is. In all likelihood he went to hide somewhere, and then…" She gulped. "Shot your dad later that night."

She looked down at the floor, not wanting to see RJ's appalled expression.

"Matt told me you'd seen someone and that you spoke to the police again." His voice was strangely hollow. "He didn't say you opened the door for him."

"He was just another person hurrying into the building on a stormy afternoon. It was right at the end of the day. I didn't really even register him at the time." Tears rose inside her. "I'm so, so sorry." She looked up, to find RJ's eyes filled with pain.

But instead of striding away, he stepped toward her and took her in his arms. "I know you'd never do anything to hurt my family, or the company." His warmth enveloped her, and the stirring male scent of him soothed her ragged nerves. "We all know that." He pulled away from her long enough to look her in the eye. "No one blames you for Dad's death. The good part is now we have a real suspect and the police can go after him." She shuddered as he buried his face in her neck and his breath heated her skin. "And I can't even tell you how much I've missed you." His words swirled around her, spoken with gruff passion.

"I've missed you, too." Her voice sounded so small. Her heart filled so fast with all the hope and love she'd locked away in the last day, thinking she'd never need it again. He'd told her he loved her! "I love you, RJ. A part of me has loved you for years, but since we became close…" Words failed her, which didn't matter because RJ's mouth covered hers in a heady kiss.

He pulled her tight against his muscled chest and she sank into his strength. When their lips parted, she felt his chest fill with a mighty breath. "God, Brooke, I couldn't stand my life without you in it. Can you ever forgive me for being such a jerk?"

His wry expression almost made her laugh. "You were under stress. You're still under stress."

"We all are, but that's no excuse for the way I behaved. I'll do anything in my power to make it up to you." His face hovered close to hers, kissing and nuzzling her, stirring sparks of arousal that mingled with her joy to create an electric atmosphere.

"I don't want anything from you." She stroked his hair, and relished the rough feel of his hard cheek against hers. "I just want you."

RJ's ragged breath revealed the depth of his emotion. "And I just want you. Will you, Brooke? Will you marry me?"

"Yes." The tiny voice emerged from somewhere deep inside her. Somewhere hope had survived during all the drama and upset of the last few weeks. "I will."

They held each other tight, half-afraid some fresh drama would fly in through the window to blow them apart again. They stayed silent for some time, then RJ spoke. "It's okay if you're pregnant. In fact, it's more than okay." He pulled back far enough to meet her eyes. "Once again I overreacted and lost sight of the big picture. I'd love to have a child with you, Brooke."

Her chest tightened, or was it her heart that swelled even further? "Me, too." She smiled. "Though there's an excellent chance that I'm not pregnant, so don't get too excited. I wasn't at the right place in my cycle."

"Then we'll just have to try again." Hope sparkled in his eyes. "Because I see us having a big family."

Brooke swallowed. She'd always dreamed of a house filled with children, so unlike her solitary childhood. "I'd love to have a big family, like yours."

"Then we'll need a big house. Maybe a historic one near downtown? Or would you prefer something out in the suburbs?"

"I love downtown. It's nice to be able to walk to the shops, and restaurants. And work." She froze. Work. Would they keep working together after they were married, or would that be too weird?

RJ raised a brow. "Are you thinking what I'm thinking?"

"I'm not quite telepathic enough to know. But I was wondering if I'm still banished from the office."

"Definitely not. But I think you should move into your own office. You've done enough time manning the desk outside mine. I think it's time you're promoted to management."

Brooke blinked. So he had remembered their conversation where she'd shared her career goals? The subject hadn't come up again so she'd tried to forget about it. "I'd love that. I'm happy to work at The Kincaid Group in any capacity, but I'd like to stretch myself and develop new skills that can help the company."

RJ laughed. "Hey, you're not on a job interview. I already know you're an organizational genius. And if things go south with Jack Sinclair running the show, maybe we can start our own company together."

She smiled. "That might be fun."

"I think anything we do together will be fun, as long as we can keep our perspective, and I promise I've learned a lot about myself over the last day or so." He took a deep breath. "From now on I'll put our relationship first and everything else second. Or even third." His dimples appeared. "Or fourth."

A sudden thought clouded Brooke's happiness. "What will your mom think about us?"

"She'll be thrilled." He stroked her cheek. "I couldn't understand why no one, including her, would tell me who the eyewitness was. Later I realized she didn't want me to know it was you. She really likes you. She asked about you several times during dinner last night."

"She doesn't mind that I'm not from local aristocracy?" She couldn't help voicing the worry that had nagged at her from the first time RJ asked her out.

"Not at all. Mom judges people on their own merits, not the arcane rules of the society she was born into.

That's why she married my dad, even though a lot of the local snobs thought him beneath her."

"I don't think I'll ever understand the rules of Charleston society."

"Don't waste time trying, because they don't make any sense." He kissed her on the nose, which brought a smile to her lips. "We'll make our own rules to live by."

Their mouths met in a kiss that melted the tension in her body and replaced it with a flush of pleasure. RJ's arms enclosed her in their protective circle. Everything they'd been through hadn't torn them apart forever, but had pulled them closer together.

"Rule number one," she breathed, when they finally parted lips for a few moments. "No shoving me off on paid leave when I get on your nerves."

RJ winced. "I made a real ass of myself. If you can't ever forgive me for that, I can understand."

"I'll let you off just this one time." She dotted a kiss on the end of his nose. "Since you're devastatingly handsome." The sheepish look in his slate blue eyes made her smile.

"That's quite a compliment coming from the loveliest woman in Charleston."

"Flatterer."

"It's all true. Best figure, too." He squeezed her rear. "And since I seem to have talked my way back from the brink of disaster, I hope I'll be sharing a bed with it tonight." He grew still and his gaze darkened. "You did say you'd marry me, didn't you?"

Brooke chewed her lip and pretended to look confused. "Did I?"

"I think you did but it might have been wishful thinking."

She shrugged her shoulders. Arousal trickled through her like hot liquid. "It's been a confusing time, lately. Maybe we should stop talking and just go to bed right now."

RJ's dimples appeared. "That's the best idea I've heard in a long time."

* * * * *

HIS SECRETARY'S
LITTLE SECRET

CATHERINE MANN

To my animal rescue pals
everywhere – especially Virginia, Sharon
and Tiffany. You bring such talent, joy and
support to this emotional journey!

One

Portia Soto's mama always said doctors didn't grow on trees. That an exotic name couldn't make up for her plain looks. And to count her blessings if she got a proposal from a podiatrist twice her age.

Clearly, Portia's mama hadn't counted on her daughter ever sitting beneath a towering palm watching Dr. Easton Lourdes hang upside down by his knees as he tried to save an ivory-billed woodpecker. An endangered species and thus warranting the wildlife preserve veterinarian's full attention. Which was convenient, since that meant he wouldn't notice he'd totally captured Portia's.

Between the branches of the ancient black mangrove, small stars winked into her vision, the lingering violet of sunset fading into black. The moments just after sunset in the wildlife preserve were Portia's favorite. Night birds trilled overlapping tunes through the dense, steamy woods. Everything seemed somehow prettier, more lush and flamboyant in the absence of sunlight—the preserve transformed into a decadent Eden. At night, the place was a mysterious beauty, far more enticing than Portia had ever considered herself to be.

Except she didn't feel much like herself when she was around Dr. Lourdes.

To be frank, Easton was hot. Really hot. Sexy in a shaggy-haired, unconventional way. An extremely wealthy heir to a family fortune, and a genius veterinarian with a specialty in exotic animals.

He also happened to be the unsuspecting father of Portia's unborn baby, thanks to one impulsive night during a tropical storm nearly two months ago.

In the time that had passed since their unplanned hookup, she'd done her best to put their relationship back on a professional level, to safeguard her hard-won space and independence. A task that had been increasingly difficult to stick to, what with him casting steamy, pensive looks her way when he thought she wasn't aware.

But wow, was she ever aware of him. Always.

So apparently, for Portia, doctors did grow on trees. But that didn't stop the chaos overtaking her life in spite of her best efforts to carefully organize and control her world. She wanted to figure out her plan for the future before she told her onetime lover about their baby. But she was running out of time.

They'd had an impulsive encounter during the stress and fear of being in close quarters during a tropical storm. Such an atypical thing for her to do—have a one-night stand, much less a one-night stand with her boss. She'd always followed the rules, and she'd denied her attraction to Easton until the tension of that tumultuous frightful storm had led her to give in.

She'd enjoyed every moment of that night, but the next morning she'd freaked out. She'd worried about putting her much-needed job and on-site housing in jeopardy—and about how intensely being with Easton had moved her. She didn't have time for messy emotions, much less a relationship. She'd been living day to day, working to keep her head above water financially, especially since her brother had started college four years ago.

Now she had no choice but to think about the future for her child. Her need to establish her independence had to be placed on the fast track for her child's sake. She refused to let her baby have the unsure life she herself had lived through because of her parents' lack of any care or planning for their children's welfare.

The thought of the future nudged Portia into movement. A small movement, of course. It wasn't as if she could just run out of here and leave her boss without the spotlight she was holding. Her hand fell to her still smooth stomach covered by a loose T-shirt layered over trim cargo shorts—her fieldwork basics. Neatly pressed, of course.

A leaf plummeted to the ground with surprising speed. Ten more fell down from the limb above her head, reminding Portia to pay attention to the man above her.

"Can you adjust the spotlight to the left?"

"Sure, how far?"

"To the left."

Ah, nice and vague. Her favorite sort of directions. "Four inches? Twelve inches?"

"Move and I'll tell you when to stop."

"That works—" Portia checked her response. She'd

been second-guessing herself more than ever since that night. Things that hadn't bothered her before now suddenly worried her.

"Stop."

Four inches. She'd moved four flipping inches. How much easier would it have been for him to say that?

She sighed. She was irritable, nauseated and her swollen breasts hurt like crazy. She needed a new bra ASAP. Under cover of the dark, she repositioned one poking end away from her tender flesh. "Can you see now?"

"Almost got it. Just have to stretch farther."

The syllables also stretched, just as she imagined his fingers were doing. Always dramatic. Which was part of his allure...

A cracking sound popped through the night. Portia looked up into the twisted web of branches, her eyes desperately trying to process the image before her. She watched Easton fall out of the black mangrove in what felt like slow motion. He was a silhouetted rush of leaves and flailing limbs, culminating in an echoing thud as he hit the ground. The chorus of nighttime birds stopped as if they too were interested in the doctor's fate.

Panic filled her veins. Her feet and hands grew numb but she pushed them into motion. Fast.

He didn't move, and from her distance, she couldn't see if his chest rose and fell. "Easton!"

His name was a plea and a command to answer all at once. His limbs were splayed out inches from the tree trunk. He'd barely missed landing on the protruding roots. From the muted light, it looked like he had barely avoided impaling himself on a decaying tree limb.

She closed in on him, crouched down to examine him.

Thank the Lord, he was breathing. She felt his pulse. It was strong, but he didn't respond to her touch.

Laying a hand on his shoulder, she gently shook him. Wanting him to be okay. Needing him to be okay. The thought of him hurt sent her mind tumbling into the land of what-if? She'd become adequate at shoving the big what-ifs aside, but with the father of her future child lying unconscious, worst-case scenarios flooded her mind.

What if she didn't get to tell him about the baby? What if he was in a coma? What if…

What if his eyes—sharp blue as lapis lazuli—opened and he continued to look at her like *that*? Her wild thoughts halted as she saw his mischievous gaze trace her outline in the dark.

"I'm alright but don't let that make you move," he muttered, the right corner of his lips pulling up with sexy confidence.

His dark hair curled around his neck—twigs and branches adorning his head like the crown of some mythical forest prince. A sexy prince at that. Her hand lingered on his wrist, making her recall the night they'd spent together. The way he'd held her. She had carefully avoided his touch since they'd woken up to safety and a return to their normal working relationship—since finding out she carried his baby. Everything felt complicated.

She wanted to bolt away. Pushing her back into the neighboring Florida buttonwood tree, she swallowed hard. She didn't know how much longer she could keep her job, living in her cabana on the refuge, and hide the truth. There just wasn't time to save all the money she would need to be independent before the truth became obvious. The panic nearly made her lose her breath, but she pushed it aside as she'd been doing for weeks.

Yes, she would tell him. He deserved to know. But she wanted to get through that initial doctor's appointment first, and each day gave her more time to organize her thoughts into the best way to balance this scary turn her life had taken.

A turn of events made all the more difficult by the way her body remembered too well the explosive passion they'd shared. Even thinking about that night, with the feel and scent of him so close now, turned her inside out with want.

He rested on his back, watching her with those clear blue eyes as he stroked a loose strand of her hair. "Damn, you're a pretty woman."

"Stop. You don't mean it." Why had she said that? It was as good as asking for another compliment and she'd sworn to herself she wouldn't spend her life wrapped up in appearances as her beauty queen mother had.

His gaze held hers and refused to let go. "Don't I?"

"Maybe you do in your own way. But you're a flirt. Get your mind on business. How's the bird?"

Though the movement made him wince, he straightened, sitting up. He had managed to protect the fragile bird during his fall. Easton held it proudly as it nestled into his hand. "Not a mark on him—not from the fall, anyway. We should get back to the clinic and figure out why he's unable to fly."

"I'll drive. Unless you object, but you really shouldn't," she couldn't stop herself from babbling, "since you did just fall from a tree."

He shrugged, rising slowly to his feet. "Of course you can drive. Why would I have a problem with your driving?"

"Most men prefer to drive." Her father always had, declaring her mother too airheaded to be trusted behind the wheel. Scrunching her nose at the memory, Portia stood, dusting off the leaves that clung to her pants.

"I'm not most men. And you're right. I did just fall out of a tree." He shed more small twigs as they made their way to the sanctuary's four-door truck.

"Then it's settled. I'll take the wheel." Driving the massive vehicle would allow her some element of control. And damn, did she need that in spades right now.

"You're a better driver than I am anyway, even when I haven't backflipped down a few limbs to land on my ass."

"Okay, seriously, I can't think of another man on the planet who would admit that." As her head moved, a strand of her normally perfectly pulled-back hair caught on her eyelash. On instinct, her hand flew upward, folding it back into her ponytail. Back to order.

He grinned roguishly. "Then they must not have my confidence."

Her eyebrows lifted. "Or arrogance."

"True." He slid into the passenger side. "You asked for an appointment with me earlier and then the emergency call came in about the ivory-billed woodpecker. We'll have some time to talk on the drive back. What did you wish to speak about?"

Telling him about her pregnancy like this? Not at all what she planned. Not at all what she would do. When she told him, it'd be in a calm setting. One of her choosing. Not in the company of a wild, injured animal. Or a wildly sexy, injured man. "This isn't the time."

"Why not? Is it that serious? If so, speak up now," he said firmly, turning to face her. Those blue eyes demanding something of her.

"Let's take care of business first." Her lips thinned into a line. Pushing him away. Her mother had depended on a man for everything and then had nothing when that man died bankrupt in prison. Portia had vowed she wouldn't let herself commit to anyone until she was certain she could stand on her two feet, debt free and independent. She wouldn't let herself think about how much harder that would be as a single mother.

His eyes narrowed and she could practically see him running through a catalog of possible topics.

"It's personal?" he asked.

"That's not what I said."

"About the night of the tropical storm six weeks ago—" A hungry smile pushed along his mouth.

Damn him for being so intuitive. He had a knack for that. All the more reason for her to be carefully guarded around him.

"Let's not speak about that now."

"You haven't wanted to speak of it since the storm. When are we ever going to talk about it? You're a determined woman, that's for certain."

She knew she couldn't delay the conversation forever, but right now her stomach was still in turmoil over his fall. And she wanted to go to her first doctor's appointment to confirm that the pregnancy was on track before turning her whole world upside down.

And yes, she was trying to think of any reason she could to delay, because once she told Easton about his baby, she would lose control of her life forever.

Dr. Easton Lourdes leaned his seat halfway back, his head still spinning. Partly from the fall, but mostly from the woman beside him and the memory of those mo-

ments he'd kept his eyes closed and just absorbed the feel
of her against him. Since she'd come to work with him
two years ago, he'd suspected there were fires burning
behind her uptight demeanor. But hell, he'd had no idea
how hot they'd blaze until that one night with her during the storm.

Portia Soto. The most organized secretary on the
planet. The woman who—until recently—had kept his
eccentric spirit in line. Until their night of passion during a tropical storm showed him just how wild she could
be once she let down that tightly upswept hair.

But the next day, she'd gathered her long caramel-
brown hair back as fiercely as ever. Tighter even.

He needed his secretary. The Lourdes Family Wildlife
Refuge was fast becoming an internationally renowned
animal research and rescue center, and he was the man
in charge of the science. To make the impact he wanted
to make on the world, he *needed* his secretary. But he
wanted Portia. And he wasn't sure how to have both.

If only he understood humans as well as he did animals. His childhood spent with rich, globe-trotting parents had exposed him to creatures around the world. He'd
paid attention and taken in an understanding of animals'
unspoken language. But even though he'd had the best
of everything money could buy, he'd lacked much in the
way of learning how to make connections with people
other than his parents and his older brother. No sooner
than he'd make a friend, his family would pack up and
jet off to another exotic locale.

Easton cracked his neck, a crescendo of echoing pops
responded in his back, the tension finally unwinding.
With his neck less contracted, he positioned himself so
he could watch her. Portia's gel manicured nails were still

quite perfect as she gripped the pickup truck's steering wheel at a "nine and three" position that would make any driver's ed teacher proud. Her doe-brown eyes were focused, attentive to the road.

Intentional. That was how he'd describe Portia. Intentional and proper.

With all her wildness contained.

Despite her manicured look, she fit in well at the wildlife preserve his family owned and funded. Easton brought his world-renowned skills as a veterinarian/scientist specializing in exotic animals. His brother, Xander, ran the family business and fund-raising.

And there sure as hell was a lot of fund-raising and political maneuvering involved in saving animals. P ortia's calm organizational skills were an immeasurable asset on that front too, according to his brother, Xander. Easton only had to show up in a tux every few months and talk about the research he loved.

For the most part, he spent his time handling the hands-on rescue and research efforts, and Portia's efficiency helped him make that happen. He was lucky his family's wealth meant he could leave the fund-raising to his brother and get his hands dirty doing what he enjoyed most.

And he tried his damnedest to entice Portia to play in the dirt with him.

Easton's eyes slid from her face to the soft, yellow lights on the road back to the clinic. The preserve stretched for a few acres on Key Largo, a small island in the archipelago south of Florida. A necessary answer to urbanization and tourist development, Easton believed, as did his new board of directors, apparently.

He was damn lucky. He lived his dream every day. Sure, some people were able to turn passion into a paycheck, but Easton was a veterinarian at his preserve solely for passion. He recognized that he'd been blessed by his family's money. It had enabled him to follow his vocation without worrying about compensation. He didn't advertise his lack of salary because, for Easton, it didn't matter. He felt honored to work for the sole purpose of helping the animals. To do some good in this world. Money had never been a big concern for him personally, but the reality of a small refuge accountable to a board of directors meant he had to worry about things like that on occasion.

As a secretary, Portia was brilliant—organized, dedicated—exactly what a free-spirited guy like him needed. But he also wanted her, as a man, and that made working with Portia increasingly challenging.

Since he'd hired her, he'd noticed her—and then he'd immediately move his attention back to business. But now, he caught himself distracted by the pinkness of her lips, the way she straightened her ponytail when she was thinking. Over and over, he'd replayed that night in his head. In a perfect world, he could have both. His kick-ass secretary and his sexy lover, too. But Portia had made it damn clear he wasn't welcome in her bed again. She'd sent him a brief morning-after text and then ignored his messages unless they were work related.

His heart pounded as he thought of the last—and only—time they'd been together. The memory ramped him up—before he deliberately pushed it aside.

Regaining focus on the present, he surveyed her tight smile. Portia hadn't said much in the past few minutes, but as if she needed to fill the space with words, she sliced through his thoughts. "So do you think the bird broke a wing?"

He blinked, troubled at the formality of her tone. "Perhaps. I'll have to x-ray it to be certain."

"Good. I'm glad we were able to help him." Matter-of-fact as ever. All business. No hint, no trace of anything more.

She pulled the truck into the driveway of the clinic, parking it. As she turned to face him, he saw concern pass through her eyes. Had she been that worried about his fall?

His fingers ached to touch her bare skin, to explore her gentle curves. Although her breasts were more generous than he remembered. What else had he remembered wrong from their dimly lit, rushed lovemaking? The space between them dwindled, electricity sparking in the air there.

Her eyes danced, and he saw that spark take hold in her, too. The same spark from the night of the storm.

He wanted to nurture that spark into a flame.

He kissed her. God, he kissed her. Tried to rein himself in so he could savor the moment rather than risking another fast and furious encounter. He didn't want to send her running as he had before. But damn, she tasted good. Felt good. He slid his hands up to cup her face.

For an incredible moment, she seemed to kiss him back. Then everything shifted. She pulled away, her skin sickly pale.

And then she opened the door and ran. More than ran. She flat-out bolted before he could even form a syllable.

This man had a way of flipping her stomach upside down on a regular day, and now that she was pregnant, her stomach didn't seem to know which way was up.

Her ballet flats slammed, skidded against the ground.

Her stomach rumbled a protesting gurgle, bile rising in the back of her throat.

She ran inside the clinic, through the side entrance and toward her office off the main reception space. She sagged back against the wall, sliding down to the floor while trying to decide if she needed to race the rest of the way to the restroom or simply stay put, calm, unmoving.

Yes, staying still was best. She drew in one deep breath after another. With each breath, she tried to focus on her immediate surroundings. At least the normally bustling clinic lacked people at this hour. All the staff and volunteers had gone home after settling the animals in for the night. Good, she'd hate to have an audience for this. Her eyes adjusted to the dim light, and she heard the creak of the door that lead to the supply closet.

Portia swallowed again, feeling unease and nausea reclaim her stomach.

A light flicked on in an adjoining office with the door open. Maureen. Easton's research assistant and sister-in-law. Like Easton, Maureen put in long hours, sacrificing sleep for the animals' sake.

She had a clipboard in her hand, and a pen tucked in her hair. Maureen must've been doing inventory. While keeping a meticulous inventory made life at the clinic run smoothly during all seasons, hurricane season made this task rise to a new level of importance. If the intensity of the tropical storm a few weeks ago was any indication of the hurricanes to come, Portia knew how vital it would be to the survival of the refuge for them to maintain plans and supplies.

But what of her own plans?

Portia took a steadying breath as Maureen noticed

her and came over. Her bright red hair bouncing in curls, Maureen crouched next to Portia, green eyes searching.

"Are you okay?" Maureen's slight Irish brogue lilted.

"I'm fine. I just forgot to eat dinner and I'm light-headed. Low blood sugar. I'll be fine."

Standing, Maureen opened a drawer in the supply room, the one where she'd stashed other sorts of emergency supplies—saltines, PowerBars and gum. "You work too hard."

Maureen tossed her a packet of crackers. To Portia's surprise, she actually caught the wrapped package, shaking hands and all. Tearing open the wrapper, Portia stood and took her time nibbling while she searched for the right words to deflect Maureen's comment.

"I enjoy my work." Not completely true.

She was grateful for her well-paying job and the adorable one-bedroom cabana that came with it. She had a dream of becoming a teacher one day, but she needed to pay for her brother's education and save enough to finance her own—

Except that wasn't going to happen. She was out of time to fulfill her own dreams. She had to think of her brother and this baby. And even if her pay doubled, there wasn't even enough time to figure all of that out before she had to confess everything to Easton.

She hated thinking about money at all. It made her feel too much like her gold digger mother. But there were practical realities to consider.

Like getting some crackers into her stomach before she hurled.

She nibbled on the edge of a saltine. Each bite settling her stomach. For the moment, anyway.

Maureen glanced around the clinic, leaning around

the corner that lead to the examination room. "Where's the doctor?"

"He's examining an injured bird we rescued." Or so she assumed. She'd left him in a bit of a hurry.

What on earth had he been thinking to kiss her like that?

More to the point, what had she been thinking to allow it to happen? To respond? Normally, she prided herself on her control. Her good sense. With Easton, it seemed, she had neither.

Maureen passed over a container of wet wipes, her bright diamond ring glittering. Recently, she'd married Easton's brother, Xander. "Here."

"What?" Portia took them, confused.

"You've got dust on your knees and on your elbows."

She looked down to check, heat flaming her cheeks as she remembered being close to Easton. Of their bodies pressed against each other on the hard ground. Not that she intended to share those details with anyone. "It's messy work out there."

As if on cue to make her cheeks flame hotter, the side door opened and she heard the long stride that was distinctly Easton's. From a distance, he glanced at her, the bird cradled against his chest in a careful but firm hold.

Maureen stepped forward. "Do you need help?"

He shook his head. "I've got this. You two carry on."

Easton headed toward the back where they did X-rays, away from other animals. His footsteps grew softer until the sound faded altogether.

Maureen turned back to her. "You seem more of the office job type. I've often wondered what made you take on this position." Blunt and honest conversation with Maureen. While normally Portia appreciated Maureen's directness, Portia didn't know if she had the stamina for this sort of exchange right now.

"The pay is more than generous and the locale is enticing."

Did that sound as lame out loud as she thought? Didn't matter. It was true. She'd needed the better-than-average pay, with housing included, to save the money she needed to pay for her brother. Her stomach did another flip and she reached for a cracker. The scents of the clinic were bothering her in a way they normally didn't—the stringent smell of antiseptic cleaner used religiously on every surface, the wood shavings lining crates, the air of live plants.

"And the pay is such because the other secretaries before you couldn't handle an eccentric boss and his unconventional hours, helping him with X-rays, the animals and fieldwork, cleaning his messy office...or they tried to put the moves on him. And yet you've put up with him even though he's clearly not your type."

Portia stiffened, biting down hard on the edge of the cracker. She chewed and swallowed before speaking. "What would my type be?"

"Did I sound presumptuous? I'm sorry if that came out wrong."

"Not at all. I'm truly curious because... Oh, never mind." The question had sounded innocent, but in a strange way, Portia began to wonder if Maureen knew, or at the very least suspected something had happened between Portia and Easton.

"I just meant I can see you with a suave, well-traveled businessman or a brilliant professor. But of course you're clearly more than capable of taking care of your own love life. Tell me about your type? Or maybe there's already a gentleman in your life?"

A gentleman in her life? Time for a stellar deflection.

Portia arched her brow and rolled her eyes. She did everything she could to visually signify that she had no connection to anyone at all. One of Portia's greatest strengths had always been hiding behind conversation.

"Tell me about your honeymoon plans." That topic ought to do it. Maureen and Xander had delayed their honeymoon trip because, after they were married, they'd realized just how deeply they cared for each other. Originally their marriage had been for convenience—he'd needed a wife to keep custody of his daughter and she'd needed citizenship—but it had since deepened into true love.

"I cannot wait, Portia. It will be hard to be away from Rose for two weeks, but she'll be staying with her grandparents."

Rose, Xander's sweet, blonde baby girl. Portia's unborn baby's cousin.

The weight of that sentiment slammed into her every fiber.

Her baby and Rose would be family. Portia's hand settled on her stomach. She was connected to this place and this family now, no matter what.

Portia's brother was connected too, through her, even though he lived in the panhandle—in Pensacola, Florida—getting ready to enter his last year of college. He had emotional support from their aunt nearby, but the older woman barely made ends meet. She had gone above and beyond by taking the two of them in after their mother drank herself into liver failure when Portia was thirteen and her brother, Marshall, was only seven.

It was up to Portia to support her family—including this unexpected baby.

Her head started spinning with how tangled everything had become.

Maureen stepped forward, concern creasing her brow. "Are you sure you're feeling alright?"

"It was a long work day. I'm hungry and exhausted. That's all."

She needed to get herself together. Wear looser clothes if need be. Give herself a chance to verify everything was alright with the pregnancy and if it was, take the time she needed to come up with a plan for her future.

She'd worked too hard for her independence to give it up now, no matter how tempting Easton might be.

Two

What the hell was up with Portia?

When he'd stepped into the wildlife preserve's main building, he had taken note of her pale face and standoffish demeanor. Leaving her alone to talk with Maureen seemed the best option. He'd heard the two women leave a half hour later, each sending a quick farewell shout before heading out.

Easton understood that Portia regretted their impulsive encounter during the tropical storm. He'd almost started to accept that it wouldn't be leading anywhere. It was one night and no more.

But then he'd seen that look in her eyes today.

Shaking his head in bemusement, he closed the clinic door and punched in the security code before turning away into the inky dark. Night creatures spoke to him through the cover of darkness, a cooing mix of coastal birds and tropical bugs. He could identify each sound as readily as he could identify different human voices. As a young boy, Easton digested each sound the way some men committed the sounds of roaring engines to memory. He knew each voice and wanted to help ensure they all continued to speak.

He'd had offers to work at other, larger clinics in more exotic locales, but the newly named Lourdes Family Wildlife Refuge was a personal quest for him and his brother. And he liked this place he called home.

As much as he'd enjoyed his eccentric life growing up, always on the move with his globe-trotting parents, he also enjoyed waking up in the same place each morning. The Key Largo–based animal preserve blended the best of both worlds for him—the wilds and home.

Even the main house reflected that balance of barely domesticated wildness. A sprawling mansion, it stood two stories tall, complete with open balconies and an extravagant, oasis-inspired pool.

Which was where Easton was headed now. His brother, Xander, sat alone on one of the lounge chairs, a glass of bourbon neat in his hand.

Easton and his brother had always been different but close. Since their parents traveled the world with little thought of creating a home or helping their kids build friendships, he and his brother relied on each other. Even more so after their father died and their mother continued her world-traveling ways, always looking for the next adventure in each new country rather than staying in one place to connect with her children.

This house represented more than Easton's commitment to preserving animals in Key Largo. This shared space with his brother represented an attempt at familial cohesion. An attempt at proving they could grow something stable, something to be proud of. The moonlight filtered through stray clouds, peppering his walk in a play of shadow and light on the well-maintained lawn.

He didn't want to blame his parents. They deserved to live their lives as they wanted, to be themselves. And even if they hadn't been conventional parents, they had more than lived up to their commitment to feed, house and educate their children.

But as much as he didn't want to blame them, he'd found his rocky relationship with them had influenced him. He found it difficult to sustain lasting relationships with women. He'd had a series of short romances. And the only time he'd even considered the altar, she—Dana—had split up with him right before he could propose. She'd said he was too eccentric, too much of a kid at heart, for a committed relationship.

Which was ironic as hell since he'd already been looking at engagement rings.

He hadn't told her that. Dana probably would have said he wouldn't have been much of a husband, or that he wouldn't have actually bought a ring. And she probably would have been right. He knew he was eccentric, and he'd worked to find the right career to blend his passion and personality with work he cared about. He got to climb trees and play in the woods for a living. Not too shabby as a way of channeling his strengths. He'd taken what he'd inherited of his parents' quirky ways and toned them down, figuring out how to stay in one place.

None of that seemed to matter, though, when it came to figuring out how to settle down, based on his history with Dana, Laura, Naomi... Damn, he was depressing the hell out of himself.

So where did that leave him with Portia?

Once on the stone ground that surrounded the pool, he grabbed a plush lounge chair and pulled it beside Xander. Easton sat in the middle of the lounger, facing his brother. Xander's ocean-colored eyes flicked to him.

Xander had taken on the wildlife preserve in memory of his wife's passing. Reviving the then struggling refuge had been her passion.

This place meant the world to both brothers.

"What's the deal with you and Portia?" Xander's tone was blunt and businesslike—the commanding voice that won him boardroom battles left and right.

"What do you mean?" The answer came too quickly out of Easton's mouth.

"Don't play dumb with me. I was out for a walk with Rose and I saw the way you looked at Portia when you both got into the truck earlier." He sipped his bourbon, fixing Easton with the stare of an older brother.

"Why didn't you say hello or offer to help out?"

"You're trying to distract me. Not going to work. So what gives between you two?"

Easton chose his words carefully, needing to regain control of the conversation before his brother went on some matchmaking kick that would only backfire by making Portia retreat. She was prickly.

And sexy.

And not going to give him the brush-off another time. She'd been avoiding him more than ever recently and he was determined to find out the reason.

"Easton?" Xander pushed.

"She's an attractive woman." Not a lie.

"A cool woman, classic. And she's been here awhile. She's also not your type. So what changed?"

She absolutely wasn't the sort to go out with a guy

like him. And yet there was chemistry between them. Crackling so tangibly he could swear he was standing in the middle of a storm with the heavens sending lightning bolts through him. She clearly felt the same way, except the next morning, once the storm had passed, she'd insisted it couldn't happen again. He'd thought if he waited patiently she would wear down.

She hadn't.

Until today. "And what would my type be?"

"You really want me to spell that out?" Xander's crooked glance almost riled Easton.

Almost. Then he reminded himself he was the chill brother normally. He was letting this business with Portia mess with his head.

"No need to spell it out. I'll get defensive and have to kick your ass."

"You can try."

Easton smiled tightly. As kids, he used to lie in wait for Xander, always trying to best him in an impromptu wrestling match. He won about half of the time, which wasn't too bad considering his older brother had shot up with height faster and Easton hadn't caught up—and passed him—until they were in high school. Now, they had exchanged the good-natured physical wrestling for well-placed banter.

Silence between the brothers lingered, allowing the chorus of nocturnal creatures to swell. Not that he minded. Easton and Xander could both get lost in their own thoughts, with neither of them rambling on with nonsensical chatter. He'd always appreciated the ability to hang out with his brother without feeling the need to fill every moment with speech.

Easton had to admit Xander was right. Easton had al-

ways dated women who were more like him, free-spirited, unconventional types.

Date?

That didn't come close to describing what had happened between him and Portia.

And maybe that was the problem. What had stopped
him from asking her out on a date? Before that night,
he'd wanted to keep their relationship professional. But
after they'd crossed that line… He'd been trying to talk
to her about that night. But he'd never done the obvious.
Ask her out to dinner…and see where things progressed
from there.

He'd always been a man of action and speed. But why
not take things slowly with her? He had all the time in
the world.

Easton didn't know where things were heading with
Portia, but he wasn't giving up. He hoped that dating was
the right plan and considered asking Xander for input.
Usually he and his brother told each other everything,
relied on each other for support—hell, they'd been each
other's only friend when they'd been traveling with their
parents. Easton needed a plan. And his brother was good
at plans, and Xander had far more success in the romance
department.

Except right now Easton wanted to hold on to the shift
in his relationship with Portia. Keep that private between
the two of them. He didn't want to risk word getting out
and spooking her.

Because, yes, something had changed between Easton
and his brother too since Xander had married Maureen,
and Easton couldn't figure out what that was. His brother
had been married before and had loved his wife, mourned

her deeply when she'd died. Still, Easton hadn't felt he'd lost a part of his brother then, not like now.

So yeah, he wasn't ready to share yet.

Or maybe it had nothing to do with his brother.

And everything to do with Portia.

Up until realizing she was pregnant, the most anxiety-inducing moments in Portia's life had been when she'd fretted about taking care of her brother and paying bills.

This morning had combined all of her anxieties. Her secret pregnancy coupled with arriving to work a half hour late. She'd been sick for what felt like hours and it had thrown her off schedule. Portia was never, ever late. Tardiness drove her insane. Since the morning sickness seemed to be getting significantly worse, she might have to move up her appointment with the doctor to next week. That made her stomach flip all the more since it would mean facing the uncomfortable reality of having to tell Easton.

Dr. Lourdes.

Her boss.

Damn.

Refocus. She pushed those thoughts out of her mind. Easton's schedule needed to be organized for the day. That wouldn't happen if she didn't collect herself right now. Tugging on the sleeves of her light pink cardigan, she stepped into the office, ready to do prep work for Easton's arrival.

Blinking in the harsh white light, her tumultuous stomach sank. Easton sat behind his desk, already at work.

His collar-length dark hair was slicked back, blue eyes

alert and focused on a stack of papers in front of him, full lips tightly pressed as he thought.

She drew in a sharp breath, another wave of nausea and dizziness pressing at her. He looked up from his desk, his clean-shaven face crinkled in a mixture of concern and...surprise? She realized *he* was the one all put together this morning and *she* was the one feeling scattered and disorganized.

This sudden reversal robbed her of her focus. His eyes traced over her, his head falling to the side in concern.

"Are you okay? It's just—you are never late. In fact, you arrive to everything at least fifteen minutes early." He set his pen down, eyes peering into hers.

She swallowed, her throat pressing against the top button of her off-white button-up shirt and her strand of faux pearls. Part of her wanted to lean on him, confide in him and get his support. But how? She didn't have much practice in asking for help.

"Uh." Stammering, her mind blanked. "Yeah. I just... I think I may have the stomach flu. I haven't felt this bad in ages."

She put a hand to her stomach as if to emphasize her symptoms. But really, her palm on her stomach just reminded her of the life growing inside her and how difficult telling Easton was going to be.

"I think that is going around. Maureen called out with the same symptoms. Should you go rest?"

"I'll be fine. I've got crackers and ginger ale on hand. Anyway, how's our little patient doing this morning, Doctor?" She added the last part to keep a professional distance between them.

"Walking around, even attempting to take flight. X-rays show no breaks in the wings and there are no missing feathers, so I'm guessing it's a strained muscle that will benefit from rest. Then back into the wild." He ran his hands through his hair, his athletic build accented with the movement.

"That's good to know. Your risky climb saved his—or her—life."

"His," he answered simply.

Oppressive silence settled between them. She hated this. There had been a time, not even that long ago, where conversation had felt easy and natural between them. But since the tropical storm, she'd looked for every reason to put distance between them. This morning was no different. "If you're busy with patients, then I'll get to some transcriptions."

"Actually, I'm not busy with patients. Let the transcriptions wait." His voice dropped any pretense of nonchalance. Determination entered his tone.

"Okay. But why?"

"Let's talk."

Every atom in her being revolted. Talk? How could she begin to talk to him? She wasn't ready. She needed more time.

"I don't think that's a good idea. We don't talk. We work." She fished the planner out of her oversize bag and waved it in the air.

"I think talking is an excellent idea." A small, hungry smile passed over his lips, blue eyes shining with familiar mischief.

Why did he have to be so damn sexy?

"Please, don't make things more awkward than—"

"Go out with me on a date."

A date? With Dr. Easton Lourdes? The world slammed still. "A what?"

"A date, where two people spend time together at some entertaining venue. Tomorrow's not a workday, so it can be afternoon or evening. I don't want to presume what you would enjoy because honestly, you're right, we haven't spoken very much. So for our date, what do you think about a wine-tasting cruise?"

She couldn't drink, not while pregnant. She winced.

"Okay," Easton said, moving from behind his desk, "from the look on your face I'll take that as a no. Concert in the park with a picnic? Go snorkeling? Or take a drive down to the tip of the Keys and hang out at Hemingway's old house or climb to the top of the Key West Lighthouse?"

"You're serious about wanting to go on a date?" What would she have thought if he'd made that request months ago? Or if she weren't pregnant now? What if he'd made that request when she had the luxury of time to explore the possibility of feelings between them?

Except she didn't have time.

He sat on the edge of his desk, a devilish look in his eyes. "Serious as a heart attack."

She could see by his face he meant it. Totally. He wanted to go on a date with her. She'd spent two years attracted to him while never acting on it in order to maintain her independence and now—when the last thing she should be doing was starting an affair with him—he was asking her out.

Her emotions were clouding her judgment. Their impulsive night of sex had flipped her mind upside down. Their attraction was every bit as combustible as she'd expected. It had stolen her breath, her sanity. She'd even entertained pursuing something with him. For a moment, she'd not cared one whit about her independence. But fears had assailed her the next morning. Heaven knew if he'd suggested a date then, she would have run screaming into the Everglades, never to be seen again.

Okay, maybe that was overstating things. Or maybe not.

But it did bring up the point that now, things were different. She really did need to talk to him soon and come up with a plan for their baby. Meanwhile, though, maybe she could use this time to get to know him better on a friendship level and find the best way to tell him about their "love child."

She just had to ignore the electricity that sizzled between them every time he looked at her.

"Key West," she said. "Let's take the drive to see Hemingway's house."

The romantic ride he'd planned just yesterday to Hemingway's house had somehow gone awry.

What should have been a leisurely scenic drive down the heart of the Florida Keys was getting him nowhere with Portia. He wanted her to open up to him, to reveal something about herself. But she was totally clammed up and he was on fire to know more about her. To find a way past her defenses and back into her bed. To pull her clothes off, slowly, one piece at a time and make love to her in a bed, at a leisurely pace rather than a frenzied coupling in a bathroom during a storm.

And she'd gone into her Ice Queen mode again.

Which had never overly bothered him before but was, for some reason, making him crazy now. Yes, he burned to know more about her than what she took in her coffee—although these days she seemed to enjoy water with fruit slices more than her standard brew. He needed to get her talking.

And he also needed to power his way past this slower moving traffic into a clearer stretch of road.

Checking the rearview mirror, he slid his vintage Corvette into the fast lane, getting out from behind a brake-happy minivan. As they passed the van, he noted the map sprawled out on the dash. That explained everything about the somewhat erratic driving behavior.

He used the opportunity of an open road to check out Portia, noting her slender face, porcelain skin and pointed nose. The edges of her mouth were tensed slightly. Her hair was gathered into a loose ponytail, not completely down, but definitely more casual than her usual tightly pulled-back twist. The hairstyle had led him to believe getting through to her today would be easier.

Apparently, he would have to work harder at getting her to reveal her thoughts. And work harder at restraining the urge to slide his hands through her hair until it all hung loose and flowing around her shoulders. He remembered well the feel of those silken strands gliding through his fingers as he moved inside her—

Hell, there went his concentration again.

He draped his wrist over the steering wheel and searched for just the right way to approach her. Often times the simplest ways worked best. Maybe he'd been trying too hard.

"When my brother and I were kids traveling the world with our parents, we became masters at entertaining ourselves during long flights. I'm thinking now might be a good time to resurrect one of our games."

She tipped her head toward him. "Oh really? What did you two play?"

Ah, good. She'd taken the bait.

"Our favorite was one we called Quiz Show. I was about ten when we started playing. I was determined to beat my older brother at something. He was still so much taller, but I figured since we were just a year apart, I had a fighting chance at taking him down in a battle of the minds."

"Tell me more," she said, toying with the end of her ponytail, which sent his pulse spiking again.

"We'd already been on a transcontinental flight and then had to spend ten more hours in a car. So we'd burned out on books and toys and homework. We started asking each other outrageous questions to stump each other."

The result? Two very tight brothers. He hoped to re-create that experience with Portia. To learn something about her. "Would you like to play?"

"Uh, sure. You go first, though, and I reserve the right not to answer."

"Fair enough." A natural quizmaster, he paused, thinking of his first question. One that would help them flow into more personal topics. "What do you do for fun?"

"Are you being rude?" she asked indignantly.

Well, hell. "What do you mean?"

"You said the questions were meant to stump the other person so your question could be taken as an insult."

"Damn. I didn't mean that at all. How about consider this as a new game, our rules. I meant what does Portia oto do for fun? To unwind? Because I don't know you well and I'm trying to get to know you better." He needed more than just raw data. He wanted her quirks, her idiosyncrasies. He wanted to figure out his attraction to her. Once he did, then he could put those tumultuous dreams to rest.

Or know whether to pursue an all-out affair.

She shot him a sideways look, her ponytail swishing, the ribbon rippling in the wind. "Okay, I see what you mean. But you have to promise not to laugh at my answer."

"I would never. Unless you tell me you make to-do lists for fun. Then I might." He kept his tone casual, his grip on the leather steering wheel light.

"I may be a Post-it note princess, but that isn't my 'fun' time. No. I actually like to draw." She said the words so quietly that they were almost swept away by the wind.

"You draw?" He spared her a sidelong glance, noting the way her cheeks flushed, even beneath her oversize sunglasses.

She nodded, pony tail bobbing. "I do."

"Well, what do you like to draw?" He pressed for progress.

She took a deep breath, hand floating in the air as she made an uncharacteristically theatrical gesture that drew his attention to her elegant fingers. "Oh, you know, the usual kinds of things. Animals mostly. Lots of animals. People, too. Their faces especially. I like the small details."

"You are just full of surprises, Ms. Soto." He bet her way of noticing made her a brilliant artist. Nothing seemed to escape her gaze. He liked that about her. He was finding he liked a lot more about her than he'd realized. Apparently before now his absentminded professor ways had made him miss things. His attention to detail wasn't as fine-tuned as hers.

Something he intended to rectify.

"Hmm. I can be... Well, how about you, *Doctor* Lourdes? What do you do for fun?"

His formal salutation felt unnatural coming from her. He knew she used it to put distance between them, but he wasn't allowing it this time. "I'm afraid to confess my favorite downtime activity is fishing."

"Really?"

In the corner of his vision, he saw her angle toward him.

"Really," he responded without hesitation. "I know some would say that goes against the conservationist, animal lifesaving oath I took, but I'm not a vegetarian and I always eat what I catch."

"It's not bungee jumping or something equally adrenaline inducing?"

"I know. I'm a letdown. I like fishing because I enjoy the quiet time to think and reflect. And I'm humbled by the way the ecosystem works—how connected everything is."

"Now who is full of surprises?" she murmured, more to herself than to him.

"My turn. What about your dreams? What do you really want to do?"

"I'm happy to be your assistant."

He shook his head. "Not what I asked."

They were only a few minutes away from the Hemingway Home and Museum, and the traffic around them increased, taillights glowing all around like a faux fire.

Portia tugged on her ponytail, thinking.

"In a perfect world? Like a money-and responsibility-free world?"

"Yep." Tall palms stretched above them, casting shadows over her face.

The bright-colored houses and tropical foliage made the island look more like a movie set than reality. Foot traffic was dense too, but the cruise ship passengers on tour for the day would be pulling out before too long and things would quiet down.

"I think I'd like to do something with art. Maybe a nonprofit for kids that focused on creativity after school. Especially for kids who don't have a strong family support system. I'd love to help them see they have the ability to create something beautiful and wonderful."

Her words touched him as he turned the corner, traffic heavier as they drew closer to the historic landmark. "That's a wonderful idea. There isn't enough of that in the world. Any particular reason you chose this need over others?"

"When I was younger, I saw a lot of kids bogged down by circumstances out of their control and they had no outlets of support. I hated that."

He could hear in her voice a more personal reason for her dream, one he felt like she wanted to share. This woman was more like the one he remembered from the night of the storm, the Portia who'd told him of her need to keep on the lights during storms as a child so her brother and her stuffed animals wouldn't be afraid. But he'd seen in her eyes that she'd craved that light and comfort then too, but even now was unwilling to admit her own need for support. Even as her standoffish ways frustrated him at times, he also couldn't help but admire her strength.

If he could keep her talking, he could win her over. What he'd do once he had her, he wasn't sure. All he knew was that he wanted her like he'd wanted no one and nothing else.

But how to tease this information out of her?

He slowed the car to a halt, the traffic in front of him growing worse.

And then the unthinkable happened, interrupting his thoughts. A crash echoed in his ears less than an instant before the car jolted forward.

They'd been rear-ended. Damn. His protective instincts went on high alert and his arm shot across in front of Portia.

Only keeping her safe mattered.

Three

Her near-electric moment with Easton ended with a resounding thud.

A minivan had rear-ended them.

Easton had flung his right arm out to protect her... and protect their unborn child. Not that he knew anything about the baby, and she wasn't any closer to being ready to tell him on this far-from-normal day.

As far as dates went, her romantic outing with Easton had been anything but typical. Yet not in the quirky up-for-whatever way that normally characterized Easton's gestures. She'd seen his protective impulses around his niece and the animals. But this was the first time Portia had been on the receiving end. If she weren't stunned—and more than a little afraid—she would think longer on how that made her feel.

His blue eyes filled with concern as his hand reached for hers, helping her step out of the car.

"I'll be fine." She waved him off, eager to get out of the Corvette and take dozens of deep breaths away from the scent of scorched rubber and brakes. "I promise, I will tell you if I feel the least need to go to the doctor."

And she would. Keeping her secret wasn't worth risking her child. Already, she could hear sirens and see cop cars, firetrucks and an EMT vehicle. She would check in with a medical tech.

"All right. I'll go give the statement to the police." He squeezed her hand quickly before walking away to check in with one of the officers.

One deep breath after another, she calmed her nerves, taking comfort in the strong breadth of Easton's shoulders. She winged a prayer of thanksgiving that he was okay, as well. This could have been so much worse than a dented fender.

In all honesty, she had been in a worse accident when she was thirteen, shortly before her mom died. Her mother had taken her to school in a little blue car. At the final turn before the school, they'd been sideswiped by a bright red pickup truck. That day, she'd needed stitches, and her mother had severely damaged her already ravaged liver. Only a few months later, her mother had died, leaving Portia and her brother alone. They'd moved from Nevada and into the house with their father's older sister in Florida.

While today's crash had only been a fender bender and there were no overt signs of damage, still, she worried. Had the crash harmed her unborn baby?

The thought brought a wave of nausea as the steady swirl of red-and-blue lights echoed in Portia's peripheral vision. How much longer until those emergency vehicles wove their way closer?

She was responsible for the life growing inside her. The life she had to protect. A little boy or little girl—

And thank goodness, one of the EMS trucks stopped on the shoulder of the road just one car up. Since there wasn't a line of others who appeared in need of emergency care, she pushed away from the light pole and moved toward the ambulance.

Smoothing her sundress in an excuse to steady her hands, she approached the younger of the two EMTs. The gold name tag read Valez.

"Uh, sir?" Stammering, she twisted her fingers together, a flush crawling across her face.

"Yes, ma'am?" Valez, a man in his midthirties with a jet-black mustache, asked, gesturing toward the back of the ambulance.

"I feel fine. But…" Oh Lord. This was the first time she would talk about her pregnancy out loud. "I'm pregnant and I just want to make sure everything is alright."

The rest of the sentence flew out of her mouth, the reality of her situation echoing back to her.

"You did the right thing in coming over here, ma'am. Please, sit down. We'll get you checked out. If you need additional care, we'll transport you to the nearest hospital. But let's hope that's not needed. Okay?" He lifted her wrist and began taking her pulse. "So just relax and let's talk. How far along are you?" He glanced at her while waving a hand for the other EMT to come over. The older gentleman handed Valez a bag filled with equipment.

"Umm. Well, not quite two months. But fairly close to that point." Portia's voice was a whisper, nearly covered by the sounds of car horns and conversations.

Valez's brow furrowed, reaching for his stethoscope. "And so far, your pregnancy is going well?"

"Yes."

He checked her pulse, nodding to her. "So far, your vitals seem just fine."

Deep breath out. Good. "What should I watch for?"

Handing his equipment back to the other EMT, Valez turned to face her. "There are two things you can watch for—bleeding and cramping. Based on your vitals, I think you are in the clear. Just be sure to put your feet up and try to relax."

Portia's vigorous nod sent loose tendrils of her hair out of her ponytail and into her face. Before she could respond to Valez, Easton strode toward them, concern wearing lines in his ruggedly handsome face.

"Everything okay?"

Heart palpitating, palms sweating, she urged her tongue to find words. "Fine, I'm just fine."

He glanced at the EMT. "Is that true? She's a tough cookie who doesn't complain."

Valez nodded, holding his medical kit. "We've checked her over and everything appears fine. She knows what signs to look for."

"Signs to look for?" Easton's brow furrowed, looking confused.

Damn.

Panic pulsed in her throat. This could not be how he found out.

The two technicians exchanged glances. Valez cleared his throat. "Yes, symptoms to look for after a car accident."

"Symptoms?"

She tried to interrupt, panicked over what the tech might give away, but he nodded at her reassuringly.

"Whiplash, for example. If your neck feels stiff in the

morning. Or aches from the seatbelt or from the impact if your airbag went off."

She inched away. "No airbag. Our vehicle was barely tapped, but I appreciate all the other information you provided. Truly." She spun to Easton. "We should clear out so they can check out any others who need help."

"Okay," Easton answered, giving a final wave to the EMT. "Thank you for taking the time to be so thorough. I appreciate it."

"Just doing our job." The tech nodded to her. "Take it easy, ma'am."

Easton turned back to her, gesturing to the slightly damaged car. A deep sigh escaped his lips, though when he turned to face Portia, a smile manifested. An easy-going smile. One she wanted to give in to. She wanted to lean on him, to rely on him, but she knew that was a recipe for disaster. She had to do this on her own. The sensible thing? Cut her losses on today—on the idea of them.

He touched the top of her arm with gentle fingertips. "This is not the way I envisioned our date going, but I'm glad no one was injured. You must be starving. I know I am. Would you like indoor or outdoor dining?"

The accident shook her ability to remain calm. Though her vitals checked out, she worried about the baby. And that worry made her realize the futility of pursuing anything personal or romantic with Easton. She would always be connected to him, but she couldn't come to rely on him.

"Honestly, I would like to pick up to-go food and head home."

"I know it's a long day driving the whole way down the Keys. Would you rather we get a hotel?" he asked, rushing to add, "Separate rooms of course, if that's what you want."

"I want to go home."

Portia felt downright foolish. She needed space—a place to think. Somewhere away from Easton.

He studied her eyes for a long moment, then shrugged, "Sure, your day. Your date. But it's going to be damn good carryout."

Thoughts of the accident still shook Easton. Though small, the fender bender replayed in his mind.

Portia's scrunched brow visibly displayed her stress. Her demeanor shifted after talking to the EMT. Easton had the sinking feeling that she wasn't as fine as she let on. Or maybe the accident had spooked her as it had spooked him. She'd been initially hesitant to accept his offer of the date. Maybe she'd interpreted the accident as a sign that they had to turn back.

He fished his soda out of the cup holder and sipped on the cola. She was safe. They were both safe. The car had received some damage, but that didn't matter. Not really.

Portia, currently chowing down on carryout, appeared pale, but her color was returning by the bite. She'd chosen a hogfish sandwich, which he hadn't expected at all, even though the delicate fish had a scallop flavor he personally enjoyed. But he'd thought she would order something grilled on top of a salad, the kind of thing she'd pick up locally when she grabbed them takeout for lunch if she needed to go into town on a workday. Yet, this time she'd chosen heartier fare and downed the sandwich like a starved woman. Even alternating each bite with a conch fritter.

This glimpse of her zest for life, her savoring of the

senses, made him hungry for a taste of her. He'd wanted
to stop for a roadside picnic, but she'd shot down the
suggestion, noting the gathering storm clouds. He had
to concur. They needed to start for home.

Traffic in the northbound lane moved moderately fast,
but allowed Easton to take in the scenery. Sometimes, he
felt like he lived at the refuge. Not a big complaint—he
loved his work, knew caring for the animals transcended
a job and landed squarely in the realm of a vocation. But
he often forgot what a normal day looked like.

Then again, his unconventional childhood had never
really allowed for normalcy either.

Regardless, the drive reminded him of just how damn
lucky he was to live in the tropical Florida Keys. People on bikes lined sidewalks. Palm trees bowed in the
summer wind. Easton could make out the turquoise of
the sea catching radiantly in the sunlight, the shoreline
dotted with shacks that were homes and shops, colorful
and scenic. The natural panoramic view was gorgeous.

But not nearly as gorgeous as the woman next to him.

Portia continued to surprise him. Intrigue him. He
had a few hours until they'd be back at the refuge. Maybe
he could restart their quiz game. Figure out more about
her. Easton wanted to tease answers from her lips. Understand more. He could ask her about her family. He
knew nothing about them. In fact, Easton didn't really
know much concerning her life before she came to work
for him.

He could ask her if she'd ever been close to marriage.
Did she want a family of her own? What was the worst
kiss she'd ever had? That could at least break the ice and
make them laugh. Or he could ask why she'd been avoid-

ing him over the last few weeks when they worked together every day, for crying out loud.

With a renewed commitment to demystifying Portia Soto, he turned his head, ready to begin the questions again.

But as he opened his mouth, he knew he couldn't continue.

Her head rested against the window, her eyes were closed and she was fast asleep. He picked up her empty food container, tossed it into the carryout bag, and decided to take comfort in the fact that she felt at ease enough to nap around him. He reached for the radio to turn on a news channel just as his phone rang, the Bluetooth kicking in automatically.

He reached to pick up fast before the tone woke her. But she only twitched once before settling back into even-paced breathing.

He spared a quick glance to the caller ID. His brother, Xander, was on the line. Easton tapped the monitor and his brother's voice filled the air.

"Hey, dude, check this out." Background noise echoed as he said, "Rose, baby girl, come back to Daddy and talk on the phone. Tell Uncle Easton what you just told Daddy."

Easton's mouth twitched. His brother was such a devoted father, and it was funny as hell watching his starched-suit, executive brother wrapped around that tiny little finger.

Easton's toddler niece babbled for a few indistinguishable sentences before she said, "Birdies, birdies."

"That's great, Rosebud." Yeah, Easton had to admit his niece was mighty damn cute. "Give the phone back to your daddy now. Love you, kiddo."

"Hey, brother," Xander's voice came back over. "That's awesome, isn't it? We have the next generation of veterinarians in our family."

"Could be, could be." His eyes flicked back to Portia. She readjusted in her seat, sleep still heavy on her brow. The warmth of the afternoon sun hit her cheekbones, making her glow with natural, sexy beauty.

Xander's baritone voice snapped Easton back into focus. "Maybe she'll add to the family portfolio with inventions the way you have."

"She'll one-up me, for sure. And how the hell did you know about that? It was supposed to be—"

Xander cut him off, a smile present in his tone. "A secret and you just invested well, I know. But one of your colleagues saw me at a wildlife preserve convention and thought I was you."

"Ouch." While the brothers shared the same deep blue eyes and broad-chested build, Xander's clean-cut executive look could never be confused with Easton's collar-length hair and slightly disheveled persona.

"It was a windy day. I didn't look like I'd combed my hair."

"I think I was just insulted."

"You were." A laugh rumbled in Xander's throat.

"Thanks."

"No problem. How's it going on your...what was it you were doing today?"

He was probing. Easton could hear it in his voice. Through clenched teeth Easton replied, "A professional run with my assistant."

"Right." Doubt dripped from Xander's tone. Easton could practically see Xander's eyebrow raise, incredulous as always. "How's that going?"

"We'll be back by the end of the day."

"Given your wanderlust soul, something makes me doubt that," Xander teased, but the joke missed its mark. Struck a nerve in Easton.

"We will be."

"That reminds me of when Mom used to say she'd have us all back to the hotel by dinner, but instead, we'd spend the night somewhere unexpected. You've got her sense of time, you know."

Easton's jaw clenched tighter. "See you in a few hours, brother."

He hung up the phone, eyes intensely focused on the road. Wanderlust was one thing, but he still struggled to be taken seriously. To prove he could stay in one spot for a long time, be dedicated to something outside himself. That he wasn't wandering aimlessly in Neverland.

"Easton," Portia's voice jolted him out of his fog. "What did he mean by invention?"

"Oh—" he shrugged "—it's nothing."

"Clearly, it's something—" she paused to sit upright again "—if it added to your family's financial portfolio." She held up a hand. "Wait. Forget I said that."

"Why? I encouraged questions today. Quiz Show, remember? The more outrageous the better."

"Most people find it rude to ask about another person's finances."

"That's not really a secret. And as for my invention…" He shot her a sidelong glance, trying to get a read on her. Truthfully, he felt exposed, talking about this aspect of his work. This idea felt more personal than any bank balance. "It's…I created a shunt to go into the liver duct. It opens and closes in a way that enables multiple testing of a sick animal without multiple sticks."

A smile warmed her face, nose crinkling. "That's really amazing and compassionate."

Eyes back on the road. He changed lanes, sunlight streaming into the car. "The animals I take care of, they're my kids."

"Until you have children of your own."

He shook his head. "I'm not going to have them."

"But you're so great with Rose, I never would have guessed you don't like kids." Shock entered her tone, and Portia cocked her head to the side.

"I do like them. I just don't plan to have any of my own. I'm crummy father material. Too devoted to the job. I expected you of all people to understand that."

She smiled quickly, fidgeting. What had he said wrong?

"You do work long hours," she said simply.

He needed to get this conversation back on track. Heat filled him as he remembered his reason for this little outing in the first place—to romance her—to woo her. To get her back into his bed. "We have spent many, many hours together."

And he hoped to spend many more in a nonbusiness capacity, sooner rather than later. In fact, there was no moment like the present. The accident left him wanting to seize the day. Talk of the invention nudged him to take things in a new direction with Portia.

He eased the vintage car over to the shoulder of the road and turned off the car.

Portia looked around, confused. "What are you doing? Is something wrong with the Corvette?" She fished in her purse and pulled out her phone. "I'll look up the number for auto service—"

"Portia?" He started to lean toward her.

"Yes," she answered without looking up from her phone.

"Stop talking." He cupped her face in his hands and pressed his mouth to hers.

Four

The taste of Easton tantalized her senses, intoxicating and arousing. This was what she'd been trying to forget from their passionate encounter the night of the tropical storm. A night she hadn't spoken of since then, except in vague references, but a night that had filled her dreams more often than not.

His hand palmed her back and drew her closer until they were chest to chest. Her swollen breasts were especially sensitive and felt the contact all the more acutely. With a will of their own, her fingers crawled up his hard muscled arms to grip his wide shoulders. She wriggled to get closer, her mouth opening wider to take the bold sweep and thrust of his tongue.

Warping her away from reality, the kiss unlocked Portia, electric sensations enlivening her awareness. Her normal laundry list of concerns were rinsed from her mind. Instead, she solely focused on the curve of his lips, his deepening kiss, the sweep of his tongue and the stroke of his hands. He pulled her closer, lifting her out of her seat and into his lap. Holding her in his broad arms, the scent of his amber aftershave mixing with faint sounds of ocean waves crashing to shore. Her fingers wandered into his long hair, silky beneath them and she relished every moment of making an even bigger mess of his normally tousled mane.

She'd slept with him—albeit a hurried encounter. Still, she knew the full extent of his appeal, and so she couldn't figure out why a simple kiss could turn her so inside out. Okay, not a simple kiss because nothing with Easton was ever uncomplicated.

Still, she knew the risks of getting too emotionally involved, of depending too heavily on a man. How could her body betray her so, especially after what he'd said about not wanting children? As quickly as that thought hit her she shut it down again. She'd ached to be in his arms again for so long she was a total puddle of hormones in need of an outlet.

In need of *him*.

Now.

His lips moved from her mouth to her jawline to her neck, until her head fell back to give him unfettered access as she reveled in his hungered frenzy. Back resting against the steering wheel, she slipped slightly, the car horn wailing into the moment. Snapping her into the present. Back to the fact that they were on the side of the road and not anywhere private enough for the thoughts shooting through her mind.

As the car horn died, they both winced, a laugh emerging from Easton. He brought his hands to his face, running them through his dark thick hair. Returning to her seat, she laughed too, watching the way his hair fell back into a sexy disheveled mess.

A smile still playing on his lips, he clicked the keys into place, engine warming back up. He steered the yellow Corvette back onto the road, and she settled deeper into the plush leather seat, warmed by their shared exchange of heated breath and hotter skin even as her worries returned.

A calm silence descended, broken only by the slight rustle of tires on gradient pavement.

An unquenchable need to understand what had just happened loosed her lips. "What made you do that?"

Bright blue eyes met hers briefly before he returned his attention to the road. "Because we're dating and you look incredible and I couldn't help myself."

"Dating? This is one date. That's all I agreed to, in case you've forgotten." She felt the need to clarify, because the thought of more scared her. She couldn't risk sliding into an emotional commitment of any kind, not with her and her brother's future so uncertain, not with the secret still looming between her and Easton. This was about getting a sense of him for her child's sake. Wasn't it? Her baby had to come first.

"One date? For today. If I'm not mistaken, you enjoyed that kiss as much as I did. Deny it. I dare you."

"What is this? High school? I'm not taking a dare."

He reached for her hand, the simple gesture sending pulses of interest through her body. Her stomach flipped, phantom traces of his lips echoing along her warming skin.

Easton brought her hand to his lips, the five-o'clock shadow scratching her hand. Teasing. "Double dog dare you."

She choked on a laugh, but kept her hand in his. "That is so…silly."

"Yes, but you're smiling. That's as dazzling as kissing you." He winked and grinned. "And make no mistake, kissing you, just looking at you, is mighty damn amazing." His grin broadened.

And stole her breath.

Her guard was slipping too fast. He was clearly trying to draw her out, and he was succeeding. She needed to erect some boundaries. Fast.

"You can be too charming for your own good sometimes." Her grumble was only halfhearted, she knew. She turned to stare out her window at the dark plumes of violet-gray clouds in the distance. Chances were they would blow northward, but the unpredictability of storms in this state still made her nervous.

"You say that as if it's bad. I'm simply being honest with you."

"How about hush up and drive so we can enjoy the sunset." Tugging her hand from his grasp, Portia leaned forward, watching the sun sink behind the whitecap crests. Easton's declarations rocked her defenses and struck a nerve in her tender heart.

"Can do."

The deep, dark clouds descended on the horizon, hungrily devouring the serenity of the sunset. Rain dripped onto the roof of the Corvette, faster and faster until the drops turned into a violent barrage of water.

So much for that picture-perfect sunset.

* * *

The bad turn in the weather had literally and figuratively reduced their momentum.

Easton gripped the Corvette's steering wheel in tight hands. For the past two hours, the wall of tropical rain had brought traffic to a crawl. Red brake lights filled the road, their colors seeming to smear as the windshield wipers worked as a frenzied metronome.

While this rain didn't mount to tropical storm level, it was bad enough to back up traffic as people navigated slowly along the packed, narrow road. Many had just pulled off to the side. So many, in fact, the shoulder was lined with vehicles as tightly as the highway.

Whatever electric moment that passed between them had fizzled, fading with each pelt of the rain.

That could be due to the intensity of the storm. Portia's eyes seemed heavy with inexplicable worry.

From beneath his fingertips, he felt a tug on the low-slung Corvette's steering wheel. A result of the piling rain and flooding streets. The tug shifted them slightly to the right, toward the shoulder of the road.

Portia's hand touched his arm, a gesture of reassurance. Her lilting voice contrasted against the harsh thunder. "This is almost as bad as the storm we drove in to rescue the Key deer that had been hit by a car."

He nodded, remembering well that night and how difficult it had been not to kiss away the tenderhearted tears she'd cried. Only the reminder that she was his secretary had kept him from acting on the moonlit impulse. "By the way, this rain is piling up and tugging on the steering— I think it might be slightly worse than the night with the Key deer."

"So more like the time we were transporting the pelican back from Pigeon Key?"

Ah, he recalled that vividly too, how her hair had lifted with the crackle of electricity from the lightning, how his fingers had ached to stroke over the wispy, fly-away strands, how he had realized he was feeling more and more drawn to her the longer they worked together.

So many experiences, long work nights, storms, had been shared between them. And now, another storm and more experiences brewed and crackled. The night she refused to address. That seemed to echo louder than the thunder.

"I'd say so. I mean, just look outside the window, Portia. The water is building on the streets. I think a flood is imminent."

She peered out her window, lips pursing together. As lightening flashed in front of them, he recalled how electric their connection had been during the last tropical storm. The undeniable chemistry had sent them slinking into the bathroom together.

He wanted to touch her like that again. To taste her. But his thoughts were interrupted by the extreme deluge. He could barely see the taillights in front of him.

He had driven in worse when he had to, but right now he didn't have to. They didn't have to. It was more important to be safe.

After the accident earlier today, he wasn't taking any chances. He blipped on the turn signal, seeking shelter on the side of the road.

She turned to him quickly, her lush brown ponytail bouncing, her eyebrows raised. "What are you doing?"

"Pulling over. This is insane to keep driving." He didn't risk taking his eyes off the road as he steered into a tourist shop parking lot with dozens of other cars. "Any problems with that?"

"You're right. No need to risk us getting in another wreck. There are plenty of people who can take care of the animals."

"Maureen is definitely capable." He pulled into an open spot and parked the car.

"Then let's stop for the night." She leaned forward to pick up her purse from the floorboards. "I'll start searching on my phone for a hotel."

"You have to know our chances of finding two rooms open are slim to none."

"I realize that." She pulled out her cell, smiling smartly. "Luckily, you're going to be fine with sleeping on the sofa."

A tapestry of blues and oceanic greens flooded Portia's vision when the door to the honeymoon suite—the only room available on such short notice—swung open.

The Sheltered Crescent Inn sat twenty feet from the ocean, providing panoramic views of the storm. Flashes of pure white light made shadows dance across the room, revealing an array of coastal-themed decorations. Entering the room, a smile lifted Portia's lips. The decorator seemed to have stuffed every free space with conch shells, sailboats and kitchy sayings about life being better at the beach.

Shuffling over a kelp-green rug, she leaned against the solid tan couch, eyes drifting to the open door that led to a luxury bathroom, complete with a spa Jacuzzi built for two.

Fresh-cut roses stood tall in a white vase on the driftwood coffee table. This, of course, was the most expensive room in the inn, and part of her felt bad about having to stay the night here, even though she knew money was no object for him.

The other part of her desired this extra time with Easton. As if by staying in such close proximity, she'd figure out the right words to say to deliver her life-altering news.

Turning her head, she surveyed his broad shoulders, the way his dark hair curled slightly. Ruggedly handsome with those bright blue eyes. His appeal, she tried to tell herself, had not motivated her decision to stay the night with him.

A quick scan revealed a single king-size bed peeking out from the bedroom. But there was no second bed. Just the tan couch she leaned against.

Easton's voice rumbled, and she caught the scent of his spiced cologne as he moved past her to the minibar. "Can I get you something to drink? A snack?"

"Just water for me, please." She pulled her tablet from her purse, the fading, rain-drenched sun just barely reflecting off the screen. "We could work. I have my phone and tablet."

"Do you carry that with you everywhere?" he asked as he poured bottled water into two crystal goblets.

"It's a part of my life," she answered defensively. "Organization is crucial."

"Why?"

"What do you mean by that? It's a positive trait." Frowning, she tugged her ponytail tighter into the scrunchie. She'd been responsible for taking care of her brother when they lived with their mother and she'd found early on that it helped to make lists, to have everything laid out ahead of time, to leave as little as possible to chance.

The crashing of waves echoed in the room blending with the *tap-tap-tap* of the smoldering storm. The deep sounds of thunder ebbed, becoming more and more distant.

He passed her drink to her, their fingers brushing, static snapping like the lightning outside. "Crucial, though? Do you really believe it's that important to be so regimented?"

"Of course I do. It's why you hired me." She caught sight of her own reflection in the glass window. Her hair now perfectly coiffed in a ponytail, but her face bore the stamp of exhaustion she felt tugging at her more and more at the end of each day. "Why are you pushing the point now?"

"Because I can't figure you out."

"Well, the feeling is entirely mutual."

"How so? I'm an open book."

Sort of. And then not at all. "When I took this job, I expected a scientist would be more…scientific."

He clapped a hand to his broad chest. "Have I ever been anything other than effective at work?"

"It's not that. I just didn't expect such a free spirit. Someone who doesn't own a comb and climbs trees." She couldn't hold back her teasing smile even as she knew she was playing with fire by flirting with him.

"I own a comb."

"Do you use it?" She crossed her arms, unable to resist teasing him.

He smiled crookedly, lines of amusement fanning from his eyes into his tanned face.

She nodded. "That's what I thought."

He moved toward the radio, abandoning the work space. She moved past him, his body gently skirting hers, teasing her senses and awareness. Portia's eyes narrowed, suspicious as she sat.

She had to carefully construct her walls, to keep him out of her mind. It would be easy—far too easy—to become undone by his gaze. "Easton…"

"What? We need to listen for weather alerts." He stepped away from the radio. "And I don't need a comb to organize my thoughts. As for organizing everything else, that's what I hire you for. You're stellar at your job, by the way, and I appreciate that more than I can say. I don't want to lose you over…this," he said, waving his hand between them, "either, so I've been taking things slow. But when I saw the look in your eyes after I fell out of that tree, I knew the waiting was over." The corner of his mouth pulled upward, a cocky smile in place. He looked at her hungrily.

"Oh really? This whole romance deal has been because in a weak moment I was actually worried about you?" She'd had no idea she was so transparent.

To him at least.

"Worried? I saw more than concern when you looked at me." His sidelong glance unsettled her.

And made her skin tingle with awareness.

"Easton, is that ego heavy to carry around?"

She tossed a sofa pillow at him. He easily deflected it with an arm.

"Fair enough. Does it help if I say I'm incredibly attracted to you? Because I am." He closed the distance between them, leaning on the other side of the couch. "You don't believe me?"

"I do—you're just…over the top."

"I'm honest. Is that so difficult to believe?" He touched her chin and guided her face toward his. "You're a beautiful woman. So lithe and elegant."

Rain continued to drum on the roof, a soothing sound. But his words gnawed at her. The tone was direct, straightforward, when normally he flirted. So his honest question tugged at her more, compelling her to answer straightforwardly.

"I'm comfortable in my skin, with my life, with my appearance." She brushed off his compliments, the image of her mother manifesting in her mind's eye. "I'm pleased with who I am, and where I'm going in my life."

"And well you should be."

"Thank you." She avoided his gaze, picking up another decorative pillow and hugging this one to her stomach. "That peace was hard-won though."

"How so?" He sat next to her, confusion coating his tone.

His thigh brushed against hers and a part of her wanted to just succumb to the attraction, to avoid this discussion, to avoid the future. But his eyes probed her with undeniable curiosity.

She didn't really like discussing this. Usually made it a habit to avoid this kind of conversation. But she'd decided to share more with him, and she intended to follow through on that. "My mother was the first runner up in the Miss Nevada pageant. She was bombshell gorgeous with pinup poster curves. She'd grown up poor, making her own dresses and costumes. She found her stiletto heels for competitions at yard sales and dyed them herself. The world thought she made a fabulous match with a wealthy casino magnate in Las Vegas, my dad."

Fabulous? More like financial. Her parents had made

each other miserable the minute his money dried up and he'd been sent to prison for tax evasion.

"But you may already know this," she added.

"I don't."

That came as a shock. She would have expected him to know all about her history. "You didn't have me investigated when you hired me? I would think given your family's money..."

"I did a work history check, and called your professional references, all of whom spoke of you in glowing terms. But we're not talking about work. And even if they'd told me personal details, that wouldn't have been from your perspective. I want to hear about your life. From you." His tone was genuine, but firm.

She wasn't used to being the center of attention, and she wasn't sure how she felt about it. But best to finish the story and get the sad truth about it out there and hope he wasn't the sort to judge her for her parents' actions the way others had.

Easton didn't seem the judgmental sort. She liked that about him.

She continued, "My father lost all his money when he went to jail for tax evasion. He died in jail a few months later of some strain of flu—he was a lot older than my mother."

Her dad had kids from another marriage and hadn't been much for the family scene. But he'd taken Portia to work and let her sort casino chips by color. God, she hadn't thought about that ritual of theirs until now.

She shook off the memory and moved on, eager to finish this convoluted history. "My mom...she drank herself into a liver crisis that was compounded by an injury in a car wreck. She died when I was thirteen and my brother was seven."

Portia had been crushed over her father's conviction, and she'd been devastated all over again when she realized her mother had only married for money. Taking the job working for Easton, Portia had been determined not to be drawn in by the wealth of the estate—or the man. And she'd managed to keep her distance from him for nearly two years, only to have her resolve crumble in one emotional night.

"I'm so sorry you had to lose your parents that way."

"Me, too." She shuddered, the memory wounding her all over again. "But they made their choices and paid a high price for them. My brother and I were lucky we had an aunt here in Florida who took us in so we didn't end up in the foster care system."

"You and your younger brother."

"Yes, she didn't want to be a mother that late in life. She was happily single." Her aunt, while kindhearted, had been career minded and set in her ways. But her aunt had given them stability if not an abundance of motherly affection. "But she did her best by us."

"You brought up your brother."

"He means the world to me." She swallowed hard, then froze as a horrible thought hit her. "I hope you don't think I would ever have made a move on you to keep my job."

"No, God no. I know you better than that. You have always been a trustworthy person in the way you've handled business, the volunteers and the animals. I trust you, implicitly."

His praise and trust should make her feel good, but given the secret between them, she could barely hold back a wince of guilt.

"What happened between us that night was impulsive."

And impulsive was not her style. She didn't know how to roll with impetuous feelings. Ever since she'd become responsible for her younger brother, she had laid out a life plan. Put structure over desire because she had to. She didn't want to end up like her mother.

"But that night did happen, so why won't you speak to me?" He linked their fingers and rubbed the back of her hand against his stubbly jawline, holding her gaze as if he knew full well what that rasp against her skin did to her senses.

As if he knew full well how deeply attracted she was to him even as she sought to keep the boundaries high.

"I am speaking to you now."

"That's not what I meant and you know it." He kissed her fingers one at a time, and then lowered their clasped hands to rest on his knee. "But we can let that go for the moment. You were telling me about your mother."

"I told you already."

"You said she was first runner up for Miss Nevada. Why was that important?"

A loaded question.

Her mother had had full lips, long curly brown hair and the perfect hourglass figure. Conventionally beautiful. A fact her mom impressed upon Portia, who lacked those qualities. Her mother reminded her frequently that she was plain, average, in need of "sprucing up" with flashier clothes and makeup. Whereas her younger brother had a more classic cute kid look that her mom had insisted would make him a child television star.

Portia settled on a benign response. "She even made

it into the national pageant when Miss Nevada got pregnant and married during her reign. Mom didn't crack the top tier at nationals though."

"You're still not answering my question."

A lump grew in her throat. "Some parents play favorites. My brother was her favorite."

"That's not cool. Parents should love all their kids the same."

"Maybe I misspoke a bit. She loved me. She just... liked him better."

"Why?"

She plucked at the pillow in her lap. "He was everything she wanted in a child."

"How so?"

"Charismatic. Attractive." Her brother's eyes were deep brown, his skin always easily tanned. He could have been a child model. Compared to him, Portia had been disappointing.

"You're mesmerizing and gorgeous, and most importantly, brilliant."

"You don't need to stroke my ego. I told you. I'm comfortable in my skin. I don't need a centerfold body." This conversation had to end. Now. She didn't like this level of flattery. It set her on edge.

"You're beautiful."

"Stop—"

"I mean it. I've been clear about that." He looked at her with intense curiosity, lifting a rose from the vase on the table. Easton handed it to her, a romantic peace offering of sorts.

"Well, I did look like a drowned rat that night—" She stopped short.

"So we're finally going to talk about that night."

He leaped on her words, like he'd been waiting for any chance to discuss the night burned into her mind.

"I was there. I remember it well. Very well." For a moment, she imagined the feeling of his lips on hers, his hand twining in her hair and wrapping around her ponytail.

"As do I."

Five

After weeks of strained silence, Portia finally looked ready to discuss the night of the storm with him. Perhaps there would be an explanation for why she'd shut him out so completely since that night, and why she squirmed away from his compliments. Because damned if he was any closer to understanding this woman.

A knock at the door stayed her lips, causing them to shut tightly into a thin line. Easton was content to ignore the door, but she tipped her head in the direction of the continued tapping.

"Room service," Portia reminded him, starting to rise.

He'd already forgotten he'd ordered them dinner—a bread basket, herb-crusted red snapper, jasmine rice and side salads.

He grabbed her hand, gently tugging it. "Please, sit. I'll get it." He gestured for her to return to the tan couch or go to the small dining table. "Let me do something for you for a change. You're always running around keeping my life in order."

"Thank you. I appreciate it."

Good. He hoped so, because he was doing his best to salvage something from this disaster of a date.

Easton opened the door, met by a nervous-looking woman with bright red hair. She wheeled the overburdened cart into the center of the room and cast a glance at the rain-slicked window. Another crack of thunder sounded above them, sending vibrations through the building's foundation. The food attendant winced. The lights flickered and she shot them a faltering smile. "I thought it would be an adventure to move here." She quickly unloaded the food onto the table, and a blend of spices steamed into the air. "I'm ready to go back to shoveling snow. Um, sorry to babble."

"Please, don't apologize. We understand." Portia lifted lid after lid on the tray, inhaling. He heard her stomach growl in response, a blush rising to color her cheeks.

Even in the smallest moments, Easton found her drop-dead sexy.

The attendant nodded to Easton, and set three candles on the table. "Just in case we lose power." She took her tip and raced out of the room as if in search of the nearest transport north.

Easton pulled away the last of the covers, pleased with the results, especially considering how busy the hotel must be with the influx of guests due to the storm. "Come on, let's eat. You sound hungry after all."

"I'm going to pretend you didn't just insult my femininity." She fixed him with a dark look, but he saw the amusement in her eyes.

"Portia, your femininity has never been in question. I thought I made that abundantly clear two months ago. Unless you've forgotten about that night."

Her throat moved with a long swallow. "Of course I remember."

Good. Very good. "The rain sure sounds like that night."

He pulled out the rattan dining chair for her.

Another whack of thunder overhead. The lights strained brightly for a moment. A strange buzz erupted and the lights winked out. Easton grabbed the candles and matches, lighting the wicks. They hissed to life.

He was suddenly thankful for the lack of light. The flickering candle flame provided intimacy. Maybe the romantic date could be salvaged? Albeit in an unconventional way. But he never liked status quo anyway.

Portia bit into her roll, chewing thoughtfully. She swallowed before responding, eyes wandering past him to the window where raindrops beat onto the storm glass. "This tropical storm's nowhere near as bad as that one."

"I know. I guess it just sounds louder since we're not in a storm shelter," Easton agreed, stabbing a piece of snapper with his fork.

"It was secluded," Portia agreed, her eyes fixed on the flame. She looked up through her lashes. "And crowded."

And that wasn't his point, but at least she was talking.

The night with Portia had been all heat and fire. One that demanded attention and kindling. A draw he hadn't felt since his teenage years when he'd fallen hard for a girl in a village his family had hung around in for a whole four months—a time that had felt like forever to him as a teen. But as always, the next move was always in the works. He'd learned a lot about starting relationships, but not too much about how to maintain them. "It's a wonder we found a place to be alone and no one noticed we were gone.

"In case you're worried about gossip, I told the others you were nervous about the tropical storm since you're from Nevada, and I was reassuring you."

"Thank you."

"I would have told you as much if you would have spoken about that night before now."

"Well, you told me now. And I'm glad you stemmed any embarrassment."

"My brother was so caught up in his newfound love for Maureen I doubt he even heard me."

"They are a beautiful, happy couple. I didn't think there was a chance your brother would find someone after his wife died. He grieved so hard for Terri." A trace of sadness edged her voice. Portia had liked Terri, and he knew she was sad for little Rose to be growing up without her mother. The loss had devastated Xander and everyone at the refuge.

"Their marriage surprised me as well, and Maureen is so different from Terri, too." In fact, Easton had been more than surprised at his brother's interest in Maureen, Easton's quirky, outgoing second-in-command. Yet somehow, Xander and Maureen managed to make it work. "But there's no doubting how he feels about her."

"That's true." Portia pulled a weak smile. A roll of thunder sounded, lightning coursing through the room, dressing her slender face in shadows. Darkness lingered in her eyes.

He moved the candle to the center of the table. "You don't look like you agree."

"I do, then and now. I was just thinking how their romance made me feel." She shrugged. "I don't know, kind of sad that night, seeing them together."

"How so?" Tilting his head to the side, he leaned on his elbows, drawing ever-so-slightly closer to her.

"My life is such a mess I didn't think I would ever feel that way about someone." Portia sighed, that weak smile intact.

Easton raised a brow, confused. "You're the least messy person I've ever met."

She chased a piece of lettuce with her fork, a frown forming on her mouth. "My parents had an awful marriage. My brother, who I all but brought up, was barely keeping his head above water in school after a diagnosis of dyslexia. My plans for my life are on hold until he finishes college, and I can help him get his loans paid down. Then I'll go back to school."

"And what about now?"

She looked at him, a quiet resignation set in her brow. Everything about her stance looked defeated. "I'm not where I expected to be at this point in my life."

"Where would you like to be?" His voice dropped an octave, becoming gentler. Serious. He wanted her to know he was interested in what she wanted. Truly captivated by her.

"In college." She held up a hand. "But let's stop with that line of discussion. I don't want to talk about it. At all."

"Portia—"

"Seriously." She took a deep breath, shutting her eyes. "No. I don't want to discuss that. Let's talk about something else."

One strike and she'd already declared him out. But he didn't give up easily or play by the rules.

With nothing left to lose, he decided to gamble. Ask the question he'd most wanted the answer to. "Okay, how about you tell me why you didn't speak to me the day after the storm?"

"We were busy cleaning up the place." Her standard response was too calculated to be real.

"You really expect me to keep accepting that answer?" he asked with a laugh, trying to inject levity into this dark moment.

"It was worth a try." She smiled so wide her nose crinkled, then her grin faded.

"Nice. But I would really like an answer."

She tore at another piece of her bread. He watched her try to collect herself. "Okay, you're right that cleaning up after the storm just offered an excuse to keep my distance. The feelings were so intense that I worried if we repeated that night, I wouldn't be able to keep working with you." She set down her plate. "Now more than ever, I'm still not sure. And that's why we need to keep our distance."

In a flash, she'd scooped up a candle and her pink purse. The chair rocked slightly from her departure, and her footfalls were lost in the sustained rumble of thunder. Portia's hand covered the flame, bracing it from the air's assault.

Easton barely stood before she strode past the Jacuzzi and into the solitary bathroom. The door closed behind her slender back, coming into place with a definitive click.

The sound of a lock.

Damn.

He heard water rushing through pipes, and he imagined her—a siren amid the water's steam and bubbles.

She clearly needed space, but that image tortured him. Especially after the intensity of their roadside kiss and the honest answers she'd given him.

Deep breath.

Another.

One more. She ran the bathwater, trying to calm herself with the sound, but her heart pounded and she found herself blinking back tears.

With shaking hands, she pulled her cell phone from her purse. Her tired eyes squinted at the intense light of the screen as she found her brother Marshall's contact information.

One ring. Two. He should be picking up soon, up late studying for a test he'd told her about. Portia knew he was at school. He'd opted to take a summer class at University of West Florida in Pensacola in order to finish in five years rather than sliding over into a sixth.

The ringing stopped and the light sound of music filtered through the connection.

"Hey, sis." Marshall's voice was hoarse and distracted.

She imagined his lanky frame hunched over his desk, his dirty blond hair buzzed shorter these days so he could sleep later in the morning after staying up late studying.

"Do you have friends over? If you need to go, that's okay."

"I'm studying. You know how I like white noise in the background."

"I do remember." Her brother had had a tough time in school and she'd worked hard to help him stay on track. His grades hadn't been good enough for a scholarship and it was taking him an extra year to graduate. But as long as he finished, she would be happy.

"What can I do for you, sis?"

An excellent question. She had no idea what anyone could do for her. She hadn't even really had a reason to call Marshall. "I'm just calling to let you know I'm okay since the weather is so bad here."

"Um, the weather's bad there? I really have been locked down studying. I didn't even know there was a problem. Should I be on the lookout for a tropical storm or hurricane to swing my way?"

"I don't think so. It's just heavy rain. And maybe I needed to hear my little brother's voice." She poured bubbles into the tub, watched them grow, blanketing the top level of water.

"You're the best. Really. I appreciate it."

"Marshmallow—um, you don't mind if I still call you that, do you?"

His rich laughter made her smile. She was so damn proud of him.

"No problem, sis. Just don't post it online or anything."

"I wouldn't dare." She tested the water in the tub, appreciating the warmth.

"Thanks. And hey, be careful, okay?" A note of concern darkened his voice. "You work too hard and deserve a rest. I've been thinking I should take next year off and get a job, sock away some money and give you a break. You could go on a cruise or something."

Panic iced her. She loved her brother as much as if he were her own child—she'd practically raised him, after all. Held his hand as he learned to walk, wiped his tears when he scraped his knees, helped him with his spelling words. She feared if he stopped with school he would never go back. She'd seen it happen with other students, and she especially worried for him given how hard his learning disability made things for him. "Don't even entertain the notion. You are so close to finishing. Once you have your computer science degree, you're going to be so much more hirable. Just hang in there."

"We can talk at the end of the summer."

"You're going to break my heart if you don't finish. Please, see this through."

"What about you make me a promise as well to take care of yourself?"

"I will." She would have to tell Marshall about the baby soon, but not until he'd enrolled for the fall. She didn't want to distract him from his studies any sooner than necessary.

And of course, she still had to tell Easton, too. As soon as she had her doctor's appointment. One more week.

"Do you promise?" he pressed.

"Yes, I promise. I will relax. I went out to dinner tonight with, um, friends, and in fact, I have a bubble bath calling my name. So I should sign off. Love you."

"Love you, too."

She disconnected the call, putting the phone back in her purse, attention fully on the bath. She shimmied out of her clothes without the least thought of neatly folding them. For once, she had too much on her mind to care. The chill on her skin urged her to get beneath the blanket of warm water.

As she slid into the filling bath, her hands instinctively went to her stomach. She and Marshmallow would have a bigger family soon, a caring, close family. Another redeeming thought? This baby would offer her another chance to be a mom, this time an older and wiser one.

And what kind of father would Easton be? Involved? Distant? A playmate or educator?

She knew how he worked with a sense of fun and creativity, and she knew how he felt against her. Intensely focused on her needs and unwavering in his attention.

All of her thoughts led back to that night. The sustained thunder reminded her of the thunder from that other storm. How soothing Easton had been, how caring.

Portia inhaled deeply, listening to the sounds of the storm, watching the flame crackle to itself until her eyes grew heavy and she slipped into sleep...

Flashes of awareness entered her vision. As a non-Florida native, the power of the tropical storm terrified her. Easton's good-natured teasing shifted into pure comfort. In the storm shelter, he slid his arm around her.

That's when she felt yet again the undeniable heat between them at a time when she was too damn vulnerable. Marshall was close to failing out of college and losing hope that he could finish. She couldn't let her hard work and sacrifice be for nothing. She was scared for her brother's future. She was scared for her own future, listening to the storm rage.

Her defenses were down, and her heart was oh so vulnerable. She simply couldn't find the resolve to resist her attraction to Easton any longer. A passion she hadn't come close to feeling in her past two relationships with men, both more conventional types like her.

The attraction to Easton had burned into her with those blue-fire eyes, and before long, she wandered into the bathroom with him, first with a pointed look, then him following down the short hall to the tiny room with a simple shower stall.

They snuck in there, peeling themselves away from the others in the storm shelter.

"Portia," he said her name simply, the syllables so sexy coming from his mouth.

"No words. Just..." She couldn't find a way to express to him what she felt without giving away too much. She'd been attracted to his good looks from the start, but the physical was superficial. She'd been able to hold out, especially fearful of being seen as a gold digger like her mother.

But over time, she'd been drawn all the more by his intelligence as well as his compassion around animals. Now here they were, acting on that attraction. She didn't want to think beyond that. She reached for him.

Or he reached for her. She wasn't sure who moved first. She only knew the attraction, the passion—the craving—was entirely mutual. Their first kiss felt like one of ultimate familiarity. Like coming home. Like one of a lover who'd known her for an eternity.

She wanted more. She wanted it all, regardless of where they were or how they'd ended up here or what tomorrow could hold because she couldn't think that far into the future. She whispered her need to him and he answered in kind as he lifted her onto the sink. She felt the ripples of his honed muscles as he managed the maneuver in an effortless sweep. He was such a fascinating mix of brains and brawn, privilege and earthiness.

"You're so beautiful, so enchanting, so sexy. You've turned me inside out countless times with those take-no-bull eyes and the confident toss of your head. I've been burning to touch your hair, to take it down and feel it," he whispered onto her skin with kisses, pressing his mouth into her flesh as his hands skimmed over her French twist. His fingers plucked at the pins and they

clinked against the sink behind her one at a time as fast as her racing heart.

Her mind blurred with passion. Their hands a frenzy as they pulled up shirts. Opened pants. Touched. Explored.

Found.

The room was dimly lit and small, his body close to hers with minimal room to step back. Yet driven by need she wriggled and he positioned. And he thrust inside her.

Her head fell back, a husky moan rolling up her throat. He captured it with his mouth, then skimmed a kiss along her ear, whispering gently shhh, shhh, shhh. Reminding her of the people a short hall away.

She dug her fingernails into Easton's shoulders, rolling her hips in sync with him, meeting him move for move. Their lovemaking ignited her every nerve, leaving her feeling, for the first time in a long time, connected.

For years, Portia had carefully constructed walls, pushed people outside to remain focused on providing a good life for her brother. She still wanted that. But she also wanted more. She wanted this. She wanted Easton.

Every kiss and every thrust reminded her of how lonely she'd been for years. For her whole life even. Each move and touch imprinted on her body and mind how exciting this was. How exciting they were together.

"Portia."

Her name sounded like a promise on his tongue, caressing her ear. Calming her senses but bringing her body to life. The beating of her heart sped up, becoming more ferocious and urgent.

And her name again. "Portia?"

No longer a promise, but a question...

* * *

Bolting upright awake, she grabbed the side of the tub and sloshed water over the sides, realizing she'd been asleep. Easton was, in fact, calling her name—but just from the other side of the door. Portia looked across the bathroom, a different and more spacious one than in her dream.

The bathwater had cooled, chilling her overheated flesh. She glanced at the door, then down to the haphazard pile of her clothes on the tile floor. Water pooled along the Saltillo squares. A lot of water. She must have splashed and thrashed during her nap in the tub leaving her clothes totally soggy…

And impossible to wear.

Easton rapped his knuckles on the door. Portia had scurried away an hour ago. In the last ten minutes, his desire to give her space ebbed, replaced by worry. He'd imagined her sick, or passed out on the floor.

"Portia? Are you okay? I'm getting worried." He called again, fingering the plush white hotel robe he held ready for her, "Portia, answer please or I'm going to need to open the door."

"I'm okay."

Finally. Thank God. The sound of her husky voice soothed him slightly.

"I'm sorry for disturbing your bath." He pressed his forehead to the door in relief, the cool wood soothing his overheated brow. "I apologize for upsetting you into bolting away earlier. I don't know what I said, but you have to know I would never deliberately hurt you."

"I'm really okay."

Still, he couldn't step away. "Are you going to spend the night in there?"

"Of course not."

"Do you plan to come out anytime soon?" He angled back and stared at the door, as if that act alone would cause it to swing open.

"I was thinking I would come back in there right after you go to sleep."

"Well, that's a problem because there's only one bathroom in here and I'm going to need to step in there before bed. Or rather before I go to sleep on the sofa."

"Oh, of course. I'm sorry about that. I'll be right out."

More rustling water sounds echoed, followed by drips of water. The lock popped open, and she stood in front of him. Damp tangled hazelnut hair, the small white towel wrapped around her, accentuating her curves.

Air pulled away from him. Damn, she was sexy. She turned him inside out in a way he remembered well from their night together but he had wondered if his memory was faulty.

He had tried his best to get answers from her. To be a gentleman. To get closer to her on a more cerebral level.

But that hadn't gotten him jack squat. He didn't understand her any more now than he ever had. But he recognized the heat between them. And damned if he didn't see that same simmering warmth reflected in her eyes.

On to Plan B.

Hungry for her touch, he reached for Portia.

Six

His lips found hers, catching her by surprise until she almost stumbled back into the bathroom.

All the tension she'd been storing in her body seemed to flood out of her as she unfolded into the moment. In the taste of his lips, the curve of his tongue. Her nerves melted, all tension over thoughts of meeting him in only a towel leaving her.

For this evening, here in this hotel honeymoon suite she could be a little foolish. Give in to the chemistry between them. Hell, she wanted him. Like with the kiss in the car, she didn't have much time to be with him, to get to know him, to explore every inch of him. Because her plan to put boundaries between them wasn't going to work. It wasn't boss and secretary time, not anymore.

She would have to find her way to a new peace with him. She would have to find a way to have him and her independence, too. And while this might seem reckless, playing it safe hadn't worked. And once the news of her pregnancy came out, her window of time to explore avenues for connecting with him would narrow. Considerably.

He sighed heavy against her, taking a step back deeper into the living area. Closer to the sprawling bed. A rush of cold air pressed against her chest and neck, a palpable absence. "I'm sorry. I didn't mean to grab for you like a caveman. I saw you in the towel and, well, damn, I couldn't think straight." He nodded past her, toward the bathroom. "I realize now your clothes are damp and hanging out to dry. You didn't have a choice but to wear the towel."

She leaned into him, the rain-fresh scent of him tempting her all the more. "If I'd wanted you to stop kissing me, I would have said so."

His eyebrows shot upward. "Really?"

"Really. I'm a mature woman. I know what I want and I am capable of speaking my mind." At least, for right now, she knew she needed his touch. All of him. Reality could wait until the sunrise.

"And what would that be? I need to hear you say what you want before I make another move."

"I want you." She stepped back, closer to the bed, unable to miss the way his eyes lingered on her long hair falling in damp and loose strands. "Right now, I want you to keep kissing me and more. I want us to explore the attraction we found that night of the tropical storm. To take it further and take our time. I wasn't planning this, but let's see where it goes."

"Well, I'm very glad to hear that since I want you, too. So damn much." He reached for her and she took another step back. He tipped his head, intensity stamped all over his face. "Are you going to drop the towel?"

"Are you going to undress for me?" Her gaze roamed over his muscled body, wanting to see and feel more of him.

"My pleasure." He began unbuttoning his shirt.

"I believe it will be mine. We didn't get to see each other before." So much of the sensations of the night had been lost to frenzy. She wanted to know every inch of him.

"No, we didn't." He tossed aside his cotton button-down, revealing the sun-bronzed chest she'd admired more than once while he'd been swimming. "I'm not arguing with you by any means, but what brought about this change of heart?"

"Do you need to know why? Can it be enough to know I want to be close to you tonight? Because I do, so very much." She gripped the towel in her fist, holding it closed as the water nearly steam dried off her warming body. "This day may not have been what we planned, but I have enjoyed being with you. I'm not ready for it to end."

"Portia…" He gritted his teeth, obviously wanting to say more.

"That's all I can give," she answered softly, honest in this much at least.

He gave in with a growl of frustration and desire. "Okay, beautiful lady, that's good enough for me tonight."

He toed off his shoes and tugged off his socks.

His hand fell to his belt buckle and then to the zipper of his khakis. He kicked his pants aside and there was nothing left between them except her towel and his boxers. His erection strained the waistband, attesting to just how much he wanted her.

The towel slid from her grip and his eyes went wide with appreciation. A step later from her—from him—and they stood chest to chest, mouths meeting.

His hand wandered to her damp hair, the movement bringing them closer. Easton kissed her, tongue exploring, urgency mounting. Her hands outlined circling swirls on his skin, enjoying the way he seemed to respond to her touch. His kiss becoming more urgent with every sweep of her fingertips.

He walked her backward toward the bed until her legs met the mattress. A gentle nudge sent her onto her back—into the downy blue duvet, pillows scattering.

She pulled back from him, eyes adjusting to the dim light, appreciating his body and the hungry look in his eyes. Portia stared up at him through her lashes, worried he might notice the changes in her body, in particular the swell of her breasts. Or would he just write off the differences to mistaken memory over time? Or perhaps to the fact that they hadn't even had the opportunity to look closely enough that night? She certainly hadn't been able to gaze her fill of him.

He leaned her back on the bed, the coolness of the cotton bedspread pressing against her skin—a stark contrast to the heat of his body. Wandering lips found her collarbone, and her hands tugged at his boxers, pulling them off. He angled on top of her.

His hand tucked between her legs, his fingers finding the damp core of her, stroking and coaxing and dipping inside. His touch slickened; he rubbed over the bud of her arousal.

Tonight was already so different from the evening of the other storm, the night they'd quickly and impulsively made love. Every kiss tonight was more deliberate, more passionate. She bit his lower lip, and he growled in response, pressing into her. She hooked her right leg around his, needing him to get closer. Her heart bolted at a maddening pace, her excitement intensifying as his hands brushed back her hair so he could kiss her neck. Her lips.

Palming his chest, she traced him with her other hand, trailing down, down, farther still until she cupped his straining need, wrapping her fingers around the length of him. A groan of pleasure hissed from between his teeth just before he pressed his lips to hers again.

He stole her breath, and she stole his right back. Their tongues met, thrusted and stroked just as their hands touched and caressed each other. Each touch brought her closer to completion and his quickening breaths between kisses told her he was equally near the edge.

She wondered when he would call a stop to this and reach for the honeymoon suite gift basket by their bed—a basket with condoms in every color imaginable. But he showed no signs of stopping.

With knowing hands, he kept touching her, pushing her toward the edge, interspersing deep kisses with roving hands. Driving her wild. He took her closer to release, then eased up, only to tease her closer again. And she reveled in tempting him in equal measure, stroking and stroking, grazing her thumb over the head of his erection. The first droplets of his impending release slicked over the tip, giving her the power to move faster, his breath speeding in time. Thank goodness. Because she didn't know how much longer she could hold back...

Bliss.

Pulse after pulse of pleasure ripped through her, and she only barely kept her wits around her enough to bring him to his release, as well. His deep groan caressed her ears bringing a fresh wave of aftershocks shimmering along her passion-sensitive nerves.

As the last tremble faded, she sagged back, gasping from the power of her orgasm. She couldn't even find the will to open her eyes just yet. She could only feel.

A rustle sounded beside her. Easton. The covers shifted as he untangled them from their feet, and then a sheet settled along her. The ceiling fan overhead sent gusts of air down to dry the perspiration along her forehead.

Easton settled beside her, and she glanced at him, rolling to her side. His arm was flung over his eyes, his chest rising and falling rapidly, each breath a hint slower but still not back to normal. She reveled in the knowledge she'd brought him the same pleasure he'd given her.

Her eyes drifted to the honeymoon suite gift basket by their bed, looking at the assortment of neon condoms. Was that glitter on them, as well? A hint of apprehension whispered through her. She wasn't ready to tell him that they didn't need condoms.

Now she just had to figure out how to deal with using glitter-covered birth control.

The moment felt like an eternity as she stared at the basket, contemplating how to proceed. Heart hammering, Portia felt her hands start to tingle, a sure sign of her anxiety.

Easton's deep blue eyes searched her face. "Come here."

He opened his arms to her.

She hesitated.

He lifted her hand and tugged her gently until she toppled to rest against his chest. His arms folded around her and anchored her there. "Sleep."

Surprise drifted through her passion-fogged mind as she realized somehow he'd understood her hesitation even though she hadn't voiced it. "You're serious? You don't want to finish this?"

"I do. But I can tell you're not ready and I'm smart enough not to make the same mistake twice. You're too important to me."

His words touched her as intensely as any stroke against her skin.

"If you're sure?"

"I am. Very." He rubbed her bare shoulder gently. "Now rest. We'll talk more tomorrow."

He draped himself around her, encircling her in his muscled arms. Protective and gentle.

She settled into him, noting the rhythmic rise and fall of his chest. The darkness in the room covering them both, shielding them from the reality of the morning. But for right now, Portia could pretend everything was fine and normal. That having someone take care of her was exactly what she needed.

And it was damn hard to deny that this didn't feel natural.

Morning sun streaking through the shutters, Easton listened to the patter of the shower and thought of the night before when Portia had been in that same bathroom, soaking in the tub.

They'd never made it to the spa in the corner of their bedroom, the ledge decorated with candles and champagne. But then this was a honeymoon suite, and they were not honeymooners.

He scratched his chest and kicked aside the covers. While all his plans for the evening hadn't come to fruition, he had no regrets. He'd made significant progress in his hopes of winning his way back into her bed.

Instinct told him the best move was to give her space. To pursue her carefully so as not to scare her off again. He wasn't risking this second chance to be with her. He knew too well how fast life could change, how quickly people he thought he could count on were gone. He also knew his own shortcomings in maintaining relationships for the long haul.

He swung his legs off the mattress, feet meeting the cool floor. He tugged on his boxers and reached into his pants pocket for his cell. After that storm, he should check in with Maureen and make sure the refuge hadn't suffered substantial damage. While he loved spending the night with Portia, he knew the staff and animals at the preserve counted on him.

Walking out to the balcony, he cued up Maureen's number. The Gulf Coast waters glistened in the aftermath of the storm. A few branches littered the beach and chairs were overturned, but he didn't see any major upheaval. Morning walkers and shell collectors were already on the sand, a few kids dodging waves in bathing suits and tiny life vests. Vacationers were getting back to normal. Hopefully he would get the same report from home. Maureen answered on the third ring, her voice bright and alert.

"How'd we fare with that storm last night?" Easton asked in lieu of a normal introduction.

"And good morning to you, too," Maureen teased. "We've been worse this year. Some debris, naturally. I'm mobilizing a team of volunteers for yard cleanup."

Easton sank into one of the wooden Adirondack

chairs, looking out onto the sun-speckled water. "How about the animals?"

"Spooked a few of them. But no substantial damage to any of the facilities and no major injuries to speak of," Maureen said, a parrot cawing in the background. "We were lucky."

"That's great to hear. I worried about them and you guys." He inhaled deeply, the scent of ocean overpowering his senses.

"So are you transporting any animals on your way back up?" Maureen asked.

"No. This isn't exactly a business trip."

He could practically see Maureen's eyebrows raising as she responded. "Yeah. I guessed that. Easton?"

"What?"

"Be careful with Portia. I think she is going through something. She's just been off lately. At first, I thought she was worried about how Marshall was doing in college, but now I'm not so certain that's the only concern in her life."

Protectiveness crept through him, making him want to scoop her up and handle any worries that burdened her. He *would* figure them out, damn it. "Thanks for the heads-up."

"We all care about her. She's more than an employee."

"I know. I'll talk to her today on our way back. See you soon." He ended the call, looking through the sliding glass door, Maureen's words echoing in his mind. He had noticed the same thing about Portia more than once lately.

But he'd failed to take action in helping her. He'd been so focused on his own pursuit, his own needs. Guilt stung.

Easton went back inside and practically ran into Portia. Her hair was damp and loose from her shower, but rather than a towel, this time she was dressed in her clothes from yesterday. They were wrinkled, but dry. He didn't want to rush her, especially not after he'd just made a point of deciding to give her space.

No caveman tactics today. He would take things slow.

But she looked gray, like the color had been leeched from her. Her eyes briefly met his, but she turned away to perch on the edge of the sofa as if ready to take flight.

With a doctor's eye—even if for animals rather than people—he studied her more closely. Looked into her eyes. Counted her respiration as well as her pulse throbbing along her neck. And still he was no closer to figuring out what had upset her.

He could heal any animal, identify birds by their songs, but determining what made Portia tick was proving to be much more challenging.

Noting the exhaustion on her pale face, he said the first thing that came to mind, "You've been putting off going to school because of your brother's loans. What if I told you that you don't have to wait?"

"What do you mean?"

"Plenty of bosses help pay for their employees' college education. So why not start classes now?"

"I'm not the kind of woman who will take money from a man she's seeing, much less sleeping with, and it's insulting that you think I would." Fire burned in her eyes.

And her response struck a nerve for him.

"I'm insulted you think I would offer for any reason other than wanting to help. I should have thought to learn more about you sooner, and I would have known the need." He clasped her shoulders in a gentle grip and hoped she would read the genuine concern in his eyes. "Clearly stress is wearing you down and if you're burned out then that's bad for me on many levels. As a boss and as a person who cares about you. So let me help how I can."

"No." She shook her head, lips tight.

"That's it? No?" His hands dropping to his sides, he stepped away, and paced for a moment until he caught his betraying restlessness and leaned against the doorframe, trying his best not to appear frustrated. Easton wanted the best for Portia. No strings attached. He cared about her.

"Yes." She tugged her hair scrunchie off her wrist.

"Good."

"No, I meant, no you can't help." She piled her hair into a high ponytail on the top of her head, pulling it tight. "And yes, my answer is still no."

"Would you care to expand on that?"

She sagged into a chair. "Another time?"

Every road led back to this with her—to him being shut out like last time. As if she was leaving before she even had a chance to inevitably head out the door. "Sure, but on one condition."

"What's that?"

"You won't close yourself off again and block me out completely," he said, a gentle demand. He searched her face to gauge her reaction.

Portia's eyes fluttered shut. For a moment, she didn't speak. A sigh escaped her, and she opened her eyes to stare at him. "That's not a promise to sleep together. Last night—"

"Was another impulsive moment." He completed the sentence for her, finding he actually agreed with her. Stepping closer, he continued, "I get that. Completely. That's why we didn't finish."

"Truly?" She played with her necklace, sliding the charm back and forth on the silver chain.

"Yes, Portia. Truly. I want you to have sex with me totally aware of what we're doing. Not swept away. Well, swept away, but for all the right reasons. And trust me, I do believe that will happen and in the not too distant future."

"You're mighty confident." The first hint of a smile shone in her eyes, tipping her beautiful lips and chasing away some of the strains of exhaustion.

"About what we're feeling? Yes, I am." He lifted her hand and pressed a kiss to the inside of her wrist, lingering, holding her eyes for an instant before linking their fingers and stepping back. "Now let's get dressed and hit the road. We're both going to be late for work."

The ride back to the refuge had been mostly silent. Portia organized her notes, working hard as they drove.

As she color-coded her tasks, she felt more settled. This process with her notes and highlighters provided order and grounding. Each precise stroke of the pen and marker helped erect her protective walls.

Easton hadn't pressed her during the ride, letting her work in silence while he guided the low-slung Corvette around the storm-tossed debris on the roads. He hadn't even argued when she'd bypassed breakfast and asked only for warm tea with peppermint. Although she had pretended to nibble on a cookie.

She looked up from her planner, the afternoon sun warming her skin. They were on the road to the refuge. Somehow, two hours had come and gone.

He pulled the Corvette into the driveway, parking beneath a tall royal palm tree. They unbuckled, each exiting the vehicle. When her foot touched the solid ground, Portia's nerve and resolve grew.

She wasn't normally a person of impulse but after last night, she wondered if perhaps she should tell him about the baby now after all.

"Um, Easton," she began, hesitantly, words catching in the air as Maureen bounded onto the scene.

Portia couldn't ignore the huge sense of relief over being let off the hook a little while longer. Yes, she selfishly wanted more time with Easton to explore this attraction before risking a possible confrontation when he found out about their child.

"Hey pretty lady, you're back. I have a surprise planned for us." Maureen beamed at her, wrapping Portia in a hug. "I'm stealing your assistant for the remainder of the day. And your brother wants to talk to you." Maureen laughed, pulling Portia to the door of the mansion.

"You two have fun. Portia, we'll talk more later." He waved. Heading toward the clinic.

Maureen tugged Portia into the mansion toward the spacious women's locker room. She put her hands over Portia's eyes as she led her inside.

Relaxing harp music sounded, and when Maureen removed her hands, Portia took in the transformation. The steel and oak-benched locker room had been transformed into a day spa, not just with softer lighting, candles and sparkling water, but complete with pink-draped massage tables, a table of dainty foods, and makeup/hairstylist gear.

Maureen spread her arms wide. "Surprise. I knew you would try to go back to work after the time away, so I caught up with everything at the clinic. Now we can enjoy a girls' getaway, complete with dinner and pampering. Facials and shoulder massages and even a hair trim."

Portia froze, indecision and old insecurities taking

control. "I appreciate your generosity, but I'm not comfortable with a makeover."

"That's not what this is about at all. You're beautiful as you are. I meant what I said about pampering only. You work too hard."

Maureen pointed to the spread of food on the far table.

Portia pursed her lips, leery of trusting Maureen. She felt vulnerable. But the food smelled divine. The long wooden table had a mixture of breads, garlic-crusted chicken, crab legs, and angel-hair pasta with lemon butter. Portia's stomach growled in response.

Now that Portia's stomach had settled and since she hadn't eaten yet today, the meal tempted her as much as the prospect of a shoulder massage.

"You have beautiful hair. Why do you keep it pulled back? It looks almost painful."

"It isn't." She touched her ponytail self-consciously.

"I'm sorry." Maureen winced. "I shouldn't have said anything. That was rude of me. I just wondered...but it's none of my business."

"I actually have my mother's hair." Portia stepped up into the stylist chair, looking at her reflection in the mirror. She shrugged her shoulders.

"And that's not good?"

"We had our differences, many of them. In fact, we were different in every way except for our thick hair—if not the same color. I want to be my own person so I chose a different style than hers."

"Then be your own person. Take charge."

"I have." Mostly. Partly. She'd brought up Marshall. She'd provided for him, a contrast from her mother's version of caring, which involved making sure they had the right "look." Their mom's pampering of her son had been almost smothering as she paraded her little boy in front of agents in hopes of landing a child star role in a commercial or television show. Portia felt that lack of a normal childhood could have been at least as damaging as the criticism she'd received. And then after their mother's death when Portia and Marshall had gone to live with their aunt in Florida, the decidedly nonmaternal woman had used what bit of parenting instincts she had to parent the younger of the two, leaving teenage Portia to fend for herself as she navigated young adulthood.

"Okay." Maureen nodded, slicing a mix of cheeses from the assortment and sliding the samplings onto the bone china plate along with fruit and crackers. She brought it to Portia, a smile resting on her lips. "Good?"

"Looks delicious." Portia took the delicate dish, wary of Maureen's easy acquiescence. "Just okay? You aren't going to push me to participate in some magic makeover?"

"Remember! Today is *not* about makeovers. It's about relaxation and letting our inner self shine through." Maureen plucked up a grape and popped it into her mouth.

"But you want to offer advice."

"Of course. I'm opinionated." She snorted on a laugh. "Just ask my husband. Or anyone who knows me for more than five minutes then, like you."

"Alright, then. Let it fly. I'm a canvas." She popped a cheese cracker into her mouth before setting aside the china. "Paint me."

Maureen sat back in her chair, examining Portia. "I would suggest you let your hair down and quit thinking about your mother. Embrace who you are. Your hair doesn't have to be up or completely down either. I realize you like it back from your face. So perhaps try some clips, have fun with jewelry."

"That's it? Let my hair down and pack some Be-Dazzled pins?" She was surprised, half imagining that Maureen was going to suggest a severe haircut or worse—bleach it as her mom had not-too-subtly suggested more than once.

Well, damn. She did think about her mother's criticisms too often.

"It's a start, Portia. If you could choose any dress you wanted, no holds barred, what would you choose?" She gestured wide with her hands, as if all the clothes in the world were actually in front of them.

"I thought you were supposed to be helping me pick."

"I will, if you need me, but I don't think you need anyone's guidance on this."

Portia glanced back over her shoulder, curious and a little suspicious of some mystery motive. "What's really going on here? Did Easton put you up to this?"

Or worse yet, after their night spent away, was Maureen attempting to matchmake?

"I'm just empowering you to be who you want to be." Maureen removed Portia's ponytail, letting her heavy hair fall. Grabbing a brush, she worked through her tangled air-dried locks. "Oh Lord, did I really just say that? Empowering? I sound like some kind of self-help book—you're the last woman who needs help. I just want to pamper you since you go out of your way to take care of others. And in case you're worried, the professional hairstylist will be here soon."

"It's kind of you to arrange all of this, and I don't mean to sound like an ingrate." She looked at her short, neat nails and wondered what they would look like with a bolder color, not long French tips or fake nails, but just something...fun. "I shouldn't have said what I did about my mother. I don't want to be someone who blames everyone else for my hang-ups."

Maureen set down the brush and took a chair beside her. "You're the last person I would assume that about. You are levelheaded and confident."

Portia didn't feel that way. She felt like she'd clawed her way through life to find confidence and a future for herself and her brother. To find the independence she craved. She didn't want this roaring frustration inside her. She wanted to be happy about this baby, her child. Instead, she was just...scared.

What did she know about being a mother? She hadn't had good examples. Maybe this spa day, and the time with Easton, would help her get her head on straight before her whole world changed.

The doctor's appointment was less than a week away. A relief.

And the ticking clock counting down her time to finish exploring this whole empowerment exercise. Soon she would take on the whole Lourdes family full force—and one incredibly charming veterinarian—and tell them she was carrying the next little addition.

Seven

Three hours later, Easton stood in the doorway leading to the women's locker room and braced his hands on either side to keep his footing. He'd heard from his brother that the women were getting dinner, massages and makeovers. And he'd expected some glammed up, artificial look. He'd prepared himself to say the right things on his way to kissing the artifice away. Had anticipated the moment with a raw sensuality that burned deep inside him.

However, he hadn't expected Portia's angled features to make her look downright ethereal. And the difference rocked him. He'd always found her attractive—her kindness, her stunning smile, her deep, dark eyes.

But with her hair falling around her ears…

How she sat relaxed and causal…

She knocked the air from his lungs. Literally.

Her eyes widened as she noticed his stare, a faint blush

rising, swirling in her cheeks. The shadowed light catching on her slender face. Damn.

"You look stunning," Easton said, his voice hoarse as he worked to drag air into his lungs again. "And I don't just mean the hair or the makeup. There's a glow to you that's incredible."

Maureen tipped her head to the side. "A glow?"

Portia shot to her feet, dismissive of his compliment. "Thank you. All the credit goes to the makeup artist and hairstylist. I just sat still and let them work."

She walked to the drink station and fixed herself a glass of sparkling water and then dropped in a lime slice from a bowl.

Don the security guard and his wife, Jessie, floated into the room. Active fiftysomethings, they were a powerhouse volunteer couple. They donated a substantial amount of time and money to the refuge. Somehow, they'd also become surrogate grandparents to Rose, poking in and out of the house. Down-to-earth people no one would suspect actually had made billions through savvy investments in the dot-com world, getting out right before it crashed. They were a regular fixture around here, often staying late. It was never a surprise to see them wander in, and the Lourdes family could never pay them back for all they'd done for the refuge.

The dim light of the room made Jessie's spotted pullover appear like a molten mix of tan and black, making her seem like a jungle cat. Elbows hooked together, they strode over to Easton and Portia who had shrugged off her robe to reveal a formfitting mint dress. All of her curves accented, the mint color brought her pale skin to life. Teasing him, tempting him.

She brushed her fingers against his. A small gesture, sure. But he found himself itching for more. A lot more.

Jessie cooed, patting Don's stomach. "Did y'all know that we are celebrating thirty-three years of marriage next week?"

"That is amazing." Portia nodded, a smile on her lightly glossed lips.

Easton nodded absently as well, eyes fixed on her. Wanting her.

"Are you doing anything special?" Easton said after a moment, shifting his weight slightly so his body would caress Portia's. She leaned into him, like a palm tree swaying in a springtime breeze. Awareness simmered between them, a slow burn.

Don combed his fingers through his snow-gray hair. "When are you planning to ask her out on an official date?"

Portia choked on her sip of sparkling water.

Easton set his drink aside slowly and lifted an eyebrow. "When did you start up a matchmaking service?"

Don shrugged, proceeding in his typical straightforward manner. He'd never been one to mask his thoughts or feelings. "Sorry to have put the two of you on the spot there, but it's obvious to all of us around here that the two of you are an item. So I was just wondering when you're going to start dating. Or if you already are, let the rest of us in on it so we can double date."

"Double date?" Portia squeaked, putting aside her own drink now.

Jessie reached her hand out to gently squeeze Portia's arm. She gave a quick wink. "Sure. Do you think married couples don't date anymore? If that's your idea of marriage, no wonder you've stayed single for so long."

Easton watched as color drained from Portia's face. He decided to steer the conversation to a different topic—anything to make Portia feel more comfortable and not derail his plan to win her back into his bed. "I know married couples have romance. I've seen my brother married twice, happily both times."

Jessie lowered her voice, holding a glass of sparkling wine in a relaxed grasp. "Then you two are dating and keeping it quiet?"

She asked so casually, as if she were inquiring about the weather and not asking for a piece of private, intimate information.

Easton folded his arms over his chest, frustrated that his friends could be eroding the progress he'd made toward getting Portia back into his bed. "No offense, Don, but why is this any of your business?"

"Wow, you're in a bad mood. Must be the barometric pressure drop," Don teased, still not getting the message. Easton saw Portia's spine grow rigid, the glow of earlier replaced by seething discomfort.

Jessie gave an exaggerated wink. "Or a lack of romance in your life."

Portia waved a hand. "Hello, I'm here and a part of this conversation."

Jessie turned to Portia, blinking. In faux seriousness, she asked, "So is he properly romancing you?"

Easton held up a hand. "Stop. Yes, I'm interested, very interested, in Portia. And I want to win her over, but that's for her to say and you're not helping matters."

All eyes turned to Portia.

"What?" She held up her hands defensively. "Things are complicated."

Jessie nodded. "He's your boss."

"True." Portia winced. "Thanks for reminding me."

Easton had kept his frustration under control when it was all good-natured ribbing, but now, as he watched Portia grow increasingly uncomfortable, he started to steam. He wanted to protect her from any upset, even something as innocent as this sort of thing.

Jessie shot a warning look at Easton before leaning toward Portia. "Has he made you uncomfortable with his advances? Because that wouldn't be right."

Easton bristled. Established, wealthy volunteers or not, there were lines and they were skirting close to crossing them.

Portia touched his arm lightly. "Easton hasn't done anything wrong. I made the first move on him, okay? So there. Yes, we have feelings for each other. Yes, we're attracted to each other. And yes, it was probably silly of us to think our private lives could be private in such an intimate work environment, but we really would appreciate some space to figure this out. Thank you."

She adjusted her weight and fixed them both with a commanding stare before striding out of the room. Her chin up.

He had never seen her be so assertive before. She'd become a force—like the storms that had brought them together—firm, unflinching and unapologetic.

Dazzling.

And he was stunned as hell that he wanted more than just to have her back in his bed again.

Drained, Portia sagged against the door after the men left, watching the stylist pack her gear, listening to the sounds of zippers and bottles of products clinking together before more footsteps reverberated along with the closing of a door. With the portable salon packed in bags, the room echoed.

She hadn't been in the mood for such prying questions from anyone, even friends like Don and Jessie. And the questions seemed to carry more weight, hit her more deeply, because of her pregnancy.

Her still secret pregnancy, made all the more complicated by that look in Easton's eyes when he'd seen her. She could have sworn she saw more than just passion, and that excited her and scared her all at once because heaven help them, this could not be a regular dating relationship. They didn't have the luxury.

Pressing a hand to her forehead and closing her eyes, she couldn't remember the last time she'd felt so alone. Then the warm press of another person sidled beside her, sweeping an arm around her shoulder. Portia looked over, the smell of peonies and powder lingering.

Jessie. A woman happily married for decades. A grandmother. Content with where she was in her life.

A painful sight for Portia right now.

The older woman patted Portia's shoulder. "I'm sorry, dear, we didn't mean to upset you. My man, he can be pushy, but he didn't mean any harm. We thought it was so obvious."

Portia found it easy to forgive the woman for her overreaching. Jessie showed her tender heart daily in how she sang to wounded animals as they underwent treatment. Which made her think of Easton's tender care of animals that could seriously injure him in their wounded, frantic state. He was such an intriguing, unexpected sort of person.

She looked down at her fingers twisted together in her lap. "Our feelings are that apparent?"

Maureen's brogue answered as she called from behind a changing screen, "Yes, they are. Especially this past week." She passed Portia a tissue. "I've never seen you cry before."

Portia sagged onto an oaken locker room bench. "I do have emotions."

Sitting beside her, Jessie stroked a lock of hair over Portia's shoulder. "Of course you do. You just usually keep them to yourself. But those feelings are tougher to keep inside when hormones are out of control."

Jessie gave her a pointed look that all but had Portia squirming in her chair. Her secret pregnancy wouldn't be a secret much longer if people were already guessing. Luckily, Maureen seemed oblivious. Still, the time clock was ticking down. Portia had to tell Easton. "I'm doing better now, but thank you for caring.

"Of course, dear, we're all a big family here. And I'll make sure Don lightens up on the teasing." Jessie clucked her tongue like a protective mother hen.

"Thank you. That would be helpful." Especially until Portia figured things out for her future as a mother.

With a satisfied nod, Jessie stood up. She fluffed her hair with her fingers, and started to walk away. She paused for a moment, spinning on her kitten heels to face Portia. "You really are lovely, and glowing. Take care of yourself, dear. Maureen, would you mind taking me to see my favorite little Key deer baby that has a broken leg?"

Maureen pranced out from behind the screen, her curly red hair falling midchest, contrasting with her white shift dress. Her gold accessories catching the light, making her look like some Celtic princess from centuries past.

"Of course. I have about an hour before I'm supposed to meet Xander. I'll take you to the baby deer."

She linked her arm with Jessie's and tossed Portia a wave and a wink.

Glowy.

Such an intentional and loaded word.

Did they know? Or at the very least suspect?

Before panic could fully rise in her chest, Portia's cell phone rang, sending her thoughts skittering. Looking down at the screen, she read *Marshall*.

Scrambling to answer, she clicked the green button, shoving the phone to her ear.

"Hey, sis. I haven't heard from you in a while—"

"Since last night."

"I know," he teased gently. "I was being sarcastic. You sounded, um, off last night. I wanted to follow up. You're not the only one who worries."

The weight of responsibility felt heavier than ever on her shoulders. Every decision she made could have such far-reaching repercussions. "Work has been hectic. How are you?"

"I'm good. Classes are good, grades are solid and I have good news for you."

"I could use good news." She couldn't keep a wobble of concern out of her voice. She was so confused, and for a woman used to controlling every inch of her life, that was a difficult and alien way to feel.

"Are you sure you're okay?"

Oh, nothing. Just my life being torn apart.

She wanted to say something like that—wanted to share her life-altering news with her brother. Instead, she looked at her nails, choosing to remain the strong, balanced force she always thought Marshall needed. "Yes, of course. Tell me your news?"

"I got a gig as a residence hall counselor after summer session this fall, which means free dorm and a break on tuition. There's been a last-minute opening and they asked me."

"That's fantastic." A shred of positive news. There'd be less to siphon away from her pay. The debt for his college education was worth it though. She needed to see him settled before she could make any plans for her future, however much she wanted to... She stopped thoughts of Easton short. For now. And she focused on her brother's words instead.

"I'm trying my best not to be a burden to you. I appreciate all you've done for me."

"It's my joy. I'm proud of you." She'd never told him of her own dreams to go to college. She was so afraid if he didn't complete his education now he never would. She needed to know he was secure in his future.

But she also had a child to consider. Life was so very complicated.

And she wanted to be with Easton again so damn much.

The next day, when Easton had asked her to have dinner by the pool after work, she hadn't even bothered making an excuse to decline. Clearly, hiding their mutual interest from everyone and each other was futile. In a way, that observation caused a degree of relief for Portia. There would be no sneaking around now. Fewer secrets. This would be their first date since their night in the inn. The night they'd almost slept together.

A night she couldn't get out of her mind.

After his date request, she'd rushed to her cabana to shower and change. As she slipped into a simple backless green dress, she felt a buzz hum through her body.

Apprehension coursed through her spine, filling her with a strange mixture of curiosity and desire. She fluffed her hair, opting to let it stay down like the stylist had done the day before.

Maybe there was something to all that empowerment talk Maureen had given Portia. A new hairstyle for a new chapter in her life. The small change felt like she'd made a promise to herself to be brave for her own future and not just for her brother.

Regardless of the attraction between her and Easton, Portia needed to get to know him better. The father of her unborn child. No. Wait. That was wrong.

Their unborn child.

That shared child meant they would forever be in each other's lives, even if he was a reluctant parent. She couldn't see him turning his back on his child altogether. And if he did? Then he wasn't a man worthy of either of them.

She left her little home and walked the path over to the pool by the main house. Easton had said he planned to walk her over, but coming to him gave her more of a sense of power.

Now she was glad she had done so as she had a few minutes to take in the dinner arrangements unobserved. Easton had hired a Spanish guitarist and a pianist to play sultry songs. The beautiful riffs filled the night air, making her forget for a moment that she was at his house and not in some fancy restaurant.

Glancing around the pool deck, she certainly felt like

they had been transported somewhere magical. High romance. No expense spared. Globe lights were strung overhead like personal stars. The whole patio was decorated in hibiscus flowers and soft green ferns—a tropical getaway in the middle of daily life.

The house was silent and unlit. Xander, Maureen and baby Rose had left for an evening getaway.

Easton stepped through the double French doors with a bouquet of peonies in his hand and stopped short once he saw her, then he picked up his pace again.

"Portia," he called out, "I wanted to escort you over."

She met him at the stairs. "I know, but I was ready early, and I do know where you live."

"That you do." He extended his hand clasping the pink blossoms. "These are for you."

"Thank you, they're lovely." She brought the dozen buds up to her nose and inhaled the sweet fragrance.

Easton took a carafe from the wet bar and slid the flowers inside, pouring water into the makeshift vase. She was touched by the way he didn't order staff around to do his every task. He was a man with the money to pay for most anything he wanted and help for every moment of the day, and yet he lived a purposeful life.

He nodded to the flowers' placement before turning to her. "I thought about getting you candy too, but I keep seeing that basket full of edible toys back in that honeymoon suite."

Laughing, she pressed a hand to her lips and finally gave up holding back her amusement. "I'll return the vase once the peonies wilt."

She would be drying them as a keepsake for their baby. Far better to explain how she and her child's father had dated and enjoyed their time together. She couldn't bear for their child to feel like the unwanted result of an impulsive night.

Easton pulled out a chair for her at the wooden table. The peonies added the perfect touch to their romantic dinner, no one but the server and the musicians around.

Soft wind whispered as Easton pushed in her chair, his fingertips lingering for a moment on her bare shoulders. He took his seat across from her, foot knocking playfully into hers. His ready smile illuminated by the Tiki torch that kept bugs at bay.

Easton tucked his ankle against hers. "You really do look beautiful. If I didn't think to tell you before tonight, I apologize."

"You told me."

"You didn't believe me, though, did you? There's a skepticism in your eyes that stuns me."

Portia leaned closer to him, so her words didn't strain against the melody of the guitar and piano. "Of course I realize we're attracted to each other."

He touched her chin and tipped up her face. "You are lovely, elegant and always have been. It's all I can do to keep my hands to myself at work."

"You've always been completely professional in the workplace."

"I'm a damn good actor, then." He plucked a hibiscus from a nearby arrangement, spinning the stem between his fingers.

She laughed, unfolding her napkin and placing it in her lap. These luxurious meals were a treat, but she would have to watch her fish intake for the baby. Still, her mouth watered with hunger, a welcome relief from the morning sickness that grew worse each day. "I do appreciate and respect that you've been restrained in the office."

He tucked the flower behind her ear near the jeweled pin, ramping up her awareness. Distracting her from the parmesan-and-herb-spiced yellowfin tuna that overtook her plate.

"So it's okay for me to touch you outside the office now?"

"I didn't say that, exactly."

He dragged another flower up her arm, until it rested on her cheek. "I can see something's holding you back. Am I simply not your type?"

"Why do people assume they know my type?" She shimmied away from the flower, picking up her fork and skewering one of the roasted tomatoes.

"Someone else agrees with me?" He lifted one eyebrow.

"I didn't say that."

"I know I'm eccentric." Laughing, he pointed to the decorations overhead.

"You're brilliant and a gifted veterinarian who manages to work with a wide variety of exotic animals." Portia rested her fork along the upper edge of her plate. "And, yes, you're also one eccentric tree climb away from having your own television series."

"You don't make that sound like a compliment."

"I only meant I'm reserved. Some have even called me prim—" She held up a palm. "I'm alright with that description. I know myself. But you *are* eccentric. I would expect you to be drawn to someone more flamboyant."

"Some say opposites attract. I think it's more complex than that. Attraction defies reason."

So true. But that didn't stop reason from interfering with attraction, reminding her how hard she'd fought to be independent, to build a life for herself outside of her parents' shadow. She couldn't afford to forget that in the long term.

And yet, still, she burned for this man. Unable to resist for this one moment at least, she lifted her fingers to stroke his collar-length, wild hair. The touch happened before she thought better of it. And maybe it wasn't so bad as long as she knew it was her decision. She was in control. "Relationships are based on common interests."

"What are your interests? You draw, but what else?"

"I'm your secretary."

"My assistant." He corrected her gently, placing his hand on top of hers.

"Whatever. It wasn't your place to know my hobbies."

"We've spent more time together than some people do when officially dating. I should have listened better." He thumbed the inside of her palm, a small smile tugging at his mouth.

"Is this going to be round two of Quiz Show?"

"I was just going to ask you what song you would like for me to request from the pianist."

"Something with a beach music flavor. I love to dance."

"You do?" His bold mouth twitched in a crooked smile. "See, we have something in common after all. Hold on while I place our request."

He pushed out of his chair, heading to the pianist, all elaborate arm gestures and flash. An intoxicating vision.

Returning to the table, he extended his hand. "If you've finished with your dinner, could I have this dance?"

How could she resist? Right now, she couldn't. "I would like that, very much."

"I'm honored." He bowed deeply before whisking her onto her feet to the makeshift dance floor.

Pressing against each other, she felt time strain and stop for this moment. The scent of his cologne mingled with sea breeze and salt. He sang softly in her ear, his hot words warming her inside out.

His soft eyes met hers, desire and electric sparks passing through his gaze.

No matter what the future held for her, or how he reacted to her secret, there was only one way this night could end. Together, tangled.

Eight

Dancing with Portia set him ablaze. His hands had touched the bare skin of her back peeking out from behind her breezy green sundress. After the music faded, she looked at him through shy eyes.

"Walk me home?" her voice quiet, eyes burning into him.

Easton's hand trailed alongside her right arm, enjoying the softness of her skin, the way she seemed to melt under his touch.

He leaped at the chance to lace her fingers with his, for the extra time together. His stolen sidelong glances at her increased the farther away they walked from the main mansion to her modest off-white cabana. Her shoulders, normally strained, seemed relaxed. A light breeze tossed her half up, half down hair, the moonlight illuminating soft traces of makeup that accented her slender face and beautiful pink lips. She seemed like a tall fairy—an extension of the landscape. His landscape.

Their footfalls on the white sand road looked like shooting stars in the night.

Portia had always been naturally beautiful, but he couldn't recall a time when she'd seemed so at ease and calm. The spa afternoon had brushed life back into her, making it all too obvious to him how she always did things for other people and didn't do things for herself. He wanted to pamper her. He wanted to protect her. But as she spoke of common interests and viewpoints, he wondered if he should be protecting her from himself and his vagabond spirit.

She fiddled with her keys, fishing them out of her pale yellow purse. Shifting her weight from leg to leg, he noticed how her strappy sandals pushed against her skin.

The cabana she'd been given as part of her pay had been stark and basic when she'd arrived. Now the little wooden hut glistened with peace and beauty, her stamp everywhere. Flowers of nearly every hue overflowed from boxes and pots. Lush ground cover filled in spaces with only jeweled step stones breaking their flourish. A fountain built of terracotta clay pots overflowed into a pool of fat orange fish.

She unlocked the bright yellow door, brushing her feet on the mat before stepping inside and clicking on the lights. Inside, a plump, inviting sofa, in what he'd heard Maureen call a shabby chic print, nearly filled the room. There was an artistic flair to Portia he hadn't noticed before, in spite of her telling him she enjoyed drawing. He could see her creativity in the way she'd planned her garden and how she'd refinished old pieces of furniture, end tables with swirls of color patterned into the grain and shape. Even her simple ice cream parlor table sported handblown glass spheres that filled a bowl like crystallized treats. Somehow, he knew she'd made those, with her patience, frugality and eye for beauty. Why hadn't he thought before about how she commented on the distinct hues of the birds and other creatures in the wild?

And how had he not stepped inside here before now?

He'd missed so much about her until that night of the storm when he'd been drawn to her with new eyes, the electricity in the air gathering around her like lightning bugs. Even in trying to get her back into his bed, somehow he'd missed important details. Getting to know her had been a selfish plan, but he was finding himself more captivated than he'd ever been by another person.

"Portia, your place is lovely." Like her.

She slipped her shoes off and nudged them in line beside the door with her toe. "It's nothing compared to your professionally decorated mansion."

"You have an artist's flair to you that surpasses anyone else we could have hired."

"Thank you." A blush on her cheeks, she stared lovingly at her possessions. Proud of her space and vision. Confident.

"I like the way you brought nature inside." He stepped to the walls lined with pen-and-ink sketches of Florida coast scenery and animals. "And your art. These sketches are yours?" he asked even as he saw her initials precisely in the corner of each one.

"Yes, I mentioned I like to draw." She tapped one of her sketches, an alligator winding through marsh grass, a wry smile on her face. She'd never seemed so sexy, so decisive. So sure of herself as she was in the arena of her art.

"I remember. But this is more than just doodling or

drawing. This is talent, a gift." He turned back to her. "I respect the work you do for me. You keep me organized and focused in a way no one has managed before. But here, I feel like I'm keeping you from your true calling."

She looked at him thoughtfully, her love of art apparent on her face. "I'll get back to it one day as more than a hobby."

"Why one day? Plenty of college students work while enrolled. I did."

Taking his hand, she led him into the living room. She sat on the bright yellow couch in lotus position, patting the seat next to her. Inviting him closer. She leaned forward, interest and surprise knitting into her brow. "Even with your family's money?"

"Absolutely. I wanted hands-on experience." He sat too, linking fingers with her. Needing to touch her.

"That's nice to hear about you. I didn't know." Her palm rested on his knee in an unspoken promise of more to come.

This was another dance they were doing now, one he could see in the awareness in her eyes, the widening of her pupils.

"It must not have come up in your Quiz Show."

"I would have expected your life growing up, traveling the world, would have given you the opportunity for vast experiences."

"We were talking about you. And your brother. And why you refuse to let anyone help you with him," Easton said, not taking the bait to talk about himself. Portia so often deferred her interests and needs to others. He didn't want her to do that now. Not as he finally glimpsed her soul and her sparkle.

"Because I can take care of him. He's my family. He

has a learning disability. He's brilliant but needs tutors. He will graduate, it's just taking five years with summers. He's even picked up a part-time job as a residence hall advisor this fall. I'm proud of how hard he's worked."

"And then it will be your turn?" He reached for her cheek, stroking it with a soft thumb. Wanting to give her all of her dreams.

She placed her hand over his, stilling the motion of his fingers, yet pressing his touch more firmly against her skin. "I thought we were coming here to make love."

"Wow, I struck a nerve, didn't I?"

She rose from the couch, headed to the kitchen as if she were considering his words. Lingering by the fridge, she cocked her head to the side and popped her hip out. "Maybe I want to start getting hands-on experience with my art right now."

"What do you mean?" His heart pushed, hammered, at the suggestion in her pose, at her yet to be articulated promise. Standing, he strode into the kitchen.

"You can be my canvas." She pulled a tub of whipped cream from the refrigerator. She lifted the lid and swirled her finger through, painting her lips before licking them clean.

He almost swallowed his tongue.

She was distracting him on purpose. Of course she was. But looking at her right now, feeling the answering heat inside him, he would gladly let her. He would find out more about why she was delaying her schooling later.

After he explored every tasty inch of her. He couldn't take his eyes off her still-damp lips. "I assume that's my cue to get undressed."

"If you want." She shrugged nonchalantly, staring at him with a certain, commanding smile.

He made a mental note to make sure her future included all the spa days she wanted. Whatever magic Maureen had worked in getting Portia to take some downtime had paid off in spades. There was a new relaxation and confidence in her.

"I want. Very much." He stepped closer, unbuttoning his shirt and tossing it aside.

She swept her finger through the dessert topping again and touched his collarbone. Her stroke was cool from the cream, and then she dipped her head, her breath warm as she said, "Ooops, I need to erase that." She swept her tongue along his skin. "I'll need to draw that over again."

"Do I get to practice my artwork on you?"

"Are you any good?"

He took the tub from her and set it on the table by the colorful glass display. "I damn well hope so."

His hands damn near shaking, he reached behind her to unzip her dress until it slid from her body to pool around her feet. She kicked it to the side. He took in the vision of her peach-colored lace bra and panty set, her breasts perfect globes calling to his hands to explore. Her eyes held his as she released the front clasp. He was quick to help her stroke free of the scrap of lace so he could "paint" a snowy cloud of whipped cream over one nipple, lave it clean before giving equal attention to the other.

Her kittenish purrs of pleasure rewarded him for his diligent effort. She cupped his face and guided him back for a kiss. The sweet taste of sugar on her tongue went straight to his senses. Before he could gather his thoughts again, they'd both stripped away their clothes in a frenzy of motion on their way to kneeling on the kitchen rug.

Taking turns, they painted each other, although his

artwork was more precise than hers, Portia's more in the league of landscapes that sent her kisses all over. He focused more on her breasts, a trail down her stomach, then settled between her legs for an intense, intimate kiss. The sweetness of her had little to do with the topping and far more to do with her. Portia. This amazing woman who'd come into his life and shaken him from his superficial dating ways.

He wanted more from her. So much more.

With each stroke and circle of his tongue, her breathing grew faster. She gripped his shoulders, her nails digging half-moons into his flesh urging him to cover her body with his. He didn't hesitate.

He settled between her legs and positioned himself at the hot slick core of her. Something tugged at his mind but before he could finish the thought, Portia skimmed the arches of her feet along the backs of his calves and hooked her ankles around his waist. The arch of her hips welcomed him inside her. Where he belonged.

His head fell to rest against hers, the bliss of being joined with her so incredible it almost pushed him over the edge. He gritted his teeth to hold back his release, to make sure she found complete pleasure, everything he could give her before he indulged himself.

Stroke after stroke, thrust after thrust, he filled her and savored her rocking motion in sync with his. They were learning each other's bodies, specifics and needs, erogenous zones. The scent of her freshly perfumed skin and some kind of massage oils along her shoulders teased his every breath.

He would drink her in if he could.

Let her know how beautiful she was. Always. No makeover needed.

She was Portia. He'd not realized why he'd pursued her so stubbornly, but this surprising woman was who he'd been waiting for. And finally he was where he wanted to be.

That thought tore away the last vestige of his restraint and sent him hurtling over the edge into a blinding orgasm. His release sent him pulsing deeper into her, faster, each pump of his body drawing a "Yes, yes, yes" from her lips until... Her back arched upward. Her head fell back, her silken hair fanned around her.

No need for them to be quiet here in her home, just the two of them. Their cries of completion twined in the way their hands did over her head. Together.

His arms gave way and he just barely caught himself on his elbows before he rolled to his side, taking her with him. He folded her against his chest, their bodies sticky with sweat and the remnant of whipped topping.

In the stillness of this cabana, he felt at peace. The rise and fall of his chest made more comfortable by the press of Portia's body against his. His fingers stroked down her side. The moment of rest as beautiful as she was.

Easton kissed her cheek before nuzzling her with his late-day beard. "What brought on this change of heart?"

Portia looked up at him through long eyelashes. "Not a change of heart. I've always wanted this. I just felt like the time was right. This is our night."

"The first of many more, I hope."

She hummed in answer and kissed him, silencing any more talk or even rational thought, for that matter.

His hammering heartbeat started to recede into normal rhythms.

"We should get clean." He said into her skin. In response, she kissed him, deeply, her tongue darting over his.

"Done so soon?" She bit his bottom lip, hand wandering down his side.

She got up, her body a dark silhouette in the streaming moonlight. Walking to the bathroom, she looked seductively over her shoulder.

He wanted her, even more than before, and he planned to have her again and again. Thank goodness he'd brought enough condoms—

A sinking feeling slammed him in the gut. Damn, damn, damn it.

He was always careful. He'd only ever forgotten one other time, the first time he'd made love to Portia and when he hadn't heard anything from her in spite of his attempts to reach out, he'd known they'd somehow been lucky.

As he followed her toward the shower, though, he snagged his pants with his wallet full of condoms to use from here on out. They could talk about the lack of birth control during those other two encounters in the morning.

Because he wasn't letting anything interfere with this night in her bed.

Bright sunlight streamed into her room, nudging sleep from her eyes. Looking out the window, she began to turn her gaze inward. To memories of last night.

Allowing Easton to come to her space had been a big step. A bold one. Portia had allowed him to glimpse her private love affair with art—the one activity that steeled her nerves, made her feel brave and resourceful. She'd channeled that creative capacity into their night, blending art with love.

She stretched fully, remembering the way their tangled bodies sought each other as if by their own volition and inclinations. Portia painted him with whipped cream, made a masterpiece of his skin and her desire. Pulled him again into the shower. Needed him.

She'd felt like wildfire last night. A rush of flame and heat so intense, one that had to burn itself out. Which was where she felt like this morning was heading. To the aftermath. He'd used condoms those last two times. She hadn't wanted to break the mood by telling him it wasn't necessary, not when she already knew they would be talking about the baby soon, likely before her doctor visit. Because it wasn't fair to keep him in the dark now that they seemed to be heading into a relationship. Once she shared the news with him, things would change between them forever.

She turned from her side to see if he was awake.

Those bright blue eyes met hers, his dark hair curling on the pillow. "Last night was incredible. *You* are incredible." He stroked his fingers through her loosened hair. "I hope you don't run in the other direction again to put distance between us. Because I want us to be together. I want to see where this is going."

"I have no intention of running." She meant that. Running with their unborn child wasn't an option. She needed to face this head-on. No matter what. She'd been running from this conversation for too long.

"That's good to know." He leaned in to kiss her, then stroked the outline of her face. "I'm sorry for losing my head last night and forgetting to protect you."

"You mean not using a condom?" Bile churned in her stomach. The conversation was already headed in the wrong direction. She wasn't ready for this conversation. Not yet.

"Yes," he nodded. "That's twice I've let you down and

I'm sorry. But I want you to know that if there are consequences, I'll be here for you."

"Consequences." The word felt clinical. Distant. Emotionally shut off. But then she hadn't wanted the conversation to get emotional. So why was she bristling? God, her emotions were a mess and she knew it had more than to do with the baby.

"Consequences. As in pregnancy," he clarified. "Unless you're on the pill?"

All of her gusto and nerve manifested into steel will to cover the hurt his words caused. Part of her did want to rely on him and make a real relationship, but now she was second-guessing herself. Yes, she needed to tell him the truth. But she didn't need his help. Didn't need him to be obligated to her. Portia always figured things out on her own, made them work for her. Even if that path wasn't the easy or conventional one. "Don't worry about me."

"Of course I will. You don't need more responsibility on your plate in addition to your brother. In fact, can we talk again about me help—"

"No." She pressed her fingers to his mouth, surprised at the depth of her remorse over realizing they didn't feel the same way about last night. He was not ready to be emotionally involved with her, not ready to be a true parent. For a moment, she'd wanted to do all of this with him by her side, and she swallowed back the fantasy of being able to parent with him. "Can you stop talking about money and responsibilities and consequences? I know you don't want children. You've made that clear."

"As I recall, I said I don't think I'll be a good father and that I wasn't ready to start a family. Now that I think back I'm not sure exactly what I said." He scratched the back of his head. "You may have noticed but my thoughts get jumbled around you."

"You said you don't want children. I remember your words, and I would think a man of your education level would know what he's saying." Anger edged out her more tender emotions as she lobbed the words at him.

He reeled back under her attack, then he sat up, grasping her hand. "I'm not trying to pick a fight, Portia, although it's clear I've upset you. I'm sorry for that."

Portia tugged her hand from his. Distance. She had to put some space between them. And quell the rising tide of nausea building in her stomach. "Please, stop apologizing. I'm an adult. I'm equally responsible for what happens between us when we have sex."

"I'm trying to be honorable. Would you prefer I was a jerk?" His sincere blue eyes punctured her, calming her for a moment.

"Of course not." She shook her head, eyes stinging with unshed tears. The world pressed on her shoulders, pinning her to this moment.

"Then let me be a gentleman."

"Gentle is good."

The words stalled on her lips, heart growing heavy as nausea took over her body in full force.

He reached out to touch her, but she bolted from his fingertips. Running to the bathroom, door closing behind her.

Her bare thighs pressed into the tile floor as she held the porcelain toilet. Two types of illness bore upon her. One from the increasing intensity of morning sickness. That sickness she could manage—that one had an end in sight.

But her heartsickness over the lost chance to be with Easton in a real relationship?

She'd parented her brother and never felt this solitude—instead she'd taken comfort from her friends. Heaven knew she had friends and support here at the refuge.

Yet none of them were Easton. The abyss of her loneliness stretched in front of her as she heaved the contents of her stomach into the toilet.

Consequences.

The word sliced through her mind. She just wanted to curl up on the cool tile floor and not move for seven more months.

What was it about him that sent Portia running to lock herself away from him?

Easton sat on the edge of her bed, scanning the room. Everything seemed to have a definitive place. Bright, cheery colors served to accent the plain white walls. Her poppy-orange bedspread added warmth and comfort to the room.

She didn't have a lot of figurines or knickknacks, he noted. A small, skinny faux marble table sat in the corner, holding a bouquet of fresh-cut flowers.

Next to him on her nightstand, he noticed a small sketchbook, the spine worn from constant use. The visible signs of wear seemed at odds with the rest of Portia's room.

Glancing at the still-closed door, he decided to pick up the black leather-bound book. Leafing through the pages, he found himself transported.

Portia's floral sketches that hung in the hallway were beautiful. But the sketches in the notebook were stunning. Haunting, imbued with reality. She'd sketched different animals from the refuge, her images playing with shading and line structure.

He was no art aficionado, but Easton knew enough to realize Portia's raw talent. He felt a renewed dedication to getting her into an art program. She'd been self-taught. If she had resources, a mentor and time…she could be downright fantastic.

He replaced the sketchbook back on the nightstand, continuing his survey of the room. The top of her dresser housed a framed picture of her and Marshall, a gold-leafed copy of fairy tales and a ring dish where a pearl necklace coiled.

He picked up the book of fairy tales, reminding himself Portia needed her space. The door was still shut, but when they'd been at the inn, she had taken a bath and come out of that experience more relaxed.

Surely this morning was the same thing. He tried to convince himself of that.

But as time passed, seconds turning into minutes and then a full half hour without any sound other than the bathroom sink running and running, he began to worry. He hadn't heard the bathwater start, and he feared she was perhaps crying.

He walked toward the bathroom door and as he drew closer he realized…she was throwing up. Retching. Again and again. Worry overtook him and he knocked firmly on the door.

"Portia, let me help you. Do you have food poisoning?"

A long pause echoed, then he heard the sound of the sink turning off and the sound of what he thought was her head resting against the door panel.

"Easton, I don't have food poisoning. I have...*consequences*."

Her words churned in his mind and settled. Hard.

He'd discussed the possibility of pregnancy with her but he'd been speaking hypothetically. This wasn't hypothetical. This was reality.

A baby.

His.

Inside her.

The sideswiped feeling stung along his skin much like a sunburn. But soon it eased enough for other feelings to flood through. Frustration that she hadn't told him before. That she had only decided to share it with him now that they were separated by a bathroom door and there was no way she could hide the pregnancy's effects. But at the forefront of all those thoughts? But at the forefront of all those emotions?

Possessiveness.

This child and Portia were now his responsibility. They were both officially a part of the Lourdes family circle. Given her independent streak, which was a mile wide, he could already envision her shutting him out.

He'd just figured out he wanted to create something real with her. No way in hell was he letting her walk away. He would keep her and their child, using whatever means necessary.

Nine

Portia pressed her head to the cool panel of the wooden bathroom door and waited for Easton's response to her poorly timed announcement. This was not what she'd envisioned when she organized the talking points for this conversation. She'd meant to roll out the pertinent details in a logical sequence. Warn him that she was prepared to take on this responsibility by herself. Assure him his child was in good hands with her.

Instead? She'd blurted out the truth in the harshest of terms possible.

Her heart pounded in her chest, slamming against her ribs that already ached from her extended bought of nausea. She could barely stay on her feet she felt so weak, a new low in her battle with pregnancy symptoms. She just wanted to crawl back in bed and hug her pillow until the birth.

With every day that passed, the morning sickness grew

worse. Although after today, she didn't know how it could be worse other than lasting all day long. Heaven forbid.

Should she call the doctor to move up her appointment date? Or...no. It was already Tuesday and her appointment was at the end of the week. Besides, she'd heard the old wives' tale that the worse the nausea the stronger the pregnancy. An upset stomach meant there were more hormones pumping through the system from her body's change. But she didn't have any scientific proof for that and couldn't risk her child based on internet articles.

She drew in deep breath after deep breath, wishing her little haven of a bathroom could be the place of peace it normally was. The old-fashioned claw foot tub had a Parisian-themed shower curtain hung from the ceiling, the whole room decorated in cream, mauve and gray. She'd painted a shadowesque chandelier on the wall with tiny rhinestone studs in the place of lightbulbs, a touch of whimsy that made her smile most days.

Rhinestones couldn't touch this nausea.

Hanging her head, her toes curled into the plush bath mat. She'd been so excited when she had come to the refuge and taken this job two years ago. The exotic locale had called to an adventurous side of herself she'd never indulged. This tiny house had been an unexpected bonus, a treat, a space to call her own since up to then she'd lived in Pensacola, close to her aunt's place, sharing an apartment with her brother. But the pay bump here had enabled her to head out on her own, and the timing had been right for her brother to spread his wings, too.

She had her own space, and now she needed to make the responsible choices that went with that freedom. Definitely she would give her doctor's office a call to see if her symptoms warranted an ER visit this weekend. They must have a twenty-four-hour service or a nurse on call to answer questions. She would not work over the weekend so she could take care of herself until that appointment on Monday. She would place the call as soon as she dealt with her baby's father on the other side of the door.

Heaven help her. She'd screwed up this announcement so badly.

"Portia?"

The low rumble of his voice pierced the bathroom door. She couldn't detect how he'd received her declaration about the baby. He'd told her he didn't want children...but the reality was, he was already a father. If he was half the man she thought he was, he would step up in some way. She'd seen him with his niece, and he was tender. Loving. She knew he would be as kind to his own child.

If she'd misjudged him, however, she could and would be a loving mother. She could take care of herself and her child. Her baby would be loved, not judged.

She swallowed hard, then took her time brushing her teeth, all the while bracing herself to face Easton. She splashed cold water on her face and toweled off.

Willing her hands to steady, she pulled open the door. Bright rays of sunshine washed over Easton, who stood, slightly disheveled, in crisp blue boxers.

Tugging on her oversized T-shirt, she really looked at him, taking in his muscled chest and abdomen. Sexy blue eyes filled with concern. His sleep-tousled hair perfectly accenting his sun-bronzed skin. Easton, the eccentric, wealthy doctor.

And the handsome father of her child.

What an exciting affair and romance they could have had if she'd only had the bravery to grasp this chance sooner. If she'd followed her instincts, which had shouted that they were both attracted to each other. Instead, she'd waited until it flamed out of control, and she had been too caught up in the moment to exercise her normal wealth of good sense. Knowing him better now, she wondered if his sense of honor had kept him from making the first move on an employee before the first storm that had brought them together.

"You're pregnant," he said, clasping her shoulders in broad, calloused hands. "With my baby."

"Yes." She resisted the urge to lean into him, to soak up the warmth of his body. "This isn't how I wanted to tell you, but yes, I am. Nearly two months along. I took seven pregnancy tests that first week I was so…stunned." Shocked. Scared. "They all came back positive. I called my doctor and she said to start prenatal vitamins, and we made an appointment for my first visit with an obstetrician. I go at the end of the week."

"Just a few days away." His voice was quiet, as if processing. He had to be feeling even more overwhelmed than she was. She'd had more time with the news.

She chewed on her lip before responding. "I was waiting until then to tell you."

"So you did plan to tell me," he said as he sat, causing fabric ripples on the bright comforter.

"Yes, God yes. Of course. What did you think I would do?" All she'd done was make plans since she had first discovered the news. Planned how to tell him. How to deal with a new addition to her family. She had a bullet list of baby needs. A monthly plan of action a mile long.

He shook his head, blinking rapidly, no words forming on his lips. After a small breath, he pressed on, "I wasn't thinking much of anything since I've had less than five minutes to absorb the news. I don't even know if you're planning to have the baby."

"I just said as much didn't I?" Heat built in her cheeks, hands growing numb.

"Not really." He grabbed her hand, studied her features. Her stomach gurgled an involuntary response and an aggressive wave of nausea threatened her again. "Portia? Are you okay?"

The scent of their lovemaking clung to the sheets. She wanted to crawl in the bed and press her head into her cool pillow and simply sleep the day away.

Another roll of nausea knocked into her along with a wave of dizziness. She fumbled for the edge of the mattress, gripping it.

Anchoring herself, she twisted the comforter in her fist. "Yes, I'm having my baby, and I plan on keeping him or her."

"My baby, too," he reminded her quietly, firmly. "I want you to put your feet up." Standing, he cleared a space for her on the bed, fluffing pillows before gently sliding his hands under her arms to prop her at one end. He also set an empty small trashcan nearby diplomatically. "In case you're feeling ill again, you can use this rather than getting up. Is this typical for how long your nausea is lasting each day?"

He went into doctor mode. She could see it in the patient way he asked her the question. Feel it in the touch he brushed on her forehead, surreptitiously checking to see if she ran a fever.

As his longtime assistant, she knew he was assessing her symptoms while trying to keep her at ease. Just like a sick deer. Or a surly monkey. How flattering.

"*Our* baby," she reminded him, remembering his possessive words. "And the nausea's gotten worse this week."

Her stomach churned again, bile rising in her throat. With a deep breath in, she tried to settle herself.

"Yes, ours, which gives me a say in the child's life." He took her wrist in one hand, his thumb squared over the pulse that she guessed was sporadic at best.

She felt like crap.

"I'm glad to hear you feel that way." She wanted to keep up her end of the conversation, tell him she didn't need his veterinarian care for her very human baby. Except she appreciated the way he tugged the blankets over her. Mopped a cloth on her forehead.

When had he gotten a damp cloth? Nerves pulled tighter inside her, making her head spin faster. She was glad he wanted to be a part of their child's life, but she could also feel her control of the situation slipping away.

"Portia, I would never abandon my child."

Determination and something Portia thought looked like hurt passed over his features, finding purchase in the tension of his expression.

"I know that." Yet while she knew Easton was kind, she hadn't been sure how he would respond to the news based on how quickly he'd bailed on old relationships. "Yet you've admitted to feeling ambivalent about parenthood. You've purposely steered clear of meaningful relationships and you climb around in trees like a mashup of Peter Pan and Tarzan."

"I'm not sure I like that analogy at all." He knelt in front of her, taking her hands in his, meeting her gaze with such earnest urgency in those mesmerizing blue depths. "But right now, the important thing is to make sure our child is healthy and thriving. Do you think you could hold down some water or ginger ale?"

She tried to answer but his concern for their baby— for her—touched her heart, and the more emotional she became, the more her stomach misbehaved. She was already so weak from morning sickness that she simply couldn't face another bout.

"I could try." She said it only to make the medical professional in him happy.

The thought of putting anything to her lips made her queasy. But this conversation was important in setting the tone for the rest of her and her baby's lives. She'd done such a poor job telling him about her pregnancy and now was her chance to set boundaries. Assure him she would be okay on her own.

Portia could hear Easton speaking, but the words grew softer as her head swirled. She worked to steady her focus by grounding herself in the beauty of his eyes, the rough velvet of his voice.

"Portia? Portia are you listening?"

"Yes, of course," she said softly, her vision growing fuzzy around the edges.

"Then what do you think?" he squeezed her hands.

He sounded so distant, fading by the moment.

"Easton?" She struggled to make sense of his words. "Think about what?"

Her fingertips seemed to lose contact with the comforter, sending her into a widening spiral. Nothing made sense. She tried to reach out for his hand. For the bed. For anything, really. But her vision sputtered, growing foggier as she tried to figure out what she thought about the proposal. No use.

More nausea, more dizziness, the room giving way like some scene out of *Alice in Wonderland*.

She fainted, her world swallowed by the unknown.

An hour later, sitting dumbstruck and numb in the ER waiting room, Easton stared hard at the window to the outside world as if he could somehow get himself and Portia back to that familiar reality. Not that staring helped. He barely registered the sway of palm trees or the glimpses of the ocean.

His thoughts kept turning inward, replaying the morning's events. Portia telling him she was pregnant, growing paler and disoriented. Portia fainting suddenly on her bed, scaring the living hell out of him.

Typically, Easton was the sort of man people liked to have around in emergencies.

When he was a teenager, he and his brother had hiked up a hill in Virginia. Their parents had let them have free range that afternoon. Easton had pushed them to explore. But as they neared the top of the hill, Xander lost his footing, tumbled down, falling on the rocks and trees, breaking his right arm in three places. Even then, Easton possessed a doctor's cool hand for dealing with injury and illness. He helped his brother to his feet, and calmly transported them both to a hospital. Fear never pushed at him once.

But today when Portia had been nonresponsive…he'd felt fear wrap icy hands around his heart and mind. The ride over to the hospital became a blur. She'd gone straight into a wheelchair, unable to stand without swaying. Seeing his beyond-competent Portia so incapacitated leveled him.

The staff's urgent and worried care revealed just how fragile and ragged she'd become. Why the hell hadn't he made sense of her symptoms earlier in the week? Maureen had told him something was off. He knew something was off.

And yet he'd ignored all those signs, too damn focused on his own goals. He was a first-class ass. By the time he'd handed her over to the hospital staff, her pale skin had felt so clammy.

The cackle of a loose parrot from outside snapped him back to the ER waiting room. He stood, wanting to be in the exam room with Portia. To do something, anything, to help her. Instead, he was out here. He sat back down, back pressing into the hard plastic of a lime-green chair. Across from him, he watched an older couple in their sixties talk in hushed tones.

The man's swollen ankle was propped up on a stool. His wife stroked his arm, love shining in her eyes along with a hint of irritation. Over what?

Not that it mattered. Easton just grasped for distractions.

Two seats away, a small girl cried intermittently. Her mom stroked her hair, cooed to her. Soothing the toddler. No father in sight.

Easton's heart seized. He wouldn't be that way with his child—an absentee father. If everything was okay.

Everything had to be okay.

Worry pushed into his thoughts again. He felt shock stiffen his joints. What if something terrible was happening to Portia right now? He clenched his hands into fists, squeezing. Trying to get a grip on the situation.

He'd been upset with her that she hadn't said anything to him before this morning. He wasn't sure what would happen with them. Her news had changed everything. But more than anything else, he wanted her to be okay.

A swoosh of the automatic doors sounded, letting in a blast of muggy heat from the outdoors an instant before a familiar voice called out to him.

Xander.

His brother had arrived, two cups of coffee in hand along with a bag of something.

"Easton? What's going on? I heard you were rushing Portia to the hospital."

"Who told you that?" Easton asked, surprised to see his brother huffing and puffing in front of him.

Xander snorted and passed over a large cup of aromatic java. "Do you think anything's a secret with all those volunteers around?" He held out the bag. "Want a doughnut?"

Clearly some things were secret since his brother made no mention of what ailed Portia. Still, Easton got the point. "No, thank you. The coffee's just what I need though. Thanks." He took a bracing drink of the nutty brew, then set the cup on his knee. "Portia's pregnant."

"What?" His brother blinked, surprise coloring his face. All that boardroom bravado gone. Xander dropped into a seat beside Easton, setting the bag and his coffee on the steel end table. "I'm…confused. Surprised. Details?"

"She's pregnant, and the baby's mine." Easton took another sip of the strong coffee. Too bad they didn't serve IV caffeine around this place.

"Congratulations, brother." Xander clapped him on the shoulder once, twice. "I assume you're happy—but hell, wait." Worry crept into his voice. "Why is she here?"

"Her morning sickness is out of control. They have her hooked up to IVs since she's dehydrated."

"All during the pregnancy with Rose, Terri battled that. You remember."

"Sort of, yes." A memory of his niece after Terri died

wandered across his mind. He'd taken her to the beach, built towering sandcastles for her. Easton told her stories of magical lands and talking animals. His flair for theatrics making her squeal with sharp giggles of uncontrollable laughter. He'd always thought his role as über-involved uncle would quell any parenting needs. Easton was crazy about his niece. But then Xander remarried Maureen and Rose didn't need him as much anymore.

For a few weeks, the lack of time with his niece had been strange. He felt like a castaway from that family unit.

But with Portia...

New possibilities leaped before him. He wanted Portia—he sincerely wanted to marry her. And he wanted to be there for their baby. To do whatever it took to be a good husband and father.

Because, damn it all, they would be a family. He wouldn't be relegated to the sidelines. He knew what it felt like to be an afterthought in his parents' lives. He wouldn't let his child entertain so much as a hint of a notion that that could be true.

He might not have planned on being a father, but he would figure out how to do this. He would be there for the baby and for Portia.

Xander angled forward, elbows on his knees. "You should be in there with her."

"They're going to let me join her soon. We're not married so I don't have a spouse's rights."

"You look shell-shocked."

"I only found out about the baby this morning." Easton combed his fingers through his hair, likely doing more harm than good. "I'm still...adjusting to the news."

Adjusting didn't even begin to cover it. He'd been set on romancing Portia, taking her out on dates, winning her back into his bed. He hadn't thought beyond that. He didn't do long-term relationships well. At all. His history spoke to that.

But now the baby—and yes, the power of his growing feelings for Portia—flipped his world upside down. He needed to think. To process. And figure out how to become someone she could depend on.

"Is she planning to have the baby?" Xander whispered, eyes darting around the emergency room.

"Yes, of course." He'd been so relieved when she had reassured him on that score. Of the million questions he had for her when he'd heard the news, that one had been the most important and she'd put his mind at ease.

"Then congratulations, brother. You're about to embark on the most amazing experience of your life." Xander slapped Easton's shoulders again.

"Thanks." He meant it. Still, he had worries and doubts.

His brother had embraced parenthood full-on. But he had always been better with personal relationships, too. He'd taken time to build something with Terri before they married and had Rose. Easton, on the other hand?

Every woman he had ever dated had been disappointed with his brand of interpersonal skills. Before, it hadn't bothered him. Much. But for Portia? He wanted to be better.

Xander leaned away, astute eyes locked on Easton. "You don't look happy."

"I'm just concerned about Portia right now." He wasn't ready to talk about his concerns and explain what a mess he'd made of things by not pursuing Portia outright after the tropical storm. He'd wanted her then, had played in his mind a million ways to angle for another night together, yet he had stopped short of acting on those thoughts. Now he wondered what had held him back. Whatever it was had made his life a helluva lot more complicated.

"Of course you're concerned about her and the baby. I understand. I'm sorry. What can I do?"

"I appreciate your coming here. You could have just called though, you know." He hated distracting his brother with personal matters. He didn't like burdening him or taking him away from his family.

"We're brothers. I was worried. You would have done the same thing if the positions were reversed."

"Truth." He nodded, meaning it all the way to his soul. His brother was his best friend, always had been. "You're right about that."

"And besides, you must have forgotten your damn phone again and didn't answer when I tried to reach you." Xander cast a sidelong glance his way, eyebrows knitting in faux annoyance.

Easton welcomed the ribbing, needing to share a laugh with his brother now more than ever. His laugh tangled up with his brother's, rumbling in the waiting room as a doctor in green scrubs stepped through one of the endless row of doors.

"Easton Lourdes?" the tall silver-haired doctor called, clipboard in hand.

Easton rose from his chair, lungs tight as he nodded.

The doctor waved a hand, motioning for him to follow. "You can see Ms. Soto now."

Portia kept her arm preternaturally still, glancing at the IV needle. Though she knew she could move her arm slightly, she felt like it needed to stay still as she processed the events of the morning.

She clenched her jaw as she looked at the ultrasound.

A tiny bean-like figure was displayed on the screen. Her baby. The future frightened her slightly—or it had until the doctor came in with the ultrasound monitor. She watched her child move, become real before her eyes.

Looking around the sterile white room, she knew she needed to plan. To figure out what direction she'd take. Her fingers itched for pen and paper...to make checklists and doodle storks.

The medicine she'd been given worked wonders. For the first time in weeks, she didn't feel sick to her stomach in the morning. That alone stabilized her.

The thin door that led from her room to the rest of the ER allowed muffled sounds to pass through the light wood. Sounds of machines beeping, a small child crying, a cart rattling down the hall. Adjusting her weight, the paper crackled beneath her, bringing her back to the stillness of her room.

The blue cotton hospital gown allowed air to kiss her back and neck, the coolness refreshing her as she leaned forward, letting her paper-shoed feet dangle off the edge. She tested her balance and found the floor didn't wobble or spin anymore.

At the sound of a quick knock, Portia raised her head and called, "Yes?"

"It's me." Easton's deep voice filtered through.

Nerves tingled but her stomach remained steady. She reached for the blanket and draped it over her shoulders and wrapped it around her protectively. "Yes, come in."

The door clicked open an instant before a wide hand swept back the privacy curtain. His broad shoulders and chest in a refuge-branded polo shirt filled her vision, blocking out the rest of the world. He shoved his hands in his jeans pockets. "How are you feeling?"

"Better, much better. The fluids help and they gave me something for nausea."

"So you're, um, both okay?" Concern furrowed deep in his brow, and for the first time since they'd met, he seemed unsure.

"Yes, we are." Lifting her left hand, she pointed to the ultrasound machine behind him. The image of the baby—*their* baby—was frozen in black and white on the screen. "You can see here. That bean is your child."

He turned to face the ultrasound machine, the profile of his face in her direct line of vision.

Portia watched the way his eyes squinted and refocused, almost as if his identity as a doctor disappeared, leaving behind a man in awe. Of course, she was aware he could read this ultrasound from a medical standpoint—note nuances, explain away the shape.

The man in front of her clearly did not process the image from such a technical angle. Instead, his lips, though pressed together, curled upward in a faint smile. His cheeks softened. She couldn't get over the expression of awe on his face. The possessiveness and pride etched into his stance. Looking at him now, she began to realize all his talk about not wanting to be a father was false or delusional. He'd already become attached. This baby wasn't just hers anymore.

And her baby's father was a man of money and power. She couldn't help but remember how his brother, Xander, had used that wealth and power to ensure he maintained full custody of his daughter after his first wife died. Portia had applauded his efforts, since in that case, his former in-laws had strange ideas about what a child needed to be happy.

But the incident worried her now as it occurred to her

Easton had the same kinds of resources at his disposal. He'd admitted he had never invested in a long-term relationship. What if he got tired of Portia but wanted more time with his child?

Easton eyed her, his rich dark hair falling in waves, catching the cold, sterile hospital room lights. "You're absolutely sure you're alright?"

"The hormones are really something else." She swiped away those worries, telling herself she was being ridiculous.

"Can I get you something to make you more comfortable?" He gestured around the room. He was trying, she could see that. "Like a pillow or another blanket?"

"Once the meds kick in a little more, how about an ice cream sundae, loaded with peanuts, bananas, cherries and fudge sauce?" Her taste buds shouted yes, but she still wasn't confident her stomach would cooperate. All the same, it felt good to dream that soon she could indulge all these cravings.

"Done. The freezer will be packed with options before we get home."

Home?

His home and hers were not in the same place, not really. Nothing was settled yet between them.

"I'm joking. Soon though, hopefully." She put her hand on her stomach, staring back to the ultrasound. To her future. "I just would like to have my simple, uncomplicated life back."

"That isn't going to happen."

"I know." She nodded, eyes drifting to the IV bag filled with fluid. Knowing that this was one of those defining moments—a moment she'd like to sketch or paint when she could.

"And I'm committed to being a part of my child's life." His voice carried such fierce determination, hinting at the kind of father he'd be.

The kind of father she *hoped* he would be.

"You're so good with Rose. You'll make a wonderful father. You're more prepared than I am."

He had a way of taking unexpected things in stride, a trait she'd always envied. His wanderlust soul necessitated quick readjustments. Portia felt like his personality prepared him differently for the trials of parenthood.

"I don't agree. You have brought up your brother. You help care for the animals. You have a great knack with the kids that come to visit the refuge. You'll be a great mom." He laced his fingers with hers, showing his sincerity in the strength of his touch. "But let me be clear, you won't have to parent alone. We'll be here for each other."

"So many details to work out." Her mind reeled. Now that he knew...well, she'd have to make all sorts of new plans. And backup plans.

"But we don't have to work them out now."

She chewed her bottom lip, confused. "How can we not?"

"Can you put the need for organization on hold for a while and let us live in the moment? We have months. Let's take things one step at a time."

"What's the first step?" She found comfort in breaking tasks into smaller portions, everything falling into neat categories and checkable boxes. She knew enough about Easton to know he didn't think so linearly. An intense curiosity burned in her as she waited for him to explain.

"First?" He stroked a thumb across the back of her hand before his blue eyes met hers. "Will you marry me, Portia? Make a real family for our child?"

Marry him?

Portia swallowed, an eternity passing between them. Words scattered from her mind, leaving her to only stare at him. What on earth was he thinking to jump into marriage so quickly? Sure, they appeared to be compatible, and maybe the relationship could go somewhere, but how could she know where for sure. They'd only had two dates!

Frustration bubbled up that he wasn't taking her concerns seriously. Their focus needed to be on parenting. Not romance. Not right now. She needed to protect her independence more than ever, for her child. Because heaven help her, she was starting to care for Easton—too much.

And didn't that thought cause the room to spin again?

"You're not going to pass out again are you?" he teased, tipping her chin up gently with one knuckle.

"No." She shook her head. Now more than ever, she needed her wits about her to withstand the will of Easton Lourdes. He might be eccentric, but he was a man accustomed to getting what he wanted. "I'm just not ready to make that kind of commitment. We have so much more to plan out."

"Fine, then. You're a planner. We'll plan." He stepped closer, wrapping his arms around her. "But just so we're clear, this time that you're taking to plan? I'm going to be using everything in my arsenal to convince you to marry me."

Ten

Two days later, deep, dark clouds encroached on the late-afternoon summer sky with threatening force. Tropical Storm Elliot rumbled in the distance, a menace that, if the forecasters were correct, would pass them by, turn into the Gulf of Mexico and eventually head toward Louisiana.

Sure, the outer bands of the storm would dump water on them with some degree of severity. But that weather shared more in common with a tropical depression—a resounding difference in destructive capacity.

Still, Easton wasn't taking any chances with the lives of the animals and people he cared about. He'd begun to organize the volunteer staff into small task forces—everyone charged with securing different aspects of the refuge. Just to be safe.

And, truth be told, he felt like he needed to keep busy while he waited for Portia to give him an answer about his proposal. Easton threw himself full force into storm preparations.

Hoisting a bag of bird seed onto his shoulders, he made his way around the atrium, opening the feeders with practiced ease. A brightly colored, talkative macaw cackled, landing on a tree limb overhead.

Easton poured the seed into the dispenser, his eyes trailing to the window where he saw volunteers scurry across the yard securing loose objects, checking shutters.

"Here we go," he said to himself. The macaw cocked its head, stretching wings wide and displaying the red underside.

"We go. We go. We go." The macaw's shrill voice made Easton laugh lightly.

"That's right. You sit tight during this storm," he told the bird as he made his way to the door of the atrium, surveying the flutter of wings. Antsy. All the animals were.

Then again, animals had a way of knowing things about storms that seemed to escape the notice of humans. Judging by their unease, Easton couldn't help but wonder if this storm would turn into something stronger than predicted. It'd been a few years since Key Largo had taken substantial storm damage, something he'd been incredibly thankful for. But as a Florida native, he knew that luck only lasted for so long.

Exiting the clinic, Easton noticed bright red hair against an increasingly gray backdrop. Maureen and his brother worked across the yard by the main mansion, checking the storm shutters. Rose bounced and waved from a navy blue carry pack on Xander's back. Her little blond curls rustled in the wind, streaming behind the toddler's face. Her expression lit up in a smile—too young to realize the severity of the situation.

His niece's peal of laughter carried on the wind, causing a wide grin to take over Easton's face. He felt it warming his eyes. She blew him a kiss, which he caught in the air. With theatrical flair, he pretended it took two hands to hold the kiss, wrestling with it. She clapped her hands, watching intently. Easton pulled his hands to his heart, patting lightly on his chest. Rose loved this game they played. He'd started this ritual a few days ago with her.

With the uncertainty brewing around the fate of his relationship with Portia, Easton felt desperate to fortify the connection with his niece.

Growing up, Xander and Easton had been well traveled, following his parents on adrenaline-fused adventures. Adventures that made him feel like the world had magic in it. When their father died in a mountain climbing accident, his mother had been like a ball that suddenly lost its tether. She skidded and skirted out of Easton's life. She'd simply checked out, a bohemian spirit that refused to settle. Another lost connection, another kick in the gut.

And Portia? Would he have to add her name to the list of the lost?

He didn't have the chance to dwell too long on that thought. There she was—barely released from the hospital, taking an active role in storm preparation. A protective desire stirred in him, drawing him to her. Making his way past volunteers carrying a kayak to one of the storage sheds, he approached her.

With the wind whipping violently, her hair loosed from her ponytail. She looked wild, fierce—a part of the stormscape. A force all her own.

She directed a group of volunteers carrying emergency supplies of water and canned food for the storm shelter.

He'd arrived by her side by the time the last member of the volunteer supply train had disappeared into the house.

Portia turned, knocking into him, her pointed features pensive but relaxed. Starting to walk, she held a clipboard in her right hand filled with a page-long checklist.

He loved that about her. *Loved?* The word caught him up short. He wasn't the kind of guy who thought that way emotionally, just that reason had ended more relationships than he could count.

He'd known Portia for two years—professionally, sure, but still a long time. Longer than most nonfamily relationships. He would have used words such as *liked. Adored. Admired.* But *loved*? He wasn't sure what to do with that word.

Easton shook off the tangent and said, "While you're deciding whether or not to marry me, let me help you."

"Help me?" She blinked at him, confused. She held up the clipboard as if to show him everything was under control.

He shook his head, holding up a hand. "Financially. You need to rest more. Put your feet up. Especially until you get the morning sickness under control. Let me pay for your brother's college and yours."

"Are you aware there's a storm brewing?" Her eyebrows shot heavenward with confusion. "I'm sure you have as much to do as I do. And furthermore..." She shook her head. "Why would you do that?"

"To ease your stress. I won't miss the money." Money was the least of his concerns. He wanted her well cared for. She worked so damn hard for everyone. She would never even think to put her needs first.

"You want to keep me closer because of the baby. You

want to put me in your debt." She met his gaze measure for measure, but her shift from foot to foot relayed her nerves.

"Of course I do. But I also want the chance for us to parent together. You and I both want what's best for all of us."

Her eyes narrowed, challenging him. "Don't play games."

Easton bristled, stopping in his tracks. He could be a lot of things—eccentric, stubborn. But he'd never been one to play games with people. He respected other living beings too much for that. "Think of the money as child support. This is what I should do, and it's what I want to do."

"You're not going to try to take the baby from me?"

The question shocked him silent for a moment. He'd proposed after all. He wanted to be a team. To tackle this together. "No. Hell, you're going to be an amazing mother. If anything, I'm worried about what kind of father I'll be. Surely you are too, after what I said about not wanting children."

Her eyebrows pinched together and she hung her head, watching their steps along the path as if thinking. "I've thought more about that, especially since our time in the emergency room, and I've decided you don't give yourself enough credit. I've seen you here with the animals. You have a tender, nurturing side to you whether you want to admit it or not."

Nurturing? "There's a difference between baby animals and human babies."

His words were practically lost to a roll of thunder. Rain, hard and determined, came pelting down on them. On instinct, his hand found hers and he gestured toward the barn on the far end of the property. She nodded in understanding, tucking the clipboard under her arm.

He pulled her forward in a brisk jog, making for the entrance of the teal-colored barn. Wind nipped at their backs, surprisingly chilly.

"How so?" she yelled as they picked up the pace, her fingers gripping his tightly.

He strained to hear her as they made their way to the barn. "There just is."

"Well, that's not very scientific," she said smartly. "I think nature kicks in either way."

And speaking of nature. He really needed to check on the animals in the barn, particularly the pregnant Key deer with a wounded hoof.

Around them, palm trees bowed to the ferocity of the wind, lightning sizzling around them like a sporadic camera flash.

They crossed the threshold into the barn. Portia closed the door, sealing out the weather.

"I'll check on Ginger Snap," she said, pressing a hand on his shoulder. He nodded, fumbling in his pocket to call his brother for a storm update.

Portia gave a small smile, heading to the pregnant deer they'd rescued a few weeks ago. Ginger Snap had a nasty cut on her right hind leg that he'd stitched. But before she could be released back to the wild, the deer needed to recuperate.

"Um… Easton?" Portia's voice interrupted his phone scrolling. He noted the urgency in her tone and jogged over to the stall door.

Ginger Snap was in labor.

"I think we're going to have to stay with her," Portia said, setting her clipboard down. No script for this.

Hell. She was right. He couldn't leave the injured deer, but his heart felt heavy. Conflicted. He wanted Portia to be in the safest place in the refuge. While the barn was up to current hurricane code, he would have felt better if she were in the storm shelter.

"Give me a second." He queued up Xander's number and pressed Call.

Two rings in and Xander's deep voice pulsed through the speakers.

"Where are you?" his older brother demanded.

"In the barn with Ginger Snap," he said, watching the deer pant heavily.

"You better stay there. Trees are falling. Debris is flying. Tropical Storm Elliot just got upgraded to Hurricane Elliot and it has turned to us. We're going to take a direct hit sometime in the next hour, brother."

Damn. The increased strength meant it was too risky to move Portia and her unborn baby.

"Thanks for the update. Stay in touch and stay safe."

Xander's voice sounded garbled. "You, too—" The connection winked out, lost to static.

"Are you ready for your first hurricane?" Easton asked, shoving his phone into his back jeans pocket as he turned to face Portia. Her face paled, eyes widening as she looked around the barn.

He pressed on. "We'll ride out the storm. We're in a safe place with plenty of supplies."

"If I didn't know you better, I would think you stirred up this storm to get me alone." Her lips twisted in a smile, spunk invigorating her. She looked at the office area in the barn—a small sofa, desk and bathroom. There certainly were worse places to be trapped. "I'm not sharing a bed with you just because we're trapped here."

"Of course you're not." He clapped a hand over his chest. "I'm going to be a total gentleman and give you the office sofa—since there isn't a bed here."

"You're being too nice. I'll feel bad if you sleep on the floor."

"I'm not going to be sleeping. There's a hurricane."

"Well, yes, there's a hurricane, so what exactly do you think you can do to hold that back? You're not a superhero."

"Good point. Although I guess I'll have to return my special hurricane cape."

A smile slipped between her teeth, then a giggle, followed by a full laugh as the tension eased from the room after their mad dash readying for the storm. Lord, he liked the sound of her laugh.

"That's better." He skimmed his hand along her arm, static easing back into the air again as awareness stirred. "You are right that we should both relax."

Her smile faded. "You make it so difficult to resist you."

He wished she didn't say that like it was such a bad thing. But he would work with what he could to persuade her. He sure as hell hoped nature would do its job for the deer. And for him and Portia.

Because the stakes were too high to consider failure.

Rain thumped and beat against the tin roof, the wind loud like the train Portia had ridden as a teenager when she went to live with her aunt. The breathy whistle of the wind felt unnatural—a sound that deeply unsettled Portia to her core.

For six hours, the storm raged, tossing debris into the metal-cased doors. It had made Ginger Snap's delivery stressful.

The tan deer's eyes had widened at the extreme noise, stress beyond labor pains visible in her deep brown eyes. So expressive.

But Easton had helped Ginger Snap. Spoke to her in calming tones, his voice seeming to have a mesmerizing effect on the doe. A beautiful fawn they'd named Cinnamon had been born about an hour ago.

So much excitement and stimulus over the last six hours had left Portia tired. She'd made sure to chug water, to stay hydrated. If she fell ill during the storm due to dehydration again, the options were limited. Her medication had been tucked away in the storm shelter. She felt fine though—and especially attentive to her body and her baby's health.

After she and Easton both washed in the small bathroom, bodies skirting and pressing against each other, they'd gathered an impromptu storm picnic. She ate like she hadn't in days, surprised by her own hunger.

Portia stretched out on a checkered blanket on the floor of the barn. Her body curved around the scattered snack plates—grapes, cheese, crackers. Easton stroked her hair, staring at the stall door.

She looked back at him. "I still can't believe I got to see that doe being born." The memory of the scene made her heart swell. Easton's practiced hands, his nurturing soul emerged in full force. Confirming what she already knew to be true about him. His parental instincts had been honed and developed by years of veterinarian care, his compassion ringing true.

"Cinnamon's a fighter. She's storm born. That's good luck and it means she's resilient." He smiled down at Portia, his tanned face warm and so blindingly handsome.

For a moment, she wondered if there was any truth

to the superstition about being born in a storm. Portia had been born in the middle of a blizzard. Good or bad?

Gathering her head into his lap, his hands massaged her shoulders. Invigorating her senses and soothing her unease about the storm. "How do you feel? Any troubles with the nausea?"

Portia leaned into his touch, his fingers releasing the ache in her muscles. Her eyes fluttered shut. "All's well. The food's amazing and the ginger ale really works. The midwife who stopped by before I left the hospital had some great suggestions. I wish I'd thought to reach out for help sooner."

"You don't have to do this alone. I'm here for you and our baby." He leaned close to her, folding his body to whisper in her ear.

"I do appreciate your saying that. And thank you for giving me space on the marriage proposal. I need time to adjust, we both do." It'd been two days since she'd been proposed to and hospitalized for extreme dehydration. Two days hadn't supplied her with enough time to make a life-altering commitment. She needed to weigh the pros and cons to arrive at the most logical course of action. She'd lived her whole life preparing to be independent. Now Easton was asking her to depend on him. She wasn't sure she knew how.

"The news is already spreading and I can't control other people's reactions."

The reactions of other people bothered her less and less. Her primary concern remained the health of her child. "Let's deal with one day at a time. For a free spirit, you're sure trying to think fifty steps ahead."

"Then let's focus on the moment," he said, pushing ever so slightly deeper into the knot in her right shoulder.

She melted into his touch, how his strong but intuitive hands knew just how to knead away the tension of the past two months. His thumbs found and worked loose a knot below her shoulder blade, then he stroked lower along her back.

And she knew—she just knew—she wanted, needed, more from this elemental moment alone with him. So beautiful in its secluded simplicity with the whole of nature at work around them, as tumultuous as her feelings for this man. She wasn't used to such a lack of control over her emotions, but right now, she reveled in it.

Angling nearer, Portia tipped her face up for a kiss, her emotions close to the surface after all they'd experienced together today. She palmed his chest, his heartbeat firm and accelerating against her touch. Her arms slid upward and around his neck, deepening the kiss, and with a hard groan he rolled her onto her back until they both stretched out on the quilt. The scent of the laundry detergent teased her nose along with the sweet musk of fresh hay. Clean and earthy and elemental all at once.

Easing her refuge-branded T-shirt off, she tossed it aside and met his eyes boldly, inviting. And as his eyes lit with fire, he didn't hesitate to unhook her bra and reveal her body to his hungry eyes. He stroked her skin, pulled away her shoes and jeans, touching and kissing and igniting her until her head thrashed on the thick quilt and she whispered pleas for him to get naked now, damn it.

A sigh of relief shuddered through him and he tossed away his clothes in a haphazard pile, his eyes staying linked with hers. Peering deep into her with fierceness.

Even in the muted glow of the barn's backup lights, she could still make out the definitions of his tanned, muscled body. Every fiber of her being screamed a possessive *mine*.

And yes, she saw how his eyes caressed all of her with clear appreciation, arousal. Desire. She'd never felt more beautiful, and truth be told, it had more to do with the way he touched her than with any look in his eyes.

Easton kissed along her neck to her ear, nibbling her earlobe and whispering, "Are you sure you feel okay? You were just in the hospital—"

Her fingers went to his sensual lips. "I'm fine, and the doctor cleared me for all activity short of bungee jumping."

"Well, then that's good for us since bungee jumping is nowhere on my agenda." He grazed kisses along her jawline back to her lips again. "But if you need to stop at any time, just say the word."

"Trust me, I will. Our baby means the world to me."

Easton's hand trailed down her side to her stomach, his eyes focused on her pale skin as he rested his hand there. A small, awestruck smile tugging at his mouth. "To me, as well."

Her heart softened at his words, and she reached for him, pulling him back over her, determined to take everything from this time together that she could.

The storm raged outside, but she and Easton were safe here together. But she knew too well the real world and worries couldn't stay at bay forever.

That marriage proposal still loomed between them, and she was no closer to feeling comfortable saying yes.

Sleep eluded him, but that was probably for the best. After they'd made love, they'd dressed and curled up on the blanket together. Portia fell asleep in an instant.

He wondered if his brother was safe or if the storm was letting up anytime soon. He'd tried to call Xander, but the cell phone reception was crap due to the storm.

They were in the oversize stall with Ginger Snap and her baby. It was the safest interior room in the barn. He watched as the deer tried to nurse her fawn, struggling to get the action right.

He picked up a piece of hay, rubbed it between his fingers and crooned softly, "You can do this, Ginger Snap. I know it's not easy, girl, but you can do it. You can be a good parent to your baby. You know what to do."

The momma deer flicked her ears toward Easton.

"I'm sorry we're not in the clinic, girl, but I'm here with you. Portia's here with you, too."

Oh Lord. Portia. He turned his gaze back to where she slept. Watched her chest rise and fall, the soft sounds of her steady breath reassuring him.

He could spend an eternity with her. And damn, but that rocked his world. And settled his footing all over again. He'd never found any woman he felt this way about, and he knew he never would again. She was... Portia.

His mind drifted back to their lovemaking and the spark between them. Incredible—like nothing he'd experienced before. He wanted to win her, to make her stay. Every moment without an answer to his proposal made him feel like she was a step closer to bolting out of his life forever.

Easton snapped the piece of hay, smiling at the deer. "And we care about you. You're not alone in this parenting. We won't let anything happen to you. We'll stay here with you all the way through. Although it's going to be a long night, I'm afraid. Care to answer? Because I could use some help on my end with being a parent."

Cinnamon started to nurse, which seemed to calm Ginger Snap. Her head rested on the barn floor as she appeared to relax, her stressed breathing becoming easier.

"You look like you don't even need my assistance right now after all. But then you deer have been having young on your own without the father around. So maybe you could tell me something about why Portia is being so stubborn about marrying me? Or hell, even talking about it?"

He watched Ginger Snap settle even more, her ears flicking attentively to Easton. The doe's eyes were deep and dark. But mostly, he noticed how calm she looked now. He tilted his head, laying a hand on the ground.

Portia stirred beside him, tossing slightly in her sleep.

He waited for her to settle before continuing, "Sure, you and she can do this on your own. But she doesn't have to. If she could just accept how much I care about her. I'm not going to leave her. I'm not like my parents. I'm steady. I've found a way to have adventures right here at home. I'm not...leaving..."

Portia moved restlessly again, stretching, then yawning as she woke. She sat up slowly, carefully, and smiled ever so slightly before pushing her tousled hair from her face. She removed a scrunchie from around her wrist and piled her hair high on her head. With bleary eyes, she reached for the water bottle, popped off the cap and took a sip.

Easton eyed her, worried. "Are you feeling alright?"

She took another sip, waited, then nodded. "All seems well." She picked up a cracker and nibbled it, as well. "Here's the real test though."

He moved closer, cautioning, "Take it slow."

"I will. Morning's close and I know what that usually means." She rolled her eyes and stayed still, waiting.

"No need to do anything other than rest." Damn crummy time for a hurricane. A sense of helplessness kicked over him even as he knew there was nothing he could do to battle Mother Nature's forces outside the barn door.

The winds sounded softer but he suspected that was merely the eye of the storm.

He stroked along her arm. "Have you given any more thought to my proposal?"

She held up the cracker in the muted light, scrutinizing it. She shook her head dismissively. "Can we talk about that later, please?"

Ginger Snap gave a huff.

"I know I said we had time to work on this during the pregnancy, but I'm wondering if that's a cop-out. We're good together. We've known each other for two years. We get along well, and the chemistry between us is incredible, beyond incredible. I've never felt this much for anyone else. Can you deny you feel the same?"

He meant it. Never had a relationship been more real to him. He'd ended other relationships quickly because he'd known they would not work out. He'd already spent more time with Portia than he had with any other woman. And even if he and she hadn't been romantically involved, he knew her.

Wanted her.

Couldn't let her go.

He wanted to provide for her. For their child. He knew he could make this work between them if she stayed and didn't bolt. How ironic was that? He'd been the king of leaving and now he could well be on the receiving end.

It scared the hell out of him. And also made him all the more determined.

"All of what you mentioned is good for dating or an affair. But it's not enough for a marriage." She set the cracker down, picked up the water again. Swirled it around as she stared at him.

"Why not?"

She put aside the water bottle. "Because it's not love. We can have everything in sync, all the chemistry in the world and without love, we won't last. That will be so much worse for our child. We have to get this right."

Ah, there it was. Portia's need for absolute perfection bubbling to the surface. That need had held her back in the past. It kept her from pursuing something if every aspect wasn't perfectly hammered down, all boxes checked. She'd waited for the perfect time to go to college too, but she'd been so busy planning, she'd never gotten around to just doing it.

"My mother and father loved each other and it didn't make them attentive parents," he snapped the truth, frustration growing. "Hell, they flat-out lost us in foreign countries more times than we can count. Most kids travel and learn words in other languages like *where's the bathroom* or *I'm hungry*. We learned *take me to the embassy*."

She cupped his face in a gentle, caring hand. "Easton, I am so sorry. That had to have been terrifying for you and your brother and it's not right, not at all. But you also have to know that as much as you act like the absentminded doctor socially, when it comes to responsibility you are always one hundred percent there for your patients. You tell yourself you're an eccentric like your parents because that keeps you from risking your heart."

"Like you're using your brother's education as an excuse to keep from living your life?" he asked quietly.

"I'm taking care of him." Her lips went tight.

"He's an adult." Easton pointed out, reaching for her hand. "He can take care of himself. It's your turn to have a life. Marry me."

She snatched her hand away, anger brewing in her eyes, making him feel like the storm had jumped inside the barn. "I don't want to be your obligation and I don't want some marriage of convenience."

"My brother and Maureen married for convenience and it's worked out well for them. No one can deny that. Portia, I care about you."

"I realize that. You're a good man. But I don't want to depend on anyone. And if I did, it would be a man who loves me wholeheartedly. I deserve that."

"And you'll have everything as my wife."

"Everything?" Her head fell back in frustration and she sighed before she looked back at him. "You're missing the point altogether."

"And what is the point?"

"You've been thinking differently since you saw those glitter condoms in the honeymoon suite. Seriously. Glitter. Rubbers. Is that any reason to get married?" Scarlet hues rose high in her cheeks, anguish mounting in her voice.

Damage control. Easton needed to calm her. "The lack of condoms—glitter or otherwise—is how this happened. Plenty of people have gotten married for fewer reasons."

"This is not funny."

"Trust me, I'm not laughing."

"This is no way to start a life together. I don't even think I can continue to work here."

His temper rose, the weight of her words surprising him. "What the hell?"

"Don't swear at me!"

He pinched the bridge of his nose and closed his eyes. "I'm trying to figure out what's going on in that mind of yours."

"I'm the logical one. This makes perfect sense."

"Not from where I'm standing. Maybe it has something to do with pregnancy hormones—"

"Don't. Don't you dare suggest I'm illogical because I'm pregnant." Tears welled, hovering in the corners of her eyes even as those same eyes spit fire and back-off vibes. "I know how I feel and what I want from life. I want my child to be happy and I want to stand on my own two feet."

"We're both parents now. We need to make compromises."

"Oh, you really need to be quiet." She shot to her feet. Her voice reaching new heights, causing Ginger Snap to bleat. "I am not some kind of compromise. I will never be anyone's second-best disappointment ever again. I deserve better."

Head held high, she headed out. Hand on the barn's wide double door, she hesitated. Rain still came down in sheets, but the hurricane's eye could hold.

A massive crack sounded, like a tree splitting, and Easton bolted to his feet, racing to Portia. He snagged her in his arms and rolled under a low-lying support beam just as a falling tree pierced the barn.

Eleven

The barn warped beneath the weight of the tree, groaning—a sickening sound of metal buckling. A small hole opened like a wound, allowing a throaty chorus of hurricane force wind to enter the safe space of the barn and rain to drip on the floor.

Another groan. The tree sank lower, its branches scraping, cracking, filling the main part of the barn.

Portia wriggled beneath Easton, craning her head to look. In the wind whipping through the hole in the roof, he couldn't tell if she was injured or not. Her eyes were wide as she stared at the impending catastrophe a few feet away from where she lay pinned to the floor.

If the roof gave way. No. He corrected himself—*when* the roof gave way—she would be in the trajectory of the crash if he didn't get them out right now. He would have to worry about any possible bruises later. The situation was too urgent.

He pulled her close and rolled to the stall with Ginger Snap. His muscles screamed at him to move faster. He barely registered the unnatural coldness of the wind swirling inside, tearing at him, working against him. He tried to communicate with Portia, but his shout was lost to the roar and the howl.

Their fight didn't matter now. The only thing that mattered to Easton was keeping her safe. He kept moving, shielding Portia's soft body, pressing on through the invisible wall of wind filled with grit and twigs. Heaven forbid if a larger branch should come their way. He willed their bodies to move as one, shoving them both to the far left side, toward Ginger Snap and her newborn baby, who cowered in the corner. The two deer cried and bleated in unison, fear rampant in those deep, dark, knowing eyes.

Finally, Easton found a solid wall under a reinforced steel beam, the other corner of the stall and the reason he'd chosen this spot in the first place. He pressed Portia against the wooden planks of the side, rain drifting in through the branches and pooling on the floor. Rain still hammered outside, beating the roof and the ground. He kept his back to the storm just as the tree crashed the rest of the way into the barn. Sliced the metal clear open as wind and sky flooded them with the unnatural sounds of raw power.

Thick, sideways rain pelted inside, and the shifting tree brought a scream from Portia. He hugged her closer. The oak moved one last time, settling, in a surreal way almost sealing off the elements beyond.

For now.

Heart hammering in his chest, Easton's body pressed against hers. He counted them lucky to have been out of the fall zone of the tree.

Easton felt her inhale sharply, holding her breath for a long time. Noted the ragged pace of her heart as she loosed the breath. The release of air seemed to rival the strength of the storm.

She leaned into him. To Easton, it seemed as though her body might melt into his. He felt the tension in her stance, the fear in her skin. Despite the near-deadly experience, he felt strangely calm as her light floral perfume wafted by him. A glimpse of normalcy.

How he wanted to protect her against all threats and hardships. Weather. Health. Finances. All of it.

Portia's messy ponytail tickled his nose, reminding him of gentler times with this sexy woman. Of being in a bed—a true bed with her.

He inhaled deeply, steeling himself against the pelting rain as he dared a look behind him to survey the damage.

The structure of the barn was intact—they wouldn't have to demolish the building. But the barn had received substantial damage from Hurricane Elliot.

But all of that could wait. Portia softened beneath his touch. She reached her slender hand for his, entwining their fingers. He squeezed tightly and then dropped her hand. Thunder and wind assaulted their senses, but they were close enough for Easton to reassure his pounding heart that Portia hadn't been hurt.

In a bellowing voice while checking her over with careful hands, Easton asked, "Are you alright?"

"Yes, yes, I'm fine." She wriggled under him. "More importantly, how are you? You're the one who put himself in harm's way."

"Not a mark on me. But I need to secure that area where the tree came in with some tarps or the whole place could flood by the time the hurricane passes."

He looked back over his shoulder, mentally planning and strategizing what needed to happen.

She chewed on her lip, eyes trailing to the damage. With a vigorous shake of her head, she pressed up. "I'll help."

A snort escaped him before he thought better of it. He appreciated her resilience, her willingness to pitch in and help out. But being knocked around by hurricane-force winds and soaking to the bone? Not an option. "Like hell. Be still and try to stay calm for your sake and for our baby. I don't want you doing anything until you've been checked over."

Her spine went straight and rigid. "I'm careful."

His jaw went tight and he couldn't resist snapping. "Careful? Like when you tried to run out into a hurricane?"

Her eyes filled with tears, and she pressed a hand to her mouth. "You're right. I wasn't thinking. Oh God, how could I have been so reckless?"

His anger dimmed in the face of her tears, and heaven knew, he didn't want to upset her more.

He clasped her fingers, trying to soothe her. "And that's why, for the baby's sake, I'm sure you'll sit over there and watch Ginger Snap and Cinnamon. We can argue until we're both soaked or you can let me get to work."

She nodded, a mixture of annoyance and defeat in the thin line her lips formed. But she didn't argue. Instead, she grabbed the quilt from the floor and walked slowly to the deer, hands extended.

Easton heard her talk to the deer. Reassuring them everything would be alright. She sat in the hay next to them, eyes fixed on the fawn.

Easton moved quickly to the small office, grabbing

a tarp from the supply closet. Scouring the shelves, he located nails and a hammer from behind a stack of toilet paper.

Knowing that he didn't have much time to make an effective barrier, his limbs sang to life. He hammered a tarp wall, reminding himself the entire time that he needed to make sure Portia stayed safe. He wouldn't have her catching her death out here.

With the help of a ladder and some rope, he got to work, using the grommets on the tarp to stretch it in some places and using nails to secure it in others. In a few places, he nailed the thing to the fallen tree, but in the end, he did a decent job protecting them from the rain.

The blue tarp wall wasn't going to win him any construction awards, but as he stepped back to survey his handiwork, he knew it'd do its job. Nothing more, nothing less.

Putting away his tools, Easton found a clean T-shirt in the barn office. He toweled off his head and walked back to the stall where he'd left Portia and the deer. He stopped in his tracks.

Like some woodland fairy, Portia was wrapped in a quilt, fast asleep. Her head cradled by her arm, which rested on Ginger Snap's rump with Cinnamon curled between them.

She'd been wiped out. That much was clear.

But something else gnawed at his consciousness as he looked at the strange scene in front of him.

For the last several years, he'd been convinced that because Terri and Xander had joined the efforts of the refuge and set up shop here that he'd been at the core of a family. He'd been more convinced after Terri passed away, leaving Easton to help with baby Rose.

He was happy here, sure. He'd enjoyed the rewards and benefits of a family without any of the investment or risk. That'd been his role.

But as he stared at Portia, watched her sleep nestled up next to a deer, he began to realize that wasn't the role he wanted. He'd been playing it safe for too long, keeping his relationships light and easy until he'd reached this point where he didn't even know how to have a deep and meaningful one. All that was about to change, however. Because Easton didn't want a sideline role anymore. He wanted something lasting, with the strong, sweetly fierce woman in front of him.

This Peter Pan wannabe was ready to leave Neverland. To follow his Wendy.

He didn't just care about Portia. He loved her.

Marrying her wasn't about the baby. It was about building a life with her, forever. And he'd sabotaged his proposal by not recognizing her most vulnerable of insecurities. He'd made her feel like an obligation rather than a precious treasure.

No wonder she'd tried to storm out of here.

He'd minced his words, convinced her that their circumstance as parents were the reason he'd wanted to pursue a relationship with her.

That formulation had been completely wrong. He loved her enthusiasm for logic and how that balanced her artistic soul. Easton loved the way they balanced each other. His love for her coursed through his veins. He didn't know why he hadn't recognized it before.

He loved her. Not for her secretarial skills. Not as a valuable employee. He loved Portia for all that she was—sacrificing, kind, artsy and wildly sexy. All of her.

Now he had to persuade her to say yes.

* * *

So after a crash in the barn and another five hours trapped in said barn, Portia had weathered her first Category 3 hurricane. Now, in the strangely bright morning sun, she sat on a kitchen barstool watching the cleanup effort through an open window, cooled by a fan running off a generator. She should have gone to the doctor by now, but that had been rescheduled due to the storm.

Both Easton and Xander refused to let her help. The ER scare and the stress of the storm had them both convinced she needed to rest. To stay away from any form of physical labor.

So here she sat on a stool in the kitchen looking out the window. And looking. And looking. Just as she'd been stuck in the barn unable to act. Sure, she'd slept. But even when she was awake, Easton wouldn't talk to her or let her exert herself in any way, physically or emotionally. As if her emotions weren't already in a turmoil regardless. Thank goodness one of the volunteers was a nurse and had checked her out or she would be in an overrun ER right now. And Portia had to admit to a massive sense of relief that Easton and their baby were okay.

And thank heaven there were no casualties, human or animal. All damage had been structural, which could be repaired with time.

She propped her chin on her elbow. She felt like a true Floridian now, down to a leveled house. Her small white cabana hadn't been a match for Elliot's relentless winds and storm surge. The majority of her belongings were probably floating to a distant shore, displaced.

Like she felt. Out of sorts.

At least not everything had been lost. Some photo albums and sketchbooks she'd tucked away in her closet remained. Some clothes, too. But there was so much damage.

Every line of sight and perspective revealed more destruction. Debris littered the lawn, pieces of people's lives from yards away. A Jet Ski, pieces of a dock, even a window air-conditioning unit. She could barely see the presence of light green grass.

She'd been through snowstorms before, when traveling with her parents, but there was a crystallized beauty after a blizzard. People holed up with hot cocoa in front of the fire. This kind of destruction and loss after the hurricane humbled her. Made her feel small and fragile. Made her question her need not to rely on anyone.

But so did being confined to the main house while other people worked to make the place habitable again. Volunteers picked up debris, moving branches and pieces of buildings with military precision. Or, she thought, a laugh pushing at her lips, with ant-like precision—moving things so much larger than the human body.

Maureen kept Portia company, pouring her a glass of water. Maureen's red curls fell in her face, making her look wild. "Anything else for you, love?"

Picking up the orange-tinted glass, Portia shook her head. "Not unless you can sneak me outside so I can be useful to somebody."

Maureen put a hand on Portia's shoulder, shaking her head. "Everyone just wants to make sure you are okay. And you are being useful. Honestly. Taking care of yourself is useful to all of us. We care about you, you know."

Portia had grown to appreciate her friend's blunt honesty. She simply nodded.

From across the kitchen counter, Portia's phone rang, vibrating like mad.

Maureen glanced at the caller ID. "It's your brother. I'll leave you to it." She gave Portia a side hug before disappearing into the house, her footfalls echoing until they were silent.

She slid over to answer the phone, steadying herself.

"I've been so worried about you," Marshall said by way of greeting.

Portia traced the ridge of the glass with a light fingertip, staring nowhere in particular. "Well, hello to you, too."

"I feel like when one sibling goes through a crazy hurricane unexpectedly, hello falls a bit short. Are you okay?"

Was she okay? Again, she didn't know how to answer that.

"Of course I am. I'm not going to lie, Marshmallow. The hurricane was the most intense thing I've ever witnessed. But I am okay. Everything here is just fine."

"You just..." Marshall trailed off. "You just don't sound like yourself. I can come see you, take a job in Key Largo and help you out."

The words knifed Portia in the chest.

"Absolutely not." Portia took a sip of her water, deciding not to tell him about her destroyed cabana. He didn't need to be worried by that. Hell, that would send him on a plane within the hour.

She pressed on. "Finish school and then kick butt. That's what would make me happiest."

He paused, sighing. "Fine. But I'm coming to see you this weekend."

She stuttered. "That's really un—"

He interrupted her. "No, it is necessary."

"Okay," she found herself saying. "Yes, please. I would like to see you. I, um, need to see you. I've missed you."

"I miss you, too. See you soon, sis. Love you."

Portia looked back outside at the chaos. "Love you, too."

He hung up, leaving Portia to her swirling thoughts about letting others into her life, accepting help and comfort. She couldn't hide from the truth. She needed other people as much as they needed her.

The realization settled inside her with a depth that went beyond just the physical implications of a hurricane, and made her question all the times she'd pushed offers of help away. She'd denied people the chance to give back the way she gave to others.

And why?

To protect herself from rejection? To give herself control over her world after a tumultuous childhood? Maybe. Probably. The whys didn't matter so much. What mattered was changing, becoming less rigid in her views and broadening her scope, letting love into her life as well as giving it.

She saw Easton from a distance. She would know his walk, his stance anywhere, even if he wore a tuxedo rather than his regular cargo pants, boots and T-shirt. Or nothing at all. Her heart squeezed with emotion.

She couldn't hide from the truth anymore. She'd fallen totally and irrevocably in love with him. Chances were, she'd loved him for a very long time and hadn't allowed herself to admit it to herself because her feelings weren't logical.

Love wasn't logical. It wasn't based on looks. Or a checklist. Or criteria. Feelings couldn't be stacked into a neat, orderly pile. Her emotions were messy and tangled and to hell with independence.

Her soul hurt so much because she loved him, completely and irrationally. Her feelings didn't make sense and they weren't supposed to. This was about leading with her heart rather than her brain. She'd worked so hard not to be like her mother, Portia had missed the whole point. Her mother hadn't really loved anyone but herself. All of her mother's relationships were based on—checklists and criteria. Portia may not have looked like her mother, but in a sad way, she'd fallen into the same trap.

How sad was that? Tragic actually.

Hopefully she wasn't too late to change things and build a future with Easton and their baby. A future built on love.

As Easton drew nearer, he caught her stare through the window. In his arms, he carried stacks of her artwork. He raised them above his head, a smile forming on his face.

But not on hers. She knew this gesture was a kind of peace offering, and oh how she wanted to accept it. But sadness blanketed her, pulling her heart into a plummet.

Because as deeply, completely and passionately as she loved him, she now understood her own self-worth.

She'd always wanted to be independent. Well, this was her test. She owed it to herself and to her child to stand up for herself. As soon as the cleanup was completed, she would demand the fullhearted commitment from Easton they all deserved.

A week later, fading sunlight washed the bruised but recovering refuge in orange hues. As Easton scanned the outside patio tables, he could barely believe that a week ago, the place had been torn apart by Hurricane Elliot.

The substantial damage to the barn and clinic had been repaired. Both Xander and Easton spared no expense, contracting the quickest, best construction companies in southwest Florida to bring the structures back up to tip-top shape.

As he looked around the gala fund-raiser tonight, he could see all of that hastened hard work paying off. Manicured grass, well-maintained buildings. Normalcy.

Which was exactly what he needed to show the collection of celebrities, politicians and socialites that bustled from table to table with champagne glasses in hand.

A snazzy pianist set up on a pop-up wooden dance floor, string lights winking on overhead, creating an illusion of stars brought down to earth. The pianist's notes mingled with the jazz singer whose sultry alto voice spit out lyrics from crooners of another more elegant age.

The brothers had agreed this event would be black-tie and impressive. They needed to be out in public view to fully demonstrate their success as an organization for the reopening of the refuge. So the Lourdes brothers had pooled their connections, hired a decorator and thrown a major event together in five days' time. Impressive, even for them.

As he watched the black-tie affair unfold in his backyard, Easton felt proud of the roots he'd laid down here. The roots he hoped to add to tonight.

The Serenade to Starlight signified the official reopening of the wildlife refuge. This event allowed them to renew their presence in the public eye, something completely essential for maintaining their facilities and the care of the animals.

The whole place seemed to twinkle in cool silver lights and accent pieces. The guest list consisted of A-list types from Miami, South Florida and the Keys. A few prominent West Coast starlets had flown in as well, lured by the promise of positive press coverage for their philanthropic efforts. Of course, the brothers made sure the volunteers could attend, too. The refuge depended on their time, effort and grit. They deserved to enjoy this evening.

Still, a moment of pride and joy turned to apprehension as Easton scanned the crowd, zipping past the women in cocktail dresses. Skipping over the heads of the politicians with cigars and whiskeys on the rocks. He spotted Maureen facilitating media coverage. Xander shaking hands with one of their big donors.

There was only one person is this crowd of people he really wanted to see, however. And that was Portia.

Since the storm, they hadn't had a moment alone. Despite living in the mansion together—under the same roof—she'd kept her distance. Their conversations had been short, quiet. An air of pensive distraction painted her face and actions all week, but he'd wanted to give her time to collect her thoughts and recover from the storm.

Some time where he wasn't pressuring her about marriage.

And she'd retreated totally.

A lesser man, one not dedicated to wooing the love of his life, might have turned tail and given up. But Easton had never been that kind of man. His bones didn't allow him to quit. He knew when to use his theatrical, eccentric, romantic heart. He'd laid down a plan to win her over. Moreover, he'd determined a way to prove how important she was to him.

Then, he spied her through the crowd.

His heart hammered, breath catching in his throat.

Portia rested a slender hand on one of the cocktail tables set up by the massive pool. Her hair was piled on her head, but not in her normal ponytail. Instead, her hazelnut hair was swept into an Audrey Hepburn bun. A slinky peach ball gown clung to her curves, suggesting her natural grace.

Damn. She was sexy.

She moved and the peach-colored dress shimmered in the lights as she leaned to talk to her brother, Marshall, who'd decided to visit for a week. That was another reason Easton had wanted to give Portia space. He knew she needed to spend time with her brother.

But tonight, it was Easton's turn. And he had to get to her.

His brother clapped him on the shoulder, a small glass of bourbon neat in his opposite hand. Easton's open stare at Portia interrupted, he turned to face his brother.

Xander winked at him, understanding what was going on.

Jessie flanked Xander, a vision in glittering silver sequins. She absently straightened Don's bow tie as she spoke. "You boys have completely outdone yourselves."

Sipping his bourbon before answering, Xander nodded. "We just wanted to express our appreciation for the hard work of the volunteers."

"We wouldn't be here without all of you," Easton added, his eyes watching the governor. A few feet away, the man paused. He stooped down, a smile on his wide, tanned face as he took a bright pink carnation that Rose offered him. She clapped when the governor stuck the flower behind his ear. Rose waved goodbye to the official when Maureen scooped her up, heading toward her husband.

Rose's bright eyes lit up when she noticed Easton. She bounced in her sunset-yellow smock dress, blond curls catching in the light summer breeze, twisting over the green wreath crown in her hair.

Rose looked over at her uncle and blew a kiss. Easton caught it in the air and pressed it into his heart. And in that moment he knew he would continue the ritual with his own daughter one day. Because yes, while he couldn't explain why, he knew without question that his and Portia's child was a girl.

A daughter. A son would be great, too. But he already could envision his and Portia's little girl in his heart's eye. And she was incredible.

The pianist and jazz singer faded, their set coming to an end. Elle Viento, a famous singer-songwriter, was up next. The brothers had flown her in from her vacation house in Destin, Florida, to sing.

Her guitar and soft vocals rippled through the crowd, giving the guests a small pause. Even Harvey Fink the movie star stopped to watch Elle play.

The gorgeous night needed to stay this way. Just a bit longer. Just until Easton could make his way to Portia.

Don interrupted Easton's thoughts. "I'll bring you another drink, dear," he told his wife, kissing her on the cheek before disappearing to the bar. Jessie looked like a schoolgirl, her eyes glowing.

"So, Easton, how is Portia? Things settling between you two?" Jessie asked in her matter-of-fact way.

He exchanged a glance with Maureen. "She's fine. And we're pregnant."

Easton wasn't concerned with hiding that truth. He loved Portia, and didn't care who knew what anymore. All that mattered was proving himself to her.

Jessie's hand went to her chest, eyes wide. "Pregnant?" Her tone questioning, prying.

Maureen nodded, saving Easton from answering every single nosy question. "Yes and she is doing well. Glowing and excited."

But Easton wasn't going to let Jessie think he needed shielding from the invasive questions. He was more than ready to declare himself.

"And I have every intention of romancing her for a very, very long time. I love that woman." Every fiber of his being sung that revelation.

Maureen's grin spread like wildfire to Xander and Jessie. She playfully shoved his arm. "Now, there's the magic word. Go get her, Doctor."

Easton winked, setting out to find Portia. He strode over to her, resting a hand on the cocktail table.

Marshall welcomed Easton with a big, toothy grin. The young man's square features contrasting with Portia's slender, angled ones. The sibling resemblance came in their slender height and inquisitive brown eyes. Easton had learned to size people up quickly after all the moving around he'd done in his childhood, and Marshall was a good kid, really bright. Easton understood why Portia sacrificed so much for him.

Easton cupped Marshall's shoulder.

"Do you mind if I steal your sister for a while?"

Marshall smiled, but pinned Easton with a serious look far beyond his years. "As long as you take good care of her."

"I promise, on my honor." He thrust out his hand for the young man to shake. He hoped Marshall would soon be his brother if all went according to plan.

Marshall nodded, his dirty blond hair flopping on his forehead. He turned his attention to a young soap opera star in a bright green dress with a vee neck open to her navel.

Laughing, Easton turned away, focusing his full attention on the only woman at this event who mattered to him. Portia. He ducked his head to whisper in her ear. "I think it's time we talk."

"Right now?" She glanced up at him, her eyes scanning his as if she were looking for something.

"We've put it off long enough, don't you think?" He touched her elbow. "Come on, I have something in the barn I would really like you to see."

She chewed her glossy bottom lip for an instant before nodding. "Yes, of course. I'd thought perhaps we should talk after the property cleanup and celebration, but there's no need delaying."

He took her hand in his, leading them beneath the twinkling paper lanterns toward the barn. The rustle of music and cocktail conversation faded the closer they got to the newly rebuilt structure, repainted teal just like the old one.

Easton placed his hands over Portia's eyes. "No peeking," he teased, nudging the door open with his foot.

They crossed the threshold, lights activated by their movement.

"And now." He took his hands back, letting her see the barn.

Framed pieces of her salvaged art work decorated the barn. Some paintings hung from the rafters and were surrounded with shimmery lights. Billowing flower stalks in sunset-colored pots lined the barn, leading toward a stall at the end of the row.

Ginger Snap poked her head out, ears moving. Portia stepped forward, eyes going from piece to piece and then to the fawn Cinnamon who stood tall beside her mother on spindly legs.

Atop a pile of fresh hay, Easton had laid a brilliant white-and-gold quilt at the far end of the barn. Then he'd covered the blanket with a tray of bright, tropical fruit and crackers. Two champagne glasses flanked an ornate bottle of sparkling water.

Easels lined the path to the blanket. He took her hand, led her to the picnic.

Bright pink calligraphy scrawled across the first canvas: You're Beautiful.

She moved on to the second, a smile lighting her eyes as brightly as the strands of twinkling bulbs illuminating the barn: You Drive Me Crazy—And I Like it.

At the next canvas, her fingers went to her lips, her gaze wide: Easton Loves Portia More Than Life.

Her hand slid away from her mouth, her fingers trembling as she traced the two words on the final message: Marry me.

Tears filled her eyes, one, then another sliding down her cheeks.

"Hormones?" he asked.

"So much more," she answered. "Easton, you are...so charming. And so ridiculously handsome."

Delicate hands stroked his tuxedo lapel, moved to his face. His heart was barely contained in his chest as he looked at her, reading the supreme tug of emotions in her eyes.

He needed that emotion to be love. His whole soul sang his love for her. If she left...he couldn't even finish the thought. Her absence would devastate him.

Easton dropped to one knee and pulled out a ring box

from his back pocket. He popped it open, letting the lights bring the solitaire diamond to life.

Portia's hands went to her mouth, tears streaming down her face.

"I love you. I never thought I would find a woman who would make me want to settle down and figure out how to really be in a relationship. But then I met you and everything changed. Portia, you are the kindest, most self-sacrificing person I've ever known. I want to spend the rest of my life deserving you. Will you marry me?"

She clasped her hands to her chest. "Yes. Yes. Yes, Easton."

Relief swept away the buzz of nervousness he'd refused to acknowledge until that moment.

He stood up sweeping her into a hug, kissing her deeply.

"I love you so much, too." She said as he slipped the ring onto her finger. A perfect fit—as they were for each other.

"No worries about me being Peter Pan and Tarzan combined?" he half joked, unable to keep from worrying. He needed her to believe in him.

"I'm thinking I may have prejudged you. You're more like Dr. Dolittle and Louis Pasteur. A doctor, scientist, tenderhearted veterinarian and amazing man."

He pulled her into him, touching her cheek. "God, I do love you, Portia, and while you've mentioned my dating history, I've never said those words to any woman before. I mean it."

"I know you do. You're a man of honor." She pressed her hand to his cheek, the facets in her diamond engagement ring refracting all those little lights into a prism around them.

"So you know I mean every word of this. I love you, with everything that's inside me. I wish I could explain why. I just know that I do—"

She pressed her fingertips to his mouth. "You don't have to explain. I get it."

"You do?"

"I understand what it means to feel something completely irrational and yet very real. Because I'm in love with you, too. In my head I understand we complement each other, our strengths play well to each other. Yet that doesn't matter because I've met other people who fit that criteria and they didn't come close to moving me the way you do with just a look."

"A look?" He eye-stroked her, taking his time.

"Yes, a look." She sidled closer, her body pressed to his. "But I have a little secret for you."

"What would that be?"

"A touch is even better," she whispered in his ear.

He prided himself on being an intelligent man, her very own Louis Pasteur, after all. Although a hint of Tarzan could come in handy every now and again.

He swept an arm behind her knees and lifted her against his chest, sinking with her onto the thick quilt he'd placed there with just this hope in mind.

The hope of celebrating their engagement, their future and their love.

* * * * *

JOIN US ON SOCIAL MEDIA!

Stay up to date with our latest releases, author news and gossip, special offers and discounts, and all the behind-the-scenes action from Mills & Boon...

 millsandboon

 millsandboonuk

 millsandboon

t might just be true love...

MILLS & BOON

THE HEART OF ROMANCE

A ROMANCE FOR EVERY KIND OF READER

MODERN

Prepare to be swept off your feet by sophisticated, sexy and seductive heroes, in some of the world's most glamourous and romantic locations, where power and passion collide.
8 stories per month.

HISTORICAL

Escape with historical heroes from time gone by. Whether your passion is for wicked Regency Rakes, muscled Vikings or rugged Highlanders, awaken the romance of the past.
6 stories per month.

MEDICAL

Set your pulse racing with dedicated, delectable doctors in the high-pressure world of medicine, where emotions run high and passion, comfort and love are the best medicine.
6 stories per month.

True Love

Celebrate true love with tender stories of heartfelt romance, from the rush of falling in love to the joy a new baby can bring, and a focus on the emotional heart of a relationship.
8 stories per month.

Desire

Indulge in secrets and scandal, intense drama and plenty of sizzling hot action with powerful and passionate heroes who have it all: wealth, status, good looks…everything but the right woman.
6 stories per month.

HEROES

Experience all the excitement of a gripping thriller, with an intense romance at its heart. Resourceful, true-to-life women and strong, fearless men face danger and desire - a killer combination!
8 stories per month.

DARE

Sensual love stories featuring smart, sassy heroines you'd want as a best friend, and compelling intense heroes who are worthy of them.
4 stories per month.

To see which titles are coming soon, please visit

millsandboon.co.uk/nextmonth

LET'S TALK
Romance

For exclusive extracts, competitions
and special offers, find us online:

- facebook.com/millsandboon
- @MillsandBoon
- @MillsandBoonUK

Get in touch on 01413 063232

For all the latest titles coming soon, visit
millsandboon.co.uk/nextmonth